CAROL LYNNE

BRANDED
BY LOVE

ELLORA'S CAVE
ROMANTICA PUBLISHING

BRANDED BY GOLD

Book one in the Men in Love series.

On the run from her stepfather, Jenny Barnes wakes up in hospital to find the two men she's loved for years are with her. Her stepbrother, Jake, and his best friend and lover, Cree, have finally been called to her side after they spent years searching for her. But when they take Jenny home to their new ranch, even they can't keep her tormentor away. With the help of their ex-Seal buddies they set out to keep the love of their lives safe and to capture Jake's own father.

Reader Advisory: This book contains references to rape and graphic violence.

BEN'S WILDFLOWER

Book two in the Men in Love series.

What would make a woman cut herself off from the town she grew up in for seven years? For Kate the answer is one man, a powerful man.

When Kate is in danger of losing her ranch to the bank, she enters into a partnership with Ben. This six-foot seven-inch, overly endowed ex-Seal is looking for a home. He finds a home and love with Kate. When problems on the ranch begin to escalate, Kate points the finger at one man, the man from her past who is determined to drive her out of town.

What's an ex-Seal to do but bring in the rest of his team? Ben summons a few members of his team to help protect Kate from a man who believes he's above the law.

Reader Advisory: This book contains references to rape and graphic violence. It also includes a brief male/male sex scene.

An Ellora's Cave Romantica Publication

www.ellorascave.com

Branded by Love

BRANDED BY LOVE
Carol Lynne

ઠ

BRANDED BY GOLD
~9~

BEN'S WILDFLOWER
~173~

BRANDED BY GOLD

ào

Dedication

ℰꙩ

To my cousin Ali and my sister Rhonda. Thank you for believing in me.

Trademarks Acknowledgement

ℰꙩ

The author acknowledges the trademarked status and trademark owners of the following wordmarks mentioned in this work of fiction:

Glock: Glock, Inc.

L96 sniper rifle: Accuracy International

Life cereal: General Mills, Inc.

Mr. Clean: The Procter & Gamble Company

Rio Chama Steakhouse: Santa Fe Dining, Inc.

Chapter One

ഌ

With rain sprinkling down on her face, she managed to open her eyes just a crack. "Where am I?" she thought. The hard surface under her was cold and wet. She tried to raise herself off the uncomfortable surface only to experience pain so intense her world clouded and the darkness once again took her.

Sirens, she heard them getting closer. She managed to open her eyes again to see a stranger's face looking down at her. "Don't try to move, ma'am, help is almost here."

Help, now she was going to get help, when she'd needed it for the past two days. It was too late for help. Her body was already dead. Killed in a dark room with a knife and a branding iron by the man she'd once called father.

* * * * *

With dust still settling on the dry New Mexico ranch, Jake and his old hound dog Blue walked toward the ranch house. Jake took the stairs two at a time then looked back for Blue. "What's the matter, old boy, did I wear you out today?" Blue slowly made his way up the stairs. He went right to the comfortable cushioned settee and jumped up. Within a minute he was sound asleep. Jake shook his head and grinned. "You'd better not let Cree catch you on the furniture, he'll make Blue stew for dinner."

Shaking the dust from his dark brown hair, he entered the kitchen tired and sore. Jake spotted Cree, the local sheriff, bent over getting a beer out of the fridge. "Damn, that's one sexy ass," he said.

Cree stood and it took his breath away as it did every time he saw him. With shoulder-length blue-black hair and eyes the color of the moss growing down by the creek, Cree Sommers was devastating to look at. He stood six-foot, three in stocking feet and had the body of the Indian warriors of his mother's tribe. Wide, strong shoulders narrowed to an incredible six-pack abdomen and lean hips.

Cree looked Jake up and down. "Oh yeah, well, why don't you come on over and give this fine ass a hello." He grinned and bent over to get another beer out for Jake.

"Gladly," he said with a smile and walked smoothly over to Cree. Jake grabbed a handful of Cree's ass and squeezed. "Man, I've missed you this week. How was the conference?"

Before Cree could answer, Jake kissed him with all the love and passion he'd been storing up. The kiss turned into an erotic game of charge and retreat with both of their tongues dueling for position.

"Boring as hell." Cree set down the forgotten bottles of beer and began tugging at the snaps on Jake's dirty chambray shirt. "God, Jake, I need to feel your skin, it's been a long week." Cree deftly removed his shirt and began licking Jake's neck. "I want you, naked and in me now."

Fantastic, just what he'd wanted to hear.

Jake gave Cree one of his smoother than silk smiles and tugged Cree's shirt out of his pants and began unbuttoning it as fast as his fingers would allow. "Take your gun and your pants off and I'll deal with the shirt."

"Oh good, skin."

Jake loved Cree's skin, all bronzed and smooth. He managed to get Cree's shirt off and then started on his own pants, which wasn't easy with his steel-hard erection pressing against his zipper. Cree was dropping his khaki uniform pants to the kitchen floor when the phone rang.

"No, no, not now. Damn.,"

Here Jake finally had Cree naked and he was gonna have to share him again.

"How about we pretend we don't hear it," Jake said, kissing Cree's stomach. His skin felt like velvet on his tongue. Numerous muscles rippled under Jake's lips letting him know Cree was affected by his touch.

"You know I can't do that, cowboy. What if there's an emergency down at the station?" Cree sighed. He reached for the phone as Jake continued on his journey down Cree's stomach to his rock-hard cock. His erection jumped up to hit Jake on the chin just as he tried to put it in his mouth.

Oh, fruit of the gods.

Cree's cock was warm and smooth. Cree reached down to grab Jake's hair enough to hold on and began a slow thrust in and out of Jake's mouth. He reached for the phone. "Triple..." Cree coughed and cleared his throat. "Triple Spur Ranch, Cree speaking."

Cree listened to the caller on the phone and stopped thrusting into Jake's mouth.

"Yes, this is Jake Baker's ranch, one moment and I'll get him for you," Cree looked down at Jake.

Jake stopped sucking to look up at him. "Jake, phone for you, it's a hospital in Kansas City."

Jake looked at Cree, trying to determine what was going on. Cree shrugged his shoulders and handed him the phone. "This is Jake Baker, may I help you." Sharing concerned looks with Cree, Jake listened to the caller on the other end.

Cree reached out and wrapped his arms around Jake. He began kissing him on the neck in silent support or pure horniness, Jake wasn't sure which.

Somehow, Jake knew this wasn't going to be good. His knuckles tightened on the phone.

"Mr. Baker, this is Mary English from St. Joseph's Hospital in Kansas City, Missouri, and we have a patient that was brought in to the emergency room with no identification."

Jake held his breath waiting for her to continue. "She was carrying a picture in her back pocket with two men under a ranch sign. The back of the picture had Jacob Baker and Cree Sommers, Junctionville, New Mexico, written on it. We contacted the state police department in New Mexico and they gave us this number."

Gripping the phone until his knuckles turned white, Jake felt the air leave his lungs for a moment and then managed to ask, "Can you give me a description of the woman in question?" *Please no, don't let it be her. Anyone but her.*

"Yes, of course. She's about five-foot, four-inches tall, appears to be in her mid-twenties, approximately one hundred and ten pounds, with long black hair and blue eyes. I don't mean to worry you but the young lady in question is in a coma and we're hoping for some medical information. It appears she has been through quite an ordeal recently and in the past."

His knees threatening to give out, Jake reached for the wall. Cree wrapped his arms tighter around Jake and held him upright. Jake cleared his throat and answered, even though at that minute he wanted to cry. "I know the woman. Her name is Jennifer Barnes and she's my stepsister. I'll be on the next flight out of Santa Fe to Kansas City."

"Thank you, Mr. Baker, I'll have the social worker standing by to speak with you upon arrival."

Cree saw the distress on Jake's face and took the phone from him and replaced the receiver.

Jake couldn't move for a minute. His thoughts swirled around in his head until he felt Cree turn his face to his and kiss him softly. "What's happened to our girl, Jake?"

Jake looked into the dark green eyes of the man he loved and tried to talk around the lump in his throat. "There's been some kind of accident and Jenny's in a coma in Kansas City. They...they got our names off a picture they found in her pocket and called the state police to track me down. Do you know how Jenny got a picture of the two of us standing

14

underneath the Triple Spur Ranch sign?" Jake blew out a calming breath. "I guess it doesn't matter now, the important thing is they found us. I have to go to the airport and get to my Jenny."

Cree looked at Jake more intently and fisted his hands in his hair. "You mean *we* have to get to the airport and get to our Jenny." Jake pulled away and started walking to the bedroom to pack a bag. Cree stopped him with a hand on his arm. "I sent that picture to my momma in a Christmas card a couple years ago."

* * * * *

Five hours later they arrived at St. Joseph's Hospital and were immediately met by the social worker.

"Hi, Mr. Baker, I'm Nancy Victor, the social worker on call tonight. I wanted to talk to you before allowing you to see Ms. Barnes. We have some questions regarding her past and present injuries that we were hoping you could shed some light on."

With Cree standing beside him holding his hand, Jake nodded, unable to answer around the tight knot in his throat.

"Mr. Baker, your stepsister has two brands, one old and one new, burned into her skin." Jake's ears began ringing and it took all his concentration to focus on the rest of the conversation. "The police have been notified and are anxious for any information you can give them regarding the identity of the person or persons responsible."

In that instant Jake saw his father's face on the worst day of his life almost five years ago. Cree and Jake thought if they left the Double B, Jenny's part in the affair would be forgiven. Jake now knew all was not forgiven. Jenny had paid dearly for their mistake and Jake knew she would never be able to forgive them. Jake looked over his shoulder to Cree standing behind him with his hand on Jake's shoulder. He could see in Cree's eyes that he was thinking the same thing.

15

Chapter Two
11 years ago

ೲ

Jenny was twelve when her mother, Helen, married Buck Baker and came to live on the Double B ranch in Oklahoma. Buck always said he'd never remarry after Jake's mother died so it came as quite a shock when he brought home Helen and her daughter after a short business trip and they were already married.

Jenny was a beautiful girl with midnight black hair and the bluest eyes he'd ever seen. She looked so delicate with her porcelain skin and tiny frame. Jenny was also a lonely child out on the ranch with only grownups for company. She began seeking out Jake and his best friend Cree Sommers. They didn't really want a twelve-year-old following them around but they both felt sorry for the sweet little girl.

They began to include Jenny in their daily activities out on the ranch. Cree even saved her life that first summer, when she fell into the deep water of the creek that ran down the center of the ranch. Jenny was picking wildflowers along the bank while he and Cree were fishing when they heard the splash of water and then the screams. Cree immediately jumped into the water to the flailing little girl. He carried her out of the creek and seemed to win her heart and devotion in that one act. That was the summer both he and Cree taught their Jenny how to swim.

The next year both Jake and Cree graduated high school and decided to join the Navy together. Jake hadn't been outside Oklahoma and wanted to see the world. Cree wanted to get away from the reservation and the bad memories of his childhood. Cree's dad was a white man who worked for the government. He met Naomi, Cree's mother and they fell in lust at first sight.

Naomi got pregnant and the elders of the tribe insisted Lyle Sommers do the right thing and marry her. Afraid for his job, Lyle married Naomi and set up house on the reservation. Lyle never wanted an Indian wife or a half-breed kid and he let them know it daily. When Naomi got pregnant for a second time it was more than Lyle could take and he left the reservation never to be heard from again. The lasting damage to Cree's self-confidence was his only legacy.

The summer before they left for the Navy they tried to do everything they could with Jenny. She was so sad that they were leaving her. Cree and Jake took her fishing and swimming almost every evening after Jake's chores were done.

Buck, Jake's father, was distancing himself from Jake even further at this point. Buck hated the thought of Jake joining the Navy. He just assumed Jake would want to follow his example and take over the ranch for him someday. When Jake tried to tell his father that he wanted to see the world before being stuck back in Oklahoma until he died Buck went crazy. "You goddamn little bastard. Are you implying this ranch isn't good enough for you? That being 'stuck' here is a fate worse than death? Just know this, you little smart-mouthed punk, if you leave this ranch you leave it. Got it, boy?"

"Yes, sir, I understand," Jake mumbled although he was sure his dad would change his mind after he was gone awhile.

As the years followed, Jenny wrote to Cree and Jake almost daily. She told them of her life on the ranch and asked about their days. It was the tone of the letters that became increasingly more despondent as the years went by that had both Jake and Cree questioning Jenny's happiness. Often the letters appeared to have tearstains on the pink pages. Whenever they questioned her about her happiness Jenny would tell them everything was fine and they needed to concentrate on keeping themselves safe so they could come back to her.

Jake and Cree became Navy Seals, which kept them away from home for the better part of the next four years. On their first leave together they decided to go back to the ranch and see their little Jenny. What they found was not their "little Jenny" but a beautiful seventeen-year-old with the body of someone much older.

"My God. Jenny, is that you?" Jake looked at the woman standing in front of him. "Where did my 'little Jenny' go?" Jake couldn't believe his eyes at the changes the past four years had made. Jenny's hair no longer hung in two loose braids on the side of her head but in a silky waterfall of black satin down to her waist. Her body had begun to change as well, her breasts had grown enormously and his body reacted on sight.

This was wrong, Jake told himself. *He couldn't have sexual feelings for his seventeen-year-old stepsister. That would be just, wrong.*

Jake glanced over at Cree who was staring at Jenny's chest with his mouth open. "Cree, close your mouth before the horseflies find it."

"I'm so glad you're home. I've missed you both so much I thought I might go crazy," Jenny cried, wrapping her arms around both men. "Please tell me you're staying awhile."

Jake and Cree stepped back from Jenny not wanting her to feel the evidence of just what her grown-up body was doing to them. "Just three days this time, Jenny. I'm sorry it can't be longer but the Navy has kept us busy and we're to report back for duty in four days," Jake said.

Jenny looked so sad it almost broke his heart. "Let's just make the most of the time we have together." Jake looked at Cree and then back to Jenny hoping to see a sign of acceptance in her eyes.

"Cree," Jenny asked softly, "can you stay here at the ranch with us or are you planning to go see your momma on the reservation?"

"My momma didn't know I was coming and went to Texas to see her newest grandbaby. So I guess if you want me, you got me," Cree said with a sexy grin.

* * * * *

That night they sat down at the dinner table just as Buck was coming down the stairs after his evening shower. Jake noticed that even at forty-five Buck Baker was still a very powerful and youthful-looking man. With dark brown hair with flecks of gray and golden brown eyes it was no wonder all the ladies in town where still keeping an eye on him, despite his married status. Jake couldn't help notice his dad had actually come to the table with no shirt on. "Dad, do you always come to supper half dressed or is this a special occasion?"

Buck stopped in his tracks and his head snapped from Jake to Cree. "What are the two of you doing here?" he asked sharply. He seemed to be surprised to find them at the supper table. "It seems to me you made your choice when you decided you'd rather be soldiers than ranchers. We've got no use for soldiers here." Buck walked to his customary place at the head of the table and sat down by Jenny. "How long are you two planning to sponge off me this time? And for God's sake, don't distract Jenny from her priorities." Buck patted Jenny's hand and then squeezed it gently. "We've settled into a nice routine, Jenny and I."

Jake was stunned by his father's hateful words. They hadn't been close since his mother died when he was eight, but he thought the Double B would always be considered his home. He guessed he was wrong in that assumption. Jake noticed the proprietary looks that Buck gave Jenny when he thought no one was looking. He figured Buck had substituted Jenny for the son that had left him.

19

Jenny's mother Helen had been bedridden for the past three months due to an unknown illness. Jenny told Jake the doctors couldn't find anything to explain the extreme fatigue Helen was experiencing.

* * * * *

The next three days flew by for Jenny, Cree and Jake. They went swimming in the creek and rode fences like they did the summer Jenny came to live on the Double B. Jake enjoyed being back on the ranch especially swimming with Jenny in a bikini. He would never forget that tiny green swimsuit. Her breasts spilled out the top and he kept hoping that he would catch a glimpse of one of the large nipples he could see straining through the thin material. Jenny seemed to be totally unaware of her sensual body.

When the three of them swam together, Jenny still jumped on them trying to push them under the water like she did when she was a kid. This Jenny, however, was definitely not a kid. One day as the three of them were swimming, Jenny swam to him and wrapped her legs around his waist, trying to wrestle him under the water. Jake's cock had immediately reacted to the soft mound pressed against it. Jenny seemed to catch on quickly to what was happening with his body. She looked him in the eye and kissed him. The kiss was all he'd been waiting for. Jake grabbed Jenny's ass and pulled her even closer, rubbing his cock on that sweet pussy as he devoured her mouth. Cree swam up and pulled Jenny out of Jake's arms and kissed her like a man dying of thirst. Jenny looked from Cree to Jake and smiled.

"Make love to me, both of you, please," she asked shyly.

Jake closed his eyes and groaned. "Sorry, Jenny, we can't yet you're still a little young for that. Save yourself for us and when the time is right it'll happen." Jake took a calming breath and tried to get his dick to cooperate.

Jenny formed her kissable lips into a mock pout. "All right, but I'm going to hold you two to that promise."

All too soon it was time to leave and Jake watched the tears run down Jenny's face as she waved them down the drive leading to the county road.

The letters they exchanged became increasingly more personal as the time went on. Both Jake and Cree began to love Jenny like the woman she had become. A year later a telegram came informing him that Helen had died from her lengthy illness. Jake and Cree both took leave to be there for Jenny.

Three days later Jake and Cree pulled up to the ranch house in their rental car. No one seemed to be around to greet them. The house was empty, so they made their way to the barn. As they entered the barn, waiting for their eyes to adjust to the light, they could here Jenny crying.

"Jenny? Where are you? Cree and I are here for ya, baby."

"Jake! I'm in the back stall. Please wait and I'll be there in a minute," called Jenny.

"Jenny, it's Cree, do you need some help?" He couldn't help but hear the sadness and distress in her voice.

Jenny came around the corner just as Cree and Jake decided to go after her. They stopped in their tracks when they saw her. The right side of her face was bruised and swollen.

"Oh God, Jenny, what happened to your face?" Jake rushed to her and touched her cheek. "Who did this to you? Tell me and I'll kill the son of a bitch!" Jake fumed.

"N-no one, Jake, I-I got thrown by my horse this morning. It was my own fault I didn't have the saddle cinched tight enough," Jenny tried to explain but looked everywhere but at the two men standing in front of her.

Jake and Cree looked at Jenny and then at each other. There was no way she was telling the truth. Jenny was the best horsewoman they knew. They wrapped their arms tight around her waist Jake in front of her and Cree behind her. They held her without words, kissing the sides of her neck, letting her know they were there for her. After a while Jenny pulled away and asked them to walk her to the house.

"I'd like to lie down for a while, if you don't mind. I have to cook supper for Buck and the hands in a couple of hours," Jenny said softly. Her hands were visibly shaking and she still wouldn't look either one of them in the eye.

"Why are you cooking for the hands, Jenny? What happened to Ms. Fitzgerald?" Jake asked. Ms. Fitzgerald had been with his family since his mother died.

"Buck fired her last October," she said with sadness in her eyes. "No one really knows why and you know Buck doesn't explain himself to anyone." Jenny shrugged her shoulders. "Since then I've been doing all the cooking and cleaning. I don't mind and with Mother gone, I feel I need to earn my keep."

Cree began rubbing circles across her back as they walked her up the stairs to the house. "Sweetheart, you're eighteen years old now. You don't have to stay with Buck on the Double B. There's a whole world out there. Get a job in town and maybe a little apartment until Jake and I get out of the Navy."

Jenny turned to face Cree. "You don't understand, Cree. I have no one else. No other family. The only friends I have are you and Jake and you're not even in the country most of the time. The ranch hands have been very appreciative of my cooking skills and it makes me feel like I have a reason to get up in the morning."

Jake and Cree kissed Jenny's cheek and sent her on up to bed. After she closed her door, Jake turned to Cree and said what they had both been thinking. "What's going on here?" He stalked toward the front door with a determined look on his face. "I'm going to go find Buck and get to the bottom of this fucked-up mess." The screen door slammed shut at his hasty departure.

Jake left Cree in the living room while he set off in search of his father. The ranch was looking better than ever. Buck had added a few buildings since he'd been gone. It looked like he'd built a new house for his longtime foreman, Rex Cotton.

He found Buck in the garage, putting away fencing supplies.

"Hi, Buck." Jake entered the big shed. "I was sorry to hear about Helen. Cree and I flew in as soon as we could. Sorry it wasn't in time for the funeral." Jake was startled by the look of pure rage on his father's face.

"What in the hell are you doing here, boy! Didn't I make it clear the last time you two came that this was no longer your home? I have Jenny now and have no use for the likes of you two," bellowed Buck.

"Speaking of Jenny," Jake stared at his father, "what in the hell happened to her face? She tried to tell us she fell off Moonbeam but we both know that just isn't possible with Jenny. So who hit her, Buck? Was it a ranch hand or some punk in town? Tell me so I can find him and kill him."

"It's none of your business, boy." Buck threw the wrench in his hand against the wall. "I handle things on this ranch," he screamed as he stormed toward Jake. "I'm the king on this ranch and you're no longer welcome in my kingdom."

Jake was shocked at his father's anger but refused to back down in regards to Jenny. "Cree and I aren't going anywhere until we know Jenny's safe here. I'll go talk to Jenny again and maybe I can get a truthful answer out of her this time." Jake spun on his heals and starting striding back to the house.

"You stay the hell away from my Jenny, you fucker!" Buck screamed.

Jake's steps faltered at that statement but he kept going, storming into the living room to find Cree sitting on the bottom step with his head in his hands. Cree looked so lost and confused. His head came up at Jake's entrance. He stood and approached him.

"What did ya find out, Jake?"

"Not a goddamn thing except that we're no longer welcome in 'Buck's Kingdom'. He said he already took care of whoever hit Jenny but he wouldn't tell me who it was. He then proceeded to order us off the ranch. I told him not until I get some answers from Jenny and we make sure she'll be safe here." Jake was shaking with rage and Cree put a calming hand on his shoulder.

Cree looked at Jake then looked up the staircase toward where Jenny was resting. "Let's go see about our girl then."

They climbed the stairs to Jenny's room and knocked on the door. "Jenny?" Cree said. "Can Jake and I come in for a minute?"

There was no answer at first then a softly spoken "Come in".

Jake and Cree found Jenny lying in the center of her bed. Her eyes were red-rimmed and her cheek was turning an awful shade of purple. "Come over here and sit with me," Jenny pleaded. "Please hold me and tell me you're not leaving me again."

"Oh baby, please don't cry. Of course we'll hold you." Jake motioned for Cree to sit on the opposite side of the bed. They engulfed Jenny in their arms and began rocking her back and forth. Kissing the top of her head Jake began questioning her further. "Jenny, you have to tell us who hit you. We know it wasn't falling off Moonbeam." He exhaled audibly. "Was it a ranch hand or maybe a boyfriend from town?" Jake dreaded the answer to that question but knew he needed to know. "Please talk to us, Jenny. We only want to make sure you're safe."

Jenny went rigid and pulled back from them. "You honestly think I have a boyfriend in town?" Jenny asked in wonder. "Don't you know how I feel about you and Cree? Jake, you guys are my entire life. The only people left on earth that I love. I know I'm only a child in your eyes but I love you both with all my heart."

"I love you too, Jenny. I've loved you since you were twelve years old. I've been in love with you since you were seventeen and we definitely don't see you as a child." Jake stopped talking. He seemed to be at war with himself. With a slight shake of his head he continued. "I know it's wrong and I've tried to fight my feelings for the past year but I can't seem to get you out of my heart." Jake looked at Cree and nodded.

"Jenny, I love you too," Cree said as he brushed a lock of hair off her cheek. "That's why we have to make sure you'll be safe when we're overseas. You're our heart, Jenny. You are the main thing that's kept us alive all these years. We'll be out of the service in two years and we hoped you would think about coming to live with us and becoming a family."

"You mean it?" Jenny squeezed both Cree and Jake. Her smile lit up her face despite the awful bruise. "I'd love to make a home with both of you. One of the reasons I've stayed at the Double B is because it's also your home and it makes me feel closer to you both when you're away." At that moment Jenny couldn't have felt more loved or special. She looked at Jake and softly outlined his lips with her finger. "Thank you, Jake." She leaned in and brushed her lips across his in a mere whisper of a kiss. Jenny turned to Cree. "Thank you, Cree." With another soft touch of her lips she kissed Cree.

Jake squeezed Jenny and fought for breath. "You are the sexiest woman I've ever met and right or wrong both Cree and I want to make love to you. The problem is we'll have to wait until we can be a family away from Buck. He's ordered us both off the ranch and we have no choice but to go." Jake pulled back from their embrace and looked Jenny in the eye. "Do you need us to take you somewhere, Jenny? We can't leave you here unless we know for sure you'll be safe." Jake feathered his fingers over the ugly purple bruise.

Jenny placed her hand over Jake's. "No, Jake, I'll be fine here at the Double B until you send for me." She suddenly looked a little uncomfortable. "It's just that Buck—"

Jenny got no further in her explanation before the door burst open with an outraged Buck storming into the room.

"What in the hell is going on under my roof?" He pointed toward the three of them on the bed. "You queer boy cocksuckers get the hell away from her. I told you to get off my ranch and I meant it," he raged, spittle flying out of his mouth. "Now, get out or I'll go and get the shotgun and blow your asses to kingdom come." He advanced toward the bed in a blind rage.

Jake and Cree both stood up and positioned themselves between Jenny and Buck. Jake and Cree looked over their shoulders at Jenny who had tears in her eyes. "It's all right. I'll be fine until I hear from you. Just go and keep each other safe for me please."

Jake looked from Jenny to Buck and tried to decide what to do. He was afraid that if he didn't leave things would get harder for Jenny. Surely, Buck would keep her safe from now on. He seemed to love Jenny like a daughter. In the end he decided that he and Cree should leave Jenny at the Double B.

Chapter Three

Present day

ဆ

Jake looked at Ms. Victor through a haze of shame and self loathing. "Wh-What are the brands of, Ms. Victor?" Jake had to ask even though he knew of only one person capable of putting their brand on someone.

"Well, there's one old brand and one fresh one with the letters BB. Does that mean anything to you, Mr. Baker?"

"Yes." Jake started to cry and Cree hugged him from behind to give him strength. "The brands are for the Double B ranch in Payne County, Oklahoma. The ranch belongs to my father Buck Baker. Your patient is my stepsister Jenny. Please contact the authorities in Payne County and have my father arrested or I swear he won't live another day." Jake took a deep breath, "Can we see Jenny now?"

"Mr. Baker, your stepsister is still in a coma. She was found on a country road about twelve miles from here. She's been severely beaten and has suffered many lacerations to her torso. It seems she was hit on the back of the head with what we think was the same branding iron used to mark her chest." She reached out and touched Jake's arm. Trying to offer what little support she could. "I can let you in one at a time to see her but you won't recognize her." She looked from Jake to Cree. "I want you to be prepared."

"When do the doctors think she'll come out of the coma?" Cree asked because Jake seemed to be in shock.

"At this point we don't know. Her injuries are very serious but we can't explain why she hasn't regained consciousness before now." Ms. Victor shook her head slightly. "Maybe she has no will to live. The human mind is still very

27

much a mystery. Her doctor does think it would help for her to hear from loved ones. It may give her something to fight for."

With that Ms. Victor took both men up to the Intensive Care Unit. "Gentlemen, I'll leave you in the care of the nurses and I'll go call the local authorities with the information you have provided. I'll be in touch, or the state police might send someone over to take a statement."

Jake was the first to go into Jenny's small curtained off room just in front of the nurses' station. What he saw dropped him to his knees. How could he have let this happen to her? The small figure in the hospital bed didn't even look human let alone like his beautiful smiling Jenny. He looked at all the tubes running into her tiny body. Machines beeped, monitoring her vital signs. After a minute Jake rose to his full height and approached the bed. Looking down at the only woman he'd ever loved, Jake felt helpless. Her lip was split and bruised, one eye was purple and swollen shut and her pretty face was marred by abrasions and various other bruises. "Baby, it's me, Jake." Jake ran his fingers through her long hair. He was so glad she hadn't cut it. "Oh baby, please wake up. Please wake up and let me spend the rest of my life making it up to you for all my failures."

Jake closed his eyes and prayed for forgiveness and strength. "Cree and I have a ranch in New Mexico called the Triple Spur. We designed and built it with you in mind. It's not complete without you in it." Jake took a breath and wiped his eyes.

The three years he and Cree had been looking for her seemed like a lifetime. "Why didn't you come to us for help, baby? You know we'd have kept you safe. Why'd you return all our letters after we told you we loved you?" Jake reached to the bedside table and grabbed a tissue out of the box. He wiped his dripping nose and wiped the tears from his eyes. Jake bent over Jenny's head to whisper in her ear. "None of it matters now, Jenny. What matters is that you wake up and tell me you still love me. Because I sure as hell love you. How could a man ever stop loving a woman as sweet and caring and sexy as you?" Jake kissed Jenny on her right temple, the only spot on her face that wasn't swollen and purple. "I only have a few seconds left and then Cree will be in to see you. Jenny, please give us another chance. We love you."

Jake kissed her again and left the room and walked straight into Cree's arms. "God, Cree, what have we done? Please go in there and make our Jenny wake up."

Cree bent his head and gave Jake a soulful kiss. "I'm going in and then we can go to the chapel and pray for our Jenny together."

"K."

Cree entered the room with a lump in his throat and revenge on his mind. In this situation he was not the local sheriff but a man in love with the victim. He would see that justice was done. What kind of justice remained to be seen.

Cree walked to the bed and reached out a hand to grab the guardrail before he too fell over. The smell of medicine and the beeping of monitors all threatened to overwhelm him.

"Sweetheart, can you hear me? It's Cree, sweetheart. Please wake up. I'm worried about you and I'm worried about Jake." Cree had never seen that particular look in Jake's eyes before today. "Jenny, I don't think he'll make it if you don't. I can't lose either of you. You're both my life, my entire world." He closed his eyes and said a silent prayer for forgiveness. "If you wake up for me, sweetheart, I'll see that you're never alone again. You'll be so tired of two lovesick men around you'll beg for quiet time."

Cree took hold of Jenny's hand and being careful of the IV tube, he gently squeezed. He was surprised when Jenny seemed to squeeze back just the barest amount. He looked at Jenny's face and saw nothing, no response. He could have sworn he felt it. Cree pushed the call button for the nurse, not wanting to leave Jenny's side. The nurse came through the curtain with a question in her eyes.

"Yes, sir, is there a problem?"

"I think I felt her squeeze my hand."

"Sometimes the body makes involuntary movements even in a comatose state. Keep watching her and let me know if she shows any more signs of waking up."

As the nurse went back to her station to consult the printouts and call the doctor, Jake came in to stand beside Cree.

Putting his arm around Cree's waist, he gave him a worried look. "What's going on, Cree? Is something wrong?"

Not wanting to get Jake's hopes up, Cree shrugged and circled his arms around Jake. "I thought I might have felt her hand move."

"My God, that's fantastic, Cree." Jake beamed.

Cree shook his head. "Don't get your hopes up. Jake, even if I did feel her move, it doesn't mean she's out of the woods."

Jake shook his head back at him. "It's something, man. It's more than they've gotten out of Jenny in the two days that she's been here."

The nurse returned and told them the doctor would be in to speak to them. After a few tense minutes of silence, Cree turned to Jake and took his hand. "Jake, you know if Jenny wakes up, we can't lose her again. It was hard enough on us the first time, we can't survive a second." Cree looked into his lover's eyes. "Jenny's love for us is what brought our love for each other to the forefront. I love you more than my own life, Jake, but our house is not a home without Jenny in it."

Jake looked at Cree and saw the love in his eyes. "I know. Jenny's the glue that will bind us all for a lifetime. I love you, Cree." He kissed Cree and then looked over at Jenny's bed. "Jenny, did you hear that? Cree and I need your love. Please come back to us, baby. Please make our house a home."

Jenny's eyes fluttered, started to open and then closed again. The nurse, who had been watching Jenny's monitors from the nurses' desk, came running in with a smile on her face. "It seems you two are just what the doctor ordered. It looks like your girl may be trying to fight her way back to you."

Jake and Cree were ushered out of the area while the doctor examined Jenny. He came out in the hall and smiled. "It looks like it won't be long now, although she will be weak for at least seven to ten days."

"Is she awake? Can we see her?" Jake asked hopefully.

"Give her some time to rest and check back in a couple hours."

Jake and Cree decided to spend the next few hours in the chapel asking God to heal Jenny's body. They didn't know about her mental or emotional state. They were afraid that would take a lifetime to heal.

It was two more days before Jenny started waking up properly. Cree and Jake never left the hospital. Even though the doctors wouldn't let them stay in her room for more than a couple of minutes at a time, they wanted to be at the hospital in case she woke up enough to talk to them.

On the third day Jenny opened her eyes to find both Jake and Cree at her bedside. She tried to smile but winced at the pain. Suddenly, she became aware of just what was happening. "You guys can't be here. Get out before he finds you." Jenny looked around the room in a panic. "He'll kill you both, don't you understand, he's crazy." Her throat was dry and scratchy but they should have been able to understand her. Why were they still here looking at her like she was crazy?

Jake bent over the guardrail and laid a hand on Jenny's head, tenderly brushing the hair away from her face. "Shh, don't try to talk, baby," Jake soothed in his deep gravelly voice. Cree and I aren't going anywhere ever again unless you're with us. We can protect you. We didn't spend six years as Navy Seals and not learn how to protect ourselves and the ones we love. Besides, Cree is a sheriff now," he said proudly looking at Cree. "That means we have the law in our corner."

31

Jenny closed her eyes, looking frustrated and edgy. "No, no you don't understand. Buck hates you both so much it's like a sickness inside him. He blames me because I don't love him." She opened her eyes and looked first at Jake then at Cree. "If you're near me he'll find you. He seems to always find me no matter where I go. I can't let him get to you, don't you understand?" Jenny tried to sit up. She winced and lay back down. "Please leave, I love you both and always will but I can't have your deaths on my conscience."

Trying to calm her, Cree kissed her on the forehead. "Sweetheart, the police are looking for Buck as we speak. They'll find him and we'll have him put away forever for all the things he's done to you." Cree took Jenny's hand and tenderly kissed it. "Now, the important thing is for you to get better so we can take you to the Triple Spur and show you the home we've built for you."

Jake bent over to press his nose to Jenny's. "Get some sleep, our sweet Jenny. Get strong so we can build a family."

For the next ten days Jake and Cree took turns sitting with Jenny. They got a hotel room across from the hospital so they could each take turns sleeping, but they never left Jenny completely alone. They were fortunate enough to have good friends back home who took up the slack for them in their respective jobs. Jake's foreman Hank assured him the ranch would be fine while they were gone and Cree was able to take vacation time without a lot of trouble. Cree's dispatcher at the sheriff's station even sent flowers to Jenny's hospital room. It amazed Jake how much their friends back home rallied around them especially since none of them even knew Jenny.

Chapter Four

ळ

The day Jenny was released from the hospital was one of the happiest of their lives. She still wouldn't go into any details of her attack, only that her attacker was Buck Baker. Jenny promised if they found him she would explain the details at that time. Without Buck being in custody she was just too afraid to talk.

The police were not having any luck finding Buck. The Double B hadn't seen the "King" for about six months. The foreman, Rex Cotton, explained to the police that Buck said he needed some time away to figure out some family issues and he would check in periodically. He hadn't heard from him in a month and didn't know where he called from the last time.

Cree and Jake went on a mini-shopping spree and bought some clothes for Jenny. They made a list of her sizes and favorite things to wear. Just like them, Jenny was fairly easy to please. Simple jeans, t-shirts and a pair of tennis shoes were all she asked for. Cree and Jake had the best time picking out new panties for her. They purposely only bought one bra because they both preferred her without one. It would be a while before she could wear one anyway, with the still healing brand on her breast. After they got Jenny dressed in her new clothes they took her home to the Triple Spur.

As they pulled up alongside the ranch house Cree looked in the rearview mirror at Jake who held a sleeping Jenny in his arms. "As soon as we get Jenny comfortable, I'm going to the station and catch up with the Missouri and Oklahoma State Police to see if there's any word on locating Buck. I shouldn't be gone for more than a couple of hours but I'll have my cell phone with me in case something should happen. I've also been thinking maybe we should call in a few favors from 'The

Team'. It would make me feel a lot better, knowing Jenny is well surrounded by men that we trust to keep her safe."

"Good idea," Jake agreed. "I'll start calling around while you're at the station and see what we can come up with. I know some of them have gotten out of the service since we left." Jake shifted Jenny in his arms. She was still bruised and sore but at least the swelling was gone. "Jenny, wake up, baby, we're home. I'm just going to carry you into the house, okay?"

Jenny slowly opened her eyes. She turned her head to look out the side window and gasped. "Oh, guys, it's beautiful. It's probably the prettiest house I've ever seen."

"Glad you like it," chuckled Cree. "We built it for you. Come in and see your new home, sweetheart." With that, Cree opened the front door and waited for Jake to carry Jenny up the fieldstone steps.

The house was set in a stand of trees. They'd taken a great amount of care to incorporate the house into the surroundings. Cree thought they'd done a good job with the stone and timber house. A wide front porch running the width of the house was bordered by flowers and furnished with comfortable seating. The ceiling fans overhead created a breeze even on the hottest day. The entire back wall of the house was mostly glass in an effort to bring the beautiful views of timber and hills indoors. Cree was justifiably proud of his design. The interior was a combination of Jake's taste, Cree's taste and what they thought Jenny would need and want in a home.

Jake carried Jenny through the front door and stopped so they could get her first impression of the great room. Done in natural woods and leather furniture the room seemed cozy despite its size. The ceiling was twenty feet high with exposed beams. The hardwood floors were wide-planked and had been salvaged from an old barn. Dark red area rugs made the large room feel cozy. The river rock fireplace took up a good portion of one wall with book-filled shelves on either side. The furniture was soft, dark brown leather and deep enough to hold two big men. Jake saw Jenny's eyes light up with excitement. "What do you think, Jenny, will it do?"

Jenny beamed at him. "You have a wonderful home, Jake. Are you sure I won't be intruding if I stay here for a little while?" Jenny looked from Jake to Cree with uncertainty on her face.

Jake shook his head. "Jenny, don't you understand what we've been trying to tell you? This house was built for the three of us. It's never been completely a home until you came into it. And for the record, you won't be staying here for a little while. You'll be here forever if Cree and I have anything to say about it." Jake took a breath and tried to think of a way to get through to her. "The things we told you in the hospital were all true, baby, we love you and we want you here with us. That is if it's still what you want?" Jake probed.

"Oh, loves, of course it's what I want." Jenny looked at Jake, the uncertainty written all over his face. "I'm just afraid it's not safe to be around you with Buck still on the loose." She shook her head. "I'd rather die than to have anything happen to either of you. That's why I stayed away from you for the last five years." Jenny could see the love and anger coming from both men. She knew they would be angry with her but better angry than dead. She still hadn't told them the details of the past five years and wasn't sure if she would ever be able to. Some things were better left to herself. "I'm feeling kind of tired. Do you mind if I take a short nap?"

Jake squeezed Jenny. He wanted answers but didn't want to push too much too fast. "All right, baby, if you think this room is wonderful wait 'til you see our bedroom," Jake said with a devilish grin. He carried Jenny up the stairs to the end of the hall. Pushing open the door he carried her to the large California king sleigh bed. Depositing her in the center, he came down beside her. The mattress dipped again and he looked over to see Cree stretching out on the other side of Jenny.

Jenny took in the room's cool blue and white tones and thought she was in heaven. "This is the nicest guest room I've ever seen."

Cree and Jake exchanged glances. "Sweetheart, this isn't a guest room. This is the master suite built for the three of us." He slid up next to Jenny and put his arm around her. "You have your own bathroom through that door, Cree and mine is on the other side. We each have our own walk-in closets. You see, Jenny, we built this house, this room for the three of us. Do you understand?" Jake looked into Jenny's eyes.

Looking suddenly uncomfortable, Jenny looked from Cree to Jake. "I'm not sure if you'll want me in here." Jenny was unsure of how much to tell them about her fears. "I will love you both until the day I die, but I don't know if I'll ever be able to actually make love to either or both of you. I don't like sex and doubt that will ever change."

Jake visibly swallowed. "Why don't you like sex Jenny?" The question had to be asked even though the thought of Jenny giving herself to another man made him see red. Jenny was meant for him and Cree. That's the way it was always supposed to be. Who had Jenny trusted enough to give them such a special gift? Or, oh my God, was it taken and not given? Jake looked at Cree. He could tell by the look in Cree's eyes that he was having very similar thoughts. He snuggled up to Jenny and continued.

"Jenny, please answer me, baby." Jake drew Jenny a little closer to his side and began stroking her hair.

"It's painful," she whispered into Jake's neck.

"No, baby, it doesn't have to be." How could he have let someone hurt her? "Who hurt you, Jenny? Please talk to us. Maybe we can help you get past this." Jake's body was as stiff as a board and thunder began booming in his head. He wanted a name even though he was afraid he already knew it.

"B-Buck. He…he forced me," Jenny said softly and began to cry in shame. She was so afraid that if Jake and Cree ever found out what Buck had done to her they would think her a dirty whore. The looks on both of their faces led her to believe she may've been right. She tried to sit up to get away from the disappointed faces of the two men she loved more than life.

Cree and Jake both held her tight, unwilling to let her flee. "Jenny," Cree said, trying to find a level of calm in his voice even though rage swept through his body. "Did you go to the police when Buck raped you?"

"No, Buck said if I told anyone he would find me and kill me and then he would find you and Jake and brag about what he'd done before he killed you both. I believed him, Cree. Heck, I still believe him. After I was healed enough to get away I left in the middle of the night and went to the only other place I thought I would be safe." Jenny looked at Cree trying to figure out how to tell him that not only had she deceived him but that his mother had helped. "Cree, please don't be angry with me but I went and stayed with your mother on the reservation. I begged her to never tell you that I was there. Naomi didn't agree with or understand my actions but I think she could see that if she told you I would've run away again. She kept me safe for another two and a half years until Buck got too close and I had to leave." Jenny took a long breath and waited for the fireworks to begin.

"I'll get back to you staying with my mother at a later date, but first I need to know when the rape first happened and how badly you were injured?" Cree slipped into sheriff mode out of self-preservation.

Jake was sure he already knew the when and the where of that particular question but he thought it was important for Jenny to talk to him and Cree about it. He closed his eyes and buried his face in Jenny's hair waiting for her to talk.

"The night almost five years ago that Buck threw you and Jake off the ranch. I was asleep after crying all afternoon when Buck kicked the door in. He was carrying something in his hand but I was too afraid to move. The look in his eyes told me that he was very drunk and very angry.

"He came over to the bed and pulled the covers off and then reached for the neck of my sleep shirt and ripped it down the center. I tried fighting him. I kicked and screamed but I was no match for Buck." Tears began to trickle down Jenny's face. "The next thing I felt was a blinding pain on my stomach. Looking down, I saw the branding iron in his hand. I looked Buck in the eye and asked him why. He looked at me with a cross between hatred and love and stated very firmly that I was his property and no one else's. He said he'd worked too many years to get me where he wanted me and no cocksucking bastards were going to take me away.

"He started grabbing me and pulling my underwear down, but by that time the pain was so bad I think I must have passed out. The next thing I knew I woke up and Buck was gone but my sheets had blood on them and I was very sore." Jenny began to cry, unable to go on.

Without thinking, Jake placed his hand on Jenny's stomach. He kissed her tear stained face and looked at Cree. Jake needed all the strength he could get from Cree at this moment. Cree, sensing Jake's struggle, leaned over and gave the man he loved a heartfelt kiss. The three of them held each other until Jenny wiped her eyes and smiled at them.

"Thank you both for not being angry with me." She lifted her face to Jake and gave him an incredibly passionate kiss. Jake's lips were so soft for a man's. It felt different than ever before. She began to feel funny all over. Not remembering the feelings swirling around in her mind and body, Jenny just held on for the ride. Jake seemed to sense her needs because he deepened the kiss. Fire caught between them and before she knew it Cree was also kissing her. Cree pulled her tighter into his arms and groaned, rubbing his erection against her thigh.

"Sweetheart, you have no idea how long we've wanted to do this. You're the sunshine in our world and always have been." Cree reached across Jenny and began rubbing Jake's butt. It had been a long time since they'd had the chance at intimacy. Jake groaned and looked at him through lowered lashes.

Jenny reached up to kiss Jake again, then looked over at Cree and gave him a sensual kiss. Cree's tongue rimmed Jenny's lips and they parted of their own volition. The kiss turned primal and Cree began pumping his tongue in and out of Jenny's mouth in a replica of lovemaking. Jake slowly placed his hand on Jenny's breast in hopes of getting her used to his intimate touch. Jenny flinched and it was then that he remembered the fresh brand on her right breast.

Jake stilled and removed his hand as if it had been burned. "Oh Jenny, I'm sorry. I got completely carried away. Are you all right? Did I hurt you, baby?"

"No, Jake, you didn't hurt me. It's just a little tender. You startled me more than anything, but I can't say it didn't feel good. Everything seems so new to me. Like I'm feeling it all for the first time," Jenny said in apparent amazement.

"You are feeling it for the first time, Jenny. This is making love with the people you love, not being forced by someone who's supposed to protect you." Jake began to stroke Jenny's hair. "Let Cree and me teach you what it means to express your love through physical intimacy. We'll go slowly and at the pace you set for yourself." Jake wanted nothing more than to go full steam ahead and undress both Jenny and Cree and show both of them how much he desired them, but, he also knew it would make Jenny shut down. He could be patient a little while longer as long as he knew he was working toward a lifetime of loving.

"Thank you, loves." Jenny needed some time alone to work through the feelings and information that had just transpired. "I really am getting tired now. Would you mind if we maybe practiced some more later, after I rest for a while?" Jenny could barely keep her eyes open.

"Rest, baby. Cree and I'll be here when you wake up." Jake rubbed her cheek until her eyes closed and her breathing slowed. Jake pointed to the hall and he and Cree slowly got up and made their way out there.

Cree grabbed Jake by the back of the neck and slammed him against the wall. Their mouths fused in a searing kiss meant to comfort and diffuse their rising anger and lust. Their bodies couldn't get close enough. Cree kissed Jake with all the love he had. Jake's body reacted to Cree's intensity and began rocking against the hard proof of Cree's desire. The kiss broke so both men could get enough oxygen into their bloodstream to continue with their bodily assaults on each other. Rubbing their erections on each other, both men went for the other's jeans. Jeans undone, Jake grabbed Cree's large cock and squeezed. Cree managed to slide his hand over the head of Jake's erection just as he erupted into Jake's hand. Cree began sliding his hand up and down over Jake's cock as Jake moaned and chewed on his neck. He reached down and fondled Jake's balls and that was all it took for Jake to follow suit. Leaning their foreheads together, the two shared a gentle kiss.

"I love you, cowboy." Cree looked at Jake and seemed to be weighing his words before speaking. "I hope we're doing the right thing by Jenny. I just can't imagine not having her with us but if it'll bring her pain, I can't do it. I would rather cut off my right arm than to hurt that woman again."

"I love you too, sheriff, and I think we're doing right by Jenny. She deserves love and, lord knows we have enough to give her. We'll just have to be patient for now. Jenny'll let us know when it's the right time for her."

Cree straightened his clothes. "I'm gonna clean up in one of the spare bedrooms. After that I'll head to the station and check on things but I won't be gone more than a couple hours. I'll bring back some fried chicken from Mabel's for dinner, if that's okay." Cree gave Jake one last kiss and headed down the hall.

Chapter Five

Jenny awoke as the sun was just starting to set. She looked around the spacious bedroom and found that she was alone. Gingerly, she rose from the bed and made her way downstairs. No one seemed to be in the house. Jenny walked through the great room to what she suspected was the kitchen. Walking into the bright and sunny room, she stood in awe.

The kitchen was a fantasy land for any serious cook. The wide-planked floors carried into the kitchen. The cabinets were white with black granite countertops. The walls were painted a sunny yellow that glowed with the added sunlight coming from a wall of windows. A fireplace with a built-in pizza oven took up the wall opposite the cabinets. Down the center ran an old-fashioned farm table with eight chairs. She retrieved a glass from the cupboard and opened the stainless steel industrial-sized refrigerator. She poured a glass of iced tea and drank half the glass, still standing in front of the open fridge. Filling her glass again, she decided to go out to the front porch and watch the sunset. Sitting on the big porch swing, Jenny smiled. How many evenings had she sat watching the sunset with Jake and Cree? They were her center growing up. Helen, Jenny's mother, never paid much attention to her, especially after her marriage to Buck. No one really paid any attention to her until the summer she turned twelve and went to live at the Double B.

Jenny remembered the first time she saw Buck Baker. Her mother had taken Jenny to a bar at the local hotel because she was unable to find a sitter. Jenny was sitting at a table eating chicken strips and her mother was off at the bar talking to some businessmen. Jenny was alone at the table when a man came and sat by her. He was huge and he had big muscles and kind light brown eyes. "Hi there, little one, my name's Buck," he'd said and smiled at her.

"My name is Jennifer but my friends call me Jenny," she'd replied, happy to have someone to talk to. "That's my mother at the bar. She had to bring me cuz no one would babysit me and she said she needed some grown-up time."

"Well, nice to meet you, Jenny. Does your daddy know you're here?"

"I don't have a daddy. It's just my mother and me." Jenny and the big man had caught her mother's attention. Helen, still a beautiful woman at only thirty, walked over to the table and sat very close to the big man.

"Hello, darling girl, are you having a nice time?" Helen had crooned at her daughter. "Hi, my name is Helen Barnes, and you are?"

"Buck, Buck Baker," he'd said and took her mother's hand and raised it to his mouth for a kiss. "I was just talking to your beautiful daughter. I must admit she caught my eye as soon as I walked in, she's breathtaking." He'd seemed to think a minute and then added, "As breathtaking as her mother."

Jenny didn't really know what happened after that but two days later Buck flew them to Reno, Nevada, and her mom and Buck got married. Buck took them home with him to Oklahoma the next day.

Jenny fell in love with Jake on sight. His hair was a dark sable brown and his eyes were the color of amber, framed by unbelievably long black lashes. He stayed away from her for the first couple of weeks, always hanging around with his best friend Cree Sommers. Cree was a local boy from the Creek Indian Reservation. Cree was taller than Jake by a couple of inches but just as handsome. The two of them finally noticed her a couple weeks later. How could they not when she always seemed to follow them around? She guessed they must have felt sorry for her because they started actually including her in their daily activities around the ranch. All too soon her only friends were leaving her to join the Navy.

The years they were gone were the loneliest of her life. She couldn't wait to get home from school each day so she could write them a letter. Cree one day and Jake the next. Jenny poured her heart into the letters.

It was about three and a half years after they left that her mother started getting sick. No one could figure out what exactly was wrong with her. She took to bed and stayed there until she died.

Jenny knew she should have been more aware of the feelings Buck felt for her. She'd childishly thought his tight embraces and kisses on the cheek were his way of offering support for a teenage girl with a sick mother. At no time, until the day of her momma's funeral, did Jenny feel afraid of her stepfather.

When they'd returned to the house after her mother's funeral she'd gone immediately upstairs to her room to change her clothes. She'd just pulled off her dress when the door had opened and Buck had come into the room. The look he'd given her had made her uneasy and she'd quickly pulled the dress in front of her.

Buck had just looked at her and said, "No sense hiding from me any more, Jenny. You're eighteen now and a grown woman. You'll have to get used to being looked at with tits the size of yours."

"Was there something you needed, Buck?" Jenny asked in an uncertain tone.

"Yeah, there's a lot I'm needin', Jenny, but I came up to tell you the ladies from the church brought supper by so you don't have to worry about cookin'."

"All right, Buck, I'll be down shortly," Jenny said uncomfortably.

The next day Buck had caught Jenny in the barn cleaning out Moonbeam's stall. He had come up behind Jenny and put his hands on her breasts. Jenny spun around with fire in her eyes. "What do you think you're doing? You're my father, never touch me again or I'll leave the Double B and you'll never see me again."

The next thing she knew Buck had backhanded her across the face. His eyes had bored into hers and he'd screamed, "First of all, I'm not your father. I'm your stepfather which means that we don't share any blood. Nothing says we can't be together in the biblical sense. And secondly, I've done too much to get you where I want ya. Don't even think about ever leaving me or ever threatening me again. You might just end up in the same place your momma's at." With that, Buck had stormed out of the barn. Moments later Jake and Cree had driven up and found her there.

Now as Jenny watched the sunset, she began thinking about Jake and Cree. What exactly was their relationship? She'd never asked but she always wondered. Jenny decided that she would have to take the initiative and ask one or both of them. No sooner had the thought gone through her head that she saw Jake coming back from the horse barn. She smiled at his lazy cowboy swagger. The man sure did look good in a pair of faded jeans.

Walking beside him was a sad-looking hound. "Who's your friend there, Jake?"

Jake climbed the porch steps and looked down at the dog. "Well, hello there, sleeping beauty. I hope you're feeling a little better." Jake went over and sat beside Jenny on the swing. He put his arm around her shoulders and leaned down to give her a soft kiss.

Leaning her head on Jake's shoulder, Jenny smiled. "I'm feeling much better, thank you."

Looking across at the hound asleep in his usual spot, Jake laughed. "That beast of burden is my friend Blue. I adopted him from the local shelter about two years ago. They were about to put him to sleep. I guess no one wanted a thirteen-year-old bloodhound but me." He looked at Jenny and smiled.

"Cree's really not all that fond of him. Blue likes to get up on the furniture out here." Jake shrugged his shoulders. "I love him. He's good company when Cree's at the station."

Setting the porch swing in motion once again, Jenny looked out toward the pasture. She felt completely relaxed. It had been a very long time since she'd felt at peace, even if it was just for a few brief moments. "I was just sitting out here enjoying the sunset. There's nothing like watching the sun set over the land. It makes the whole pasture a delicate shade of pink." Jenny lifted her head off Jake's shoulder and looked into his warm amber eyes. "You have a beautiful ranch here, Jake. You should be very proud of yourself."

"I am." He nodded. "There's nothing like owning your own piece of the world to make a man feel good." Jake's eyes looked out over the pastures to the new horse barn and timber and stone bunkhouse.

Jenny took Jake's hand and ran her fingers along the bulging veins of his hand and arm. "Jake, can I ask you a question? If I'm out of line please just say so, okay?"

"Jenny, you can ask me anything. There's nothing that's off-limits between us as far as I'm concerned." Jake pulled her hand up for a kiss which then turned into a lick.

Jenny giggled. She was suddenly nervous about asking him about his sex life. The last thing Jenny wanted was to offend him in any way. "Jake what exactly is your relationship with Cree and how can I fit into your lives if you're gay?"

Jake chuckled, his eyes crinkling at the corners. "I wondered when we were going to get around to this discussion. Well, baby, it's like this." He pulled her hand to his heart and just held it there. "Cree and I are in love, but we're most especially in love with you."

Jake shook his head trying to come up with the right explanation. "You see, I've always loved Cree. We pretty much just had each other growin' up. Oh sure, we fooled around a little here and there. Most farm kids do I think, but it wasn't until we joined the Navy that we fell 'in love' with each other. As time went on and our feelings for you began to change, we realized that we wanted you with us. Cree and I didn't seem to be a complete family without you.

"That's when we called the Double B and talked to Rex Cotton and were told you no longer lived there and no one knew where you'd gone. I asked him how long you'd been gone and was floored when he told me almost two years. I asked him if he knew anything about the letters that were returned to me unopened and he said that Buck took care of all the mail in and out of the ranch.

"We hired private investigators to help us find you but never had any luck. I honestly think that's why Cree became sheriff once we moved to New Mexico, so he could continue to use legal resources to search for you." Jake stopped talking and looked deeply into Jenny's eyes. "Jenny, you have to believe we never would have given up looking for you." He kissed the top of her head and looked around the ranch yard.

"We built this ranch for the three of us. We're hoping someday you'll be comfortable enough to marry us." At Jenny's look of confusion he decided he'd better clarify. "We know the law only recognizes one husband but we were hoping we could also have a ceremony under the stars that would unite the three of us."

Jenny was crying by the time Jake finished his explanation. "Oh Jake, I didn't mean to cause you and Cree so much trouble." She stroked his chest as she talked. "I thought the only way to keep you safe would be to disappear." Jenny knew she had been wrong to stay away from Jake and Cree so long. "I hope that I can eventually become the woman you want me to be for the two of you. It may take a little time but please don't ever doubt how much I love you both. This is your home and I want to make sure you don't change things between you and Cree because I'm here. The only way I'll ever feel comfortable with the three of us is if I know that you and

Cree aren't suffering while waiting for me. Does that make sense to you?"

"That makes perfect sense to me, baby." Jake gave her another kiss. This time the kiss went a little deeper. When Jake wrapped his arms around Jenny, she seemed to breathe a sigh of relief. Jake touched her lips with his tongue and she parted for him. The kiss became hungry. He couldn't get close enough. He wanted to crawl inside her body, so he pulled Jenny onto his lap. Their tongues dueled as Jake ran his fingers through her waist-length hair.

"Is this a private party or can anyone join in?" Cree said, coming up the steps with a couple of takeout bags in his hands. The sight that greeted him warmed his heart and his libido.

"Not just anyone but you can, sheriff." Jake grinned, breaking the heated kiss with Jenny.

Cree leaned over and gave them both long, deep kisses. "Well, as much as I'd like to continue, I say we'd better eat before our dinner gets cold."

Chapter Six

❦

Over dinner, Cree informed them that the police still had nothing on Buck's whereabouts. "Don't worry, Jenny, no one is giving up the search. Since it may take a while Jake and I have decided to call in a few Seal buddies to help protect the ranch. According to Jake they should start straggling in over the next couple days." Cree reached across the table and took Jenny's hand in his. "I want you to know you can trust any man on this ranch to treat you with the respect you deserve."

"Do we really need outside people coming in, Cree? What about all the ranch hands already on the Triple Spur?" Jenny asked.

Jake answered for Cree. "The ranch hands are all good men, every one of them, Jenny. We just need a few trained friends around to concentrate solely on making sure you stay safe. Ranch hands can't always be around if they still have jobs to do. Besides they're trained for taking care of horses and cattle, not for stopping psychotic assholes."

They finished dinner and played a couple hands of cards while discussing the upcoming week. "Cree will have to go to the station every day but I'll be here along with the ranch hands and the four guys that are coming in to town. You should be absolutely safe around the house but make sure you aren't alone outside even though you're on the ranch. I don't want to take any chances," Jake stated.

They finished up downstairs and all three went up to the master suite. "Um, would you rather I slept in a guest room so that you two can be alone?" Jenny asked shyly.

"Hell no!" Jake spun around to face her. Realizing he had startled her, Jake softened his voice. "I don't want you out of my sight, baby. Cree and I'd like a chance to hold you and be with you. We won't pressure you, but we want you to get more comfortable with us and the way to do that is by including you not excluding you," Jake declared.

"All right. I'd like that very much. It's been a long time since I've had a chance to sleep in relative safety. I usually sleep with one eye open. It may take a while to get used to sleeping with someone else though. I've never done it before." With that, Jenny headed for her bathroom to take a quick shower before bed. She stopped and turned around looking at both of them sheepishly. "Um, do either of you have a shirt I could borrow to sleep in?"

"Sure, sweetheart, I have a shirt you can have. Although I must admit I'd prefer you slept in nothing like Jake and I do." Cree grinned and wagged his eyebrows in a lecherous gesture.

"Please give me time, loves. I'm not ready to expose either of you to the mess of scars my body has become," Jenny confessed.

Walking into her bathroom was a pleasure. Done in pink and white marble, it was a bathroom fit for a princess. A chaise lounge sat in one corner along with a makeup vanity and pretty pink stool. A walk-in shower big enough for three and a whirlpool bath big enough for six sat on the other side of the large bathroom. Jenny could tell Jake and Cree spared no expense on her private space.

Taking off her clothes, Jenny noticed herself in the large mirror over the sink. Healing wounds littered her stomach. Like crosshatches, one for every time Jenny had refused to denounce her love for Cree and Jake.

Running her finger over the healed brand on her stomach, Jenny tried to look at herself the way a man would see her. She shook her head — no, that wasn't right — the way Cree and Jake would see her. The brand was pretty small, only one and a half inches by two inches, but the skin was raised and puckered a bit. If it had been on either Cree or Jake, would it make her sick? The answer came to her immediately. "No," she said out loud.

Jenny took her time in the shower thinking about everything that had happened in the last few days. "Don't be such a scaredy cat, Jenny," she admonished herself. She knew the two men in the other room would be with her forever if that was her choice. Jenny decided to push herself to get beyond her fear of intimacy. Besides, everything she had done with her two loves thus far had felt right and absolutely fantastic.

With her new outlook in place Jenny got out of the shower and dried off. She still had some self doubts and dressed in the extremely large flannel shirt Cree had given her. It went past her knees and she had to roll up the sleeves but at least she felt well covered. She turned the bathroom light off and made her way to the big bed.

Jake and Cree were already in it and in a heated embrace it seemed. Jenny stood beside the bed not quite sure if she should interrupt them. Their hands seemed to be all over each other petting and pulling. The kissing was like nothing she had ever witnessed. Jake and Cree looked like they were actually chewing on each other's lips and neck. Their bodies rubbed together and moans filled the room. It was the most erotic thing she'd ever seen. She must have made a noise because the men stopped what they were doing. "Darn!"

Jake glanced up and smiled. "Get on in here, baby." He pulled the covers back in place and climbed to the end of the bed so Jenny could crawl into the middle between him and Cree. Jake crawled back up to Jenny's side. Stretching his arm across Jenny, Jake gave Cree's abdomen an affectionate rub then a grazing brush to Cree's erection and sighed. He turned on his side to face Jenny and kissed her tenderly. "Goodnight, my loves, thank you both for completing my world."

Jenny's heart warmed. These two men were nothing like Buck. They would never hurt her, so why shouldn't she reach for all the love life was finally offering her. Jenny made her decision and turned her back to Jake's front and scooted back against him spoon fashion. She pulled on Cree's arm, silently telling him it was okay to move closer. Both men reacted to her silent commands. Jake began kissing the back of her neck as Cree took her mouth in a lustful open-mouth kiss. The feelings these two men stirred in her were like nothing she had ever thought possible. Jake's hands came to rest on the front of her shirt, silently asking permission to continue. Jenny covered his hand and moaned. Jake took that as a yes and began unbuttoning her shirt. Cree got into the act, while still devouring her mouth and started from her bottom buttons, working his way up. Very soon her shirt was totally open and she felt very exposed. She made a small squeaking noise but Jake was there to reassure her.

"It's okay, baby." He ran his hand down the front of her shirt. "I think it might be best if Cree turned the light on so you can see for yourself who is making love to you. You'll be able to see our faces and know that nothing about you could ever disgust us." With that, Jake turned Jenny onto her back while Cree turned on the small bedside lamp.

Jake slowly separated the front of the shirt, while keeping an eye on Jenny's face, searching for any signs of distress. What he saw when he looked down threatened to break him in two. Jenny's chest and abdomen looked like a roadmap of scars and brands. Even though the wounds were not completely healed yet, the stitches had been removed at the hospital and they were healing as well as could be expected. Knowing his reaction to the sight would directly reflect on their future, he lowered his head and began softly kissing each scar.

"I'm so sorry, baby. If I could take the pain away and pull it into myself I would in a heartbeat." Jake ran his tongue along one incredibly long pink puckered area of skin. "Please tell me if I hurt you or if you are uncomfortable with anything we do, okay?" Jake looked into her eyes once more. When he saw the tears pooling in her eyes he started to get worried that

51

he had already hurt her. He stopped and held her face in his hands. "Jenny, you'll be honest with us, won't you?"

Jenny nodded her head. "Yes, Jake. I'm not crying because of pain. I'm crying because of the love and acceptance I'm experiencing right now." Jenny tried to think of a way to make him understand the roller coaster of emotions she was going through. When Jake kissed her chest for the first time and her nipples pebbled, she knew that nothing these two men did to her would feel wrong. She would never feel like a whore when it came to making love with Cree and Jake. "I think I'm ready to continue. I want to learn everything you and Cree can teach me about my own body's desires as well as what I can do for you both. I want you both to feel just as good as I do."

A groan sounded from the other side of Jenny and Cree took her mouth in a blistering kiss. "God, you amaze me, sweetheart. To trust me and Jake to the extent you do after everything you've been through is a testament to your love. I hope that in time you can forgive us for failing to keep you safe so long ago. We should've never left you at the Double B that night and we'll spend the rest of our lives regretting our decision."

Jenny put her fingers to Cree's lips. "Shh, don't talk like that. No one could have known that Buck would go crazy. Let's just move forward with our lives."

"I love you, Jenny." With those words, Cree began kissing Jenny again at full force, wanting to climb inside her body. He lowered his hand and began stroking her torso in tandem with the caresses Jake was already bestowing on her. Their hands traveled up and down, always aware of the bandage on her right breast, where the most recent brand was. When Jenny arched into their hands, trying to get closer to the heat in their palms, Cree knew she was ready for more.

As Jake lowered his lips to the raspberry-tipped nipple of her left breast, Cree began wandering down her torso to the black patch of her womanhood. Jenny moaned and began moving restlessly on the bed. Cree found the heart of her and began to probe with a soft but sure touch. Jake reached down and subtlety spread her legs farther apart. Jake continued the assault on her breast with teasing nips and licks as his fingers worked in cooperation with Cree's to bring her to heights she had never known. Cree found her clit plumped and ready. He began drawing her moisture up from her channel to lubricate the area around her clit. He drew circles around her clit with tiny flicks to the hard nub thrown in. Jake probed her heated entrance with his finger as Cree assaulted her clit. Jenny's moans were the best aphrodisiac they had ever known. Things escalated quickly and Cree left Jenny's mouth to move down to the hard nub demanding his taste. Jake continued to move his finger within her helping to prepare her for their imminent joining. One finger became two and Jenny's arousal kicked up a notch. Jenny's breath panted out of her body between moans of pure satisfaction.

"Oh God, *Oh God, OH GOD!*" she screamed as her orgasm took her for the full ride. Her breathing slowly returned to normal. When she looked down her body, two pairs of eyes looked up at her in smug satisfaction. "Wow, can we do that again?"

Cree and Jake looked at each other and started laughing. Their laughing increased to belly rolls as their tension slid away. Jake withdrew his fingers from inside Jenny and slowly brought them to his mouth. Licking them clean, his eyebrows raised. "Mmm, better than maple syrup." For someone known around the area as having a major thing for pancakes with hot maple syrup it was quite a compliment.

Cree, not wanting to feel left out, went straight to the source and pierced his tongue into Jenny's channel. Jenny's sensitized body registered the new invasion in another mind-blowing climax. Closing her eyes, Jenny's exhausted body slipped into sleep.

Jake reached down to Cree and grabbed him by the hair, pulling him up and across to his side of the bed. "Come here, sexy." Jake's mouth slammed into Cree's, thrusting his tongue into the moist depths as if he was dying of thirst. Jake's hands traveled down Cree's body to the waiting erection. Cree broke the kiss and began biting and licking Jake's nipples. Jake starting rubbing against Cree's erection but he wanted to be closer. "I need you in me, sheriff."

Cree reached immediately to the bedside table and retrieved the bottle of lube. Kissing Jake, Cree squirted a generous amount of lube on his fingers and reached down to find Jake's puckered hole.

"Oh God…yes…yes, that feels so good, sheriff. It's been too damned long."

Cree started rimming Jake's hole with his lubed fingers and then pushed one, then two inside Jake. Using a scissor action with his fingers, he quickly stretched Jake out preparing him for the invasion of Cree's rock-hard cock. Cree's breathing was so fast he was afraid he'd pass out before he could get inside Jake. Jake spread his legs farther apart and began begging Cree to hurry.

"Now…God, now please."

Cree lined up his cock with Jake's ass and plunged in to the hilt. He liked making love to Jake this way, face-to-face. They both moaned a sigh of relief. Cree couldn't go slowly. It had been too long since he'd been with Jake. He slammed their bodies together in a force that drove them to the top of the bed. Jake grabbed the headboard so they wouldn't hit their heads. Thrust after thrust, there was no stopping Cree. "Oh, cowboy… I'm gonna."

"Me too, gonna."

"Uhhh!" Cree thought his head was going to blow off. He reached down and took Jake's cock in his hand and began pumping it. He gave Jake another blistering kiss and Jake's cum spurted up between their bodies.

Cree collapsed between Jake's spread legs with his head resting on Jake's chest.

"Too long, Cree. It's been way too long," Jake's head landed back onto the pillow. "Let's get cleaned up and get some shuteye. I have a feeling we're going to be busy for the next couple days."

* * * * *

Jenny tossed her head from side to side, dreaming.

Buck was there hiding behind her car when she got off work. She thought she'd run far enough this time. He grabbed her from behind and put something over her mouth. Jenny woke up in a dark room that smelled like dirt and mildew. Where was she? She remembered Buck and sat up. Her head began to spin and reached a hand out to steady herself. He was there in the dark, she could hear him breathing. A light blinded her, was that a lantern? Naked, Buck stalked toward her with a knife. "NO, BUCK!" Jenny tried to fight him off but he was so much stronger. He tied her hands and feet to the bedposts. Sitting on the bed beside her, Buck's face looked totally void of sanity. "Here's the way it's going to be, Jenny. I'm going to ask you a question and every time you don't give me the answer I'm looking for you'll get a cut. I'll come back every four hours and ask you the same question again. If you still can't give me the answer I want I'll cut you again. We'll continue the routine until you've learned your lesson. In the end, I'll be the only man you love. Got it, Jenny? Now, tell me who you love?" Jenny thrashed out at him but the ropes holding her wrists and ankles were too tight. "I love Jake and Cree," Jenny shouted at him. "Wrong answer, my sweet." Jenny felt the cold steel of the knife against her skin and then the warm trickle of blood as the knife cut into her flesh.

"No...no...Buck...Stop..."

"Wake up, baby, it's all right, you're safe now. Come on, Jenny, open your eyes for me."

Jenny gasped and sat up in bed. She turned her head around the room in confusion. Cree reached over and turned on the lamp. "Where...what happened?"

Jake and Cree enveloped her in a tight embrace, lowering her back until her head hit the pillow. Jake smoothed the hair out of her eyes. "It's okay, baby, it was just a nightmare. You're safe. No one is going to get past us baby." Jake continued to soothe her with his deep bass voice.

Wrapping his arms even tighter around her, Cree leaned in and kissed the tears from her cheeks. "Can you talk about the dream, sweetheart? Sometimes bringing evil into the light vanquishes it." He rubbed her arms and waited patiently.

Licking her lips, Jenny fought to calm herself down. "Buck t...tied me to a bed in a basement in some abandoned house out in the country. He had a knife. He...he would come into the room every four hours and ask the same question over and over. If I didn't give him the answer he wanted he would cut me with the knife and then leave the room for another four hours. It went on and on for two days." Jenny took a breath and wiped her tears. "Finally, at the end of the second day I was too weak to answer him at all. Buck was so angry that I'd failed his test that he brought in the same branding iron he'd used before and put it to my breast. I think Buck thought I was going to die. He became enraged and hit me in the head with the iron. The next thing I remember was waking up on the road. He must have dumped me on the side of the road like a bag of trash." Jenny sobbed into Cree's chest.

Cree kissed the top of Jenny's head and rubbed her back. "What question did he ask you?"

Closing her eyes, Jenny took a deep breath and exhaled slowly. She opened her eyes and looked from Cree to Jake. "He wanted to know who I loved. Every time I said your names he cut me."

Cree closed his own eyes and tried to breathe through the rage that rolled through him. Jake leaned over and kissed Jenny softly. "Go back to sleep, baby. I'm just going to go check on one of the mares that's about to foal." Jake got up and slipped his jeans on, closing the door softly behind him.

Jenny looked at Cree with fresh tears in her eyes. "Did I do something wrong? Is Jake mad at me for what I said?"

Cree was quick to reassure her. "No, sweetheart, you've done absolutely nothing wrong. You remained true to your love for us. Hell, most men I know wouldn't have been that strong without breaking first." Cree kissed her hair and ran his hands up and down her arms soothing her. "Jake just needs a little time to digest everything you told him. Don't forget Buck's his father. Believe me, it takes a lot out of a person to hate their own father. He'll be fine in the morning, sweetheart. Now close your eyes and go to sleep. After you're asleep I'll go and check on Jake."

Thirty minutes later Cree entered the horse barn. He found Jake curled up in the corner by the mare's stall. Jake's sobs broke Cree's heart. To see such a strong man break down and cry like a baby was almost more than he could stand.

Kneeling beside him, Cree put his hand slowly around Jake's neck and pulled him close. Jake grabbed on to Cree like a lifeline. "It's okay, cowboy. I've got ya now." Cree sat on the dirt and pulled Jake even closer.

Jake couldn't control his emotions. Every time he began to talk nothing would come out but more sobbing. Finally, after a good fifteen minutes Jake leaned back and looked at Cree. "Why? How can anyone deserve to be loved that much? I don't think I deserve her, Cree. For so many years I put my own wants and needs first. Now I find out that Jenny paid the price for my own selfishness. How can she still love us?"

Cree looked into Jake's eyes. He knew Jake was looking to him for answers. "Because she's our Jenny. There is no other person on earth like her. Why don't we just thank God that she finds us worthy." He kissed Jake and hugged him tighter. "Let's both make sure we spend the rest of our lives living up to that kind of love, okay?"

Wiping his eyes, Jake nodded. "Yeah, why don't we do that?" Jake got up and pulled on Cree's hand. "Come on, sheriff. Let's go wrap Jenny in her very own security blanket while she sleeps."

Chapter Seven

&

Jenny opened her eyes the next morning to sunlight streaming through the windows and two gorgeous men in bed with her. She took a minute to study her loves. Jenny had never really looked at a naked man besides in a magazine she saw once. Buck didn't count because he never got fully naked and she was too busy crying to see anything. Now though, she had the time and the opportunity to look her fill. Both men were gorgeous, both tanned and muscled. Jenny noticed that neither one had hair on his groin. That was strange. As she studied the differences between the two cocks, she decided that both were going to be way, way too big for her. Cree's cock had to be at least eight and a half inches long with a rather large circumference. Jake's was a little shorter than Cree's but he definitely had him beat in circumference. There was no way she would even be able to get her hand around that fat beast. Jenny was in her own little world studying the two cocks in front her when all the sudden they both began to grow. "Oh my," Jenny said, fascinated at the changes being made before her eyes.

"See something you like, sweetheart?" Cree grinned down at her.

Embarrassed by getting caught looking, Jenny looked up at Cree. "Uh…I'm sorry. I've never really looked at a real live one. I hope you don't mind?"

"As you can see, I don't mind at all and from the looks of it Jake doesn't seem to mind either," Cree chuckled.

"Can I ask you a question?" At Jake's nod she continued. "Why don't either of you have any hair down there?"

"We have our groin area waxed. It enhances our pleasure. Don't you like it?" Jake suddenly looked a little worried.

"No, I mean, yes, I do like it. It looks so soft and smooth. Can I feel it?" Jenny asked shyly.

"Baby, I would love for you to feel it…lick it…and nibble it…whatever you'd like to do to it but I think right now I hear a car coming up the drive," Jake groaned.

"Later you can take us both for a test run." Cree reached down and hauled her up for a morning kiss. He smacked her lightly on the bottom and climbed out of bed. "Up and at 'em, lazybones. That means you too, Jake."

While Jenny and Jake were dressing, Cree went downstairs to see who had arrived. It was Remy Boudreaux, the "Crazy Cajun", and Ben Thomas, both ex-Seals and good friends. Remy was living down in Key West now. Cree didn't know about Ben, he'd heard that he'd become a mercenary after retiring five years ago. Ben was at least ten years older that Jake and Cree.

"Hey there, long time no see," Cree greeted his old friends. The men shook hands and sat down at the kitchen table. "I'm getting ready to make up some pancakes. Could I interest either of you in some breakfast?"

"No thanks, Cree. We ate in town at Mabel's before coming out here. We both could use some coffee though." Ben flashed his white teeth and reached down to pet Blue.

"Comin' up. Blue, you'd better get out to the porch where you belong." Cree opened the screen door and let the dog out. "And stay off the furniture." Cree started making coffee while the griddle heated for the pancakes. "So did Jake fill both of you in on why we need your help?"

"Jake say yer honeychile in trouble," Remy returned. "Tell me and Ben what do now."

"Before Jake and Jenny come down, let me fill you in on Jake's crazy daddy. It seems Buck has been torturing our

Jenny. It started five years ago but she managed to get away from him and then he found her again a couple weeks ago. We didn't know until recently but Buck claims to be in love with Jenny. The first time he attacked her he branded her with the Double BB logo and raped her." Cree took a drink of his coffee hoping his voice would return to normal.

"She ran away and managed to stay one step ahead of him until he found her again just recently. He did the same thing this time. Raped and branded her but this time he got creative with a knife to her chest and damn near killed her. Put our poor Jenny in a coma."

Cree emptied his cup and got up to poor himself some more. "Buck's under some delusion that she's his property and can do whatever he wants to her. I don't think I need to tell you how much Jake and I love Jenny. Hell, you guys have heard us talk about her for the last ten years. The police have been searching for the bastard but haven't tracked him down yet. I have my department helping with the search locally just to make sure every one is watching out for him. What I need from the two of you is to stick close to the house and keep Jenny safe. We've got ranch hands all over the damn place but they've got their own work to do. I'll be gone most days at the sheriff's station. We've told Jenny not to go out of the house unless she has an escort. That's where you two will come in. Sound good?"

Both men nodded their agreement as Jake and Jenny came into the room arm in arm.

"Hey, guys, I'd like to introduce you to the love of my and Cree's life. This is Miss Jenny Barnes. Jenny, these two rascals are Remy Boudreaux—don't worry if you can't understand him, he's Cajun no one can understand him—and this tall bald guy is Ben Thomas."

Jenny held out her hand to both men. "Thank you both for putting your lives on hold to come to my aid. I tried to tell Cree and Jake that if Buck wants me he'll find a way but they think you two can help keep me safe." Jenny smiled at the two men. *What does the Navy feed these men?* she thought.

Remy was every bit as big as Jake and Cree. He was gorgeous, with overly long black curly hair, deep green eyes and naturally tanned skin. Ben was older than the rest of the men. He was a giant, standing at least six-feet, seven-inches. The muscles in his arms and chest strained his black t-shirt. His eyes were a steel gray and not a single hair was present on his shiny head. He looked tougher than Mr. Clean. He even had the small gold hoop earring.

Ben took Jenny's hand and placed a kiss on it. "Think nothing of it, ma'am. Cree and Jake have talked about you for so many years we feel like you're part of the family. Family sticks together no matter what in the Seals."

"*Weh*," seconded Remy.

Jenny looked at Cree in confusion at Remy's reply.

Cree laughed. "That means 'Yes' to this crazy Cajun. Remy, if you want Jenny to be able to understand, you speak English."

"Okay, boss man." Remy grinned, also bending over to place a kiss on Jenny's hand.

After breakfast, Cree left for the sheriff's station and Jake went out to the horse barn to give out the day's duties to the hands.

Jenny cleaned the kitchen then wandered around the house. The house had five bedrooms. She wondered if they were all guest rooms or if Jake and Cree were hoping to fill them up with children. Jenny hadn't really thought about children. She wasn't sure if she would make a good mother, but she was positive both Jake and Cree would be excellent fathers and role models. Jenny began to wonder what they would tell their children about the relationship the three of them had. Would they be honest about it and "let the chips fall were they may"? Yes, she decided. She wasn't in the least bit ashamed of loving two men.

A couple hours later Jenny began to get really bored. Looking out the window she saw a hot tub outside the French doors leading from the family room. The hot tub had a privacy fence on the other side of it, so she wouldn't have to worry about anyone outside seeing her. Ben was working on the computer in Jake's office and Remy was taking a nap on the sofa. Slowly, Jenny opened the doors to go outside. She didn't have a suit but no one would be able to see her. She grabbed a towel from the little rack just inside the door. Once outside, Jenny peeled off her shirt and shorts and left on her panties. Slowly lowering herself in the water, Jenny let out a relaxed sigh. God, this felt good on her sore muscles. She must have dozed off because the next thing she knew she heard Remy open the door and call her name.

"Honeychile, don't you know better than to be out here by yourself?"

Startled, Jenny sprang up out of the water and grabbed for her towel. When she realized that she had just exposed herself to Remy, she spun around and put her back to him.

Remy swore, "What that *bon rien* do to you, honeychile? I never saw the likes of it. Dat bastard better hope de cops find him before any of us do. Shor nuff!"

Jenny quickly put her clothes on after a quick dry off and tried to hurry past Remy. "I'm sorry. I didn't think anyone would see me out here. I won't do it again."

Remy reached out and gently stopped her progress. "Do not fret yer pretty head, we'll get de bastard." With that, he let Jenny flee into the house.

Late in the afternoon, Jenny began fixing a big dinner for her loves and her protectors. She decided on pot roast, potatoes, carrots and homemade rolls.

At five o'clock, she was just taking the roast out of the oven when two arms circled her. Jenny gasped and nearly dropped the hot pan.

"Whoa," Cree cried, helping her to regain balance of the pan. He reached over and put it on the table. "I'm sorry if I startled you, sweetheart. I've been thinking all day about getting you back into my arms and I guess I just made a bad decision with the whole 'grab you from behind' thing. Forgive me?" he asked sheepishly.

Jenny turned around and put her arms around Cree's neck. She leaned in and ran her tongue over his lips. "It's fine, Cree. I've missed you too."

Cree smiled and held her tighter. Leaning in, he took her mouth in a provocative kiss. The kiss escalated into a tongue bath on the side of Jenny's face and neck. Cree licked and sucked on her neck while his hands mapped out her stomach and breasts. He put his hands around her waist and lifted her onto the counter.

Jenny spread her legs so Cree could get closer. She took a chance and went with her emotions and began rubbing her mound against the large, hard bulge in his jeans. She was so caught up in her feelings she wasn't even aware that Cree had unbuttoned her blouse. His tongue began traveling down her neck to her breast. Cree reached her bra and pulled her overly large breasts out and began suckling. Jenny moaned and began panting and begging—for what, she wasn't sure. "Please."

Cree's hand came up to rub against the crotch of her denim shorts. Moving back and forth across her hard nub, Cree moaned. "Oh God, sweetheart, you feel so good. If we weren't in the kitchen I'd take these shorts off and bury my face in your sweet pussy."

That seemed to snap Jenny out of her fog, just as she heard the kitchen door shut. She looked over and saw Jake standing there with lust in his eyes.

"That's the prettiest picture I've ever seen in my life. As much as I'd like to join you, I guess I'll have to just settle for a kiss because I hear Ben and Remy headed this way." Jake came over to Jenny and Cree and gave them both big wet kisses. He couldn't resist and bent and took Jenny's nipple into his mouth for a quick suck. "Okay, I'm officially horny now, thanks, lovers."

Jenny giggled and began righting her clothes. She was just being lifted off the counter when Ben and Remy walked in with knowing grins on their faces. "All set for dinner?" Remy smiled with a quick grin at Jake and Cree.

After dinner, Jake took Jenny's hand. "The peanut gallery can do the dishes. I have a surprise for you and by the sound of it, it's here. Come on." With that, Jake pulled her up from the table and led her outside.

From the porch she could see a bright red king-cab pickup pulling a horse trailer coming down the drive. "Who is it, Jake?"

"That, my dear, is the rest of the cavalry but they also brought a surprise for you that I asked them to stop and pick up for me."

The truck stopped in front of the house and two large men got out. "Man, they grow them big in the Navy," she murmured to herself. The men came up the porch steps and shook hands with Jake and Cree, who had joined them. The first man, tall and gorgeous with military short brown hair introduced himself as Gabe Whitlock. The second man seemed hard as stone and very wary of his surroundings. He was Latin, with the dark black hair and skin to go with it. His eyes were deep brown pools of distrust.

He reached out to take Jenny's hand. "*Buongiorno.* I'm Niccolo Bellinzoni, nice to finally meet you, Jenny." Even with his aloof manner his hand was warm and hard. A tingle went up her arm, surprising her.

"Very nice to meet you both. I'm very grateful for your help." Jenny looked past the men at the horse trailer and then back at Jake. "Jake did you say you had a surprise for me?"

Jake chuckled and put his arm around Jenny. "You never could wait to open your presents." He bent down and brushed a kiss across her lips. "Well, come on then, let's go see what

Santa Gabe brought ya." He led Jenny to the horse trailer. "I figured since this was to be your home you might be able to use this old nag."

"Moonbeam!" Jenny's face lit up as she rushed to open the trailer gate to get to her beloved pure white mare. "Oh Jake, I can't believe you did this. I thought I'd never see her again. How did you manage to get her?"

"Easy. I called and talked to Cotton over at the Double B. I informed him of what was going on with you and told him in no uncertain terms that one of our friends would be by to pick up Moonbeam. Cotton was happy to oblige and said to tell you he was thinking about you."

Jenny led Moonbeam to the barn with Jake and Cree in tow. "Can I ride her in the morning? I know I'll need guards but surely one of those men in the house can ride."

"It just so happens that both Gabe and Ben are good horsemen but I'll go with you. You can take your pick as to which of the two you want to accompany us."

Chapter Eight

ॐ

The next day by sunup, Jenny was riding through the pasture with Jake on one side and Ben on the other. She had to pick Ben because he'd been cooped up in the house longer than Gabe. The morning was beautiful. The sun just coming up was slowly burning the morning fog off the hills. The wildflowers were in full bloom and she couldn't remember ever being happier. "This is just what the doctor ordered, Jake. I feel totally free on the back of Moonbeam. I'm glad I've kept up on my horseback riding otherwise I'd be getting saddle sore by now."

"Good to hear you've been keeping your hand in the horse business. I could sure use your expertise on the Triple Spur. Besides it'll be nice having you with me all day." Jake brought his horse, Sergeant, closer to Jenny so he could lean down and kiss her. The kiss reminded him of last night. God, he was getting hard just thinking about it. Jenny had come alive in their arms. She had sucked and licked both him and Cree to completion. A shiver raced up his spine. He dropped his hand to his cock and gave it a good thump. No way could he stay on horse back for long with a steel pole in his jeans.

Jake looked over at Ben. "Doin' okay, Ben?"

Ben looked like a man at peace with himself. "This is great, Jake. It's been too long since I've felt like this. I don't suppose there are any ranches around here for sale? I've been thinking about starting up my own spread. I've never owned my own place but I've done my share of working them in my younger days."

"You know, I think the old Crawford place is for sale. It's only about ten miles from here. You could buy it and we could be neighbors. It has a real nice setup. A two-story farmhouse with barn and about a thousand acres. No bunkhouse though, so you'd either have to build one or plan to do all the work yourself. I'm not saying the place doesn't need a few repairs but the bones are good. I can put a call in to Kate Crawford to see if she's still going to sell. Sad story, Kate's folks died in a car accident five or six years ago. Kate's an only child so the ranch and mortgage all went to her. Poor Kate loves the ranch but she knows she can't run it by herself. I heard some strange things have been going on over there. Might work in your favor though. I'm sure Kate's ready to be rid of all the headaches."

"Give her a call, if you would, and when this mess is over I'd like to take a look."

They rode through the east valley headed toward the creek. Suddenly, the hairs on the back of Jake's neck stood up. Jake looked around, watching the hills. "Ben, keep a look out. Something isn't right."

"I've got the same feeling, Jake."

"Jenny, head Moonbeam over to those trees as fast as you can. When you get there, get off and hide behind the biggest tree you can find and wait for one of us to come and find you. I love you, baby, now go." Jake slapped Moonbeam on the rump and the horse took off at a full run.

Just as Jenny took off shots were heard and the dirt around them felt the brunt of the bullets. "Split up!" Jake yelled. Drawing his rifle from the scabbard he starting firing into the hills where the shots were coming from. Ben joined in, firing just to the left and then just to the right of where Jake was firing. When the gunshots died off Jake looked around, trying to figure out what in the hell was going on. That's when he saw it. Moonbeam and Jenny were both lying on the ground about a hundred yards away. The breath left Jake's body and he was temporarily paralyzed. Ben took in the scene and raced past Jake to get to Jenny. Jake shook himself and followed Ben. Ben had just gotten to Jenny when Jake jumped off his horse. "So much blood. Oh God, there's so much blood. Jenny...oh God...Jenny, baby." Jake grabbed for her.

"Jake, I think the blood's coming from the horse not Jenny," Ben surmised.

Jake ran his hands all over Jenny's body searching for bullet holes. When none were found, he lifted Jenny into his arms and turned toward Ben. "Go up into the hills and see if you can find that bastard. If you shoot him, well, I guess that might be the easiest way out for him because if I ever catch him I won't be as humane."

Ben nodded, saying nothing and rode off toward the hills. Jake kissed Jenny's forehead. "Baby, wake up. I'm here and I'll get you home." He looked over at Moonbeam who was covered in blood. It was obvious the horse was already dead. Jake lifted Jenny and out of pure determination lifted them both up onto Sergeant. Riding for home, Jake took in Jenny's pale complexion. She was so still in his arms, he thought he might die before he ever got her back to the ranch.

Remy saw Jake ride in hard from the pasture with Jenny in his arms. "Not good," he said to himself as he took off toward the barn. He dialed Cree's cell as he ran. "Cree, get home now, something's happened to Jenny. Jake just rode up with her in his arms like the fires of hell were chasin' 'em." Remy disconnected before Cree could say a word. He made it to the barn just as Jake pulled to a stop.

Jake handed Jenny to Remy and hollered for Gabe to bring the truck around to the barn. "Call Cree and have him meet us at Doc Nelson's office in town." Jake knew she probably needed a hospital but the closest one was over seventy miles away.

Remy handed Jenny back to Jake once he was seated in the truck. "Gabe'll drive. What can I do, Jake?"

"I know you aren't used to riding a horse so get the four-wheeler out of the shed and go just past the east valley. Up in those hills to your left you'll find Ben. Help him track down Buck. Ben will tell you what to do from there."

Gabe pressed the gas pedal to the floor and they took off toward town.

Jenny started to stir on the way to town. She gasped and tried to sit up. "It's okay, baby, just relax and put your head back down. We're just taking you into town to get checked out by the doc. You fell off Moonbeam when she went down. You probably just got another good bump on the head but better safe than sorry." Jake ran kisses over her face. He was finally able to breathe and now the shakes started. *Why couldn't he just keep her safe?*

They made it to town in record time thanks to Gabe's lead foot. "I'm going to pull up front and let you out and then I'll park the truck and be back."

Cree was pacing out in front of the doctor's office when Gabe pulled up. Cree ran to the truck and threw open the door. He took Jenny from Jake. "What happened?"

"Let's get Jenny inside and then we'll talk."

Cree carried Jenny through the doors and the nurse was standing there waiting. "Remy called and said you'd be bringing us a patient. The doctor is in the examination room waiting for you." The nurse showed them the way to the exam room.

Jenny was awake and able to answer the doctor's questions, so the nurse escorted Jake and Cree out to the waiting room. Cree turned to Jake and put a hand on his shoulder. "Now tell me what happened."

"Jenny, Ben and I were riding in the east pasture and Buck started shooting. I knew he was in the hills so I told Jenny to head for the trees. When the shooting stopped Moonbeam and Jenny were down. Moonbeam's dead, shot through the back of the neck. The bullet must have barely missed Jenny in order to go in by that angle. When we got to Jenny she was unconscious but with no apparent injuries. I sent Ben and Remy up into the hills to find that son of Satan." Jake closed his eyes, reliving the entire event once again in his head. He opened them to find a strange look on Cree's face. "Are you okay, Cree?"

"No, not when I think about what could have happened to either one of you or both of you. I want to pull you into my arms so badly I can taste it but now's not the time or place." He squeezed Jake's shoulder a little tighter. "I love you, cowboy," Cree whispered.

"Ditto, sheriff."

Doc Nelson came out to the waiting room and looked at both men. "She has a slight concussion, maybe a few more bruises to go along with the ones she's already got. What in the hell has that poor woman been through?"

"Hell," Cree stated simply. "Her stepfather abused her and I reckon he's found her again." Cree shook his head at the implications.

Jake and Gabe took Jenny home. Cree wanted to swing by the station and call the state police to see if he could get some backup. After all, with the day's activities Buck was wanted in three states now.

* * * * *

That night, Cree and Jake ate dinner in the master suite with Jenny. She kept insisting she was well enough to eat at the kitchen table but they'd put their foot down. They both told Jenny to stay in bed for another day. Just like Doc Nelson had ordered.

Jenny finished her soup and put the spoon down. "He's found me again, loves," she sighed. "Buck won't stop until I'm finally dead." Jenny realized that Jake and Cree might think she was blaming them for not keeping her safe. "I know you're all doing everything you can but it won't be enough. He'll find a way to get to me eventually. Your friends can't put their lives on hold indefinitely. Sooner or later they'll leave and Buck will come again." Jenny said, sounding very resigned to the fact that Buck would kill her.

Cree got up and took the dining tray from her. He set it down on the dresser and climbed into bed.

Jake, who was already in bed, put his arms around her and kissed the salty tears from her face. "We aren't going to let Buck win this thing, Jenny."

Reaching out to embrace both of them, Cree thought his heart would break. Jenny was starting to slide back into depression and Jake was starting to follow her. Cree couldn't let Buck do this to his family. Hoping to take their minds off Buck for a while, Cree started undressing first Jenny and then Jake. When both of his lovers were naked he tackled his own clothes. The three of them curled into each other and began petting and kissing. Cree's hand traveled down the long line of Jake's muscled back to his butt. Smoothing his hand around the tight twin globes, he slowly began probing his back entrance.

Jake moaned around Jenny's breast and started to push back into Cree's hand. "So good, sheriff, so good."

Cree reached across and grabbed the lube from the drawer. "I need to fuck you, cowboy."

"So good."

Jake ran his hand down Jenny's abdomen, feeling smooth skin over sleek muscle. He parted her nether lips and began preparing her for his cock. They hadn't had intercourse with Jenny yet but it seemed to be the right time. Jenny was pushing against his invading fingers, trying to get closer.

"Oh, Jake, that feels good. More please."

Cree had Jake well lubed and began to position himself. Jake stopped him, "Wait, Cree, I need to position Jenny first. I want us to all fuck each other this first time." Jake spread Jenny's legs and climbed between them. Positioning his cock at her entrance, "Are you ready for me, baby?"

"Yes. Now, Jake." Jenny wound her hands in Jake's hair and held on.

Jake plunged his cock into Jenny's channel as Cree took him from behind. God, Jenny felt good. She felt so tight around his cock, milking him as he pushed in and pulled out in an age-old rhythm. Cree pumped into him in at a steady pace, reaching over him to caress Jenny's breast. They found their rhythm and the room was filled with "please" and moans.

Jenny clenched the walls of her channel around Jake and threw her head back in a scream of ecstasy. Jake completely lost it at the same time and Cree spurted his seed into him. All three collapsed back onto the bed. Both men curled around Jenny. "I never knew that sex could feel like that. I think you two might have just created a monster." Jenny looked at them with a mischievous grin on her face. She reached up and licked both of their faces.

"Let's get a little rest. It's my turn to be in the middle next." Cree reached out to pat both of his partners on the butt.

* * * * *

The next morning Cree came to the kitchen thirsty for his morning coffee. Nicco and Gabe were sitting at the table. "Mornin', guys. Have you heard anything from Remy and Ben?"

Nicco set down his cup. "They got in about two o'clock this morning. No luck though. They lost his trail south of Santa Fe. It seems he was headed out of town. Ben said they were going to get a little shuteye then fill you in later."

Cree nodded. "When Jake gets down here tell him I'm heading into the station but I'll be home early. Jenny is supposed to stay in bed today as per the doctor's orders. I warn you though, she can be a feisty little thing, so watch her." He put on his hat and headed out the door toward his sheriff's SUV.

73

As he drove in to town he couldn't shake the feeling that
Buck was gone for a while. It seemed to fit his pattern of hit
and hide. Cree decided to give Rex Cotton, the Double B
foreman, a call and have him keep a close lookout for Buck. He
knew Cotton would cooperate with him, Cotton always liked
Jake and no one approved of the things that Buck had done to
Jenny.

* * * * *

Jake woke up with his typical morning wood and looked
at the woman sleeping next to him. Jenny was so beautiful and
peaceful in sleep. Black lashes fanned out over her cheekbones.
Her nose was perfect and her lips plump and swollen from the
night before. The more he looked the hornier he became. He
needed to taste her, to reaffirm that she was indeed safe and
finally in his bed. Jake slowly pulled the covers away and
scooted down the bed so he was eye level with her pretty
pussy. He snaked his tongue out and licked up her slit. Gently,
he pulled apart her pussy lips and French-kissed her channel.
Jenny shifted on the bed, beginning to wake up. Jake swirled
his tongue around her clit and sucked the hard nub into his
mouth.

Jenny began grinding her pussy into his face.
"Mmmm…now that's what I call an alarm clock. Oh, Jake, you
make me feel so good."

Jake was devouring her cunt when his cell phone started
ringing. Without even lifting his head, he snagged the phone
off the nightstand. "Hello."

"Jake, it's Cree, what are you doing?"

"I'm just having breakfast which includes eating a
beautiful pink pussy. Why? You wanna join me?"

"God, Jake, you know I do but I'm getting ready to go
into a meeting with representatives from the state police in
New Mexico, Missouri and Oklahoma. Thanks for making my
dick stiff enough to pound nails though. I wanted you to know

that it looks like I won't be home until after dinner tonight. We're trying to set up a task force of sorts. Now, that said, why don't you tell me exactly what that sweet pussy tastes like first thing in the morning?"

"Well." *Lick.* "It's better than maple syrup," *lick,* "and hotter than the Fourth of July." *Lick.* "Maybe if you're a good little sheriff today I'll save you some for dessert."

"I hope I can get a serving of both of you for dessert. I love you, Jake. Keep our girl safe today."

"Bye, sheriff, see and taste you tonight." Jake chuckled and hung up the phone. "Now where were we, baby. Oh yeah, right here." Jake stabbed his tongue into Jenny's channel giving her the best French kiss of her life.

Jenny reached down and grabbed Jake's head, holding it to her as she pumped her hips toward his mouth. "That feels good, cowboy, but now I wanna taste you."

"I aim to please, ma'am." Jake swung his body around so they could both indulge in their favorite flavors.

Jenny giggled and settled in for breakfast. She took the tip of Jake's cock and swirled her tongue around the large, dark, plum-shaped head. Jenny knew she must be doing a pretty good job as she heard him moan. She wrapped her fingers around as much of it as she could, but the man was huge. Pumping in a rhythm that he seemed to enjoy, Jenny swallowed the head and took as much of him as she could without gagging.

Jake's hips started pumping to the rhythm Jenny was establishing. Around licks to her pussy Jake moaned and inserted two fingers into her tight cunt. He followed her movements so they work in tandem on each other. "Feels so good...so good."

Jenny reached down and started fondling Jake's testicles. She scooted a little and took one of his balls into her mouth and sucked hard. Jake jumped and started fucking her hand even harder. Jenny went back to his cock and swallowed as much of it as she could while she reached between his legs and ran her finger around his anus.

"Gonna blow, baby."

Taking a breath, Jenny barely got out the words. "Yes, give me all you've got, cowboy."

"Uhhh."

Jake came so hard Jenny must have thought she was swallowing Niagara Falls. Her body tensed and shook just as he was getting air back into his lungs. He quickly and efficiently sucked up the proof of her orgasm.

They moved positions so they were spoon style and enjoyed their afterglow. Jake kissed Jenny behind the ear. "I've got to get up and head to the barn, Jenny, but you are staying put today. I'll come up and check on you at lunch and I'll expect you to be in this bed. No arguments."

"Yes, sir!" Jenny saluted and giggled.

Jake smacked her ass and strode to the door. "Sassy little thing, aren't ya?"

Jenny just laughed and buried her head under the covers, completely content and in love.

Chapter Nine

ಊ

The sun was setting when Cree finally got out of the station and strode to his sheriff's vehicle. He was tired and stiff from sitting in a meeting all day with his newly formed task force. The other police representatives seemed to be on the same wavelength as Cree. Detective James Scott from the New Mexico State Police thought they had a lead on Buck that ended at the Mexican border. He was sending inquiries to the Mexican police to try to find out if Buck Baker had really been spotted in Ciudad Juarez, Mexico. Cree had begun to think Buck'd decided to take a little vacation until things cooled down at the Triple Spur. With any luck the Mexican authorities would pick him up or at least the border police would seize him upon reentry into the U.S.

Cree drove down the county road toward home. A level of calmness came over him when he thought about home now. Jenny was finally where she should have been for the last three years and he would do everything in his power to make sure she stayed safe. Five years was too long for anyone to be on the run.

Cree remembered he still needed to call his momma to thank her for keeping Jenny safe for the two and a half years she stayed with her. He shook his head and chuckled to himself. It was just like his momma to keep a secret like that from him. Even though he probably should be angry with her he just couldn't do it. Naomi Sommers was loyal to the people she loved. If Jenny made her promise not to tell Jake and Cree she was on the rez, nothing would have made Naomi go back on her word.

The sky was a deep magenta when he pulled in to the ranch. The weather was starting to turn cooler in the evenings.

Cree stopped his SUV in front of the barn. He wanted to talk to Jake alone for a minute.

Cree got out and made his way to the barn, stripping off the piece of rawhide he used to tie his hair back for work. The breeze felt good blowing through his long hair. He sure didn't miss the mandatory short hair that the military required. Cree noticed the other members of his old team, with the exception of Gabe and Ben, also liked the feel of longer hair. Maybe it was just a way to rebel against authority for men in their thirties. Cree entered the barn. Letting his eyes get used to the dim lighting, he called for Jake.

"Back here, sheriff," Jake called from the back of the barn.

Cree made his way to Jake and found him in a stall with one of their pregnant mares—although from the looks of things she wouldn't be pregnant for much longer. Jake was sitting by Miss Candy's head and crooning softly in her ear while stroking her neck.

Jake looked up briefly and continued his calming crooning. "It's okay, sweet girl...that's it...just stay calm and before you know it you'll be a new momma." Jake once again looked up at Cree and smiled. "Ready to be a daddy, Cree? It looks like Miss Candy is ready to drop her foal. I was thinking maybe you could go get Jenny and bring her out here. She always loved watching births."

Cree nodded, knowing that the horse would prefer no talking while she was in distress. He headed toward the house. Jake's comment about becoming a daddy still lingered in his mind. Cree always hoped he would make a good dad someday, even though he didn't have a good role model growing up. He shook his head to get rid of the thought. "Plenty of time for that later, dumbass," he said to himself.

Cree entered the house. Although he didn't see anyone he could hear what sounded like a party coming from upstairs. "What the hell is goin' on up there," he said as he started climbing the stairs. He walked down the hall and stood outside the door of the master suite.

"Pay up, Seal-boy!" Jenny's laughter came through the door.

"No way. You cheated," answered Remy.

"Man, just pay the lady and deal the next hand," Nicco's voice chimed in.

Smiling, Cree opened the door and looked at the scene before him. Jenny, Remy, Nicco and Ben were all sitting on his bed playing poker. From the stack of money in front of Jenny, Cree could guess who was winning. She looked so young and carefree at that moment. She looked like the Jenny before Buck had put the wariness in her eyes. "Uuh-um," Cree cleared his throat and leaned against the doorjamb. "What are you yokels doin' on the bed with my woman?"

Remy looked over and grinned. "Just losing our shirts. Why? Is there something wrong with that?"

Cree looked over to Jenny and smiled. "How much you take 'em for, sweetheart?"

"Oh let me see." Jenny put her finger to her mouth and looked down at the pile of change in front of her. "Yep, I'm pretty sure we have enough to run away to the French Riviera," she giggled. "Or maybe just the Riviera hotel in Vegas for a night. No matter, I'll get the rest tomorrow."

"Cree, this woman is a card shark, did you know that?" Ben got up from the bed and shook his head. "Try to keep a girl company and she cleans you out. Isn't that just a hell of a thing?"

"That's okay, let's see what she does for fun tomorrow when we all take our marbles and go home," Remy added with a mock pout on his face.

Cree entered the room and stood beside the bed. "Well, I came up to get my girl and take her to the horse barn. Miss Candy is having her foal. Are you interested?" He bent down and kissed her.

"I'd love to go to the barn but what do I do about all my winnings? I'm not sure that I can trust these unsavory characters you have floating around here." Jenny stood up and went to each of the men and kissed them on the cheek. "Thank you, gentlemen, please come back and play with me again sometime." Jenny looked at the proprietary look on Cree's face and smiled.

The other three men laughed and filed out of the room.

Cree wrapped Jenny in his arms and kissed her. "I hope you had a nap today because I've been suffering a hard-on all day thanks to Jake's little image this morning. And tonight I plan to get my own taste."

"Okay, if I have to." She smiled mischievously and kissed him back. "Now take me to the barn."

Cree led her to the barn where they found Jake still talking softly to Miss Candy. The gray broodmare was lying on her side breathing heavily, her eyes taking in the scene around her.

Jake looked up and smiled. "Hey, beautiful, come on over and sit with me and help me keep Miss Candy calm."

Jenny inched closer to Jake, not wanting to upset the mare. She sat down in the straw beside Jake and put her hand on top of his as they stroked Miss Candy together. Cree joined them after retrieving a blanket from the storeroom to put around Jenny's shoulders.

Jake turned his head to Cree and kissed him, using a lot of tongue for such a brief kiss. Jenny loved watching the two of them. She could feel her panties getting wet. When Jake and Cree slowly turned their heads toward her and gave her the same kind of kiss in turn her panties were soaked. "Hey, guys, stop doing that or I'm not gonna be much help with Miss Candy." At their devilish grins she stuck her tongue out. "I told you two you'd created a monster."

The three of them sat with the mare most of the night. At about three in the morning a beautiful new foal came into the world. Gray with a black mane and tail she was the spitting image of her mother. Jenny's eyes grew moist. "She's so beautiful, Jake." She looked at Jake and he reached out his thumb and wiped the tears that had trickled down her face.

"You're beautiful, Jenny. It amazes me that with all you've been through you can still see the beauty in the world. Do you realize this is the first foal to be born since you came to the Triple Spur? I'd say this foal will always be special to us. Our first production as a family and to mark this special occasion I think you should name her."

"Hope, her name should be Hope." Jenny said softly, remembering Moonbeam. Cree reached over and took Jenny's hand. "That's a perfect name, sweetheart. My wish is for our children to grow up riding Hope."

"I think mother and daughter can take it from here. They both look good and healthy. Let's go back to the house, I'm pooped." Jake stood and stretched out his legs then reached down to help pull Jenny up who pulled Cree up.

The three of them walked arm in arm toward the house. Jake looked over at Cree. "What did you find out today in your meeting? Are there any leads yet?"

Cree shook his head. "No, I didn't find out much but we do have a few theories. I'll fill you in tomorrow when I brief the rest of the team. Tonight I'm just too tired."

* * * * *

The next morning around the dining table Cree filled the men in on what the task force had discussed the previous day. "So until we can get official word that Buck has fled to Mexico I'd say business as usual. I know you guys all have lives of your own but I should hear something by the end of the week and then we can take it from there."

"We're here for as long as you need us, brother. Remember our motto, 'Loyalty to Country, Team and Teammate', that hasn't changed for any of us just because we're not Seals anymore." Nicco stood and walked out the door toward the porch.

Cree watched Nicco leave the room and shook his head. Nicco was one of the most loyal men he'd ever met. Cree knew there had to be an enormous heart behind the aloof manner and haunted eyes. Nicco had always been a loner but it had gotten much worse since he got out of the military. He hoped someday Nicco found happiness again.

* * * * *

Three days later the Border Patrol confirmed that Buck wasn't spotted coming into Mexico, but the Mexican Police did find his car abandoned just outside Ciudad Juarez. Because all had been quiet for nearly a week it was time to have another meeting with the team.

Cree sat at the head of the table. "I think it's safe to say that Buck must be taking a break to regroup. However I don't think the threat is totally gone. Buck will be back, I have no doubt. I've been talking to Jake and with your approval I'd like to set up a schedule of two weeks on, two weeks off. We know you all have your own lives and responsibilities. Jake and I were hoping that this would be a good compromise. If any of you can't meet the schedule there will be no hard feelings. We know you've done everything you could and we couldn't be more grateful to all of you." Cree looked around the table and made eye contact with each man.

Ben pushed his chair back and stood. "Cree, I hate to sound like a sorry piece of shit but I don't really have anything else waiting for me. I've rented an apartment in Missoula, Montana, since getting out of the Seals but that's it. I don't really have a job or responsibilities. I've just been living off my investments trying to decide what I want with the rest of my life. So if it's okay, I'd like to stay here until we deal with Buck once and for all. I figure that way Remy can go back to Key West and run his bar until we need him."

Cree looked over to Jake who nodded. "We'd appreciate that, Ben. Maybe the police will catch up with Buck before long but we'd be grateful for you help."

"Uh. Cree, I'm pretty much in the same boat as Ben so that could let Nicco off the hook for a while too." Gabe looked at Cree and Jake for their nod of approval.

"Good, then that's settled. Remy, you go back to Key West and run your bar and Nicco, you go back to…whatever top-secret stuff you do." Cree smiled at Nicco who gave him a sharp nod.

* * * * *

Two weeks later the ranch was finally calming down and they were all starting to get into a routine. Jenny had grown very fond of her two constant shadows, Gabe and Ben, and found herself opening up to them. She was coming out of her shell more every day. With a trip to Santa Fe under her belt to get more clothing, she felt she had finally found the one place on earth that she was meant to be. Her days were busy with the house or the horses. Jenny enjoyed working with Jake out in the corrals although, at times, Jake could be a little overprotective. She had been around horses since she was twelve years old but some days Jake treated her like a greenhorn. Whenever she questioned him about it he would hold her and tell her he just didn't want to take chances.

On one such day, Jenny sat on top of the corral watching Jake work with a mean-tempered stallion named Satan's Son. Jake had a lead rope on the stallion and was trying to get him calmed down enough to try a saddle. Jenny lowered herself into the corral and went to hold the lead rope for him so he could get the stallion saddled. When she approached Jake, the stallion reared up, pawing at the air. Jake pushed Jenny out of the way and got the horse calmed down. He marched the stallion back to the corral gate and tied him off. Jake spun around with fire in his eyes. "What in the hell was that, Jenny? Are you trying to get yourself killed? Do you have any idea what that mean son of a bitch could have done to you?" He reached out and grabbed Jenny to his chest, blew out a breath and just held her.

Jenny pushed him away. "Yes, I knew what I was doing. I'm a damn fine horsewoman, Jake, have you forgotten that? I was just trying to help. It could have happened with anyone, it just happened to be me this time." Even though she was furious with him she understood his fears regarding her. Jenny shook her head. "You can't wrap me up in cotton wool, Jake. I finally have a life worth living. Please, cowboy, just let me live it."

Jenny gave him a kiss on the cheek and left the corral without saying anything else. She went to the house looking for Ben or Gabe. Jenny found Ben reading a ranching magazine. "Hey, Ben, do you want to take a little ride with me and go swimming in the creek? I need to get out of this house for a while and the corral is not an option."

"Sure, I could go for a ride and swim but are you sure you wouldn't rather wait for Jake to take you?" Ben looked a little uncomfortable with the idea.

"Jake is the reason I can't go to the corral. Right now if I saw him I might be tempted to wring his gorgeous neck." Jenny ran up to her room to change into her two-piece bathing suit. She put her jeans and t-shirt over the suit and went back downstairs.

Jenny found Gabe in the kitchen baking. "Hey, Gabe, what're you baking for me today?"

"I got a new cookbook in town so I thought I'd experiment a little. I've got a chocolate soufflé in the oven so don't make any sudden movements." Gabe grinned.

Whispering, Jenny smiled back. "Okay, I'll tiptoe out of here and go find Ben. If anyone asks we're going swimming in the creek."

Jenny found Ben waiting for her on the porch. "Let's go swim, buddy. The day's a wastin'."

It was a beautiful day for a ride and Jenny raced Ben to the creek. They dismounted alongside the creek. Ben took the horses to the shade and ground tied them so they could graze.

Jenny undressed and walked toward the creek. She turned around to tell Ben to hurry when she heard his audible gasp. Jenny's hands immediately went up to cover her stomach and chest. She looked at Ben and closed her eyes. "I'm sorry, Ben. I should've prepared you for the sight of me. I didn't think about it, I guess. Jake and Cree don't seem to notice so I guess sometimes I forget about all the scars." Jenny looked down sheepishly, unable to look Ben in the eye.

Ben did something he'd never done to her before. He walked up to her and gave her a hug. "Don't ever be ashamed of something that wasn't your fault. Cree and Jake don't notice your scars because you're beautiful inside and out. They love you no matter what. Hell, I've known them for quite a few years and besides each other they've loved no one else but you. So dry those pretty blue eyes and let's go for a swim."

They walked hand in hand into the cool, flowing creek. It wasn't deep enough here to really swim so they both sat on the pebbled bottom and let the water rush around them. Relaxed and content, Jenny looked over at Ben. "Ben, can you tell me why Nicco is so quiet around me? Does he not like me or do I just make him uncomfortable?"

Ben took a minute before answering. "It's not that he doesn't like you, Jenny, he's that way with everyone. I think he's still figuring himself out like the rest of us. Nicco came to the Seals with his ghosts. The rest of us got them while in the Seals. He cut himself off from his emotions a long time ago but maybe if he's lucky...damn, if we're all lucky, we'll find someone as special as you who can exorcise our demons."

"Thank you."

Standing up, Ben reached down for Jenny's hand. It looked like a child's hand in his big tanned paw. "We'd better get going or I'll have Jake mad as hell at me for keeping you out too long."

They dressed and rode back to the ranch. Jenny felt at peace once again. She knew Jake loved her. It would just take him a while to calm down enough to let her live her life. He'd been patient with her in everything else. She guessed it was her turn to learn patience.

They rode into the ranch yard and were met by a sheepish-looking Jake. "Did you enjoy yourself, baby?"

Jake looked like he really wanted to know. Maybe it was his way of smoothing things over. Jenny let him lift her off her horse. "Yes, thank you. Ben and I had a wonderful time." Jenny smiled and reached her arms around his neck and kissed him. He parted for her and her tongue stroked the inside of his mouth.

Jake squeezed her tighter. "Well, if that's what swimming does for you I think we'll have to put in a pool," he chuckled and nipped her bottom lip then soothed it with his tongue.

Jenny sighed and put her head on his chest. "We okay, cowboy?"

"Good as gold, Jenny girl."

Chapter Ten

Three weeks later they still hadn't heard anything from Buck. Jenny was happier than ever until about a week before when she started getting sick in the mornings. She knew what it was but didn't want Cree or Jake to know yet. Jenny hid her sickness from them and when they asked about her pale complexion she would pass it off one way or another. She had a lot of thinking to do before she talked to her men about her suspicions. Jenny played hooky from her chores one day so she could think. She took a pillow and a blanket out to the hayloft one afternoon to do some serious thinking. Sneaking up the ladder to the loft, she spread out her blanket. Lying down with her favorite goose-down pillow behind her head she settled in.

As Jenny lay upon the hay she thought on her life, more precisely her future. What would happen if she was pregnant? She wasn't even married yet and she didn't know which man to marry. Would Cree and Jake be jealous of another man's child? Jenny didn't think so. They loved each other too much for jealousy. She ran her hand down her body to rest on her stomach. Jenny knew in her heart that she was pregnant. She had a follow-up doctor's appointment in a few days for her injuries. Maybe she could get an official pregnancy test run then. Thinking about the reason for the doctor's appointment made her sit bolt upright. "Oh my God. What if the baby is Buck's?" she whispered to herself.

Tears began falling down Jenny's face. Wondering whether the doctor would be able to give her a precise date for conception, Jenny tried to count her days. She had just finished her period when Buck raped her. She had sex with Cree and Jake two weeks after that. "Boy, does that make me sound like

87

a slut," she mumbled. With everything going on she hadn't given her lack of a period a second thought but she was thinking now.

How was she going to tell Cree and Jake that their enemy could be the father of her child? Jenny decided to wait and tell them when she had more information. Hopefully the doctor would be able to help her. The questions in her head got to be too much and Jenny closed her eyes and drifted off to sleep.

"Sweetheart, are you up there?" Cree's voice brought Jenny out of her nap. She could here him walking the barn floor calling her name.

"I'm up here in the loft, sheriff." She could hear him climbing the ladder and then his head poked up above the floor of the loft. Jenny smiled a sleepy smile. "I'm sorry, I hope I didn't worry anyone. I needed some time alone to think."

Cree yelled to the men outside the barn. "I found her, guys, and she's all right." Cree finished crawling up the ladder and walked over to Jenny and lay on the blanket beside her. Taking a piece of hay in his fingers, he ran it up Jenny's arm very softly. "Well, you did worry us but I can understand a person's need to get away once in a while. At least you came to the safety of the barn, but next time, please tell someone where you're going, okay?" Cree bent down and kissed her nose.

"Okay, I'm sorry, Cree." Jenny lifted her hand and traced the shape of his face. He was so handsome. His face was chiseled to perfection and his eyes were the windows to his stalwart soul. She ran her finger over his lips. The bottom one looked too good to pass up so she reached out and licked it. He seemed to catch fire.

"Oh, Jenny, what is it that you do to me." Cree took her mouth in a passionate kiss. His hands roamed down to her buttons and one by one they sprang loose. Cree undid the front clasp of her bra and her breasts sprang free. "God, I love your breasts," he said as he began raining kisses and licks upon them. Cree held her left breast in the grip of his fist and suckled like he was starving.

Jenny squirmed on the pallet of hay, grabbing handfuls and thrusting upward. "Please, Cree. I need you."

Cree let go of Jenny's breast and sat back on his haunches and unbuttoned his shirt, throwing it in the corner. He gave her a sexy smile and took off his gun belt and jeans. Jenny didn't see where they went because she was looking at the most beautiful erection she'd ever seen. She reached her hand out and touched the tip of his cock, swiping the fluid pearled there and bringing it to her lips. Jenny slowly opened her mouth, while maintaining eye contact with Cree and licked the tip of her finger.

Cree groaned and closed his eyes. "That's one of the most erotic things I've ever seen. Let me take a minute or I'm not going to last long enough to get in that sweet cunt of yours." He stretched himself out beside her and kissed her neck. "How do you want it, sweetheart, slow and sweet or fast and hard?"

"You're always slow and sweet. How about we go for what's behind door number two."

Cree positioned Jenny onto her stomach and then up onto her hands and knees. Her pink pussy lips were dripping with desire. Cree bent down and swiped her pussy with his tongue. "Damn, that's good." He placed one hand on her hip and held his cock with the other lining it up with her channel. One strong thrust and he was seated to the hilt inside her. They both froze for a second just enjoying the sensations they were each experiencing.

Cree began to pull out slowly. He smiled when Jenny made a protesting sound. He slammed back in and ground his pelvis against her. Picking up the speed, sweat began running in rivulets down Cree's face and chest. Cree pumped into Jenny with no mercy. He felt her pussy tightening around his shaft as she let out a scream of pleasure.

"Good. Oh so good, Cree. Uhhh!" Jenny would have collapsed if Cree hadn't held her up. Stroking faster Cree managed another couple of pumps before his seed was spilling into the woman he loved. They drifted off to sleep in each other's arms.

Jake finished his work for the day and went looking for Cree and Jenny. He strolled out to the barn after having no luck in the house. He spotted Gabe sitting outside the barn on a stool. "Hey, Gabe, have you seen Cree and Jenny?" The man went red-faced and pointed to the barn.

"Uh, yeah. They're up in the loft, Jake. I'll...uh...just go on back to the house."

Shaking his head at Gabe's strange behavior, Jake entered the barn and climbed the ladder to the loft. He swallowed a deep breath. On a pallet of hay lay two entwined naked bodies. Jenny's face buried in Cree's neck. Cree had his mouth open snoring. God, he loved these two people. Jake looked down at Jenny. Even though her burn was mostly healed he worried about dirt from the loft getting into the wound.

Jake undressed where he stood. That completed, he crawled over to his two lovers. He kissed Cree's neck and worked his way down the bumps and ridges of his spine ending at his sweet ass. He held the twin bronzed globes in his hands and separated them to get to the sweet little pucker he called home. Jake could tell that Cree was playin' possum so he decided to give him a bigger wakeup call. With Cree's cheeks spread wide Jake rimmed his asshole with his tongue. Jake stuck his fingers in his mouth and put first one then two slowly up Cree's hole. Thrusting them in and out, Cree finally started to move.

"I hope that's you, Jake."

Chuckling, Jake inserted a third finger. "And just who else were you expecting to stick their fingers up your sweet ass?"

"Just you, cowboy. It feels so good. As you can see Jenny and I are kinda worn-out but come on up here and we'll see if we can't accommodate you." Cree reached down and pulled Jake up by his hair, kissing him when they were finally face-to-face. "Good evening, cowboy. How was your day at the corral?" Cree smiled and kissed Jake's face and neck before moving on to his nipples.

"Hot and sweaty just like any other day. Can I tell you that what you're doin' is really helping."

Jake looked over to find Jenny watching the two of them. "Come here, baby, and get in on this Jake smorgasbord. Eat all you want for a very low price, satisfaction guaranteed."

"Okay, although you know I enjoy watching the two of you." Jenny reached out and wrapped her fingers around Jake's erection. Not wanting Cree to feel left out she wrapped the other hand around Cree's cock. She slid down and took first Jake into her mouth and then Cree. They both started thrusting upward as she swallowed them in turn.

"Just like that, baby. You're getting so good at that Cree might have to worry about his championship title."

Cree let go of Jake's nipple and laughed. "Well, we'll just have to see about that, won't we." Cree slid down Jake's body to press himself against Jenny's side. "Scoot over, sweetheart, let me show this cowboy that no one can take my title." Cree flicked his tongue up one side of Jake's cock and down the other. He made his way back up to the head and devoured him.

Jenny watched in awe as Cree took all of Jake's incredible girth into his mouth and down his throat. Cree began to swallow around Jake's cock. Jake moaned and pumped into Cree's face. Seeing her chance, Jenny bent her head and took one of Jake's balls into her mouth, sneaking her finger back until she actually had the nerve to insert a finger into Jake's rectum. Jake jerked up off the blanket with a roar as loud as any lion's, shooting his cum down Cree's throat. Cree swallowed every drop of seed Jake gave up.

"Yeah, Cree, I had a great day."

* * * * *

Jake noticed at the dinner table Gabe wouldn't look any of them in the face. Concern knitted his brow as he followed Gabe out to the porch after supper. "Got a minute, Gabe?"

Gabe turned toward Jake but looked over his shoulder instead of at his face. "Sure, Jake. What's up?"

"I just wanted to apologize for this evening in the barn. I hope we didn't offend you. Believe me that was never our intention."

Finally looking into Jake's eyes, Gabe shook his head. "You didn't offend me."

"Then what seems to be the problem? You can hardly look at any of us."

"Problem. No, there's no problem, Jake. It just makes me feel... Ah hell, I don't know."

"Disgusted?"

"No, never that." Gabe looked at his boots and said softly, "Envious."

"Envious? Are you saying you want to be with Cree and Jenny?" Jake's voice was starting to get a little louder and whole lot meaner.

Shuffling his feet from side to side, Gabe shook his head again. "I don't want your family, Jake. I want my own. I look at the three of you and get jealous. Why can't I find what you've been lucky enough to find?"

Cooling down quickly, Jake patted his friend on the shoulder. "Open yourself up to all possibilities and you'll find it, buddy. And you're right, I am one lucky son of a bitch."

He slung his arm around Gabe and walked him into the house where a game of cards was getting under way. Not poker. No one would play poker with the little card shark he loved.

Chapter Eleven

It was finally Thursday. Jenny's doctor's appointment in Santa Fe had her jumping out of bed before Jake or Cree awoke. Slipping under the hot spray of the shower, Jenny worried about the day ahead. She had to make sure neither Cree nor Jake accompanied her to Santa Fe. If the doctor did a pregnancy test she wanted to stay for the results. Cree and Jake would worry about a supposed routine appointment taking so long. Jenny decided to tell the guys she needed to do some clothes shopping while in the city. That would convince them to stay home. Neither one of them liked shopping of any kind. "Good plan, Jenny," she whispered to herself.

The shower door opened and Cree and Jake both stepped inside. Jenny licked her lips and got a wicked look on her face. "'Step into my parlor', said the spider to the flies."

"Did you hear that, Cree, we've been downgraded to flies now." Jake reached for Jenny and pulled her into his arms. Kissing her soundly, he murmured, "Good morning, Miss Spider, you can eat me anytime." He began grinding himself against Jenny's mound and pulled her leg up to his waist. "Wrap your legs around me, baby. I want to get closer."

Cree moved in behind Jake and reached for the lube they kept in the soap dish. "I do love our morning showers." He squirted a liberal amount on his fingers and set about slicking up his lover.

Jake found Jenny's entrance and thrust, seating himself to the root. "God, you feel good in the morning. You're all warm and soft. I could do this every day for the rest of my life." He proceeded to pump into Jenny's channel while delivering equally forceful thrusts into her mouth with his tongue.

Once Jake was prepared for him, Cree stilled Jake's ass enough for him to plunge into his hot, tight heat. Working like a well-oiled machine the three lovers kissed, touched and pounded their way to completion.

Afterward, soaping each other clean, Jake asked what the plans were for the day. "I have to go into the feed store and pick up an order but I should be back in time to take you to Santa Fe for your doctor's appointment."

Jenny worried her lip. "Thank you, Jake, but I was hoping to go into the city early so I could do some shopping and go by the hair salon. I know you guys did the best you could with my clothes shopping when I came but I'd like a few more things."

"Oh yeah…okay, so do you want to take Ben and Gabe? I mean, I can send someone else to the feed store if you want me to go." God, he hated shopping, just stick bamboo under his fingernails.

Stepping out of the shower, Cree handed both of them a towel from the warming rack. "I have to go into Santa Fe on business today how 'bout I meet you somewhere and we can grab a bite to eat before coming back?"

"That sounds good. I should be done with everything by four o'clock. Meet us at that Rio Chama steak place I've been hearing about. Then we can drive back together. I'm sure by then Gabe and Ben will want a break."

Cree kissed her. "Sounds good, sweetheart." Cree crossed to his closet and pulled on his jeans, *sans* underwear as usual and a uniform shirt. Patting Jake's ass on the way out of the room, he called over his shoulder. "Better luck next time, Jake. I got myself a date with a red-hot woman today."

"Oh you're a real comedian, Cree." Jake dressed in his customary ranch clothes jeans, boxer briefs and snap-front shirt. "Jenny, are you sure you don't want company at the doctor today?"

"No, Jake, I'll be fine. It's just a routine follow-up. My wounds are almost healed and the burn is no longer tender." Jenny chewed on the inside of her cheek, contemplating her next question. "Jake, do you think I should ask about being referred to a plastic surgeon for the scars? They might even be able to do something about the brands. I know you've said they don't bother you but it can't be easy to look at what Buck did to me every day."

Crossing the room in a couple long strides, Jake reached out to hold Jenny in his arms. Kissing the top of her head and letting him calm down before answering her. "Baby, when I see those scars I don't think about Buck anymore. I think about the strength of the woman wearing them. You've been to hell and back yet you're still my sweet happy little Jenny. Why cause your body more pain? Cree and I hope to put our own brand on you someday soon in the shape of a wedding band. That's the only brand we care about, baby."

Jenny looked up into Jake's eyes, her own brimming with unshed tears. "That's the nicest thing you could have said to me Jake and I'll be proud to wear your 'brand of gold'."

Jake kissed her nose, then eyes, licking the tears that had escaped under her lashes. "I love you, Jenny."

* * * * *

Ben drove to Santa Fe with Gabe riding shotgun and Jenny in the backseat. Jenny looked out the window in contemplation. The scenery was majestic and she knew she'd found a new home. "Hey, guys, I'm going to be going to the outlet mall for some clothes shopping but it shouldn't take long. After that I have an appointment with a salon down the street for some pampering. I thought you guys could hang out while I shop and maybe grab something to drink while I'm at the salon. Sound good?"

Ben looked at Jenny in the rearview mirror. "Sounds good to me. You did say something about meeting Cree after the doctor's appointment, right? My mouth is watering for a good thick steak," he said with a smile.

"Yeah, the appointment is at one-thirty. I told Cree I should be done by four."

"If you don't mind me asking, Jenny, why do you think the appointment will last that long?" Gabe finally spoke up, turning around in his seat to face her.

"W…well, I'm going also to get a pregnancy test and I want to wait for the results. Please don't tell Cree or Jake. There are extenuating circumstances at play what with the rape and everything. I just need a little time to prepare them both. I'm hoping the doctor will be able to give me a best-guess conception date." Jenny looked down at her lap and worried the tissue she held.

Ben slowed the car so he could focus on Jenny through the rearview mirror. "We won't tell, darlin', but do you think it will matter to them whose child it is?"

"No, it won't matter to them but I need to deal with my feelings if I'm carrying Buck's child." Jenny turned to look out the window, cutting off any further discussion of the matter.

* * * * *

After the mall and the salon Jenny took a deep breath and entered the doctors' building at the local hospital. She looked at the directory and found where she needed to go. Douglas A. Higgins, Family Practitioner, Suite 223. Jenny decided to climb the stairs to the second floor office with her bodyguards in tow. Ben and Gabe sat in the waiting room while she was ushered to the exam room after filling out papers and showing proof of insurance.

Dr. Higgins gave her the all-clear sign in regards to her most recent injuries. "I'm sorry such a thing can happen in this day and age" was his only comment regarding the scars and brands.

Jenny asked him about a pregnancy test and about a conception date.

"Well, the test is easy enough. It shouldn't take too long to get the result back. As for the conception date, that might be a little trickier to determine. All I can do at this point is to examine you and try to determine a date by the size of your womb."

The test came back positive, as she knew it would. The exam results weren't as comforting.

"I'd say by the size of things you're well into your second month of pregnancy. If I had to guess I'd say six to seven weeks."

Jenny didn't remember much after that. The nurse gave Gabe instructions for a follow-up visit with an obstetrician and Ben and Gabe got her to the car.

Ben looked at Gabe and then at Jenny. "Are you going to be okay, darlin'? We can call Cree and have him come here to pick you up."

"No, Ben, that's all right. It'll just take me another minute to get my bearings. I wanted to stop off at a restroom somewhere along the way and change into the new dress I bought. I think if I do that it will perk me up. D-Did the doctor tell you anything?"

Gabe looked at her with a slight smile. "Not the doctor but the nurse did. I think she thought I was the father."

Jenny's head snapped up to face him. "I'm sorry to put you through that, Gabe."

"Don't be sorry, hell, I was flattered. Anyway, the nurse told me your test was positive and you're about six weeks along. Is that a good thing, Jenny?"

"No, I don't know. The rape happened seven weeks ago, two weeks before I moved into the ranch house with Cree and Jake." She was still a little dazed by the whole thing. She put her hand on her stomach. "Even though it's possible that Buck is the sperm donor, I will be this child's mother and Cree and Jake will be its father. Right?"

Grabbing her hand, Ben knelt in front of her, looking into her eyes. "That's absolutely right, Jenny. Just keep thinking that way and everything will be fine."

* * * * *

Ben stopped off at a clean-looking gas station so Jenny could change into her new dress. When she was done they headed for the restaurant.

Rubbing his belly, Gabe chuckled. "I'm so hungry I might need to order two steaks."

"I'm sorry you two didn't get a proper lunch. By the way, have I told you both thanks for everything you've done? Not just today's counseling session but for everything all along this terrible ordeal."

"No need, Miss Jenny, that's what teammates do for each other. Just because we're out of the service doesn't stop us from still being a team," Gabe said with pride.

Cree was waiting for them when they pulled into a parking space in front of the restaurant.

Ben laughed, "Look at this great parking place just for you, Jenny."

Jenny laughed back, already feeling much better.

Cree opened her door for her and whistled. "Wow, sweetheart, you look fabulous. I'm glad you went shopping after all today. I hope you got a few more of these sexy outfits in the trunk." He leaned down and kissed her neck. The canary yellow sundress was cut halter-top fashion with no back. He walked her into the restaurant with his hand drawing circles on her spine. Her skin was so soft he just wanted to skip dinner and take her back to his vehicle so he could lick her entire body.

Dinner was very nice, the food was good and the company even better. When they'd finished their dessert Cree led them out to the parking lot. "I'm going to take my lovely woman with me. You guys head on back and we'll be along eventually. I want to take Jenny up to the hills and show her the city lights and maybe do a little necking before I have to take her back to the ranch and share her with Jake." Cree winked at Jenny and waved goodbye to Gabe and Ben.

Cree took Jenny up into the hills above Santa Fe to a scenic lookout and parked his SUV. "C'mere, you sexy woman. I've been waiting all evening for a taste of that skin you're showin'." Jenny slid over and snuggled up to Cree, putting her head on his shoulder. "So, sweetheart, talk to me and tell me how your appointment went today."

Jenny thought about telling him all through dinner about the pregnancy but decided to wait and tell Cree and Jake when they were all three together. "The appointment went well. Doctor Higgins said although I need to keep an eye on the burn for a little while longer, everything seemed to be okay." She didn't want to talk about her appointment so she brought up a subject she'd been wondering about.

"Cree, has Naomi ever been to the Triple Spur?"

Head snapping around to face her, Cree looked puzzled. "Where did that question come from?"

"I'm sorry, you don't have to answer. I was just wondering and I really miss her and thought maybe we could invite her down for Thanksgiving this year."

"Well, to be perfectly honest, Jenny, I've never really invited my momma to the Triple Spur. After what happened when I confided in my sister Tori about my relationship with Jake, she cut me off. I guess I didn't want to take the chance with momma. I don't think she would approve of my relationship with Jake and I'm too in love with the man to hide it. I guess it's just been easier to talk to her on the phone and send cards back and forth." Jenny thought Cree looked a little ashamed of himself.

"You know you're wrong. Naomi does know about you and Jake and she's happy for you. She's the one that told me. I imagine she never said anything to you because she wanted you to be the one to bring it up but, Cree, she loves you very much."

"Really? Damn, I guess my feelings for Jake are apparent even over the phone. Is that where you got the picture of Jake and me under the ranch sign that the hospital found in your pocket?"

Jenny nodded and slipped her arms even tighter around Cree's neck. "Yes. She gave it to me the last time I stopped in to see her about a year and a half ago. I can't tell you what that one picture meant to me. It was the only thing I owned that never left my sight. Too often I'd have to leave wherever I was at a minute's notice but I kept the picture in my pocket at all times so it would never get left behind.

Reaching out, Cree pulled Jenny onto his lap. "You don't need that picture anymore, Jenny. Now you can see and feel the real thing whenever you want." His mouth took hers in a heated kiss that set her eyebrows on fire. They eventually broke the kiss when oxygen deprivation became an issue. "Let's get home and show Jake this pretty new dress."

Chapter Twelve

❦

They drove toward the ranch in a comfortable silence. Jenny sitting next to Cree with her hand on his thigh. Cree kept both hands on the wheel. He wasn't about to take any chances with Jenny's life.

About twenty miles from home driving down the old county road the windshield shattered. It all seemed to take place in slow motion. Jenny turned her head to Cree and she heard him scream to her, "Get down." The SUV swerved off the road into the ditch and flipped over onto its roof and back down onto its tires.

Jenny came to almost immediately. She looked at Cree and saw all the blood. Cree's head was resting against the driver's side door but he was unconscious. Blood was running down his face and neck onto his shirt, Jenny tried to get him awake. Aware that she shouldn't move him, Jenny touched his face. "Cree, come on, honey, please wake up. You can't do this to me now, Cree, come on, you have to be here for our baby." When it was obvious she wasn't helping him she looked around for her cell phone.

Calling Jake, she continued to touch Cree's arms and hands. "Come on, Jake, answer the damn phone."

The phone was finally answered on the seventh ring. "Hi, baby, when are you two getting home?"

Jenny started to cry into the phone. "Jake, please help us. Cree's unconscious and he won't wake up." Jenny began to ramble into the phone out of shock. "Jake, there's so much blood. The windshield just exploded and Cree won't wake up. Jake, ple—"

Jake cut her off as he ran toward the front of the house where Gabe and Ben were watching TV. "Jenny…baby…calm down and tell me where you are. Please, Jenny. I can't help if you don't tell me."

"Ah yeah, okay. We're about twenty miles from the ranch, I think, on the old county road. Please, Jake. I don't know what to do."

"We're on our way, baby, just stay calm and stay on the phone with me." He gestured to Gabe's cell phone. "I'm having Gabe call the sheriff's station. They'll get an ambulance out to you." He motioned for the men to follow him out the door.

"Oh, someone's coming. I'll call you back."

The phone went dead just as they started the truck. "Damn it!" Jake tried to call her back as the truck pulled out of the drive, but the phone rang and rang. "Come on, Jenny, pick up, baby, please pick up." The call switched to voice mail. "Goddamn it. She cut me off. She said something about someone coming."

Ben looked over at Jake with an intense look on his face. "Did she say what happened?"

Shaking his head, Jake tried to calm down enough to drive the twenty miles. "No, just that the windshield exploded and Cree is bloody and unconscious."

"Sounds like a gun shot through the windshield to me." Gabe looked at Ben silently, asking him if they should tell Jake about the baby. Ben nodded his head for Gabe to continue. "Jake, I know you don't need to hear this right now but make sure they take Jenny in the ambulance with Cree."

"Why? Jenny sounded fine. A little shook up but that's to be expected."

Gabe once again looked at Ben. "Um…Jake I know she's going to kill me for telling you this but Jenny found out today that she's pregnant."

"WHAT!" Jake almost drove off the road. "Oh fuck." He threw the phone over to Ben and told him to try to call her again.

"Jake, someone stopped to help us." Jenny was still frantic.

"No, honey, this is Ben. Jake's busy drivin' but we should be there in about three minutes. You need to sit down and try to slow your breathing, honey. You're too excited it can't be good for the baby."

"Oh I...um I forgot... Yes, you're right. I'll...um...just go sit next to Cree and hold his hand."

"One minute, baby, hang on," Jake shouted hoping she would hear him over the phone Ben had to his ear.

They pulled up at the accident scene. Someone was talking to Jenny through the passenger side door. The helpful citizen turned and ran to Jake's truck.

"I just came upon it. I didn't want to move the driver but I did check and he still has a pulse." The elderly man looked from Jake back toward the SUV. "The little lady is finally calming down a little. She was hysterical when she flagged me down."

Jake jumped in the passenger seat and slid over to Cree and Jenny just as the Life Flight helicopter touched down. Jake gently slid Jenny out of the vehicle and passed her off to Ben. "Please take care of her for a minute." Jake jumped back into the SUV and touched Cree's face. From what he could tell he hadn't been shot, but the side of his face was split from brow to just under his chin. He must have either hit either the window or the steering wheel during the rollover.

Jake squeezed Cree's hand and exited the vehicle so the medical technicians could take over.

The technicians put a collar around Cree's neck and checked his vitals. Speaking in hushed tones to each other, they signaled for the backboard. They loaded Cree and rushed toward the waiting copter.

"Wait, where are you taking him? Tell me he's going to be okay?"

One of the technicians looked over at him. "We're transporting him to County General and his pulse is good. Keep your fingers crossed and get to the hospital as soon as you can."

Jake ran to Ben and retrieved a crying Jenny. "Ben, you and Gabe stay here and wait for the deputies. Fill them in on all that we know and then get to the hospital. Oh shit, I almost forgot you won't have a car. Ask one of the deputies to drive you back to the ranch to pick up another car and then get to the hospital."

Jake gently got Jenny into the car and took off down the road. "Jenny?" Jake reached out and took her hand kissing it over and over. "Jenny? Talk to me, baby. Are you sure you're okay?"

Jenny looked over at Jake with a bewildered look on her face. "I think I'm all right. Cree pushed my head down as soon as the windshield exploded. I think I might have cut my back though. I'm sure they can look at it when we get to the hospital."

"Lean forward, baby, and I can take a quick look."

Slipping out of the shoulder harness, Jenny leaned forward. Jake saw a piece of plastic embedded in her lower back. It wasn't bleeding very much, but he decided it would be better to wait for the doctors to remove it rather than for him to touch it. She had some minor cuts and scratches on her arms where she had covered her head during the crash but that was all he could see.

"Okay Jenny, you've got a piece of plastic in your back. My guess is that it's a piece from the dash. Do you think you could just stay bent where you are until we get to the hospital?"

"Yes, I'm fine, Jake. What about Cree? There was so much blood, Jake. I couldn't tell where it was coming from it was just too much blood. I'm sorry I'm not handling this very well." Jenny looked at Jake, tears still streaming down her face.

Shock, Jenny was in shock. Jake kept telling himself to drive safely, but his foot kept pushing a little harder on the accelerator.

By the time he got to County General some seventy miles away Cree had already been there for almost thirty-five minutes.

Jake pulled up to the emergency entrance and ran inside to get someone to come out and look at Jenny. He didn't really want to move her just in case the piece of plastic was more serious than it appeared.

A nurse came out and looked at Jenny's back and then signaled for a gurney to be brought out.

"Please be careful with her, she's pregnant." He looked over at a startled Jenny. "Sorry, baby, Gabe told me. He felt it might be relevant in getting you medical attention."

"I was going to tell you and Cree together." Tears started streaming down her face again as they wheeled her into the ER on her stomach. "I will be able to tell him, won't I, Jake?"

Bending over the gurney, brushing her hair back, Jake kissed her cheek. "Yes, baby, we'll tell him together."

It was a long night. The emergency room doctors' removed a small piece of the rearview mirror out of Jenny's back. Luckily the sliver hadn't hit anything vital and she ended up with only a few stitches. They treated her for shock and released her to Jake.

Cree was in surgery to repair his face. The hospital called in a plastic surgeon because the injury was so extensive. He had a concussion that would probably keep him in the hospital for a couple days but then they would release him. Jake and Jenny could care for him at home better anyway.

* * * * *

"*Hey, goddammit, someone get up here!*" Cree was yelling down the stairs from where he lay naked in bed.

The three people around the kitchen table all look up toward the screaming then around the table at each other.

Gabe finally was the first to speak, "Ben. Go see what the hell Cree wants now."

"I'm not going to do it, you do it." Ben looked at Gabe like he was crazy.

"I'm not going to do it. Hey. let's get Jenny. She'll do it. She'll do anything." Gabe looked at Ben and chuckled, remembering back to his youth and the Life cereal commercial.

"What do you say, Jenny?" Ben gave her that heart-stopping smile of his. "It's only fair you go. It's your turn. Besides, Cree loves you more than he does us so he doesn't yell as loud at you."

Throwing down her cards onto the table, she looked at both men. "You just know I had a better hand than either one of you but I'll go." Jenny got up from the heavy antique butcher block table and headed for the stairs. "If I'm not back in fifteen minutes call the cavalry or at least Jake to come and rescue me."

Jenny walked up the stairs, mumbling to herself. "Some men are such babies. You'd think no one else had ever had stitches before." She made it to the bedroom just as Cree was winding up again.

"Hey, doesn't anybody care about me anymore."

"Of course I care about you, sheriff. Now stop whining or I'm going to buy you a pretty pink nightgown and call you sissy." Jenny walked over to the bed and sat down beside the grumpy but deliciously naked man. "What can Jenny do for her little baby?"

Cree narrowed his eyes at her and stuck his lips out in a pout. "First thing you can do is stop making fun of me. Second thing you can do is to get me some clothes to put on so I can get the hell out of this bed. And the third thing you can do is to get closer to me and give me a poor baby kiss to make me feel better."

"I'll take what's behind door number three." Jenny stretched out onto the bed beside Cree and closed her lips over his.

Sighing, Cree brushed her lips with his tongue and Jenny opened right up for him. He swirled his tongue in her mouth and groaned. "As much as I love door number three, sweetheart, I need some clothes. I know you and Jake think it was really funny to take all the clothes out of the closets in here but I need to get up now. I need to check in with the station and I need to check in with the task force."

Jenny kissed his eyes and his nose then moved carefully over to the left side of his face and feathered kisses all along the six-inch line of sutures that ran down the side of his face from brow to chin. "Cree, you know you still need to rest. Jake and I are just trying to get you well and the only way to do that is to keep you in bed for one more day."

Cree put his arm around Jenny. "Okay, then you be my girl Friday and tell me what's going on?" Cree nibbled on the side of Jenny's neck down to the hollow of her throat. His wicked tongue made swirling patterns down her neck to the top of her breasts as he burrowed beneath her shirt. "Take this off, sweetheart. I want to see those beautiful breasts."

Blushing, Jenny pulled her shirt over her head and tossed it to the chair in the corner. Cree evidently didn't need help with her bra because that soon followed and sailed through the air toward the chair.

Drawing slow circles around her nipples, Cree watched them stand up and demand his attention. He withdrew his hand and substituted his tongue. Using just the tip, he drew circles around her nipple until he latched on and sucked so powerfully the tension in her womb brought her up off the bed.

Grabbing handfuls of his hair, Jenny cried out, "Cree, that feels…mmm." Sweat beaded on her brow and her legs were restless. Jenny needed this man inside her now. "Please, I need you inside me, love."

From the doorway they heard a throat clear. "So while the cat is away the mice will play, huh? Jake entered the room and began to undress. "You both know I have other things I need to be doing. Ben said you needed rescuing, he didn't say you needed fucking."

Jake crawled into bed on the other side of Cree. "How's our patient today, nurse?" He looked over at Jenny and grinned.

"He seems to be doing much better but I'm concerned about the swelling I feel." Jenny looked, Jake drawing his eyes down to where her fingers were wrapped around Cree's cock. "I think maybe it would be wise to drain some fluid, don't you agree?"

"Drain away," Cree said, stretching his arms out and spreading his legs.

Jenny gave each man a kiss and rose off the bed. "I think you two need a little time together so I'm going to go win some more money from your boys and start supper."

"You don't have to leave, sweetheart. There's plenty of me to go around." Cree began stroking his rock-hard erection.

"I know I don't have to leave, love. Sometimes it just feels right to give you two one-on-one time." Jenny kissed Cree again and withdrew from the room.

Turning away from the door toward Jake, Cree licked his lips and wiggled his eyebrows, slightly wincing from the pull of stitches. "Well, how about it, cowboy." He looked down at his cock and started stroking it again. "This swollen piece of love isn't going to drain itself."

"Oh yummy, Cree's horny." Jake licked his lips and proceeded to lick his way from Cree's ear to his cock. He swooped down on his cock in one deep-throated swallow.

Grabbing Jake's hair, Cree thrust in and out of his hot mouth, begging for more. "Mmm...yeah, cowboy, just like that."

Slowly withdrawing the cock from his mouth, Jake licked down the length to the root. He used one hand to caress Cree's sac. Jake took one of the smooth hairless orbs into his mouth and sucked. His other hand was probing Cree's tight puckered hole. As he sucked, his finger began pumping in and out of his hole.

"Suck my cock, cowboy." Cree was wild with lust, thrashing his head from side to side on the white satin pillowcase. "Damn, Jake, you sure know how to give a man a big head."

Taking a breather from the cock in his face, Jake looked up at Cree and narrowed his eyes. "Oh ha ha, very funny, sheriff."

"Okay, I'm sorry just please continue your ministrations on my cock before I explode," Cree cried, thrusting his cock against Jake's cheek.

Jake swirled his tongue around Cree's cock head a few times before once again swallowing him whole. Cree seemed to want to thrust so Jake stayed still and hummed an old Willie Nelson tune around his cock.

That did it. Cree shot his cum all the way down Jake's throat in a roar of release. "God, I love you." He pulled Jake up beside him and thrust his tongue in his mouth. Jake tasted of cum and it was damn sexy. They stroked and kissed and nibbled on each until their heart rates came down.

Cree looked over at Jake. "What did you find out today?"

"Well, it was definitely a shotgun shell that hit the windshield. The state police found the shell casing about eighty yards from where the truck rolled. They're sending it off to the lab to see about prints." Jake looked Cree in the eye. "You and I both know it was Buck and that means he's back."

"Yeah, I figured that's what they'd find. Well, Jake, I guess it's time to call the team back in on this one. Buck isn't going to give up until one of us or all of us are dead."

Reaching over, Jake turned Cree's head to face him. "I can't lose you, sheriff. When I got the call from Jenny my heart stopped beating. I don't think it started again until you were out of surgery and they said you'd be fine."

Cree lifted his fingers to the side of his face. "Does this look fine to you? Hell, Jake, I'm going to look like Frankenstein's monster." Cree shook his head and looked away.

Turning his head to face him once more, Jake softly kissed the stitches all the way up Cree's face. "First of all, I think it'll make you even sexier. Kinda like an Indian warrior with a battle scar. Secondly, do you think any less of our Jenny for her scars?"

"Of course not, but Jenny's aren't on her face right there to scare little children and old women."

Jake looked into Cree's eyes and petted his chest. "You're right. Jenny's scars aren't on her face. They're on her soul."

"Damn. Okay. I'll get off the pity party wagon and start thinking about ways to take down that bastard Buck."

Grinning, Jake bent over and kissed Cree again. "Now you're talking, sheriff. I...um...have one more thing I need to discuss with you if you feel up to it?"

"I'm fine really. What else is going on?"

"I found out that Jenny's pregnant. She didn't tell me, Gabe did the night of the accident. Jenny confirmed it but she hasn't talked to me about it since. I've been worried about her so I asked Ben and Gabe if they knew what was wrong with her. Cree, the doctor told her his best estimate was that she was six to seven weeks along. That puts conception right about the time of the rape. She first had sex with one of us five weeks ago so it's not impossible that the child is one of ours but we won't know until she's a little further along and the doctor does more tests."

"Pregnant? Our Jenny is going to be a mother? Jake, don't think I'm a bastard for saying this but I don't really care who the father is. Jenny's going to be our wife and she's going to be a fabulous mother. If we find out that Buck is the father of the baby at least it will still have your blood running through its veins." Cree's eyes were closed and a single tear ran down his chiseled cheekbone.

Drawing Cree closer, Jake licked away the tear. "I don't think you're a bastard. I totally agree with you but Jenny is having a hard time dealing with it right now. I think she's ashamed of the rape. Even though everyone's told her she didn't do anything wrong it still bothers her. Let's keep this conversation between us until she comes to us with her concerns."

"Okay, cowboy, I can do that. Now can you please get me some damn *clothes*?"

Chapter Thirteen

୧୨

The team came together over the next several days. After Nicco finally arrived on the third day the team sat at the long dining room table and discussed their options for finding Buck.

"Has Cotton heard anything from Buck?" Remy looked from Jake to Cree.

"No, nothing, but he's still keeping his eyes and ears open for us. It's like Buck has totally abandoned the Double B." Jake shook his head. What had gotten in to his father? Jenny told him that Buck thought he was in love with her, but it wasn't love, more like a sick obsession. He doubted anyone would ever be able to understand what went on in Buck's head that he would willingly give up a lifetime of work for a woman that couldn't stand him. Jake looked around the table at his friends and teammates. They were all damn good men to put their private lives on hold to help him, Cree and Jenny out. He hoped when this was all behind them there would be a way to repay each and every teammate.

Cree spoke up, "I think we should set up watches twenty-four hours a day. I was thinking two men taking shifts in the hayloft using night scopes after dark and two men circling the house in shifts. That leaves Jake and the two men not on shift still in the house with Jenny. I'll be in and out during the day working with the local and state police departments. We got word two days ago that Buck slipped through the US border when one of the regular border patrol officers was out sick and a part-time guy was taking his place. Of course we already knew that information since Buck decided to take a potshot at Jenny and me the other day." Cree ran his fingers through his long hair in frustration.

"What can I do?" Jenny stood in the doorway, having come in while Cree was outlining the plan.

"Nothing, sweetheart. Your job is to stay indoors and stay safe." Cree met Jenny's eyes with a "don't argue" thrust to his chin.

Jenny shook her head, "Not good enough, sheriff." She entered the room closer to the dining table. "I've got a stake in this too. I won't have all of you putting your lives on the line while I sit in the house doing crossword puzzles."

Jake got up from his chair and went to her. Slipping his arm around her he pulled her up next to him. "Baby, listen." He kissed her temple. "Keeping you safe is the reason every one of these men is putting his life on hold. Just let us do our jobs. We're all damn good at it." He kissed her on the top of the head.

Looking at Jake through narrowed eyes, Jenny pulled from his embrace. "I know you want to keep me safe but I know more than anyone in this room about Buck's way of thinking in the last five years. I evaded the man for five years before he found me again. Do you think it was just luck? Give me a gun and tell me what I can do in this operation. And Tell. Me. Now."

Cree drew in a deep breath. "Jenny, think about all of these men in front of you. If you insist on doing this not only will you be putting your life in danger but their lives too."

Jenny looked at the men around the table. She reached down and pulled apart the snap-front shirt, exposing her scars and brands to the men at the table. Shocked faces met hers, some of the men began to squirm in their chairs and at least one, Nicco, looked as if the image before him would haunt him forever.

"Gentlemen, this is why I deserve to help hunt down that son of a bitch. Now who can look at me and tell me I don't have the right?"

All four men looked at Cree who leaned his elbows on the table and buried his face in his hands. "You can have a gun and we'll include you in the planning sessions but I will not—I repeat, will not—put you on patrol outside." Cree raised his head and looked at Jenny in need of a compromise.

"All right for now, but don't try to hide anything from me." Jenny took one of the empty chairs and sat down, snapping her shirt up as she went. "Are there any questions I can answer for any of you? From now on, ask me not Cree, not Jake, if you want to know something about my past with Buck."

Gabe softly cleared his throat. "I have a question, Jenny. Do you know why he's doing this to you?" He leaned toward her with compassion in his eyes.

"Not really. I mean he says he's in love with me but it didn't feel much like love when he raped and branded me. He told me I was his property and that he married my mother for me. You see… I met him first. Let me tell you the story of how Buck came in to my life." Jenny told the story of meeting Buck in the hotel bar. When she was finished she saw a look of surprise on Jake's face.

"I never knew that's how things went. I just always assumed Buck and Helen fell in lust at first sight. Buck has always been popular with the ladies." Jake walked over to Jenny and put his hands on her shoulders. "I don't think I ever told you I'm sorry that Buck's my father." He bent down and kissed Jenny softly on the cheek.

* * * * *

Later that day, Cree found Jenny baking bread in the kitchen. She looked so cute with her hair up in a haphazard bun with a dusting of flour on her cheek. The state-of-the-art kitchen he and Jake had designed for her looked even better with her in it, more homey. Cree strode over and wrapped his arms around her. "Hey, sweetheart, it sure smells good in here. The bread doesn't smell bad either." He turned her around and brought their bodies together. Cree never got tired of kissing her so he began a path that went from her forehead to her chin. "I brought you a gun from the safe. It's a Glock semiautomatic. I know you're already good with a gun after all the target practice Jake and I made you do growing up but I want you to get used to this one. Hold it. Feel the weight. Let your hand become accustomed to it. We'll go out with the guys after supper and do some more target practice. I'm going to have them secure the area first and then one of them will come back in and get us. Okay?"

Leaning in to him, Jenny rested her head on his chest. "I'm sorry if I embarrassed you today in front of your friends. I'm just tired of being a victim. It's time I stopped running and started fighting now that I have something to fight for. This home and you and Jake are mine and I won't let anyone run me away again."

"I understand. I really do. Jake and I just worry about you, that's all. You're our reason for living, Jenny. We love you."

"Amen to that, sheriff," Jake said, coming into the kitchen to give them both a kiss. "You've grown up, Jenny, but you'll always be 'our little Jenny', got that?"

"Got it, cowboy. Now you two get out so I can finish supper. I made a turkey and all the trimmings. I know it's not Thanksgiving but I wanted a way to let the men know I was thankful for all of them." Jenny grinned and kissed them both saucily. She grabbed the towel off the counter and winding it up, gave each man a snap on the ass with it. She turned around and started separating her dough for rolls.

Cree and Jake left the kitchen chuckling at her and her good mood.

Supper was a real feast, Jake thought. The men really seemed to appreciate the thought and effort that went into it. After he finished he sat back and rubbed his belly. "I do believe I just put five pounds on this old body."

Rolling his eyes, Cree looked over at Jake. "Well, then I guess you just need some exercise. I think it would be a good workout for you to straighten the loft and drag that mattress in front of the loft door for Ben and Gabe." He looked at the two men with mischief in his eye, looking for backup.

Ben turned the knife a little deeper. "Yeah, Jake, that would be great. If I'm gonna have to be on my belly peering out through hay bales for twelve hours a day I'm gonna need a mattress."

Gabe joined in the fun, "Coffeepot and a blanket for when it gets cold and a—"

Jake cut him off. "All right. I get the idea, you pansy-ass little girls."

* * * * *

Working on the books sucked as far as Jake was concerned. Still it was all a part of horse ranching. Jake decided to send the bulk of the horses along with the ranch hands to the far pasture for safety. There was a small cook cabin up there, big enough for the hands to get out of the rain if need be. Most of the men took their bedrolls, preferring to sleep under the stars on a nice night.

The team thought it might be easier to spot Buck without all the horses and cowboys milling around the barn and corral. Of course that left them to tend to the mares that had either just foaled or were getting ready to foal but Ben and Gabe seemed to love the work so more power to them.

He was just finishing up printing out the payroll checks for the week on his computer when Cree knocked at the door. Jake looked up and smiled.

Man, that guy is hot. Hair just as black as a crow's wings and soft as silk. Cree'd left it loose and just looking at it made Jake hard as a fence post. "Hey, sexy, got something for me?" Jake pushed his chair back from the desk and spread his legs. He reached down and started rubbing at the steel spike in his jeans.

Eyebrows lifted, Cree swaggered over to Jake and knelt between his legs. Running his long-fingered hands up and down Jake's thighs, he grinned. "That would depend on what you have for me."

Jake reached down and unbuttoned his jeans, letting his erection spring free. "Is this enough for you, sheriff?"

Reaching for Jake's cock, Cree bent and swiped the head with his tongue. "Just about right, I'd say, but I think I need to taste it to make sure." Cree took Jake's cock in a single swallow all the way to the base. He began pumping up and down on the big, fat beast. Cree slid his mouth to the head and released him, going instead down to Jake's balls. He licked and nibbled, sucking first one and then the other into his mouth.

Jake managed to get his boots and jeans off while Cree was busy playing. He grabbed Cree's hair and slid farther down into the big red leather office chair, giving him better access.

Pulling Jake's legs onto his shoulders and down his back, Cree inched his tongue toward Jake's sexy puckered entrance. Cree rimmed the hole with his tongue and moved his tongue inside.

Jake grabbed his own cock and started pulling. "More...oh sheriff....more....need."

Cree pumped his tongue and out of Jake's ass ,groaning. He needed his cock inside this man now. He sat back and looked down at Jake. "Do you still have stuff in here? I need to be in you, cowboy. I need to ride you."

Jake reached up and opened the top drawer of the desk, grabbing the small bottle of lube. Handing it to Cree, he opened farther and adjusted his legs on Cree's shoulders. Cree got him lubed up and positioned his cock at the entrance to Jake's hole.

"Ride me, sheriff."

Cree thrust his cock inside and immediately started pumping in and out, hard and fast. Cree knew he wasn't going to last long, he needed this too badly. "Sorry, cowboy, it's going to be short and fast." Cree continued his assault on Jake's ass.

Pumping his own cock, Jake quickened his pace, timing his jerks to the thrust of Cree's hips snapping in and out of him.

Neither one of them saw Nicco standing in the office doorway. Nicco's eyes fixed on the pair with an unreadable expression on his face.

Cree let out a roar and Jake felt the wet heat deep inside him. A few more pumps of his cock and he shot his seed into his hand. Both men rested their heads together and Cree slipped out of Jake. "That was damn good, cowboy." He leaned in and gave Jake a passionate kiss.

Nicco slipped back out into the hall and cleared his throat. "Um…Jake, are you in here?"

Jake and Cree broke apart and scrambled for their clothes, laughing. "Yeah, Nicco, I'm in here, just give me a minute." He finished pulling his jeans and boots on, looked to make sure Cree was covered and called for Nicco to come in.

"Sorry to bother you two but Rex Cotton just called. It seems he got back after a night in the city and the house on the Double B's been boarded up. He figures that's a sign that maybe Buck will be gone a while. Cotton said he would stay on in his foreman's house and take care of what he could until the money ran out or he heard differently from you." Nicco looked from Cree to Jake, nodded and left the office.

Looking over at Cree, Jake smiled. "Uh…did you notice something funny about Nicco?"

"If you mean the hard-on he was sporting and the red face, I'd say yeah." Cree's eyes twinkled. "I guess he must have gotten a little more show than we thought. It also explains a few things about Nicco."

Jake looked at Cree, confused. "What things?"

Cree sat back in his chair and smiled. "The aloofness and the broodiness, you know, the all-around sour disposition of our friend. I think maybe Nicco's gay but doesn't want to admit it to himself or anyone else."

"Huh, do you think one of should talk to him about it?"

"No, I think he's finally starting to work it out on his own. We'll just let him be unless he wants to talk." Cree looked at Jake and thought of another problem they had. "Do you think it's time we talked to Jenny about the baby?"

Scratching his head, Jake nodded. "Yeah, I know that she knows we both know about the baby. I'm afraid if we don't talk to her about she'll take it we don't want the child and nothing could be further from the truth. We also need to decide which one of us is going to be her lawful wedded husband."

"I've been thinking about that and I've got an idea. I need you to be totally honest with me if the idea I have offends you in any way." At Jake's nod, Cree continued to tell Jake of the plan for the future he'd come up with.

"Sounds good to me, Cree. I agree with you about the whole name thing. It will also solidify us as a family."

"Good, now let's go find our girl and propose." Cree jumped up from his chair and walked out of the office with a spring in his step.

Chapter Fourteen

ဢ

They found Jenny watching television with Nicco asleep on the couch. "Jenny, can we have a word with you? We thought maybe you'd like to go out to the corral and see Hope and Miss Candy." Cree pulled her up out of the chair and began walking to the door.

"Sure, I'd love to see Hope. No one has let me out of the house long enough to see her since the birth." Jenny snuggled up between Jake and Cree as they walked to the corral. Hope was the prettiest little thing she'd seen in a long time. Dark gray with black mane and tail she was a little spitfire. Bending down to nuzzle the skittish foal's neck, Jenny sighed in contentment.

"What did you two want to talk to me about?"

Jake and Cree came up on either side of her and pulled her up from the ground. Cree looked at Jake and nodded for Jake to tell Jenny the news about Buck. "Couple things really. First we got a call from Cotton over at the Double B. It seems Buck boarded up the house. Rex thinks it means he won't be back for quite a while."

"Is that a good thing or a bad thing?" Jenny questioned, looking from Jake to Cree.

Cree took her into his arms and kissed her nose. "Well, it could be either. On one hand maybe Buck has decided that there's too much heat to stay around and is going back to Mexico or it could mean he's planning on camping out around here for a while waiting to get to you."

At the sad and troubled look Jenny got on her face, Cree knew it was time for the next part of their discussion. He looked at Jake and Jake came up against Jenny's back and wrapped his arms around both her and Cree.

Jake kissed Jenny's neck and moved his arms down to rest on her abdomen. "We need to discuss the baby, Jenny. I know you wanted time but Cree and I are about to burst with happiness over it and we want to share that with you."

Jenny looked over her shoulder at Jake. "But you don't understand everything, Jake. There's a very real possibility that this baby was fathered by B—"

Cree interrupted Jenny with a kiss. "That baby belongs to the three of us, no matter what. Do you understand? Baker blood is Baker blood. Jake and I will be the best daddys you'll ever see."

Letting out the breath she'd been holding, Jenny placed Cree's hands on top of Jake's on her stomach and then placed her own hands over them. "Thank you both for understanding."

"Next thing on the agenda is to get married." Cree kissed her soundly. Jake and I've discussed it between the two of us and now it's time to get your reaction to the proposition. But first let me do this." He separated himself from Jenny and went down on one knee. Jake came around Jenny and knelt beside Cree.

Both men took a hand and kissed it. Finally Cree spoke, "Jenny, would you do us the incredible honor of becoming our wife? We promise to love and cherish you every day of our lives."

Tears pooled in Jenny's eyes. "I love you both more than my own life, of course I'll marry you." She got a troubled look on her face. "How am I supposed to choose between the two of you? Legally I can only marry one man."

Getting up, Cree took Jenny into his arms once again. "We've decided for you. We knew it wouldn't be fair to you to have to do it. You'll marry me and become Jenny Sommers and Jake is planning to legally change his last name to Sommers. That way any children that we are blessed with will have both our names." Cree smiled at Jenny, proud of himself for finding the perfect solution to their problem.

"Can Jake change his name just like that?" Jenny looked to Jake for answers.

"Well, not 'just like that' but we can get an attorney and have him file the necessary papers with the court. It'll take a little while but it can be done." Jake squeezed Jenny and kissed Cree.

"Okay, then let's do it. Um…when are we going to get married? Because I'm going to start showing before long and even though I don't want a big wedding in a church, I do want pictures." She chuckled and looked at the two men. "I don't think I want to advertise to our baby my condition before our wedding."

Nuzzling her neck, Cree stopped and looked into Jenny's eyes. "How about next week? We could do it here at the ranch with just close friends."

"Sounds perfect to me," Jake said. "Then after the reception is over we can come back out to the pasture just the three of us and you two can marry me."

"Oh it all sounds so lovely." Jenny's face took on the troubled look again. "Cree, what about the people in Junctionville? Will they approve of their sheriff living with two other people?"

"Absolutely, Jenny. Junctionville is kind of an artists community. Most of the people here have their own idiosyncrasies. That's why Jake and I moved here. You'll see, our baby won't be treated any differently because of our living arrangements."

* * * * *

That evening Remy and Jenny were on cleanup duty. Jake had grilled steaks and corn on the cob so she volunteered to do the dishes. Jenny washed as Remy dried. She looked over at the man beside her. He was so devastatingly handsome. Black curls against perpetually tanned skin. She began to wonder what his life was like away from the Triple Spur. "What is it you do for a living, Remy?" She looked over at him and passed him another plate to dry.

Remy looked at her and took the dish Jenny handed him. "Well, I grew up outside New Orleans but wit de hurricane I had ta find a new base o' operation. My best friend Anton and his wife owned a bar in Key West so I went dere and bought into de business. About two years ago Anton was killed in a boating accident. Since den I run de bar wit his widow Corrine."

Jenny looked over at Remy. He had a very sad and troubled expression on his face like he was suddenly lost in thought. "What's the name of your bar?"

His eyes came back to her with a little headshake. A smile spread across his face showing two of the deepest dimples she'd ever seen. "'The Crazy Cajuns'. Jake came up wit dat name while we were in de Seals and it jus kinda stuck."

Remy put the dishes away and just stood looking at Jenny like he wanted to ask her a question but didn't know if he should. "*Cherie*, why would a woman feel guilty if a man abused her? I mean, it's not like dat was her fault, right?" He ran his fingers through his hair and looked down at the floor.

Jenny saw the need to really understand in his eyes and on his face. She thought about it and pulled on his hand until they were both sitting at the kitchen table. Licking her lips, Jenny wasn't sure of how to make him understand.

"I can't speak for anyone but me, Remy, but I can tell you my feelings and you can judge for yourself if it fits whatever situation you're asking about, okay?"

Remy reached across the table and took her hand in his. "Please."

"When Buck hurt me I couldn't help feeling guilty because I feel I should have seen the signs. He was my stepfather, for God sakes. I never knew my real father. Heck, my own mother told me when I was fifteen that she'd never loved me but I thought Buck did love me. He was always so attentive. He was always pulling me down on his lap for a morning or nighttime hug. I just assumed that's what all fathers did. If Buck found out I wanted something it was in my hands that same day." Remy's hand raised and wiped the tears from her face.

"You don't have ta go on, *cherie*. I'm sorry I brought it up. Come, let's go see what everyone else is doin'." He got up from his chair and tried to pull her up.

Jenny shook her head no and pulled him back down. "No, Remy, I need to talk about this with someone." She dried her eyes and took another deep breath.

"I thought Buck was doing all those things for me because I was his daughter. I was wrong, he…he was courting me. He was just waiting for me to turn eighteen so he could marry me." It was strange how she'd misread him for so many years. "When Jake and Cree showed up at the ranch five years ago Buck finally saw that my love was not for him but for them. He went out of his mind and branded me that night. He punched me and kicked me until I thought I was going to die."

Remy continued to squeeze her hand while Jenny wiped more tears. "The guilt comes from knowing I loved someone capable of such violence and not seeing it in time." Jenny looked at Remy and knew she was somehow hitting close to home.

"Remy, I don't know why you need to understand this unless someone you care about has been abused. Is that it, Remy? Do you know someone like that besides me?" Now it was Jenny's turn to squeeze his hand.

"*Oui, cherie*, de woman I've loved all my life." Remy let out a weary breath and continued. "I've tried being patient wit her but she's always doin' sometin to try to get me riled up. She looks at me wit de same haunted eyes dat I see in you at times."

Jenny thought about Remy's situation for a minute and smiled. "She's testing you."

"Testing me for what? I love her, I'd never lay a hand on her in dat way."

Standing up, she crossed to the fridge and got out two cold colas. Passing one to Remy, she wound up their conversation. "She wants to see you get mad to see if you can control your temper in a nonviolent way. Get mad, Remy, and show her that you won't raise a hand to her. That and patience will win her in the end if she loves you."

Draining the cola, she threw the can in the trash. "I'm lucky I've always known Jake and Cree would never physically harm me but some women have to be shown." Jenny kissed Remy on the cheek and went to find her men.

Chapter Fifteen

ഇ

Jenny couldn't find Cree or Jake in the house so she grabbed her gun and asked Ben to take her to the barn. The evening was awash in pinks and oranges as the sun set across the pastures. The air smelled of horses and dust and home. She loved this place. Jenny couldn't wait until Buck was found so she could work the horses alongside Jake again.

On the way to the barn Jenny heard a loud popping sound. Her body was forced down into the dry yard. Ben was on top of her, shouting for help. More shots rang out. Too many for just one gun, evidently the good guys were shooting back. The longer she lay there, the harder it became to breathe. Jenny tried to push herself up but Ben wasn't budging.

"Stay down, Jenny. Buck's shooting at us."

She could hear Jake calling her name but she was starting to get dizzy. The yard was suddenly quiet except the sound of running feet. Ben crawled off her but Jenny still couldn't get a good breath.

Jenny looked up at Ben to thank him when she saw the look on his face. Uh-oh. Ben's eyes widened and he began screaming for Jake.

"Get over here now, Jake. Remy, call for an air ambulance. The rest of you find Cree and go after that SOB." Ben brushed the hair off Jenny's forehead. "It's going to be all right, Jenny, we'll get him. Just lie still."

Jake reached Jenny's side and crumpled beside her. "Oh God, baby, what has he done?" Jake was crying and pushing his hand down hard on her side. Damn that hurt. Jenny looked at where he was pushing and saw all the blood. It seemed

Buck had got her again. When would she be allowed to stop paying for not loving him?

"Ben, come over and keep pressure on this wound for me." Jake stretched out beside her and wrapped her in his arms. "That's better, baby. I need to hold you."

Blue came over and flopped down at Jenny's side. Resting his head on her leg, Blue whimpered and licked Jenny's jeans.

Jenny could feel her breath getting shallower every second. She struggled to speak. Jenny had to let Jake know how she felt in case she didn't make it.

"C-Cowboy, I love you. I have since I was twelve years old." She paused to catch what little breath she had. "Please take care of Cree for me. Even though he's the sheriff I don't think he's as strong as you. Tell..." Jenny couldn't seem to catch her breath. "Tell him I love him and I'm sorry about the baby. He wanted it so b-badly." The darkness claimed her.

"Jenny? Jenny, baby, don't you die on me." Jake looked at her pale face and he was sure that Buck had finally won. "Where the hell is that ambulance?" He was so angry nothing more would come out of his mouth. Jake curled against Jenny's side and whispered his love to her. "Don't leave me, baby. Please, baby, don't leave me. I've finally found you again. You need to be here to help me take care of Cree." He heard a vehicle drive up and slam on its brakes. The next thing he saw was Cree kneeling down at Jenny's head.

Jake looked at Cree, the tears making it hard to see his face. He blinked and reached for his hand. "It's bad, Cree. It's so bad. There's too much blood. Help us please."

Cree let out an anguished sound and dropped his forehead to Jenny's. "No, not again. Jenny Barnes, I will not give you up. Wake up, Jenny, and look at me."

Jake reached for Cree and pulled him down beside him so they could both hold their Jenny. They must have been in shock because they didn't even hear the air ambulance land.

Jake felt someone tugging on his shirt and looked up. It was Ben.

"Come on, cowboy, you need to let these people work on her." He tugged at Cree and Jake until they shook themselves off and became aware of their surroundings.

Jake stood up and helped Cree. Wrapping his arms around him, Cree rested his head on Jake's shoulder and continued to cry. Jake rubbed his back and waited while the medical technicians worked on Jenny. They were carrying her toward the helicopter when Jake managed to extricate himself from Cree and catch up to them.

"Please tell me she'll live?" Jake held his breath waiting for the answer.

"Sorry, too soon to tell. She's got a collapsed lung and is losing blood fast. I normally wouldn't say this, but get to the hospital as fast as you can."

Jake grabbed Cree's hand and headed for his brand-new sheriff's SUV. "You can arrest me after if you need to, but I'm driving with the lights and siren on." Jake got Cree in the passenger side and went around to the driver's side. A big hand stopped him from opening the car door.

"Neither one of ya are in any condition ta drive. I'll take ya. I've always wanted ta ride wit de light and sirens." Remy opened the back door and Jake got in.

The ride to the hospital was ninety miles. Jake crossed his fingers that Jenny would still be alive when they got there. He reached up to the front seat and took Cree's hand and patted and soothed him.

They got to the hospital in next to no time thanks to Remy's excellent driving skills and the lights and sirens. Remy pulled up at the emergency room entrance and Cree and Jake ran inside. Jake looked around the crowded room for a nurse.

Spotting one, he rushed over to the plump, gray-haired woman. "The helicopter brought in a patient with a gunshot wound. Where can we find out how she is?"

The nurse looked over the top of her glasses at them with a sympathetic look on her face. "They took the dear child up to the operating room after we inserted a chest tube. Her breathing was much better when they took her up." She reached out to touch Jake's arm. "Take the elevator to the second floor and turn to your right. You'll see the OR waiting room and when they know something someone will be out to speak to both of you."

Remy came running through the door. "What ya find out?"

Cree relayed what the nurse had said and Remy nodded. "I'm gonna get a taxi and head back to de ranch. I'm sure dey could use all de help dey could get." He shook Cree's and Jake's hands and went outside to find a taxi.

Instead of waiting for the elevator, Cree and Jake ran up a flight of steps. They found the waiting room and began to pace. The room was small—only about twelve by twelve feet with lime green vinyl seating and beige walls.

After they'd had many cups of coffee and an equal number of trips to the restroom a doctor finally came into the room and called their names. He introduced himself as Dr. Ross Hamilton, shook their hands, guided them to a more secure room and sat them down.

"Miss Barnes is a very lucky lady. She had a collapsed lung upon arrival which the ER dealt with before she was brought up to surgery. We had to go in to repair the lung but she was lucky the bullet passed through her body without hitting any other vital organs. The loss of blood concerned us as well as her pregnancy. We gave her two pints of blood and did a sonogram and mother and babies seem to be doing all right for now."

Jake's eyes just about popped out of his head. "Babies? As in plural?"

"Yes, didn't you know? Miss Barnes is approximately six to seven weeks along. We almost missed the second fetus but it's definitely there."

Jake looked at Cree and then back at Dr. Hamilton. "Dr. Hamilton, according to Jenny's family doctor she should be more like eight to nine weeks pregnant. How can that be?"

He looked a little surprised and then smiled. "Well, if all he did was a physical examination he could have very easily been a couple weeks off on his estimation. You see, with twins the uterus becomes larger than with a single birth. Usually most doctors determine the age of the fetus by measuring the uterus. It isn't until later that an actual sonogram is performed."

Jake got up from his chair and enthusiastically shook the doctor's hand. "Thank you so much, Dr. Hamilton. When can we see Jenny and take her home?" He was sure he must have been looking at him like a begging puppy.

"Miss Barnes is in the recovery room right now. She should be moved to a private room in about an hour or so. We want to watch her closely for a while in case there are complications with the pregnancy. We'll be keeping her here at the hospital for several more days at least. Better safe than sorry I always say."

Doctor Hamilton patted Jake on the shoulder. "I don't know the lady's full medical history but her body's been through about all it can stand. When you get her out of here take care of her." *A little better.* Jake heard what he was implying, but didn't know how to defend himself. Luckily, Cree stepped up to the plate.

"It's her stepfather and we do plan to catch him one way or another."

The doctor nodded his head and, taking in Cree's uniform, shook their hands one last time. "You do that, Sheriff."

* * * * *

Jenny tried to open her eyes but they wouldn't cooperate. Her throat felt like she'd swallowed sandpaper. "Thirsty," she managed to croak.

She could hear rustling noises around her and then Cree's voice so low and melodic. "Here, sweetheart." He lifted her head a little and put something cold against her lips. "Open your mouth, Jenny. It's just ice chips but it'll help."

Jenny fought again to open her eyes as the cold ice melted in her mouth. After several attempts she managed to get her eyes open. To the side of Jenny's bed stood Cree and Jake, looking at her anxiously. "Good. Thank you."

Cree bent over her and brushed the hair out of her face. "I'm going to put your hair into a braid, sweetheart. There's no sense fighting with it while you're in bed." He pulled Jenny's hair to the side and began to lovingly braid it. She knew he needed to feel useful so she just smiled at him.

When he was finished he took the rawhide thong from his own black silky hair and tied the end. "There, all better. Would you like some more ice?"

"No thank you, love. Seeing your faces is enough." Her men looked tired, worn-out and strung out. She started feeling guilty for everything she was putting them through.

"I'm sorry about this...about the baby. Did the doctors say if we could have more?" Jenny couldn't believe what she was seeing. Both men were smiling at her, practically bouncing on their toes like little boys at Christmas.

What's wrong with them? Have they no heart or did they really detest the thought of her carrying Buck's child?

They both bent down and kissed her and then turned to each other and kissed. Jake got a grin on his face and looked at Cree and then Jenny. "You didn't lose the baby. In fact you added another one." He chuckled like he'd just told a big secret.

131

What did he say? How is that possible? "I know my head is still a little funny but what are you talking about?"

Cree looked over at the childlike look on Jake's face and rolled his eyes. "He's trying to tell you that we aren't having one baby, we're having twins!"

"Oh my God, twins? I'm going to have twins. Oh my God. I'm going to have *twins*." Now she understood Jake's bouncing glee. "You're saying I'm having twins and they're both all right?"

Jenny couldn't take it all in. She had been sure she was going to die. Jenny knew she would lose the baby at the least. But this!

Jake kissed her again. "That's not all we found out. According to the sonogram you're only six to seven weeks along. That means Buck can't be the father." Jenny's head started swimming again. She tried to focus on Jake and Cree, willing them to pull her back to earth.

"That means Cree and I both get one to play with." Jake was still bouncing and Jenny began to giggle.

"You mean you both get one to wake up with in the middle of the night when it's feeding time."

Cree's brow shot up at that remark. "With those boobs you're packing I assumed you'd breastfeed." He seemed to realize what he'd said and tried to dig himself out of the hole. "I mean, sure. Whatever you want, sweetheart. Jake and I can get up in the night with them."

Jenny couldn't help but feel sorry for the poor goofball. "Relax, I'm actually planning to breastfeed but I'll want help getting the babies' diapers changed and then brought to me to feed. I'd much rather stay in bed between the men I love and feed our children. Wouldn't you like that too?"

Knowing he was forgiven, Cree decided to try to be funny again. "With boobs like those I'm not completely sure there will be enough to go around after Jake and I get our milk and cookies before bed."

Thinking he'd made the funniest joke in the world, Cree looked at Jake and poked him in the chest. "Isn't that right, Jake?"

Jake looked at Jenny with sympathy in his eyes. "Please forgive numb nuts. He's working on very little sleep."

They did look so tired. Jenny began to feel guilty all over again. They didn't have any of these troubles until she came back into their lives. Jenny looked at Cree, so strong and beautiful, her own private Indian warrior. Jake with his shaggy hair and amber eyes, how could a girl get so lucky as to have both of them love her?

Letting out a contented breath, Jenny reached out and touched both her men. "Go home, loves, and get some rest. You can see what your team found out about Buck. I'm fine for the night. In fact, I'm feeling really tired and sore. I think I'd sleep better knowing you two were taking care of yourselves as well."

They both looked at her and scowled but they all knew she was right. "We'll let you sleep, sweetheart. One or both of us will be back first thing tomorrow morning." Cree bent and kissed her softly. He stepped back and Jake bent and kissed her a little more hungrily.

"It's almost midnight, baby, get some rest. We love you, Jenny." With that, Jake and Cree walked out of her room.

* * * * *

"What did you guys find?" Jake asked into the cell phone. Even though it was after midnight he knew the guys would be waiting up for his call.

"Damn, it's about time you called, Jake," Ben said with a heavy sigh. "How is Miss Jenny? We tried to call the hospital but no one would give out any information."

"She and the babies are doing fine. Did you get that, Ben? Babies as in plural. Jenny's having twins and they both came through the shooting just fine."

133

"That's fantastic, Jake. Here's some more good news. We captured Buck. We'll tell you all about it when you get here."

"Roger on that, Ben. We'll be home in about thirty minutes, put some coffee on, will ya? We're both beat but we'll want to hear every detail."

Cree and Jake arrived to a kitchen smelling of coffee and bacon and eggs. As they sat down at the table Gabe handed each of them a cup of coffee and plate with bacon and egg sandwiches. "I thought you two might be hungry since you missed supper. I'll go round up the guys."

Cree reached across the table and took Jake's hand. "We've got damn good friends, cowboy."

Jake squeezed back and leaned in for a taste of Cree's mouth. Tasting Cree filled him up more than the plate of food ever could. "I love you, sheriff."

"Geez, you two, can ya give us a break fer once." Remy chuckled but came up and pounded each man on the back. "Congratulations on de twins."

"Thanks, Remy. Now who's going to tell us about Buck? Nicco, why don't you fill us in. I know I'll get the facts from you with no wishy-washy stuff thrown in." Cree chuckled and sat back in his chair rubbing his belly.

Nicco looked a little surprised and cleared his throat. "Well…uh…after you left to go to the hospital we split up and started searching the tree line where the shots had been fired. Remy caught sight of a blood trail, so we knew someone hit him. We followed the trail to the hills in the east valley. There we found the trail leading into a small cave about half the way up the hill. It wasn't hard to get him to come out. He was passed out from blood loss by the time we found him.

"Ben called the state police on his cell phone and we carried him back to the ranch. The police were here along with an ambulance. You have good friends, Cree. They refused to call in the helicopter for him. They said he could ride in the ambulance to the hospital."

Jake nodded his head in thanks to the team. "So how bad was he hurt? Critical, I'm hoping. Am I right?"

Nodding his head, Remy put down his coffee. "Sorry, buddy, it looked like de bullet grazed his temple. Lots of blood but I'm thinking very little damage."

Cree looked around the table. "Please tell me they didn't take Buck to the same hospital they took Jenny."

He waited for an answer and only got uncomfortable looks. Ben cleared his throat, "Uh...yeah, Cree, I think they did."

Cree stood up so fast his chair fell back and crashed onto the floor. "Shit. I gotta call the hospital and check on Jenny. I can't believe she's there alone with that bastard." Cree was so angry it took him several attempts to dial the correct number.

Finally, he was put through to the nurses' station on Jenny's floor. He asked the nurse if she was okay. "Yes, Mr. Sommers, I gave her some pain medication and a good sedative in her IV not a half-hour ago. She'll be sleeping like a baby until morning."

Cree thanked her and hung up the phone. "Jake, do you think one of us should go watch her room until they get Buck locked up?"

Nodding his head, Jake got up from his chair. "I'll go. I'd like to take a quick shower first to wake myself up a bit." Jake nodded to his team and headed upstairs.

Cree sent the other men off to bed and followed Jake up the stairs.

* * * * *

Jake was already in the walk-in shower when Cree got undressed. Opening the door, Cree saw the lost look on Jake's face. "Come here, cowboy," Cree opened his arms and Jake walked right in.

Wrapping his arms around Jake, Cree only meant to comfort him but evidently his cock had other ideas. Springing up between them Cree's cock was heavy and full. "God, you feel good."

Jake's cock must have been thinking the same thing because it too became hard and thick. Jake grabbed Cree and urgently began thrusting his tongue into his mouth. They couldn't get close enough.

Rubbing their cocks together, Jake and Cree began pinching each other's nipples. Cree left Jake's mouth and bit and licked his way down his neck to his chest. Sucking up marks around Jake's nipples, he swirled his tongue and bit the ever growing nub. Cree continued down Jake's chest to his navel and laved and sucked the tiny hole.

Head thrown back, Jake grabbed two handfuls of Cree's long black hair and held on for what he knew was coming next. Cree's lips nipped their way down to the bulbous head of Jake's cock.

"Oh that's good, sheriff."

Taking as much as possible into his mouth, Cree nodded his agreement. Jake shifted his hips and began thrusting into Cree's mouth. "Do me, Cree."

Cree looked up at Jake and pulled off his cock with a loud pop. "Turn around, cowboy."

Jake turned around and braced his hands against the tile wall. Cree reached up and found the tube of lube on the top shelf of the shower. Squirting a liberal amount onto his fingers, Cree went to work on Jake's ass.

While he prepared Jake's hole he used his other hand to massage Jake's heavy sac. Jake fucked the air while Cree stretched him.

Lining up his cock with Jake's well stretched and relaxed hole, Cree shoved in to the hilt. "Oh, cowboy...so tight...so good...gonna make me come."

Pushing back into Cree's thrusting drives, Jake took his own cock in hand and began pumping. He threw his head back and Cree bit his neck. "Gonna, sheriff...gonna...uhhh." Jake came in a blaze of glory.

Jake's orgasm milked the cum right out of Cree's cock. "Oh it's good, cowboy." Cree and Jake both collapsed onto their knees both still shaking with aftershocks.

"Love you, cowboy." Cree kissed and stroked Jake lovingly.

"Love you, sheriff." Jake stood and rinsed himself off, reaching down to pull Cree up when he was finished. "I've gotta get back to the hospital. Did you want to come or do you want the second shift?"

Rinsing off, Cree shook his head. "No, I'm coming with you. No tellin' what you might do with Buck in the same hospital. We can send one of the guys for the second shift."

As they were drying off they heard the phone ringing. Cree looked at Jake. "It's past two in the morning, that can't be good news."

Cree wrapped the towel around his waist and ran to the phone. He reached for the phone just as Gabe knocked on the bedroom door. "Cree, the state police are on the phone for you, they say it's urgent."

Closing his eyes, Cree took a deep breath, afraid of what he was about to hear. "Thanks, Gabe, I got it in here." Cree picked up the phone. "Sheriff Sommers. What's wrong?"

Chapter Sixteen

ဆ

Jake could tell something big had happened by the red in Cree's face and the white of his knuckles as he clutched the phone. He could only hear Cree's side of the conversation but it was enough to make him break out into a sweat.

"Assholes! What about Jenny? Is she safe? So help me God, if you assholes let him get her there will be hell to pay!"

Cree nodded and walked to the closet and withdrew a pair of jeans, t-shirt and a clean pair of socks. "Okay, put me on hold while you have someone check on her but don't you dare hang up on me."

Looking grim, Cree nodded his head toward the closet. "Get dressed, Jake. The assholes let Buck get away from them at the hospital. They're checking on Jenny right now."

Cree got dressed with the phone tucked under his chin. "What! What do you mean you can't find her? Fuck! Of all the incompetent... Fuck it, my crew will find her and you can expect a full report on your commanding officer's desk as soon as we find her." Cree slammed the phone down and looked at Jake with fury in his eyes.

"Better stick your head outside the door and yell for the team to get dressed. Full battle gear. That bastard's taken Jenny from the hospital. Meeting in the dining room in five minutes."

Five minutes later the team assembled in the dining room in full military gear. All six of them checking and loading their numerous weapons. Knives went into boots, guns into ankle straps and shoulder straps.

Nicco was the sharpshooter of the bunch, so he was cleaning and testing the scope on his L96 sniper rifle. As always, Nicco seemed to be in a zone.

Jake looked up at Cree. "I called my foreman Hank and told him to leave two men with the horses. The rest of them are to fan out around the hills in that section of the ranch and look for any place Buck could have taken Jenny."

Cree gave him a quick nod. "I think you were right to do that. My thinking is that Buck wants to torment us with the fact he has Jenny. What better place than on our land?" Cree stood up to address his team. "Okay, guys, here are the plans. I'll need two of you to go into the city and check out the hospital. Find out how in the hell a man could just walk out carrying an unconscious woman. See if you can pick up any kind of trail. Talk to everyone you can. I'd say Remy and Gabe would be the best to go. Ben and Nicco are too unapproachable. That leaves Ben and Nicco to help Jake and me cover the front half of the ranch.

"Take your cell phones and your hands-free communication radios. I'm not taking any chances with missed calls or dead batteries. If you get in a situation with Buck and you see no other option, shoot to kill. The only thing that matters is that Jenny gets out of this safely."

Cree nodded to the men and the table emptied as each man went about his assigned tasks. Cree grabbed his radio and phone off the table and grabbed his rifle. "Come on, cowboy, you're with me."

* * * * *

Jenny woke the next morning to the musty smell of dirt. She opened her eyes and looked around. "This isn't my hospital room," she murmured to herself.

"Damn straight it's not."

The bottom fell out of her stomach and she snapped her head around to see Buck sitting on a chair in the corner. Even though there was very little light in the room Jenny could see the sweat-dampened pale face of Buck. "Please not again, Buck. Please don't do this to me. If you've ever really loved me as a daughter you'll let me go now."

Buck got up from his chair and staggered over to her holding a gun. "Dumb bitch. Haven't you figured it out yet? I've never loved you like a daughter. When I walked into that hotel bar and saw you at the age of twelve I knew you were meant for me. You were supposed to be mine. The only reason I didn't take you then was because I was afraid you'd sic the law on to me."

Looking into his eyes, she could tell something was wrong with him. Not just the fact that he'd gone completely insane but something else. Jenny saw the bandage on his temple. That along with the clammy look about him and the feverish flush to his face told her that infection had set in to Buck Baker's body.

She knew the longer she kept him talking, the weaker he'd become. That would give her guys more time to find her. "What about Helen? Didn't you love her?"

"Christ, you're dumber than you look, aren't you? I hated that woman. The only reason I married her was to have some kind of legal right to you. I told her as much a couple months after we were married." He gave Jenny a leering grin. "Your momma liked my money too much to put your welfare first."

Jenny remembered a conversation she'd had with her mother when she was fifteen Jenny was in her room changing her school clothes so she could go help with the chores. Helen came into the room and looked at Jenny disdainfully. "If you want to keep a roof over our heads you need to stop putting so many clothes on. Try not wearing a bra once in a while, you prude."

Jenny was shocked at her mother's outburst. "Momma, I can't go out there without a bra."

Helen's eyes blazed. "You're so selfish." She stormed across the room to Jenny and slapped her across the cheek. "Listen and listen good. You will do whatever it takes to keep us here on this ranch. Now get outside and show your stepdaddy how much you love him."

Walking out the bedroom door, Helen turned once more to face Jenny. "You have always held me back. I should have aborted you when your father refused to marry me. Who wants a woman with a kid around all the time? It's no wonder I've never loved you. Be thankful that someone does and that someone is Buck Baker."

Jenny had always thought her mother meant Buck was the only one that felt parental love for her but more recently she had learned differently. Buck was staring down at her like he was ready to pounce. She tried to sit up but grabbed her side in pain.

"My momma was always looking out for herself." She looked at Buck. "You were perfect for each other."

Buck was in front of her in a flash and backhanded her across the face. "You bitch. Don't try to get me mad enough to kill you. I've got my own plans for you."

Pacing back and forth across the floor, Buck pinched the bridge of his nose. Jenny could tell the infection was getting worse. "Where are we, Buck? What are these plans you mentioned?"

Buck stopped fingering his nose and his head shot up to stare at Jenny. "Just sit tight. We're going to wait for Jake and that faggot friend of his to come lookin' for you. I can't wait to see the look on his face when he figures out I brought you home where you belong. When he and that queer sheriff show up I've got a plan to trap 'em. Once they're tied up they're going to watch us making love before I kill them both.

"You see, Jenny, all this could have been avoided if you'd just remembered where your loyalties should have been. Now you won't have a choice because they'll be dead. Then I can fuck you all day long every day. I haven't fucked since the last time you gave it up for me." Buck reached down and started rubbing his erection.

Bile rose in Jenny's throat and she thought she was going to faint. "I gave up nothing to you. You took it with force. Didn't you get enough sex from my mother and every other woman in town?"

Buck chuckled and rubbed his chin. "Sure, I fucked your mother. What else was I supposed to do with the hard-on you gave me every day? Fucked practically every woman in town at least twice but none of them was a proper substitute for you, blue eyes."

Disgusted, Jenny spat out, "You're sick."

"Yeah, so I've heard. That's what finally did your momma in. Helen started getting mouthy about wanting more money to keep you around." Buck shrugged his shoulders. "So I had to get rid of her."

Frozen, Jenny looked at the monster before her. "What do you mean you had to get rid of her?"

"Hell, girl, the woman was only thirty-six years old. Do you really think she died of heart failure?" Buck smiled to himself. "Well, okay, she did technically die of heart failure but I guess you could say it wasn't because of natural causes. Do you have any idea how many poisons there are around a ranch?"

Buck stalked toward the door. "I'm going to find me something for this headache. Don't try to get out or I'll chain you to the bed. Don't bother screaming either. The house has been boarded up and the cowboys have all been let go." Buck left the room and locked the basement door.

* * * * *

As he was guiding his horse over yet another expanse of rock, Cree's cell phone rang. He grabbed the phone and looked at the caller ID. "Hey, Gabe, what've you found out?" He brought his horse to a stop beside Jake.

"Nothing really, Cree. The nurses on Jenny's floor didn't see anything. I found a janitor that saw Buck leave with her though. He said he questioned Buck about the unconscious woman in his arms. Buck pointed to his own bandage and told him that Jenny was his daughter and they'd been in a car accident and he was taking her home."

Cree was gripping the phone forcefully and Jake placed a hand on his thigh. Cree took a breath and rubbed Jake's hand. "What else have you found? Anything about where they went after the hospital?"

"I'm not sure. I got a report that a guy was seen getting into a cab with a woman about the same time Jenny went missing but I haven't been able to track down the driver yet. He should be coming back on shift in about an hour."

"Keep on it, Gabe." Cree disconnected the call and relayed the information to Jake.

Leaning over his saddle, Jake gave Cree a sympathetic kiss. "We'll find her, sheriff."

Nodding his head, Cree took one more quick kiss. "Yeah, cowboy, we will. Riding around here I've been thinking. If Buck wanted to torment us with Jenny, where would be the best place?" Cree tilted his head sideways, his eyes in thought. "Do you suppose he boarded up the Double B for a reason? That's the place he considers Jenny's home, after all."

"Damn, Cree, you may be right. Do you have Cotton's number on ya?" Jake grabbed the little bit of hope Cree was offering.

Pulling out his phone, Cree found Cotton's number and called it.

143

"Cotton."

"Hey, Cotton, it's Cree. Say have you seen anything of Buck? He kidnapped Jenny from the hospital after he shot her and we're trying to find him."

Cotton exhaled loudly. "Sorry, Cree, I've not been to the ranch for a couple days. I've been helping a friend. I'll go over now and check it out."

Cree knew he could trust Cotton but he didn't want Buck to take off if he saw him snooping around. "Play it cool, Cotton. We don't want for Buck to see you or he might take off."

"No problem, Cree. I can ride my horse over there. The friend I'm helping bought the old Sampler Nursery that butts up to the Double B. If Buck's there he won't see me. I'll call as soon as I know."

Cree disconnected the call and looked at Jake. "I think we should call in Nicco and Ben and regroup up at the house."

Chapter Seventeen

ℰꙨ

After Buck left the room Jenny tried once again to get to her feet. She had to get some of her strength back if she was going to go toe to toe with Buck. The stitches pulled as she sat up but so far so good. Taking a deep breath, Jenny eased her feet to the floor. Putting one hand on the old white iron footboard and one hand on her side to keep pressure on the wound, Jenny managed to get to her feet.

Pain shot up and down the side of her body. Jenny took a few calming breaths and started to walk toward the door. It was slow going but she reached the door and tried the knob. She knew it was locked but she was trying to determine what sort of lock it was when she heard footsteps coming down the stairs.

As quickly as she could Jenny made it back to the bed. The door opened and Buck came in carrying a lunch tray. "I brought you something to eat, my dear little bitch."

Buck set the tray down beside her and sat back in his chair. "So have you decided to be a good little girl? Because you know bad little girls get punished. You've already been punished enough, Jenny. It's time to know your place."

He was right. She sure had been punished enough and she had the scars to prove it. Jenny didn't even want to think what being a "good little girl" would entail, but she needed to keep him talking to buy more time. She knew Cree and Jake were searching for her.

Rex Cotton called back within an hour. "I think he's there. I didn't see his pickup but I did see what appeared to be fresh tire tracks leading into the tool shed. I tried to check out the shed but it was locked up tight. Tell me what you want me to do."

Cree looked across the table at his team. "Stay put, Cotton. I don't want to bring the police in yet so don't call them unless you see or hear something. We're headed to Oklahoma now. We should be there in about three to three and a half hours depending on how fast we drive."

"Sounds good, Cree. I'll stay put behind the barn so don't shoot when you see me."

"Ain't gonna happen, Cotton. Just don't remember names or faces after my men leave."

Pushing *end* on his cell phone, Cree turned to Jake. "She's there with Buck. Let's go. We need to take two vehicles because Jenny's riding home with you and me."

* * * * *

"So tell me, Buck, what is it that makes a man fall in love with a twelve-year-old girl? Was I just special or do all little girls strike your fancy?"

Buck exploded out of his chair, pointing his finger at Jenny. "Stop trying to make me out to be some kind of pervert." He backhanded her once again. "What I always felt for you was true love. I waited for you to turn eighteen, didn't I? Hell, your momma would have let me have you at twelve if it meant she could keep spending my money."

Jenny dabbed the blood from her split lip and scooted back a little farther on the bed. "Okay, I get that you love me but I love your son and Cree. I'm sorry, Buck, but I didn't plan it. Sometimes things just happen and no one is to blame. Forget about killing Jake and Cree. It won't make me love you. Nothing will."

Buck grabbed Jenny by the hair and hauled her off the bed. "Get over to the sink and clean yourself up." He shoved her toward the sink.

Jenny lost her balance and slammed into the sink, hard. The pain was unbearable in her side. She looked down and saw the blood seeping through the hospital gown she still wore. "Fuck!"

Another backhand to the face and Jenny was on the floor. "No woman of mine is going to talk like trash. Get your ass up and clean your face. I'll go get some bandages for your side." He stalked out of the room and locked the door.

* * * * *

Jake and Cree arrived a couple minutes ahead of the rest of the guys. They were strapping on their weapons when Ben's black SUV drove up. Everyone quickly readied themselves and looked to Cree for further instructions.

Cree drew a map in the dust on the hood of Jake's truck. "The house is around the bend. The tool shed is on the back side of the house, the barn is on the side of the house. Spread out and use what you can for cover. Put your headsets on. Gabe, Ben and Remy meet behind the tool shed and wait for further instructions. Nicco, I want you in the hayloft with your sniper rifle. Jake and I'll go to the back of the barn and meet up with Cotton. Good luck and stay safe."

The men headed out. Jake couldn't believe the state of the Double B. How could a man become so obsessed with a woman that he'd let everything he'd worked his whole life for go to shit? That more than anything clued him into Buck's mental state.

They made it to the back of the barn and found Cotton. They shook hands with their long-time acquaintance. "Anything new?"

Rex shook his head. "Nothing that I can tell. I've been sitting here thinking about how odd Buck acted before he disappeared this last time. I remembered Buck had me pick up a new doorknob and deadbolt for the door to the storeroom in the basement. Now why do you suppose he'd need those things?"

"Fuck, not the basement. He kept her in a basement the last time he kidnapped her." Jake rubbed his forehead, thinking. "Gabe, you guys sit tight until you see me unlock the front door. Nicco, keep that rifle aimed on the front door. If Buck comes out without one of us, shoot him between the eyes. Got it?"

"Roger that," Nicco replied.

"Roger," came from Gabe, Ben and Remy.

Jake turned to Cree. "I'm going in through my bedroom window. We sprang that lock so many times growing up, it's a piece of cake. You come in the front door with the rest of the team."

Cree shook his head. "No, Jake, I don't want you going in there by yourself. I'm coming with you, no matter what."

Jake thought about it for a second. "Stay behind me and only step where I step. The house has a lot of creaks but I know them all."

Jake started to walk off and stopped suddenly turning toward Cree. "No matter what happens in that house, know that I love you, sheriff." He grabbed Cree and gave him a quick kiss.

"Ditto."

* * * * *

When Buck brought back the bandages, he also brought his electric branding iron and plugged it in to the electrical outlet. Jenny's eyes grew big as saucers. "Please, no more branding, Buck."

Buck shook his head in apparent disgust. "It's not my fault you keep forgetting whose property you are. If it's the only way to show you then I have no choice. Now take off that gown and clean yourself up."

148

When Jenny just sat there without moving, he became impatient. "Goddamn it. Do you need me to teach you another lesson right here and now? Now strip and clean yourself up."

Slowly, Jenny rose to her feet and untied the hospital gown. She pulled it off her shoulders and went to the sink where Buck had put the bandages. Using a washcloth, she gently cleaned the blood off around the wound. Jenny placed four thick gauze pads over the wound and used some first-aid tape to secure it in place.

She started to replace the gown, when Buck ripped it out of her hands. "Don't even think about it. Now go lay down on the bed." He gestured toward the bed and began taking his clothes off.

Jake successfully unlocked the front door and let the team in. Putting his finger to his lips, he led the way down the basement steps. At the bottom of the steps he assessed the lock. Looking back at the men, he drew his weapon and pointed it toward the lock.

Unplugging the red-hot branding iron on the way to the bed, Buck smiled. "So tell me where you want this reminder located, Jenny? Shall I put it on the other tit or maybe on your cute ass? I'll let you choose today but make it quick. My dick's hard and as soon as I mark you I'm gonna fuck you."

Buck sat down on the bed, branding iron in his hand. Jenny knew it was now or never for her. She looked sweetly at Buck and kicked him as hard as she could in the balls. Buck bent over wheezing.

Jenny rolled off the bed screaming and reached for the dropped branding iron. She swung it at Buck and knocked it against the side of his head. Jenny felt empowered. She straddled Buck and brought the branding iron down on his forehead just as the door blew open.

Buck was screaming bloody murder by the time Jake and the team filed into the small room. Cree had his gun aimed at Buck's head. Jake noticed the look in Cree's eyes and the barely controlled fury at seeing Jenny naked.

Jenny saw it too. She had to stop Cree from killing Buck in cold blood. "Cree, put the gun down. Buck isn't worth it. As a matter of fact I can't wait for him to go to prison and suffer." Jenny glanced at Buck. "He's a pretty man for a psycho. I'm sure all the men will be fighting over him, don't you think? Cree, look at me. I'm all right. Buck deserves to suffer slowly, don't give him the easy way out."

Cree flicked his eyes toward Jenny and took a deep breath. Slowly, he lowered his gun. Turning to Ben and Gabe, he motioned toward Buck. "Could you two please take out the trash until the police get here?"

Ben easily picked Buck up and threw him over his shoulder like a fifty-pound bag of dog food. His head was bleeding and he had a nice BB brand on his forehead. Jenny was happy with that one. She was proud of herself. She felt vindicated.

Jake and Cree pulled her into their arms and they all collapsed onto the floor in a tangle of limbs. Jake kissed Jenny and wiped the tears from her eyes. "How are you, baby?" Taking in her bruised face and split lip, Jake began to worry all over again. "Please tell me he didn't rape you again."

Jenny put her hands on either side of Jake's face and looked him in the eyes. "I'm fine and the babies are fine. Buck didn't rape me this time. I kicked him in the nuts when he got close enough to try. Then I hit him with the branding iron and branded his forehead. All in all, I'd say it's been a pretty productive day."

Jenny smiled and they both knew she'd be okay. She had finally taken control of her fear and fought back.

Chapter Eighteen

ε)

Sitting in a hospital bed the next day, Jenny could finally relax. Buck had been taken to jail in Oklahoma City awaiting state charges to be filed. He also faced charges in Missouri and New Mexico. They currently had him on suicide watch.

Jenny reached down to rub her stomach. "It's over, babies. We can finally get on with the rest of our lives."

Cree and Jake strolled in at that moment. Cree looked at Jake and smiled. "So are you about ready to make an honest woman of yourself, sweetheart?" He bent down and kissed her.

"Of course. What took you so long? I've been ready since I was twelve." Jenny giggled and squeezed his hand. "They're going to let me out tomorrow for good behavior. But no sex for one more week until the stitches come out. So I guess I can marry you two a week from tomorrow. How does that sound?"

Jake took hold of her other hand and kissed her. "Perfect. Just like you." He pulled up a chair and sat beside the bed opposite Cree.

"We need to talk about what to do with the Double B. I was talking to Gabe and he'd like to put an offer on the table to buy it. I was wondering what you thought of the idea."

Jenny smiled and tilted her head toward Jake. "I think that's a wonderful idea. He told me he really enjoyed living and working on the Triple Spur so it makes perfect sense for him to buy it. I do feel a little guilty about Rex Cotton. He's been at the Double B for twenty-five years. It's really the only home he's ever had."

"Well, we'll just have to think of something then. I totally agree that we have to find a way to let him keep his little foreman's house."

Jenny sat up with a sparkle in her eye. "That's it! Why don't we sign over the foreman's house to Cotton and make a stipulation in the sales contract that he is foreman as long as he's able and willing. Do you think Gabe would agree to that?"

Rubbing his stubbly jaw, Jake thought about his old friend. "I think it would put his mind at ease. I'm sure he's going to need all the help he can get. He may be a good horseman but I don't know how much he knows about raising cattle and Cotton's the best. I'll talk it over with him tonight after supper."

Jenny smoothed the blankets over her legs. "Now let's talk about the wedding."

* * * * *

The following week was full of activity. Jenny drove herself into Santa Fe to see her new obstetrician. While she was there she went shopping for a wedding dress. She ended up with a simple off-the-shoulder ivory tea-length dress with a lavender sash around the waist. She also made a trip to the salon. Jenny had her hair trimmed and a special treatment done as a wedding gift for Cree and Jake. Jenny smiled wickedly to herself as she left the salon.

The wedding was in two days and Nicco and Remy would come back into town tomorrow. They'd gone back home for a few days to try to catch up on their own work. Ben was still in talks with Kate Crawford about buying her parents' farm. Things didn't seem to be going as smoothly as he'd hoped.

Jenny caught up with Ben when she got home from shopping. "So, how are the talks with Kate going?"

Ben got a funny look on his face and shook his head. "Not so good, Jenny. I feel bad because she really doesn't want to sell the ranch but she just can't do it all by herself."

Rolling her eyes at Ben, Jenny shook her head. "Why is it that a woman always has to come up with good compromises? Here's what you do. You buy half of the ranch. Kate gets to keep half and you two become partners. I'm sure you two can figure out the living arrangements easily enough. You're easy to get along with and you'd be better than a guard dog at keeping the place safe." Jenny smiled mischievously at that last comment.

Slapping his palm to his forehead, Ben laughed. "Why didn't we think of that? I don't need the whole ranch. I just need somewhere to belong. Something physical to do. I'm not cut out for desk work."

Ben grabbed Jenny up in a fierce hug and kissed her on the forehead. "God, you're smart, Jenny."

"And damned sexy too." Cree came strolling into the kitchen. "Now can you tell me why you have your hands on my woman or do we need to take this outside?" Cree looked at Ben with a stern expression but blew it when his lip couldn't help twitching into a smile.

Ben backed away from Jenny and put his hands up. "Hey, man, I was just thanking her for solving my real estate problem."

"Yeah well, you've thanked her, now get out." Cree looked at Ben then looked at the door through narrowed eyes.

Backing toward the door, Ben still had his hands up. "Okay, I can take a hint. Do you want me to post a guard so no one comes in to interrupt anything?" he said with a smiling face.

"Just tell everyone to stay the hell out for a while."

Ben left snickering and Cree pulled Jenny into his arms. "Have a good day, sweetheart?" Before she could answer he ran his tongue over her lips seeking entrance. Jenny's lips parted and he thrust his tongue inside the hot depths of her mouth.

Jenny tasted coffee and mint and Cree. She broke the kiss and smiled up at him. "My day was fantastic. Dr. Warner said next month when I go in for my appointment you and Jake should come with me. We should be able to listen to the heartbeats then. I'm not scheduled for another sonogram for two more months though." Jenny stopped talking and nibbled his neck.

Suddenly she thought of something and looked up at Cree. "What are you doing home? Is there something wrong?"

"No, nothing's wrong, Jenny. Everyone at the office told me to take off early because I was growling like a bear." He shrugged his shoulders. "I can't help it. I know you're here and there's no other place I want to be."

Kissing him again, Jenny rubbed her hands up and down his chest. "I kinda like you being here too but you're going to have a lot of mouths to feed before long. You need your job, sheriff. Besides, Cree, I'll always be here when you get home."

Pulling her even closer, he sank in to her mouth once again. "I'm sorry we're not going to get a honeymoon, sweetheart. I've had to use all my vacation time in the last month." Cree bent his head and nibbled her neck. When he rubbed his erection against her soft mound, she stiffened and made a small squeak. Stilling him immediately, Cree drew back and looked at Jenny's face.

"What's wrong, sweetheart, did I hurt you? Is it your side? Please tell me what I did, Jenny?"

Jenny looked toward the floor. Oh boy, this was going to be embarrassing. "No love it's not my side. I um…I had a little procedure done today as a wedding present for you and Jake. It's still sore that's all but it should be fine by the time the wedding night gets here."

With a puzzled look on his face Cree put Jenny at arm's length and tilted her chin up with his finger. "Exactly what kind of procedure, Jenny?"

Gosh, now he was looking really worried. She'd have to tell him her surprise before he gave himself an ulcer. "I uh...had a wax job done. I thought you and Jake would like that."

A smile of relief passed over Cree's lips. "Like it? We'll love it. And kiss it and lick it and eat it. Let me see, Jenny."

Cree was as giddy as a schoolboy. Jenny just shook her head, resigned. "Okay, but don't touch it. I had no idea I would be this sore."

Cree lifted her onto the kitchen counter and pulled her skirt up. "Damn, sweetheart, you aren't even wearing underwear. Guess it's my lucky day." Looking at Jenny's bare pussy made his mouth drool. Flicking his tongue out to wet his lips, Cree swallowed. "It's the prettiest thing I've ever seen."

Backing up on the counter, Jenny put her hand out. "Cree, you promised no touching."

Looking up from her pussy to her face, Cree smiled. "I know I promised it's just hard. Hell, I'm hard. It does look a little too red though. Have you put anything on it since you left the salon?"

"No, I can't get myself to touch it."

"Stay right there, sweetheart. I've got some salve that Jake and I use."

Cree walked off, leaving Jenny on the counter with her skirt around her waist. "Hey, you can't just leave me here. What if someone comes in? Cree?"

Striding back into the kitchen carrying the salve, Cree grinned. "Not that anyone would mind the sight of you sitting half naked in the kitchen but I told them to stay out. Now scoot your butt back up here and lean back. Believe me, it won't hurt it'll make it feel much cooler."

Jenny nodded her head and got into the position he asked. Putting a good dollop of salve on his fingers, Cree leaned over her pussy. "Just one lick." He snaked out his tongue and licked in between her lips, getting a good deal of her previous arousal.

"Mmm, good." Cree stood and replaced his tongue with his fingers covered in the salve. He drew little circles on her bare pussy. "See, doesn't that feel a lot better?"

"Heaven."

When he was finished he washed his hands in the sink and dried them on the towel nearby. Going back to Jenny, he slowly lifted her off the counter and held her in his arms. "Thank you for doing this for us, sweetheart. Jake's going to flip his lid. He's the one that got me to finally try it. You'll see. You'll be a lot more sensitive. You'll think your pussy's never really been touched before."

Jenny looked up at Cree. "Speaking of Jake. Promise you won't give away my surprise?"

Reaching back to swat her ass, Cree laughed. "As much as I'd like to brag to him what I got to do this afternoon, your secret is safe with me, sweetheart."

Chapter Nineteen

ဆ

Jenny's wedding day finally arrived. The weather was perfect for the outdoor ceremony. She stretched and yawned as the sun slowly lit the sky. "I do believe this will be the best day of my life so far." Of course she said it to no one since she'd slept apart from the men for the past week. Jenny told them she wanted their wedding night to be extra special and it would be better if they missed her for a while first.

Both men had been walking around with a hard-on and a bad attitude all week but they'd agree with her choice after tonight. She sat up and reached for her robe when someone knocked on the door.

Looking at the door through narrowed eyes, she called out. "If that's Jake or Cree don't come in. It's bad luck."

The door opened and a petite blonde came through the door carrying a breakfast tray. "Hi, Jenny. I'm Kate Crawford from down the road. Jake and Cree asked me to bring this up for them."

Jenny was a little surprised to see a stranger in her bedroom but Kate looked as uncomfortable about it as she did. "Come in, Kate. You can just put the tray on the bedside table. I need to get my robe on."

Kate smiled and put the tray down. "Um...the guys wanted to know if there's anything I can help you with today." She looked down at her feet seeming at war with herself. "To be totally honest," Kate took a deep breath, "I wanted to know if there's anything I can do for you. Ben's told me a little of what you've been through and it doesn't sound like you have many female friends. So I thought maybe you could use one today."

"Well, Ben's right, I don't have any female friends except for maybe Cree's mother who I lived with for a while." Jenny chewed her lip and thought about letting Kate into her life. "I'd like your help." Jenny looked at Kate through narrowed eyes. "Even if you are the most beautiful woman I've ever seen in my life. I'm just glad I trust my men or I might've had to run you off. As it happens I do trust my men and I could really use a girlfriend in a house full of testosterone."

Kate's face lit up like a full moon on a dark night. "Thank you, Jenny. To be perfectly honest with you I don't have any real friends at all. I've spent all my time the last seven years trying to make a go of the ranch." Shrugging her shoulders Kate continued. "Working fifteen-hour days hasn't left me any free time for socializing. Not that I had a lot of friends when I was in school either. The girls would have nothing to do with me and the boys only wanted one thing."

Jenny looked at the gorgeous woman in front of her. Long blonde, naturally curly hair and eyes so dark they almost looked black. Kate's body would have put a centerfold to shame. She was only about five-foot-two, but with her double D breasts she sure didn't look like a child. She looked worn-out and a little sad. "Well, I'd say you're well on the way to having a good friend now. It sounds like the girls and women around here are all just jealous of your beauty." Jenny shrugged her shoulders. "How are the negotiations going with Ben on the sale of the ranch?"

Rolling her eyes and taking a deep breath, Kate sat down on the bed. "We agreed on being partners in the ranch. I've tried to do it by myself but it's just too much work. I can't leave the ranch. I've spent my whole life there and it's my home. What we can't seem to agree on is the living arrangements. Ben wants to fix up the house and have us both live there but I don't think I could ever live with a man." Kate looked into Jenny's eyes for understanding. "Men scare me. They're so much bigger and stronger than I am." She shrugged her shoulders. "They can make you do things you don't want to do just by their superior strength."

Kate stood and started pacing the room. "Ben appears to be a very nice man but appearances can be deceiving and I'm just a little afraid to take the risk. Besides, Ben is the biggest and strongest man I've ever met. He makes me feel all shaky when he's around."

Lost in her thoughts Kate stopped talking and sat back down on the bed. "Well, enough about that, what would you like help with today?"

Jenny hated the lost and lonely look on Kate's face. She thought Kate might've been a little more like her than she'd previously thought. "For starters, you can be my maid of honor. I thought of asking one of the guys but I didn't figure any of them would go for it. Jake's standing up with Cree for obvious reasons so unless you say yes it will look out of balance."

Smiling, Kate got up and hugged Jenny. "If you're sure about it I would be honored. I've never been in a wedding before." Kate pulled away from Jenny with a hint of moisture in her eyes. "Well, we'd better get you ready."

* * * * *

The sun was low in the sky. The few guests that had been invited to the wedding waited on the front porch under the ceiling fans and Jake and Cree were in their bedroom. Cree was trying to tie his tie and not getting very far. "Jake, can you help me with this blasted thing? My hands are shaking so badly I'm about to strangle myself with it."

Smiling, Jake came across the room to stand in front of Cree. He took the tie out of Cree's hands and quickly tied it into a neat Windsor knot. "Why are you so nervous? Are you having second thoughts about getting married?"

Cree looked at Jake as if he'd lost his mind. "Hell, no, I'm not changing my mind. I've wanted this day for seven years.

I'm just really horny and anxious for the wedding night. I hope I can keep my hard-on under control until all the guests leave tonight." He flashed Jake a quick smile.

Brushing his hands down Cree's suit jacket, Jake leaned in for a very welcome kiss. "Do you want me to take the edge off for you, sheriff? Don't forget your momma is in the audience. You wouldn't want to shock her with that impressive bulge you're sportin'."

Cree looked at Jake and then at his watch. "We don't have much time, Jake, but I'd appreciate any help I can get."

Jake smiled and kissed him again, undoing Cree's belt and then his zipper. Cree's erection sprang out of his opening. Typical of Cree there was no underwear to act as a buffer. Stroking Cree's erection, Jake went down on his knees and took Cree's cock into his mouth.

Eyes rolling in back of his head, Cree moaned. "Yes, just like that, cowboy. Oh man, it feels so good."

Pumping Cree's cock with his mouth and throat, Jake fondled Cree's sac. His other hand snaked back to find the hole that was waiting for attention. Jake inserted his finger and found just the right spot to make Cree go wild. Cree started bucking and thrusting into Jake's hot moist mouth.

Cree was delirious with pleasure. "Good. Good, cowboy...I'm gonna...oh....uhhh."

Jake licked him clean then got to his feet and held the man he loved through his aftershocks. "Why don't you go into the bathroom and clean yourself a bit? I'll see you downstairs in five minutes. Oh and Cree, I love you."

Cree met Jake five minutes later and ushered their guests to the wedding awning put up to shade people from the sun.

Approaching his mother, Cree wasn't sure how he felt. He'd blamed his mom for a lot in the past, but she'd helped Jenny out so maybe it was time to forgive and forget. As he bent down to give her a kiss on the cheek, her scent brought back memories. Vanilla, his mother had always smelled like vanilla.

"Hi, Momma. I'm glad you came. I wish Tori had come too but she still doesn't agree with my lifestyle choices." Cree shrugged his shoulders and looked over his mother's head.

Naomi patted Cree on the cheek and wrapped her arm around his waist. "Son, it doesn't matter what anyone thinks but the three of you. Tori will come around eventually. I guess I had a hard time accepting it until Jenny stayed with me. I grew to love her as much as one of my own. All anyone has to do is to look at you, Jake and Jenny together to see the love you three share."

"Thank you, Mom that means a lot to me. Jenny wanted me to ask you before things got too crazy around here if you'd come back for Thanksgiving?"

Naomi eyed him up and down. "Of course I'll be here for Thanksgiving. I have to keep up with that child growing in her."

Cree's jaw dropped. "How do you know she's pregnant?"

Rolling her eyes at her son, Naomi chuckled. "I wasn't born yesterday. I know what a pregnant woman looks like even if she is just starting to show."

"Well, here's something you don't know. Jenny's going to have twins. They should be here by St. Patrick's Day."

Naomi threw her arms around Cree. "Congratulations, son."

Jake came strolling down the aisle and took Cree's elbow. "Come on, Mr. Groom, it's time."

Cree kissed his mom again and seated her in the front row. Of course there were only three rows of six chairs with an aisle down the middle for Jenny to walk. They'd only invited the cowboys from the ranch and their girlfriends or wives. Then there was Naomi and the team.

Speaking of the team, Cree saw all of them except Nicco. Surely he didn't leave to go home before the wedding? Cree was sure he'd heard him down in the kitchen that morning. *Oh well,* he shrugged to himself, *I guess he must be around somewhere.*

The minister from town stood on the little stage the cowboys had built. Jenny didn't want any fancy flowers or decorations. Instead wild flowers and sunflowers sat in tin buckets on either side of the stage. It was perfect. Perfectly Jenny.

* * * * *

Jenny heard the music begin. She'd opted for Lester, one of the hands, to play the wedding march on his fiddle. She turned and gave Kate a quick hug. "Thank you for all your help today."

Hugging her back, Kate wiped a tear from her cheek. "Believe me when I say it was my pleasure. I've always wanted a sister and today I felt as if I had one."

Kate walked slowly down the aisle followed by Jenny. She felt beautiful today and two times lucky. This may be the legal part of the ceremony but the real ceremony would happy tonight under the stars. That's when she would marry Jake and Jake would marry Cree.

Jenny got to the end of the aisle and took Cree's hand. The music stopped and the minister began the service. Jenny wasn't sure about everything he said because she was mesmerized by the looks on both Cree's and Jake's faces.

She turned to face the minister, still holding hands with Cree. The minister got to the part about objections and a shot rang out above everyone's head. Cree grabbed Jenny and folded his body over her.

Buck ran down the aisle with a gun pointed at Cree and Jenny. He started shouting incoherently. "You won't have her. I'll kill you all. She's mine…"

That was as far as he'd gotten. One minute he was running toward Jenny and Cree, the next he was facedown in the grass, a bullet hole between the eyes.

The whole thing had lasted about ten seconds. When the chaos died down Cree looked around him. Ben was comforting a shaken Kate under a shade tree. Buck was dead, but how? Then Cree spotted Nicco in the hayloft with his sniper rifle. He motioned Nicco to come down.

Jake bent over Buck's body and gently lifted his father off the ground. Taking him to the side of the house, he called the state police. Jenny could hear Jake screaming into his cell phone.

"What do you mean you didn't know he'd escaped? You're the police, for Christ's sake!" Jake paced around the side of the house around his father's body. "Just send someone to pick up his body. I've got a wedding to attend."

Jake walked back to the front of the aisle. He stopped in front of Jenny and Cree. "Can we please finish the wedding? Buck's ruined enough of our lives. Let's not let him ruin this."

Cree looked from Jake to Jenny. "I say we continue and deal with the mess afterward."

Jenny nodded and the minister began again. Luckily, no one at the wedding thought badly of the strange turn of events. Everyone there either knew of Buck's atrocities or had seen them firsthand.

When the minister turned to Cree and said he could finally kiss the bride, Cree practically devoured her mouth. Jenny could hear a lot of oooing and aaaahing from the small audience.

Cree let her go so Jenny could kiss Jake. By the time she came up for air the ranch was swarming with law enforcement. Looking around at the guests, Cree spotted Nicco sitting in the shade talking to someone from the state police.

"I'll be right back, Mrs. Sommers. I need to speak with Nicco and the police for a minute." He kissed her once again and left her in Jake's hands.

Cree made his way through the crowd and joined Nicco in the shade. The policeman was just finishing up. As the policeman walked away Cree looked over at Nicco and raised his eyebrows in question. "How?" was all he said.

Nicco looked at Cree and gave him a hint of a smile. "Gut feeling. I just had a feeling that Buck wasn't through. Thought I'd take a chance and watch the wedding from the loft through my scope."

Cree gave a slight nod. "Appreciate it, friend." He got to his feet and Nicco did the same. Both men shook hands and nodded at each other. Cree knew there would be an investigation of the shooting but it would turn out fine. Nicco was co-owner in a renowned safety and security business.

The rest of the festivities went on as planned. When the last guest left the ranch, Cree turned to Jenny and kissed her lightly on the cheek. "Why don't you go up to the bedroom and take a good soak in the hot tub? Jake and I have a few more details to take care of for our ceremony tonight."

Smiling, Jenny stood on tiptoes and kissed each of her men. "That, my loves, sounds like a perfect plan. Come up and get me when you're ready." Jenny turned and went inside the house.

When she got to their room, Jenny saw a large white box on top of the bed. It was tied with a cream-colored ribbon. Walking over to it, Jenny couldn't keep a smile off her face. She picked up the note on top of the box.

Tonight is our real wedding. Please wear the enclosed gown for our midnight ceremony. Jenny looked at the clock beside the bed. It was only ten-fifteen. She would have plenty of time for a good long soak.

Carefully, Jenny took off her wedding gown and hung it in the closet. She walked into the bathroom to start the water for her bath. When she reached the threshold of the bathroom she stopped suddenly.

Jenny put a hand to her mouth and started to giggle. The Jacuzzi was already filled. The steam still rising from the water. The tub was filled with multicolored rose petals dancing in the swirling water.

She looked around the room, candles covered every available surface. The guys had outdone themselves. Jenny felt like a pampered princess. She slowly lowered her body into the bubbling water. "Heaven on earth must have been the work of two beautiful angels."

After about an hour Jenny forced herself out of the soothing bath. She had just enough time to dress and do her hair before the guys came to get her.

Standing in front of the full-length mirror a half an hour later Jenny couldn't believe it was her. The gown the men had chosen was a dream of ivory silk. The bodice was ivory lace with spaghetti straps. The dress fell to the floor in a full swishing skirt. Jenny left her hair down. The shine of her black hair contrasted beautifully with the shine of the ivory silk.

A knock on the door startled her out of her daydream. The door opened and Cree and Jake stepped into the room wearing nothing but white silk lounging pants. They immediately stopped and dropped their jaws. Jake came toward her and held out his hand. "Will you marry me Jenny Sommers?"

* * * * *

In front of the house sat a big white Cinderella-style carriage pulled by two white horses. Jenny's eyes grew big as saucers. She turned to the men standing on either side of her and smiled. "It's perfect. How did you know that when I was a little girl I dreamt of this?"

Jake got a sheepish look on his face. His ears turned red around the edges. "Actually I heard you talking to your doll

Francine one day when you first came to the Double B. I guess I just have always remembered that part of your dream wedding." Jake looked into the blue depths of Jenny's eyes. "You're making all my dreams come true tonight so I thought I could make some of yours come true at the same time."

With tears pooling in her cornflower blue eyes, Jenny put her hands on both sides of his face. "Thank you, Jake, but I didn't need the horses or the carriage to make my dreams come true. All I need is you and Cree and the babies growing inside me."

Jake took her hands off his face and brought them to his mouth, kissing her fingers one by one then opening her hands and kissing each palm. "I promise tonight will be magical, my princess." Jake bent at the waist in a deep bow. "Your carriage awaits, your highness."

Cree stepped up and ushered Jenny to the awaiting carriage. Jenny gave a startled squeak when Cree picked her up and placed her on the royal blue velvet of the cushioned carriage seat. Cree climbed up to the driver's seat and Jake joined her in the back.

Leaning her head against Jake's shoulder, they took off toward the pasture. Looking around, Jenny felt like a giddy schoolgirl. "Where are we going to do the ceremony?"

Kissing her nose, Jake smiled and shook his head. "Out in God's country and that's all you're going to get out of me until we get there."

The carriage bounced and bumped along the rutted ranch road. Jenny didn't think the owners were going to be too happy if they broke one of the carriage axles. It was worth taking the risk though. After about twenty minutes they pulled up next to the creek. The water sparkled in the moonlight.

Looking around, Jenny's breath caught in her throat. To her right a canopied tent glowed with more than a hundred candles set in buckets of sand as a precaution against fire. In the center of the big tent sat a real king-sized bed up on a raised platform. The bed was dressed in a white comforter and fluffy down pillows. A garland of wildflowers draped the headboard. The buckets of wildflowers from the wedding had been brought down here and placed on little tables beside the bed. "Oh, my loves, it's the most magical setting I've ever seen."

Jake and Cree took Jenny's hands and drew her over to a grouping of rocks beside the creek. The rocks were covered in little votive candles in jewel-toned glass holders. They stopped in front of the rocks and both men moved to stand in front of her.

Clearing his throat, Jake took hold of Cree's hand and then Jenny's. Jenny held hands with Cree forming a circle. With tears in his eyes Jake began the ceremony. "Tonight I vow under the heavenly stars to protect and love you both until the day I die. I'll do everything in my power to be a good husband to both of you."

Lifting Cree's hand to his lips, Jake softly kissed Cree's palm. "Cree, will you take me as a partner and husband? I promise to love you and work beside you all the days of my life."

Cree lifted Jake's palm and kissed it. "I will take you for my husband, Jake. I love you with my heart and soul." Cree wiped a tear from his eye and reached over to kiss Jake. The kiss was a seductive melding of tongues and teeth.

The kiss broke and Jake looked over at Jenny. Raising her palm to his lips, Jake kissed her. "Jenny, will you take me as your husband and lover? I promise to be a friend when you want one and to be a lover when you need one. I promise to cherish you every day and to keep you safe from harm."

Wiping the tears from her face, Jenny took a deep breath and kissed Jake's palm. "I would love to be your wife, Jake. I promise to love you, work beside you and try my best to fill those five guest rooms with children." She smiled a teasing smile at Jake and reached up to kiss him. Jenny's kiss was also full of passion.

Breaking the kiss with Jake, she turned toward Cree and kissed him passionately. Jake withdrew rings from his pocket. Jenny and Cree also had rings for Jake.

Jake and Cree had talked about what to say to Jenny at the ring exchange portion of the ceremony. They both agreed that in order to move forward with their lives they would need to erase some of the past and substitute it with new beginnings. He hoped what he was about to say would help Jenny and not cause her more pain.

Jake took Jenny's hand and slipped the band of gold with his name on it onto Jenny's finger. "With this simple band of gold I brand you into my heart forever." Jake bent and kissed the ring on Jenny's finger.

Turning toward Cree, he withdrew another ring and slipped it on Cree's finger. "With this simple band of gold I brand you into my heart forever."

Cree took Jake's hand and repeated the words to him, slipping the ring on Jake's finger. Cree handed Jenny the ring he had held for her.

Jenny took the ring from Cree and took Jake's hand. Looking deeply into his amber eyes Jenny placed the ring on his finger. "With this simple band of gold I brand you into my heart forever."

All three of them looked down at the rings resting on their fingers. They had decided on gold bands with a twist. Instead of having an inscription on the inside of the ring, they had the jeweler inscribe their names all around the outside. So when Jenny looked down at the two rings she now wore, they said Cree and Jake.

Holding out her hand toward Cree and Jake, she sighed. "Perfect. They look absolutely perfect on my finger." Another look of mischief passed over her face. "Now let's see how they look from atop that big bed over there."

Picking her up in his arms, Jake carried Jenny to the awaiting bed. Cree pulled back the pristine white bedspread and Jake laid her down.

Jenny stretched out on the bed and held her arms out, noticing the way their cocks had tented the silk pants they were wearing. "Come and get me, husbands. Tonight I want both of you to hold nothing back from me or each other. This is about us. There will be no right or wrong, just feelings."

Cree had to practically wipe the drool from his chin. "Lord, I can't tell you how much I've been looking forward to this night." He moved onto the bed in sync with Jake. Both men wrapped their arms around each other as they clung to Jenny.

Touching his lips to Jenny's, Cree closed his eyes. "I love you, sweetheart, let me show you how much." Cree kissed her mouth, her cheeks and eyes. Slowly he nibbled and licked down her neck to the hollow at her throat. He couldn't resist so he sucked a mark on her throat and swirled his tongue around the hollow.

Moving down, his tongue blazed a wet trail down her chest to the bodice of the gown. Cree outlined her nipples through the lace with his finger. Soon he substituted his finger for his lips. Soaking the beautiful lace over her nipples, he reached up and pulled the spaghetti straps down her arms. Cree pulled the bodice down to her waist and went back to the hard raspberry-colored nipples.

He shifted his eyes to Jake who was sampling Jenny's mouth. Jake's hand was slowly pulling up the gown from the bottom. Cree reached over while still suckling Jenny's breast to run his hand along the outline of Jake's huge cock through the silk of his pants. Jake moaned and a drop of moisture made the pants translucent where it touched.

Jake was getting closer and closer to revealing Jenny's surprise and Cree couldn't wait to see Jake's reaction.

Reaching his hand toward Jenny's pussy, Jake groaned and pulled away from the kiss and looked at Jenny's face. "Baby, what have you done?" He sat up, still allowing Cree's hand the room to explore his cock.

Jake reached over and managed with a little help from Jenny to pull the gown down her hips and off. Jake's breath hissed out between his teeth. "Damn, that's a pretty pussy." He ran his hands over the now bare pussy and slipped a finger between her bare lips.

Squirming around on the bed, Jenny opened her eyes to look down at Jake. "That's your wedding present, cowboy." Jenny looked down at Cree still attached to her breast and fondling Jake's cock. "Cree's present is on the other side."

Cree looked up with a questioning expression on his face. "Ooooh, really? Can I see?" Cree moved to the foot of the bed with Jake. They turned Jenny onto her side so that Jake could still play with his present. Cree grinned and looked up at Jenny. "Are you trying to tell me something, sweetheart?"

Cree reached out and squeezed the white globes of Jenny's ass. Peeking out the crack was an electric blue butt plug. Cree gave the plug a little wiggle.

Jenny moaned and pushed her butt into his hand. "That feels wonderful, Cree. I've been wearing it all week so I'd be ready for tonight." She moaned, looking down. Jake began to eat her pussy and Cree was moving the plug in and out slowly. "Tonight I want both of you to fill me at the same time."

Cree looked over Jenny to watch Jake circle her clit with his tongue. Two of Jake's fingers were pumping in and out of her pussy while his mouth was latched to her clit. It was so hot he had to touch Jake.

Sitting up, Cree kept one hand around the plug, continuing the movement Jenny seemed to love and with the other hand he reached over and pulled Jake's pants down and off. Jake gave him a quick glance and smiled, spreading himself out for

Cree. Cree bent down and took Jake's cock into his mouth and down his throat.

Pulling up and off Jake's cock, Cree pumped it a couple of times. "You taste good, cowboy." He went back down to swallow him once again.

Trying to see over the tangle of bodies, Jenny raised her head. "Hey, don't forget me. I want to taste too. Isn't there someway we can all get in on the fun?"

Cree and Jake raised their heads and looked at Jenny. Cree shrugged his shoulders and Jake cleared his throat and winked at Jenny. "Daisy chain!"

They repositioned themselves so they were in a circle, each eating the pussy or cock in front of them. Jake continued to lick and nuzzle Jenny's soft pussy while Jenny explored Cree's cock and Cree continued his ministrations on Jake's cock.

Before long they were all three thrusting into the other. Jake raised his head and looked from Jenny to Cree. "I can't wait any longer."

Sitting up, Cree looked to be in the same boat as Jake. "I think that's an excellent plan, cowboy. Are you ready for us, Jenny?"

At Jenny's nod they repositioned themselves. Jake got on his back in the center of the bed with Jenny straddling his pelvis. Cree reached over to the little table beside the bed and grabbed the tube of lubricant.

Cree's hands were shaking so bad it took him longer that usual to get the lid off. Squirting a generous dollop onto his fingers he removed the blue plug and replaced it with first one finger and then two. Jenny had done a good job of stretching herself. Cree used a little more of the lube and slicked down his rock-hard and dripping cock.

Nodding to Jake that he was ready, Jake pulled Jenny down onto his cock. Jenny arched her back and moaned. "Damn, that's sexy." Cree positioned his cock and slowly entered Jenny's virgin ass. "You're so tight, sweetheart. I don't know how long I'm gonna last."

Jake and Cree found their rhythm. Jake pushed in as Cree pulled out of her. The position allowed both men to feel the other's cock through the thin membrane that separated them.

Jenny began to shake and moan. Her head thrown back, she climaxed. The tightening of her body brought both Jake and Cree to their orgasms. Grunts and howls filled the air as both men pumped their seed into their wife.

They all collapsed in a pile on the center of the bed, too spent to move for several minutes. Finally, Cree scooted over to lie on Jake's side. Jenny rolled in between her husbands. "Thank you both for a wonderful day." She held her hand up to the candlelight. The two rings reflected the light of the candles. They read Cree and Jake. Jenny pulled the hand with the rings to her lips and kissed them. "Branded by Gold," she whispered to herself as she drifted off to sleep.

BEN'S WILDFLOWER

☙

Acknowledgements

❧

I would like to thank Helen for her tireless work. You'd never know we live on two separate continents. Thank you for believing in me when I needed it most.

Trademarks Acknowledgement

❧

The author acknowledges the trademarked status and trademark owners of the following wordmarks mentioned in this work of fiction:

Bon Jovi: Bon Jovi Productions

Charlie Brown: United Feature Syndicate, Inc.

Denver Broncos: Empire Sports, Inc.

NASCAR: National Association for Stock Car Auto Racing, Inc.

Wrangler: DaimlerChrysler Corp.

Chapter One

৪৩

The crowing of the rooster just before dawn woke him. Ben Thomas rolled over and hit his alarm clock and went back to sleep. The rooster crowed again and once again a big beefy hand slammed down on the poor clock. The third time the rooster sounded Ben sat up and reached for the electrical cord. Coming out of the hazy feeling from too little sleep, Ben shook his head. His brain still felt a little foggy but at least he laughed. "Damn rooster."

Ben had lived on the Crawford ranch for two weeks. He'd bought half of the ranch and had gone into partnership with Kate Crawford. Kate was insisting that they change the name of the ranch. Ben was just too tired to care about the name of his new home.

Ben fell back down on the bed. Kate. Just thinking about her got him tied up in knots. He remembered the first day his friend Jake drove him over to meet Kate. He'd wanted to talk to her about buying her ranch. Jake had told him she might be willing to sell. It seemed she'd been having trouble running the ranch on her own. The bank was only months away from foreclosure and Kate was trying to do it all on her own.

The problem with the ranch wasn't the ranch itself. The problem was things kept mysteriously breaking that needed to be fixed. Fixing farm and ranch machinery could get very expensive and from talk around town poor Kate had the worst luck. Every time she'd save up enough money to help pay down the mortgage loan something else would break and she'd get further behind.

Jake had brought Ben over to meet Kate and see if she was ready to throw in the towel. The late summer day when they'd pulled into the ranch yard changed Ben's life. Jake had pulled up to an old two-story farm house.

The house needed work but it appeared to be well cared for. Flower boxes brimming over with pretty red geraniums and dark purple petunias sat under every window in the front of the house. A freshly painted dark green porch swing sat beside two equally green rocking chairs. The green was further carried out on the shutters bracketing every window. As soon as Ben saw the house he could picture himself sitting in one of the rockers drinking a glass of iced tea after a long day of ranch work.

Jake walked up the front porch steps and knocked on the door. When no one came to the door Jake turned and looked toward the barn. "Maybe Kate's in the barn."

Ben followed Jake to the big red barn with white trim. Walking through the door into the barn, they allowed their eyes to adjust to the dim light and called for Kate. When no answer came Jake shook his head. "I've no idea where she could be. She never leaves the ranch. Let's keep looking."

They checked out a few of the smaller ranch buildings and headed back to the truck. "Let's take a drive out into the fields. There's a dirt road of sorts we can follow."

Ben got in the truck beside Jake and they headed toward the gate to the pasture. Ben got out and opened the gate for Jake to drive through. Shutting the gate, Ben hopped back into the truck and looked around as Jake drove down the narrow dirt path. Once they were over the second hill Jake spotted Kate.

Kate was putting up hay in the field. The problem, Ben thought, was that she was doing it all by herself. She'd drive the truck and pick up about five bales and then stop and climb up onto the truck and stack them. It would take her forever at this rate. Ben could see about a hundred acres worth of hay here. So far Kate had only done about twenty acres. Ben shook his head. "Too much heavy work for a woman."

Jake laughed and pointed toward Kate. "Don't let her hear you say that. That right there, my friend, is the hardest working woman I've ever met. She does everything by herself on this ranch and has for the last five or six years since her dad and mom were killed." Jake took off his hat and ran his fingers through his hair. "Cree and I both have offered to help but she's too stubborn for her own good."

Ben looked across the field as they drove toward the hay truck. "Well, maybe she's had enough of this hard life by now and will agree to sell." Ben watched Kate stack more hay on the truck. As they got closer it appeared the bales were almost as big as she was.

Jake pulled his pickup beside the hay truck and got out. Ben was getting out of the truck when Kate stopped what she was doing and turned around. The air seemed to leave Ben's lungs. Before him stood the most beautiful woman he'd ever seen. Kate was a tiny thing—only about five two. She wore old faded jeans that fit her ass to perfection and a long-sleeved chambray shirt that snapped up the front. In her struggles with the bales of hay the top three snaps had come open. A bright red bra greeted Ben's eyes. The suntanned globes spilling out of the cups made Ben's mouth water.

Immediately he was rock-hard, which for a man of his size was definitely not a good thing. Ben had to turn back toward the truck and reposition his cock to run down the leg of his jeans. If not the damned thing would be sticking up out of the top of his pants for everyone to see. Ben's ten-inch cock had always been the bane of his existence.

Kate took the old straw cowboy hat off her head and wiped her brow. A cascade of golden curls fell to her waist. "Hi, Jake. What brings you out here today?"

Jake smiled at Kate and motioned toward her open top. Kate looked down and turned just one shade lighter than the fancy bra she was wearing. She quickly turned away and refastened her shirt.

Turning back around, Kate shrugged her shoulders. "Sorry about that, Jake. Not a very good first impression to make on your friend I'm afraid."

Jake chuckled and took off his hat. "I'd like to introduce an ex-Seal buddy of mine." Jake heard Ben clear his throat. "Actually he was my Commanding Officer. Kate Crawford, let me introduce you to Ben Thomas."

Ben walked, a little stiff-leggedly, up to the hay truck and held out his hand. Kate bent slightly to shake his hand. The moment her small hand was enveloped in his large one, a zing raced through Ben's body straight to his cock. Ben looked into her eyes and was left speechless. Her eyes were so dark a brown they appeared almost black. Ben swallowed around the lump in his throat. "It's very nice to meet you, Miss Crawford."

Kate swallowed visibly. "Please call me Kate and it's very nice to meet you too, Ben." Kate looked into Ben's eyes and smiled.

Their mutual trance-like state was interrupted by Jake. "The reason we came by, Kate, was to see if you'd be interested in selling Ben your ranch. I'm sorry if it was a little presumptuous of me but I'd heard in town that you'd been thinking about it."

Kate broke eye contact with Ben and straightened. "Sorry, Jake and Ben," she smiled down at Ben again, "but I'm not leaving this ranch until they throw me off. Which if things keep going the way they have been around here won't be that much longer."

Ben narrowed his eyes. "Exactly what kind of things have you been having trouble with, Kate?" Ben shifted his stance a bit to make more room for his cock.

Kate looked out over the lush hay fields. "Typical stuff I guess. Tractors breaking down almost daily, leaks in my holding tanks, and my windmill on the south side of the ranch stopped working last week. I know breakdowns are a part of owning a ranch. I just can't figure out why it's suddenly happening daily."

Jake and Ben looked at each other. Jake put his hat back onto his head and sighed. "It doesn't sound like normal wear and tear, Kate. Do you have any enemies? Maybe someone else is trying to buy you out?"

Kate shook her head. "It's hard to make enemies when you never leave home. I only go into town when I have to and only for as long as I need to. Although with things breaking down the way they have I've been to Junctionville more in the last two weeks than I have in the last two years." She seemed to consider the rest of his question. "As for anyone wanting to buy the ranch the answer is no. Besides Ben no one has even asked about it."

Ben withdrew a card from his wallet and handed it to Kate. "Here's my card with my cell phone number on it. If you need anything or change your mind about selling please give me a call. I'm staying with Jake for now over at the Triple Spur."

Kate nodded and slipped the card into her back pocket. "Thank you for the offer, Ben, but this is my home. It may be getting too much for me to handle but it's still my home."

Ben and Jake thanked her once again and drove back to the Triple Spur. Ben turned to Jake, thankful his cock was only half hard now. "What do you suppose is going on with Kate's ranch?"

Jake shook his head and turned down the stereo. "You got me, Ben, but that little gal surely has had a rough time of it. When her folks were killed in a car accident she got saddled with a mortgage on a ranch that has been in her family for generations. Apparently her father took out the mortgage just before he died. It wasn't that big a sum at the time. When her parents died without any insurance Kate had to take out a second mortgage to cover the funeral expenses and the inheritance taxes on the place."

"How much does she owe? Is she really in danger of foreclosure?"

Jake looked over at his friend. "I don't know, Ben. I've heard she's missed a couple of payments lately from Clint down at the bank but I can't say how much she still owes or how much longer the bank will give her."

Ben stared out the side window for a few minutes. "I'd like to help her. Do you think she'd let me?"

Jake laughed. "Didn't we just see the same woman? Kate doesn't accept help from anyone, Ben. She's got too much pride."

"Well, I'm gonna try."

Chapter Two

ஐ

The rooster sounded off again and Ben looked at the clock. It was only five-fifteen in the morning but like the rooster said, it was time to get up. Ben remembered the solution to Kate's financial problems and Ben's lack of a home problem came from sweet little Jenny Sommers.

It was a warmer than usual summer day when Ben went in search of Kate with his latest proposition. He found Kate in the barn mucking out stalls. "Good morning, Kate, how're you doing?

Kate stopped what she was doing and backed up against the stall. Pitchfork held to her side in a tight-fisted grip. He could see the stress in her body language. "He-hello, Ben, what can I do for ya?"

Ben shifted his feet, suddenly feeling very nervous. "Well… I was talking to my friend yesterday and she suggested a solution to our problem. You see I need a place to call home and a clear purpose for what's left of my life and you love this ranch but are struggling financially to hold on to it. The solution Jenny came up with is perfect. She suggested that I buy half of the ranch from you. That way you have a good-sized injection of cash and I have something to do with my days." Ben stopped and looked at Kate for any sign of agreement. He didn't see any signs at all. Kate's face was totally blank, showing no emotions, good or bad

"I appreciate your offer and it does sound possible but there's a very big problem in your solution, Ben. There's only one house. Are you planning to live on the Triple Spur and commute to the ranch every day?"

Okay, thought Ben, she didn't turn him down. That was a good thing. Now he just had to convince her they could both share the farmhouse. "Well no. I wasn't planning on living anywhere but here. I thought I could pay to renovate the house and we could share it. I could have an addition added on to the back of the first floor for my bedroom. You could have the second story all to yourself. I could even renovate the floor plan if you'd like."

Kate looked at him warily. "I'm sorry to sound suspicious but what would be involved in living in the same house? I mean… Do we share kitchen duties? Do we eat together? I just need some very clear boundaries set up before I think about your offer."

Ben's eyebrows rose at her questions. "Well, I hadn't thought of all the boundaries but I'd appreciate it if we could share household chores. I would definitely enjoy eating meals with you. I've spent a good portion of my life eating alone and since I've been at the Triple Spur I've come to really enjoy the easy conversation at the kitchen table. Does that answer some of your questions, Kate?"

Kate took a deep breath. "Yes, all but one, what about sex? You won't expect it just because I'm a woman, will you?"

"No," Ben stated firmly. "I'll never approach you regarding sex. I'm looking for a home, Kate. Not a wife or a girlfriend."

Kate chewed on her bottom lip. "I'll give you an answer in a couple of days. Is that acceptable?"

Ben nodded. "It is." He tipped his hat and started to leave but stopped and turned back toward her. "Kate, would you like to come to Cree and Jenny's wedding this Saturday?"

Kate's eyes lit up. "Yes. I would like that, Ben. Thank you for inviting me." Kate chewed her lip again. "I know a little about the situation with Jenny but could you tell me basically what happened so that I don't stick my foot in my mouth at the wedding?"

Ben turned and sat down on a bale of hay. He motioned for Kate to take the bale across from him. "Well, Kate, it's a pretty long story but I'll give you the condensed version. Jenny's stepfather Buck, who also happens to be Jake's father, raped and tortured her when she was eighteen. Cree and Jake were away in the Seals at the time."

Ben picked up a piece of hay and stuck it in his mouth. "By the time they got out of the service Jenny had disappeared. A couple of months ago Buck found her again and again raped and tortured her. That time however he put Jenny into a coma. Jake was called by the hospital in Kansas City. Seems they'd found a picture with his name in her pocket. Anyway, Cree and Jake flew to Kansas City and when Jenny was well enough they brought her home. I came into the picture when Jake called and asked if I could spare some time to help protect Jenny. Buck was still on the loose and they were afraid he would try to take her again. That bastard managed to still hurt her even though she's been surrounded by ex-Seals. He shot her horse, he shot out the windshield of Cree's SUV and he shot Jenny in the side. All separate occasions, but the team caught up with Buck after he shot her and he was arrested."

Ben took the piece of hay out of his mouth and threw it on the floor. "I shot Buck during the gun play that injured Jenny. We found him unconscious in a cave on their ranch with a slight head wound. When the police took him to the hospital he managed to escape and kidnap Jenny from the hospital. He took her to the Double B. That was his ranch. My friend Gabe is planning on buying it now. When Buck took Jenny to the Double B he had every intention of killing Jake and Cree and making Jenny his wife. Buck knew they'd come after her. He knew that Jake and Cree wanted Jenny to be their wife. In his own sick and twisted mind I guess Buck thought if he got rid of them Jenny would agree to marry him. Like Jenny would ever love, let alone marry, a sick fuck like Buck Baker."

Ben stopped and took off his hat and rubbed his shiny head. "Jenny ended up turning the tables on old Buck and kicked him in the balls and branded his forehead. We got there just as she was done. Buck's now in some jail in Oklahoma." Ben shrugged his shoulders. "That's it and now Cree and Jenny are getting married Saturday evening. I understand that Saturday night Cree and Jenny will both marry Jake in a private ceremony."

Kate's face was very pale by the time Ben finished his story. "I know I'd like to go to the wedding. Do you think Jenny might like some help from another woman the day of the ceremony?"

Ben reached over and held her hand. "I think she'd love it."

* * * * *

Ben ran his hand down to his stiff cock and squeezed. He'd been around Kate for almost three months now and it got harder every day. The renovating still wasn't done but at least his new room added to the back of the house was finished. Ben began a slow rhythm of pumping his swollen cock. Every minute he was around Kate was torture on the poor thing. He'd had to give up wearing underwear. When his cock got hard, as was the daily occurrence lately, underwear was painful. Ben had no choice but to jerk off every morning and night.

Kate seemed to feel the pull of attraction between them but was very skittish around him. As for him, he'd promised himself he'd never try to fuck her. It wasn't that he didn't want to, because the pulsing cock in his hand sure as hell wanted to. It was because he'd never hurt Kate. Ben had discovered when he was seventeen just what kind of damage a cock as big as his could cause a woman, especially a woman as petite as Kate, and the experience had permanently scarred him.

Since that horrible day he'd fucked only big, very, very experienced women. Besides the size of his cock Ben enjoyed his sex pretty rough. He wasn't into any kind of bondage or anything. He just liked to fuck a woman when and where he felt like it and to fuck her hard. The women of his past had put up with his sexual demands simply to get to his mighty cock.

Kate was a forever kind of woman. That he didn't have a problem with because he was more than ready to become a forever kind of man. It was the thought of bringing pain to such a sweet young woman that he couldn't stomach. He knew deep down that he was being irrational, but every time he looked at Kate and her tiny precious body the old fears returned. Once again he was thrust back to that night years ago when his girlfriend had called him a monster as she tried to stop the bleeding from her poor ripped pussy. He'd been young and inexperienced with women and had tried to force his cock into a too tight hole. Ben tried to shake off the painful memories and pictured Kate in his mind. Although petite, Kate's body was sexy as hell. Breasts made for a man's hands with a tiny waist and nice sized ass. He tried to picture her naked.

Ben's thoughts of his lovely sweet Kate helped bring him to a mind-blowing orgasm, his cum shot all the way up his chest to land on his jaw. Grabbing the washcloth he now kept beside his bed, Ben wiped his face and got up. He wandered into the shower to begin another day.

* * * * *

Kate woke that morning with sand in her eyes, or at least that's what it felt like. She couldn't seem to get comfortable with a man in the house again. It wasn't that she was afraid of Ben, far from it, Kate trusted Ben more than she'd trusted any man. He was just so damn big.

After getting bacon out of the fridge, Kate got out the cast iron skillet and turned on the new gas stove. She looked around her new kitchen and smiled. Besides Ben's room, the kitchen was the only room so far to get renovated. They'd decided to do away with the dining room and make the kitchen much larger. It was now the classic country kitchen she'd always dreamed of. White cabinets with soapstone countertops and a large marble slab built right into the corner of the counter. Perfect for making bread and rolling pie dough.

Kate chose to have the old linoleum ripped up and the old wide plank floors refinished. She picked a light fern green for the walls and white eyelet cotton curtains for the windows. Her favorite part about the kitchen was the long farmhouse oak table Ben found at a farm auction.

Kate smiled and finished the bacon. She'd heard the shower in Ben's room come on when she came down earlier so she knew he'd be ready to eat any time. She got the egg bowl out of the refrigerator and cracked six eggs for Ben. Kate shook her head. They would have to get a few more chickens to keep up with Ben's egg consumption. At six foot seven inches tall Ben had a big frame to fill and consequently was a big eater.

She thought about Ben a lot these days. He still made her a little nervous but it wasn't because he'd done anything to her, it was just the size of the man. It was a shame she couldn't get over the past. He was an absolutely gorgeous man. His gray eyes seemed to look deep into her soul whenever he spoke to her. The tiny lines around his eyes were the only sign of his age. Ben's totally bald head was a choice, not an act of nature. It looked good on him too. Hair would have detracted from his beautifully sculpted face. His hands had to be her favorite part of him. Very large with well-shaped fingers and those bulging veins that she loved so much. Just one of his fingers had to be at least two or three of hers. She'd never seen anything like it.

Despite his size, Ben was very gentle with all things. The horses loved and respected him as well as the cows. He'd even made a new best friend in Charlie, her blue healer. Charlie waited for Ben on the porch every morning and for the rest of the day you didn't see one without the other.

Yes, she sighed, looking out the window, he was a damned fine man. Too bad Clint had spoiled her for all men.

Kate rubbed her left arm and then, realizing what she was doing, Kate mentally shook herself and got back to fixing breakfast.

Eggs, bacon, toast and coffee were on the table when Ben walked into the kitchen. "I'm sorry. I hope you weren't waiting for me to eat. I'm moving kind of slowly this morning." Ben pulled out a chair and sat down. He quietly bowed his head in prayer then took a drink of his morning coffee.

"I made you six eggs today. If it's still not enough please don't be afraid to say so. I'm not used to cooking for someone of your size." She realized what she'd said and bit her lip. "I'm sorry. I didn't mean that the way it sounded."

Ben chuckled and took the platter of eggs from her. "Don't apologize, Kate. Most people aren't used to cooking for someone of my size. Except maybe the caterer for the Denver Broncos."

Kate laughed and felt more at ease. "What've you got going today, Ben?"

Ben swallowed a mouthful of eggs and took another sip of coffee. "Well, first I need to get the fence fixed in the west pasture. I noticed it was down again last night. I did a temporary patch job but I'll go back this morning and fix it right. Then after lunch I need to go into town to the bank. Would you like to go with me? I thought we could set up a mutual ranch account for feed and supplies."

Kate visibly stiffened in her chair. "No. I don't go to the bank. I do all my business with them through the mail or online."

"Why would you do that when town is so close by?" Ben asked with genuine curiosity.

Kate looked everywhere but at Ben. She waved his concerns away. "It's just a complete dislike for one of the bank employees, nothing to be concerned about. It happened many years ago. He's probably forgotten about it but I never will. I promised myself that I may have to do business with that bank but I'd never step foot in it again and I haven't since the age of eighteen." Kate stopped abruptly, realizing she'd said too much. She closed her eyes and took a deep breath. Opening them, she rose from the table and started gathering the dishes.

Ben reached out a hand to stop her from taking his plate and Kate jumped and pulled back her hand. "I'm sorry, Kate. I didn't mean to scare you. I was just going to tell you it's my turn to do the dishes."

Kate's face turned red. "No, I'm sorry. You didn't do anything wrong. I'm just a little jumpy this morning that's all." She turned and set the dishes in the sink. "I'm going to go take care of the horses. I'll see you at lunch, Ben."

Ben nodded. "Okay, Kate, have a good morning." Kate practically ran out of the kitchen and out the back door. Ben stared after her. "What in the hell was that about?" he mumbled to himself.

Ben decided to stop and see Jenny on his way to the bank. She was always a wealth of information on the opposite sex. And it didn't hurt that she'd become quite friendly with Kate over the past several months.

* * * * *

Ben pulled up to the Triple Spur ranch house and got out of his black quad cab truck. Jenny was sitting on the front porch snapping green beans. Ben smiled and climbed the porch steps. Bending over to give her a kiss on the cheek, he also rubbed his hand on her protruding stomach. "Hi, Miss Jenny. How are my honorary nieces or nephews doing today?" Jenny was five and a half months pregnant with twins.

Jenny smiled and rubbed her belly. "Hi, Ben. The babies are playing soccer this morning I think."

Ben sat down on one of the wicker chairs. "How come you're up here and not helping Jake with the horses today? Are you feeling okay?"

Jenny blew out a frustrated breath and began snapping green beans a little quicker, clearly taking her frustrations out on the defenseless little beans. "My husbands have banished me from the corrals for the rest of the pregnancy. Can you look at me and tell how happy I am about it? You'd think a horsewoman had never given birth to twins before. They're driving me crazy already. I might just end up staying the next four months at your place." She looked serious until her lip twitched.

"You and those babies you're carrying are the most important things in the world to those two men. It's only natural they're going to smother you after all you've been through. Please be patient with them." Ben smiled and patted her knee. "They're only men after all."

"I get ya, big guy. So what brings you here this afternoon?" Jenny went back to her green beans.

Ben shifted uncomfortably in his chair. "I wanted to ask you a couple things about Kate."

Jenny raised a single eyebrow. "What about Kate?"

Ben relayed the morning's breakfast conversation to Jenny. When finished he looked at her, puzzled. "Has she told you if I've done something to frighten her? I don't want to break her confidence in you but I can't stand the thought of scaring her again."

Jenny reached out and held Ben's hand. "I don't think you specifically did anything wrong, Ben. She hasn't come out and told me much but I get the feeling she's been physically hurt by a man. I know she was wary of moving into the same house with you because you're a man. It's not simply because you're so much bigger than most men in America, it's just that you're male." Jenny squeezed his hand a little harder. "If ever she gives you the opportunity to ask about her past, do it. Believe me. Unless she talks to someone about it she'll never be able to get over it. Other than that just be patient with her. If she pulls away please try not to take it personally. That'll only make her feel worse."

Ben leaned over and kissed her cheek again. "Thank you, Jenny."

"Well, well, well, isn't this cozy. Ben, why is it that I'm always finding you alone with my wife?" Cree stepped up onto the porch and came over to stand in front of him.

Ben smiled and shook his head. "Calm down, Conan. I was just asking a piece of advice from your lovely bride." Ben stood and released Jenny's hand. "Well, I've got to get to the bank." He started down the steps and stopped. Turning around, he looked at Jenny. "Who do you think she's avoiding at the bank?"

Jenny shrugged her shoulders, but Cree spoke up. "Clint. My money's on Clint Adams. His dad owned the bank before he died last year and Clint is vice-president. I heard some scuttlebutt when we first moved here about him. It seems he has a history of violence toward women but his daddy always bailed him out of trouble."

Ben tipped his hat to Cree and Jenny. "Thanks for the information, Cree. Thanks for the advice, Jenny." Ben stalked to his truck and roared out of the driveway toward town.

Jenny looked at Cree. "Do you think he's going to do something foolish?"

Cree looked at Jenny and kissed her. Looking at the dust being thrown up by the speeding pickup, he sighed. "Nothing that I wouldn't do. I've had my eye on Clint since I became sheriff of Junctionville. He's a good-looking guy but he's got an ugly soul. He won't be getting away with hitting on women anymore if I have any say in the matter."

* * * * *

The closer Ben got to town the angrier he became. What kind of animal would hurt a sweet, beautiful woman like Kate? Ben didn't know Clint Adams very well but he'd always seemed kind of full of himself. Well, after today Clint would be put on notice in regards to his Kate.

His Kate? Where had that come from? Ben knew he was in trouble sexually where Kate was concerned but could he be in trouble emotionally as well? Ben had never been in love with a woman. The closest he ever got was Mary Sue Jenkins, his high school girlfriend back in Missoula, and that was just a very lusty kind of relationship.

By the time Ben got to the bank his hands were shaking. He walked in and walked into Clint's office. His secretary tried to stop him but one look from Ben and she sat right back down. The door was open to Clint's office so he went in. Ben walked over to Clint's desk and leaned down so his face was right in Clint's. "What did you do to Kate Crawford?"

Clint pushed back from his desk away from the irate giant in front of him. "What did she tell you? Whatever it was, she's lying. No one would believe her silly made-up story seven years ago and no one's going to believe it now." Clint stood up and straightened his tie. "Now if you'll excuse me I have a board meeting to attend."

Clint started to walk out but was brought up short when Ben reached out and grabbed his arm. "Don't ever let me hear or see you talk to Kate again. Do you understand me, boy?"

Clint pulled away and stormed out of his office. Ben stayed where he was until he could get his anger under control. No sense in scaring the rest of the bank staff. Hell, he lived in the community now. Ben finished his business at the bank and left.

He decided to stop on the way out of town and buy Kate some flowers. He entered the little flower shop on Main Street and looked around. Most of the arrangements he saw seemed wrong for Kate. The older woman at the counter introduced herself as Melanie Donovan and asked if she could help him with something.

Ben looked around again quickly. "I want to buy a bouquet of flowers but everything seems too frilly."

"Can you tell me a little about this lady and perhaps I can come up with something?"

"Well, she's a confusing mix of tender and tough. She's an outdoors type of woman. She loves her land more than anything in the world and works it harder than any man but she's still a woman. She's soft and gentle with injured animals and stubborn horses." Ben shrugged his shoulders. "I'm sorry. I can't describe her in just words very well."

Mrs. Donovan looked at him and smiled. "Are you by chance buying flowers for Kate Crawford?"

Ben looked at Mrs. Donovan like she was psychic. "Yeah, how'd you know?"

She just smiled and nodded her head. "Because the words you just spoke are Kate Crawford to a T and I happen to have a great idea for the perfect bouquet."

Mrs. Donovan disappeared into the back room and came out ten minutes later with a beautiful arrangement of flowers. They were a combination of wildflowers, sunflowers and roses.

Ben paid Mrs. Donovan. "They are absolutely perfect. You've gained a lifetime customer today, Mrs. Donovan."

She gave him his change and smiled. "I hope so. I believe this is the first bouquet anyone has ever given Miss Crawford from my shop. I hope that lovely girl gets many more from now on. If anyone deserves a spot of sunshine it's that one. She's always been such a polite little thing. It's too bad what happened so long ago. It just closed her right up tight. We don't see nearly enough of her anymore."

Ben weighed the pros and cons of what he needed to ask. Finally he decided to just do it. "Mrs. Donovan, do you mind if I ask you what exactly happened to Kate? I keep getting conflicting stories."

Mrs. Donovan sighed. "Please don't let on to anyone that I told you this. It's purely speculation on my part, you understand, but when Kate was in high school Clint Adams started following her around town. She never gave that boy the time of day and for someone like Clint who was used to getting everything he wanted it was just too much. I don't know what happened on her eighteenth birthday but Kate was never the same fun-loving girl after that day. I saw her the day after at the doctor's office here in town and she had a black eye, split lip and a cast on her arm. Lord knows what else was done to her but that was all that was visible.

"I know she went to the sheriff that same day and tried to press charges against Clint Adams but the sheriff just happened to be his uncle and the president of the bank was his daddy. The same bank that had just given a mortgage on the Crawford ranch. Well, needless to say nothing was ever done to Clint Adams. Kate was the only one who paid a price for that boy's sins. She locked herself up out on that ranch and has pretty much stayed there since."

Ben closed his eyes, his heart breaking for the eighteen-year-old girl Kate had been. He thanked Mrs. Donovan again and left for home. By the time he pulled into the ranch yard the sun was setting. A more spiritual sight he'd never seen. The sun was just slipping down over the pasture's horizon. The horses in the pasture were silhouetted against a canvas of a vibrant pink and purple color wash. Ben picked up the flowers and headed into the house.

Kate was in the kitchen setting the table. She looked up as Ben came through the door. "Just in time. Dinner will be in about ten minutes."

Ben pulled the flowers out from behind his back and handed them to Kate. "I'm sorry about breakfast this morning. I didn't mean to frighten you. I'm just a very touchy-feely person. I won't touch you again without your permission. Can you forgive me?"

Kate had tears pooled in her deep brown eyes. She shook her head. "It wasn't your fault, Ben. I've been kicking myself all day about it. I even felt so guilty I made your favorites for dinner. Pot roast with potatoes, carrots and homemade gravy.

Please sit down and let's forget about this morning." Kate took the flowers and set them in the center of the table. She touched the silky petals of the various flowers. "No one's ever given me flowers before." Her eyes filled with tears and she wiped them away. "I truly thank you, Ben Thomas."

Ben swallowed around the lump in his throat. The fact that she appeared so touched by his gesture solidified his growing affection for her. "The flowers remind me of you." Ben started pointing out the various flowers. "The sunflowers are like you on a bright sunny day, standing tall and proud. The roses are beautiful with a delicate but pure smell. The individual petals are fragile but when held tight and wrapped around themselves they provide safety for its inner core." Ben looked at Kate who began to cry again at his descriptions. "The wildflowers are my favorite. They grow and adapt to their environment. They reach toward the sun and flourish. They can grow out of the smallest crevice in a rock's surface or out from beneath a log. They survive by their own will. The will to grow and face the sun." Ben slowly covered Kate's much smaller hand with his. "The wildflower reminds me of you the most. Whatever life seems to throw at you, you pick yourself up and raise your face to the sun."

Kate wiped her eyes with her free hand. She squeezed Ben's hand and brought it to her lips for a soft kiss. "That's the nicest thing anyone's ever said to me, Ben. I don't know if I deserve your praise though." Kate exhaled audibly. "I'm tough when it comes to the hard work required on this ranch but I've been living under the log you spoke of in my private life. I was hurt seven years ago and haven't given many people the chance to get close." She chewed her lip and nodded her head. "I think maybe it's time to see if I can grow out from beneath that log."

Ben looked at Kate. He felt a little uncomfortable. His cock was rock-hard from the innocent kiss she'd placed on his hand a minute earlier. He knew he needed to tell her what he'd done and what he'd found out in town. Ben just hoped the confession wouldn't break the fragile relationship forming between them.

Ben cleared his throat and looked into Kate's eyes. "I have a confession to make. I spoke to Mrs. Donovan in town while I was getting your flowers. She told me a little about what went on seven years ago. Before that I'd talked to Jenny and then Cree."

He looked away uncomfortably. "I was afraid that I'd done something wrong at breakfast. I don't want you ever to be afraid of me and I didn't know what I'd done to put that look of fear on your face. Jenny told me about your fear of men. She didn't know why you were afraid of them but she'd picked up from what you'd told her that you were. I asked about the bank and Cree said if anyone at the bank was at fault it would be Clint Adams."

Ben looked at her sheepishly. "I was so angry that I went to town and walked right in to Clint's office. I told him never to talk to you again or he'd deal with me." Ben shrugged his shoulders. "I must have gotten my point across because he practically ran out of his office to an alleged board meeting."

He raised Kate's hand to his lips this time and kissed it gently. "I'm sorry if I've betrayed you in any way. I can't help wanting to protect you from whatever it is that still haunts you."

Kate gave Ben a watery smile. "No one but Clint, his father Bruce and I know the real story of what happened on my eighteenth birthday. Someday soon I'll be able to open up and tell you all of it but I need to work a few things out first."

Ben patted her hand and looked around the kitchen. "Sounds fine, Wildflower." Ben smiled and removed his hand. "Now how about some dinner? I'm still a growing boy who needs his meat and vegetables." He laughed and got up to get the iced tea out of the refrigerator.

Kate smiled and set the food out on the table. They talked of the day's work they'd accomplished and talked about what needed to be done tomorrow. After dinner they decided to watch a movie. Ben stretched out on the new couch he'd had specially made for him. It was big enough so he could stretch out fully and deep enough for the wide width of his shoulders. The couch was covered in nice buttery yellow leather with red southwestern designed throw pillows.

Kate took her normal chair beside the couch. Shortly after the movie started Ben looked over to find her sound asleep curled up in the chair. Ben looked at the tiny woman. She was his dream woman. Never once did she complain about the hard work involved in running a cattle and horse ranch. Kate just did what needed to be done and accepted it. He wished she would let him take over some more of her chores but she was firm on a fifty-fifty work load.

Ben watched Kate sleep and his cock began to stir. The way she was sitting caused a gap in her sleeveless blouse that perfectly showed one demi-cup bra-covered breast. The bra was lavender and if he looked closely he could see the pale pink nipple peeking out over the top.

He looked away and tried to get his cock under control. Ben tried to watch the movie but it was a different movie playing in his head that held his attention. Ben could see himself kneeling in front of Kate's chair, slowly unsnapping the remaining snaps of her shirt. Reaching out to take the heavy weight of her breasts in his hand, he could bend closer and wrap his tongue around her huge pink nipple. Swirling his tongue around the areola, he would nip and suckle her until her cries filled the room.

Ben shook himself and looked down at his jean-covered cock. His cock had come alive to the point of pain. A wet spot appeared on the leg of his jeans. He quickly looked over at Kate to make sure she was still asleep. Wrong thing to do, he told himself. Kate's soft pink pouty mouth was open slightly in sleep. Ben looked at her lips and could easily imagine them stretched around the girth of his cock. Groaning, Ben quickly got up and went to his private bathroom.

Once there Ben quickly pulled his jeans down and took his cock in a tight fist. He pumped his cock quickly trying to alleviate the pain. It only took about five tight, hard jerks before his cock erupted in a stream of cum that seemed to never end. Falling to his knees, Ben cursed his own cock. He wanted Kate, not just for sexual relief but for a lifetime companion. He could never have her sexually though. His cock was just too damn big for the tiny woman asleep in the chair. He would hurt her like he'd hurt Mary Sue. Ben would never forget the blood and cries coming from Mary Sue. He'd split her tiny pussy so badly the injury had required stitches. Ben had vowed to himself that day, at the young age of seventeen, never to hurt another woman. The women who came after were little better than whores. Well stretched and experienced. They seemed to take great joy in the length and width of his cock.

Ben swore and buried his face in his hands. "You can't have the only one you truly want. Now pick yourself up and go on." Ben cleaned himself up and went back to the living room. He clenched his fists at the sight of Kate. He needed to get her upstairs to bed but he didn't think he could touch her and not want her again.

"Kate? Wake up, Wildflower. It's time for you to go to bed." Ben looked at the still sleeping Kate and reached out to touch her arm. "Kate? Come on, it's time for bed." She was still asleep. Ben drew in a deep breath and reached down to pick her up. The feel of her soft body cradled in his arms nearly dropped him to his knees again. He started walking toward the stairs when she stirred and opened her eyes a fraction.

Kate seemed to tense for a moment and then relaxed into his arms. "I'm sorry if I fell asleep. It was a tough day for me. Both physically and emotionally." She lifted her arms and put them around Ben's neck and rested her head back onto his massive chest.

Ben's steps faltered. He held her more securely as he made his way up the stairs. Opening her bedroom door, Ben carried Kate over and carefully put her down on top of the bedspread. He let her go and started to back away.

Kate's arms continued to cling to his neck. She put her lips against Ben's and spoke. "Please hold me for a little while, Ben. You make me feel safe and protected. It's a feeling I've been without for years." She parted her lips and touched his mouth.

Ben didn't even think about what he was doing. He crushed his mouth against Kate's and swept the interior with his tongue. He stretched out beside her and pulled her against his length. How could someone so much smaller than himself feel so right?

Kate's long hidden passion seemed to come alive in his arms. She ate his mouth with a vengeance. Her hands began to wander down his chest. Rubbing and circling his nipples. She drew away from the kiss and looked into his eyes. "I never knew. Why have I never known it would feel so good to be in a man's arms?" Kate kissed his stubbled jaw and moved down to deliver open-mouth kisses on his throat.

Ben groaned and pulled her body even closer. His hands went to the snaps on the front of her shirt and pulled. The shirt opened fully with one tug. Ben closed his eyes at the beautiful sight and prayed for control. He slipped his finger under the front bra clasp and in seconds the heavy weight of her breasts spilled into his hand. "Magnificent. Wildflower, you're breathtaking." Ben lowered his head and took one beaded nipple into his mouth. He groaned and adjusted his cock. She tasted like strawberries and cream. He licked and suckled at her breast for what seemed like a lifetime.

Kate's fingers held his soft bare head and she arched her back in a moan. "Oh God, Ben...more please...it's not enough...never enough."

Ben reached down and unbuttoned her jeans. Opening the waist fully, he was able to get his large hand down her pants. Her pussy was smooth except for a small tuft of hair at the top. Ben groaned again and thrust his cock against her body. He swallowed as much of her breast as he could and bit down lightly.

Kate's breath hitched in her chest. "More, Ben." She raised her knees and opened her legs for him.

Ben pulled her jeans down and off. He left her breast and trailed his tongue down her flat stomach. He stopped at her bellybutton and smiled. Kate had a tiny gold hoop piercing her cute little navel. "Damn that's sexy."

Kate laughed. "If you think that's sexy just wait."

His curiosity got the better of him and he continued downward. He buried his nose in her pubic hair and inhaled. Even here she smelled of sunshine and flowers. Ben continued down until he was eye level with her pretty pussy. He spread her lips with his fingers, preparing to get a taste of her essence, and stopped. Ben looked up into Kate's eyes and then back down. She had a tiny hoop running through her clit. "My God, Kate, that's the hottest thing I've ever seen."

Kate smiled and ran her fingers over his soft head. "You're the first man to ever see it. Before tonight it was my private secret. I went to Santa Fe to have it done two years ago."

Ben swiped her pussy with his tongue. He moved to her clit and carefully wrapped his tongue around the small gold hoop and pulled gently. Kate's body immediately stiffened. Afraid he'd done something wrong, he pulled back and looked into her face. It was then that he realized she was in the grip of a powerful orgasm. Pleased with himself, he went back down to drink up the fruits of his labor. Ben reached his tongue as far inside Kate as he could. He'd never get enough of the taste of her.

Kate's body relaxed back on the bed and she shifted her hips toward his face. "Make love to me, Ben."

The words snapped Ben back into the present. What was he doing? He stopped eating her pussy and crawled up and wrapped her in his arms. "Oh Kate, you have absolutely no idea how much I'd love that but it can never be. I'm much too big a man for a tiny slip of woman like you. I'd cut off my own arm before I'd ever hurt you, Wildflower, and it would hurt you." Ben placed a kiss on the top of her head and held her.

Kate lifted her head from his chest and looked almost embarrassed. "Ben. I've never been with a man but medically I'm no longer a virgin. I…uh…get lonely sometimes and take care of things myself. You wouldn't hurt me."

Ben reached down and unsnapped his jeans. Pushing them down past his knees, he gently took her hand and brought it to his erection. "Now do you see what I'm talking about, Wildflower? My cock isn't the normal size for a man. The only other woman besides you that I ever cared about was torn by this damned cock of mine. I'll never forget the blood or the screams as long as I live. After that I stuck to very experienced woman. Hell, Kate, most of them were little better than whores. I'm falling in love with you, Kate, but I will never make love to you with my cock."

Kate swallowed at the gigantic erection against her hand. Ben was built more like a horse than a man. "I think I'm falling in love with you too, Ben. We'll take the physical day by day. Maybe I could work on stretching myself like the other women in your past?"

Ben put his fingers to her lips quieting her. "Don't ever compare yourself to the women of my past. You aren't anything like them. You're my dream woman, Wildflower. I've never known a finer woman." He embraced her again and kissed her lips tenderly. "I know it's an irrational fear of mine that I need to get over and I'll try. We'll work it."

"Would you stay with me tonight, Ben? Wrap me in your arms and keep the bad dreams at bay?" Kate laid her head back onto Ben's chest.

Ben was flooded with a wealth of emotions at her questions. "I'd like to spend every night for the rest of my life in your bed, Wildflower. There's no need for bad dreams any longer either. I'll not let another man touch you as long as there's a breath left in my body."

Her hand still rubbing his erection, she kissed his chest. "Would you like me to take care of this for you? I've never tried it but I'd like to."

Ben chuckled and rubbed her back. "Maybe tomorrow, Wildflower. It's time for sleep now." He kissed the top of her head and continued to rub Kate's back until her breathing evened out and she fell asleep.

Ben closed his eyes happily thinking about the recent turn of events in his life. He smiled to himself. He couldn't believe Kate said she was falling in love with him. What had he ever done in his lifetime to deserve such a special gift? He inhaled her scent and drifted off to sleep.

Chapter Three

ဢ

In the wee hours of the morning the phone rang. Confused as to where he was, Ben couldn't find the phone. Kate's hand reached across his chest to the bedside table and picked up the phone.

"He-Hello?"

"Kate, it's Cree. I just got a call from one of my deputies. It seems you've got cattle out on the county road. I'm going to load my horse and I'll be over to help you both round them up."

Kate sat straight up in bed. "Thanks, Cree. We'll meet you there." She hung up the phone. "Our cattle are out on the county road. Cree's going to load General and meet us there."

Kate and Ben jumped up from the bed and began pulling clothes on. Even in their haste to get moving Ben noticed that Kate hadn't put on a bra. Oh man, was he in trouble. "Kate, I realize we're in a hurry but could you please put your bra on? My cock is already hard and it's damn uncomfortable to ride this way." He adjusted his hardening cock to get his point across.

Kate giggled and took her shirt back off. "Okay if that's what it takes to make you happy I'll gladly put on a bra." She gave him a wicked look and went to her dresser drawer and pulled out a black lace bra. Kate put the bra on and smiled at him.

The bra had big cutouts where her areolas were. Her pretty pink nipples standing right out of the bra begged to be tasted. Ben went to her and obliged. He gave the nipples one last taste and put her shirt on for her. "You are a truly evil woman sometimes, Kate."

She just laughed and stood on her tiptoes, pulling his head down for a passionate kiss. "I'm sorry, Ben. I've just got a lot of time to make up for. I'm like a child with a new toy."

Ben swatted her ass on the way out the door. "Come on, Wildflower. We've got cattle to round up."

Ben and Kate rode to the county road, Kate on her beloved buckskin gelding Ripples and Ben on his newly acquired Tennessee Walker, Too Tall. They met Cree on the road. Cattle were spread out across the road and on the other side eating grass. Kate and Cree took the job of rounding them up as Ben tried to fix a temporary patch on the barbed wire fence. As the cattle were rounded up and run back through the broken fence Ben kept them in by holding the wire across the opening. Every time more came back through he'd step out of the way and let them through then close up the opening again. After nearly two hours all the cattle were back on their own side of the fence. Cree and Kate climbed down from their horses and went to help Ben with the fence.

Kate held a flashlight on the wire as Ben and Cree stretched it across the opening. Kate looked at the wire that had been damaged. "Hey, guys. It looks like this wire's been cut."

Ben finished with the strand of wire he was working with and went to investigate Kate's claim. He took the flashlight from her and shone it on the ends of the wire. "I think you're right, Wildflower. Cree, what do you think?"

Cree examined the wire and nodded. "Looks like a clean cut to me. Unless your cattle are carrying around wire cutters I'd say someone's a little pissed at one of you." Cree raised his eyes to Ben and smiled. "I bet we both know who that someone is."

Ben nodded, "What can we do about it legally?"

Cree shook his head and sighed. "Well, not much unless I can get a judge to give me a search warrant for Clint's house and car. If we could find the wire cutters involved a lab might be able to prove they were the ones to cut the fence." Cree shook his head. "Unfortunately I don't really have enough to ask a judge for a search warrant. I'm sorry, Ben, but unless he tips his hand some other way I'm afraid the law can't be of much help in this."

Ben nodded his head and pulled Kate against his side, wrapping an arm around her waist. Cree's eyebrows rose at the embrace but he just smiled and winked at his old friend. "Personally, I'll help you in any way I can. I'll just have to leave the badge at home."

Ben and Kate shook Cree's hand and he loaded his horse back onto the trailer. As his tail lights disappeared around the bend Ben looked down at Kate and kissed the top of her head. "We'll get through it, Wildflower." Ben picked her up and sat her back on her horse with no more effort than lifting a child would take.

He climbed back up on Too Tall and pulled up next to Kate. Stretching out, he cupped her cheek in his hand and kissed her. Kate opened her mouth to his invading tongue and returned the favor by invading his mouth. The kiss caught them like wildfire. Ben groaned and picked Kate right off her horse and deposited her in his lap. Ripples stood quietly next to Too Tall.

Kate adjusted herself more comfortably and straddled his pelvis. Wrapping both legs as far as possible around the huge man, she took the kiss to the next level. She broke the kiss and unsnapped his chambray shirt. Kate stroked his bronzed skin with her fingers and tongue. She circled his nipples and took joy in seeing the little nubs stiffen and protrude even more. She took one and then the other in her mouth and sucked.

Ben threw his head back and groaned. "You're going to kill me, Wildflower." He reached down and began rubbing the seam of her jeans against her clit. Kate's breath hitched and she began thrusting her pussy against his hand.

She sucked the tiny earring from his left ear into her mouth and moaned. "Oh God, Ben, I feel like I'm on fire." She quickly reached down and unbuttoned Ben's jeans. Reaching her hand down his pants leg, she held and withdrew his cock. Kate used both hands to pump the enormous cock. Running her palm over the top to catch some of the pre-cum she needed for lubrication, she set up a steady rhythm.

Ben unbuttoned Kate's jeans and managed to get his big hand in the small opening. He parted her pussy lips and thrust a finger inside her. "God, Wildflower, you're so wet for me." He pumped his finger in and out a couple more times then dared to put in another. Two of Ben's fingers were as big as most men's cocks. He realized that Kate was able to take both of his fingers and smiled with joy. "We might be able to do this, Wildflower. I don't know what kind of toys you've been playing with but maybe if I got you some new ones we could work on it."

Kate held on to Ben's cock and continued pumping. She pulled away from his kiss to bend her head down and swipe the tip of his cock with her tongue. She found the slit in the top and stuck her tongue in, sucking as much pre-cum as she could get.

It was too much for Ben and he raised her head quickly. "I can't hold it anymore, Kate, and I have a feeling it's going to be a big one." Kate kissed him, sharing his own taste with him as she did. Ben jerked and plucked the tiny hoop on her clit. They both came at the same time. Ben's orgasm was so powerful that they were both soaked when his cum shot up between them.

Ben slowly withdrew his fingers from Kate's pussy and put them into his mouth. "Mmm...kiss me and taste yourself, Wildflower. Nothing has ever tasted so good." Ben brought Kate's mouth to his and swirled his tongue around her tongue.

Kate moaned and held his face, her fingers still dripping with his cum. She looked at her hands and started to giggle. "Maybe we should get off the road before people start driving by on their way to work. Not to mention the poor horses standing here so patiently all this time."

Ben seemed to bolt upright, realizing where they were. "I can't believe I just did that to you where anyone can see. I apologize, Wildflower. Forgive me?"

Kate kissed his chest. "As long as we can ride back home like this I'll forgive you anything, Ben." She snuggled in against him and Ben grabbed Ripple's reins and headed for home via the pasture.

They got back to the ranch and brushed down the horses. Deciding to go ahead and take care of the morning chores, they began mucking out stalls and feeding the horses grain and flakes of hay. Once the horses were taken care of Ben climbed into the big ranch truck and set off to fix the fence properly. Kate fed the chickens and gathered the eggs before heading in to start breakfast.

Kate washed the fresh eggs and put them into the refrigerator. She got out bacon and sausage to cook for Ben this morning. He'd used a lot of calories since supper last night. Kate giggled to herself. She didn't know when she'd ever felt this happy. It seemed like she'd been lonely her entire life. The girls in school never wanted to hang around her. Kate never knew if it was because of her looks or because she was more interested in horses than people. The boys played with her until she turned thirteen and started getting boobs. Then the boys wanted to play a totally different kind of game with her. Kate wanted no part of those games so she isolated herself on the ranch after school.

It was her senior year of high school when Clint Adams saw her again at the Junctionville Fair. He'd been away for the past few years at college and had come home for the annual fair. Kate was showing her prize black Angus bull Jolly. She also entered the barrel racing competition with Ripples.

Clint approached her after the barrel racing competition and asked her out. She remembered Clint from school. She was a lowly freshman when he was a senior. Kate remembered the way he seemed to treat his girlfriends and declined his offer.

Clint looked at her like she was joking. "What do you mean no? I'm a college guy." He looked Kate up and down and then concentrated his eyes on her breasts. "You do know who my father is, don't you, little girl?"

Kate cleared her throat and looked him in the eye. "I know very well who your father is, Clint, but I don't want to date him either. Now if you'll excuse me I need to brush down Ripples." She tried to move past him.

Clint reached out and grabbed her arm and pulled her face close to his. "This isn't over, sweet cheeks. You will go out with me before the week is over." He let her go and stormed off.

Kate didn't see Clint again until the following week on her eighteenth birthday. Her father had given her a new saddle and she was in the barn showing Ripples his new saddle. She heard footsteps and turned around to find Clint Adams standing in the doorway.

Kate closed her eyes, squeezing out the painful memory. She finished cooking the bacon and sausage and put some rolled biscuits in the oven. Kate reached over and turned the radio on. She needed to get her good mood back. Clint had taken enough years from her, she wouldn't give him another day. Kate turned the radio up and began swaying her hips to the music as she fried Ben's eggs.

Ben entered the back door and smiled. His wildflower was happy, it seemed, singing to the radio and dancing a bit as she finished cooking breakfast. He walked in and caught her attention. She stopped singing and dancing and smiled at him. "Don't stop on my account, Wildflower. I liked watching you move. As a matter of fact I think I'll join ya." He walked over and took the spatula out of her hand and turned off the eggs.

"Wait, Ben. Just let me get your eggs out of the grease and onto your plate." When that was done she put the spatula down and washed her hands. Turning toward Ben, she curtsied and reached for him. Ben found a slow song on the radio and began dancing Kate around the kitchen. The differences in their height didn't seem to bother them. Kate rested her head on Ben's chest as he held her tightly and moved to the music.

When the song ended Ben bent over and lifted Kate up his body for a kiss. She wrapped her arms and legs around him and hung on. The kiss deepened and Ben played with Kate's ass. Breaking the kiss, Kate slid down the length of his body, noticing the hard ridge of his erection as she did.

She pulled the biscuits out of the oven and put them on a plate. They were a little dark but still edible. She brought the rest of the food to the table and sat down. "Thank you for the dance, Ben. I haven't danced since my daddy died."

Ben could see the memories playing out in her eyes. "There's a dance at the Lodge this Saturday. Would you like to go with me? I imagine Jenny will be there with Cree and Jake."

Kate's face lit up like the sun on a spring morning. "I'd like that, Ben." She chewed her lip in thought. "I'll need to go to town and buy a dress. I haven't bought a dress since the funeral. I'd say I'm due for some girl shopping." She came up out of her chair and kissed him. "Do you think Jenny would be interested in going into Santa Fe with me this afternoon?"

Ben chuckled and kissed her again. "I'm sure Jenny is up to shopping any day that Cree and Jake let her out of their sight. Why don't you call her and ask?"

Kate bounced to the phone to call Jenny. Ben shook his head and smiled. He'd never seen this side of Kate. She was as happy and free as a bird soaring through the canyon. Kate got off the phone and started immediately clearing the table.

"I'm glad I called early. Jenny happens to have a doctor's appointment this morning. She said if I went with her we could shop and have lunch afterwards." She started to run water into the sink.

Ben's hands stopped her and turned her around. "I'll clean up in here, darlin'. You go get ready for your girls' day." He lifted her up and kissed her. Setting her back onto her feet, he turned her and swatted her butt. "Go get ready."

* * * * *

Jenny picked Kate up an hour later in her new minivan. They drove toward Santa Fe talking about nothing and everything. Just as they hit the Santa Fe city limits Jenny turned to Kate. "So tell me, my dear friend. What is happening between you and Ben? Cree mentioned to me that you two seemed quite close early this morning."

Kate blushed from her ears to her chest. "Well I...um...well...I think I'm falling in love with him."

Jenny smiled and patted her hand. "That's terrific news, Kate. How does Ben feel? Do you know?"

"Ben says he feels the same way about me." Kate worried her lip with her teeth. "He um...he say's he won't have intercourse with me though." She put her hands over her face. "I can't believe I just told you that."

"Hey I'm the woman married to two men remember. Talking about sex doesn't bother me at all anymore. So why is it that Ben won't have intercourse with you? Are you still a virgin?"

"Well, I've never been with a man." Kate blushed again. "But I have indulged quite a bit with the battery-operated kind of man. To answer your first question no, that's not why Ben won't f-fuck me. You see he's built more like a horse than a man. I guess he hurt a girl badly in his younger days and since then he's only screwed well-stretched sluts." Kate buried her face in her hands once again.

"Wow. I wonder if Jake and Cree know about Ben's cock size? What are you gonna do about your situation, Kate?"

"I thought maybe later today after I buy something pretty to wear for the dance maybe we could find an adult shop. I'd like to upgrade my battery-powered friends. Maybe find something in a bigger size." Kate looked out the window and laughed. "God six months ago I would have never talked about this kind of thing with anyone."

"Don't be embarrassed about it, Kate. You're a twenty-five-year-old woman—it's time." Jenny pulled into the parking lot of the doctors' building. "Come up with me. I'd love you to hear the babies' hearts beat."

Kate got out and came around to Jenny's side of the vehicle. Her friend was almost six months pregnant and with twins she wasn't getting around as fast as she used to. Kate took Jenny's arm and they walked into the doctor's office.

The visit was just routine but they did let Jenny and Kate listen to the heartbeats. Jenny looked up at Kate with wonder in her eyes. Kate looked down at Jenny with tears in hers. "Why are you crying, Kate?"

Kate kissed her friend's hand. "It's just so beautiful. I've never heard anything so beautiful."

Jenny squeezed her hand. "Someday you'll be on this table and I'll listen to your baby's heart beat."

"One can only hope."

They left the doctor's office and headed to the minivan. When they got to the parking lot the van had a flat tire. Jenny looked at the tire and shook her head. "A flat. How can I have a flat tire on a brand new car?"

Kate shrugged and opened the back hatch of the van. "Maybe you ran over a nail or something. It's okay. I'm pretty good at changing tires. Why don't you go over and sit on that bench in the shade. It won't take me long."

Jenny was surprised at how fast Kate managed to get the tire changed. Like everything else she didn't complain when work needed to be done. She just gathered her waist-length blonde curly hair into a ponytail and got to work.

After they dropped the tire to be repaired Kate and Jenny had a nice lunch and then went clothes shopping. Kate found a beautiful pale green chiffon dress. It fit her snugly on top and fell to her knees in a bounty of fabric. Kate looked at herself in the mirror. "Jenny, do you think this dress is too formal for the dance?"

Jenny eyed the gorgeous woman in the mirror. "Well, maybe a little but I think you should get the dress anyway. Maybe Ben will take you out somewhere fancy one day. It would be nice to already have a dress. Let's keep looking for something a little more appropriate for the dance."

They settled on a short, off the shoulder pale pink dress made of jersey material that fit Kate's body like a glove. "Oh girlfriend. Ben's not going to know where to put his eyes when you come out in that."

They left carrying several bags each. Their next stop was the adult sex shop. Jenny was wide-eyed as she entered the store. Kate had almost become a regular to this particular store. "Hi, Kate," the young woman behind the counter waved.

Jenny raised her eyebrow at Kate who just shrugged. Kate went directly to the vibrator section. She looked at the selection and picked up a big blue one. Kate eyed the vibrator and put her hand around it, measuring it.

Jenny looked at her and laughed. "You've got to be kidding me. No way is that thing going to fit."

Kate smiled and looked at the vibrator again. "Mmm. That's what Ben says but I'm going to graduate up to it." Kate chose two more vibrators in decreasing size from the big blue one. "Okay I'm ready."

The women left the store and went back to the tire shop. Jenny asked the man at the front desk about her tire. "I'm sorry, Mrs. Sommers, but we weren't able to fix your tire. It looks like someone took a blade of some sort to the back side wall. If you can wait another thirty minutes we can have a new tired installed though."

Jenny agreed and went outside to call Jake or Cree. Jenny came back into the shop and asked the man if they could please put the damaged tire in the back of the van. Jenny looked at Kate and motioned for her to follow her outside.

When they got outside the shop Jenny turned to Kate. "I talked to Cree and he wants to see the tire. He thinks it might have something to do with your cut fence."

Thirty minutes later they were on their way home. Jenny glanced over at her friend. She could see the worry on Kate's face. Jenny decided to lighten the mood. "I'm soooo going to ask my husbands tonight about the size of Ben's cock. I mean when you pulled down that blue vibrator I thought I would choke on my own tongue. That just can't be natural, Kate."

Kate looked at her a little too thoughtfully. "It makes Ben very sad I think. I mean…that he's so much different from most men. He still carries the scars of hurting his first girlfriend. That's why I want to stretch myself for him. I need to show him that he can make love to me without pain. That it can be pure pleasure."

Jenny didn't say anything else until she pulled up to Kate's farm house. "Thank you for a lovely day, Kate. It's nice having a girlfriend to just hang around with."

Kate smiled back at Jenny. "Thank you for letting me hear the twins' hearts beating. You three will meet us at the dance, won't you?"

Jenny rolled her eyes. "I should say no after seeing you in that pink dress but I can see you only have eyes for Ben, so sure we'll be there."

Chapter Four

ℬ

Kate waved to Jenny as she disappeared down the drive. Kate took her bags up to her bedroom and went to look for Ben. She found him patching up one of the watering tanks. He was bent over and the seams of his jeans looked like they were straining. He had a skintight black t-shirt on with a black bandana on his head in place of his usual cowboy hat. What a sight he made. Kate smiled and whistled.

"Looking good, Mr. Thomas."

Ben lifted his head and smiled. He stood and wiped his hands on his work rag and shoved it back into his pocket. Ben strode over to Kate and picked her up for a welcoming kiss. "You're not looking so bad yourself, Miss Crawford." He kissed her soundly. "So tell me about your girls' day."

Kate didn't want to really talk about the flat tire so she tried to distract him. "Oh you know, the usual. Listening to babies' hearts beat and buying extra large blue vibrators. By the way, what kind of look are you going for today? Biker or perhaps a pirate? You know I've always loved pirates. Do you have any black leather pants?" Kate ran her tongue around his gold earring and bit.

"Ouch you little brat." Ben kissed her and smiled. "Now enough about my choice of wardrobe. Let's get back to the heartbeats and the vibrator. Did you enjoy listening to the babies' hearts beat and will I enjoy watching you with the blue vibrators?"

Kate put her finger to her chin in a show of contemplation. "Yes and yes. The visit to the doctor's office was very moving. I actually embarrassed myself by crying."

Ben squeezed her a little tighter. "Do you want kids of your own, Wildflower?"

Kate tensed a little in his arms. "When I was growing up I wanted about six kids. I knew I'd be living right here on the ranch and I wanted to fill it. After my eighteenth birthday I shut down all my dreams. I thought I'd be content to live and work by myself for the rest of my life. That's why I bought Charlie after my parents' accident. He was supposed to fill the empty void in my life."

Kate wiped moisture from her eyes. "But today at the doctor's office. I don't know, Ben. A feeling overcame me. I think I'd like my dream back. The happily ever after dream from my childhood." Kate stopped talking and just shrugged her shoulders. "I'm sorry. I'm just feeling a little melancholy right now."

Ben carried Kate over and set her on top of the corral fence. "Wildflower, don't ever apologize for having a dream. The thought of you even giving yourself the chance to dream again makes me want to fall onto my knees and thank God. I know I told you I was falling in love with you but I lied."

At Kate's sudden look of sadness Ben hurried to finish his statement. "No, Wildflower, don't look sad. Let me finish. I was about to say that I thought I was falling in love with you but what I should have told you was that I love you, Kate. I don't know how I let it happen but you burrowed into my heart the first day I met you. You were in the hay field putting up bales all by yourself and not complaining a bit. I knew then that you were going to become my everything." Ben licked Kate's lips and delved inside for a taste.

Kate pulled Ben closer and wrapped her legs around him. "Take me inside, mighty pirate man." She giggled when Ben picked her up and carried her to the house. They managed to get inside and down the hall to Ben's new room before all their clothes came off. Ben had taken her shirt off on the porch steps, she'd taken his off in the kitchen and both of them had their jeans unbuttoned on the way through the living room.

When they crossed the threshold to Ben's room he laid Kate on the bed and finished stripping off her jeans.

He was pulling his own down when Kate held up her hand. "Ben, would you like for me to run up and get my new toys?"

Ben's nostrils flared as his cock sprang free of the confining jeans. "I'll save that little treat for after dinner." Ben positioned her at the edge of the bed with her legs draped over the side. "First I want a taste of your pussy. Then maybe your breasts and then I'm thinking a quick sandwich and then toys."

Kate sighed and spread her legs even farther. She loved the feel of Ben's tongue on her clit. It felt so much better than her fingers. "By the way if I forget to tell you later, this bed is amazing."

Ben licked her pussy and smiled. "Thanks." *lick* "I" *lick* "had" *lick* "it built" *lick lick* "specially." Ben spread her pussy with his fingers and fucked Kate with his tongue. He inserted one finger and tested her cunt and then quickly moved to two fingers pumping into her pussy. Ben continued with two fingers and sucked her clit into his mouth. Kate stiffened and screamed, her orgasm flooding his fingers with her sweet cream. When she was at the height of her orgasm Ben shoved a third finger inside her. Ben started to feel pretty excited about the odds that someday he'd finally be able to fuck her.

Ben removed his fingers and replaced them with his mouth. As he tasted the proof of Kate's orgasm a kind of peace overcame him. He licked his way up her abdomen to her nipples. He sucked and plucked them until she began writhing on the bed once again. Ben smiled and stood. He picked Kate up and repositioned them on the center of the bed.

Kate gave Ben a devilish smile and reached for his erection. "My turn to taste."

Ben's eyes rolled and he stretched himself out on the center of the bed. "Do your worst, Wildflower."

Kate didn't waste time on anything but getting straight to his cock. She grabbed the bottle of lube off Ben's bedside table on her way down to his thick, heavy erection. Kate looked at the huge penis in front of her face. She knew her mouth was in no way big enough to suck him down her throat, but maybe she could think of something he'd like just as much.

With a gleam in her eyes Kate straddled Ben's thighs and sat up. She looked him in the eye and opened the bottle of lube. "I know you're too big for me to do your cock justice with just my mouth so how about a titty party."

Kate squirted the lube over her breasts, still maintaining eye contact with Ben. She brought her hands to her chest and rubbed the lube in between her breasts. With a greedy smile on her face, Kate bent over Ben's cock. She wrapped her big boobs around his cock and began moving up and down.

It didn't take long for Ben to moan and thrust his cock back and forth between her breasts. "Oh God Wildflower. That is so hot. I could come just from the image of your gorgeous breasts wrapped around me. Oh… It feels fantastic…"

Kate continued to hold her boobs around the straining, thrusting cock. She bent her head and swiped the tip with her tongue. Every time Ben thrust up into her chest she opened her mouth and let the head of his cock disappear in her hot, wet mouth. Ben's taste was wonderful. Kate had never tasted a man before and she wanted more. "Come in my mouth, Ben."

Kate's plea sent Ben over the edge. "Here it comes, Wildflower. Oh! Uh-uhhh…"

Ben shot his cum deep down Kate's throat. She tried to swallow the entire load but she was inexperienced and there was just too much of the white creamy liquid. Kate coughed and looked at Ben and shrugged her shoulders. "Guess it will take some more practice."

Ben laughed and hauled her up into his arms. He kissed her with a voracious appetite. Tasting himself on her tongue was so damned sexy. "I love you, Kate. Please don't ever leave me. I don't think I'll be able to let you go."

Kate kissed him back. "I love you too, Ben, and I don't plan on going anywhere. This is our home now."

Ben kissed the top of her head and tightened his embrace. "Thank you." They held each other until they both drifted off to sleep.

* * * * *

The phone woke them an hour later. Ben reached over to answer it and Kate snuggled up to his side. Kate listened to Ben's side of the conversation. She had a feeling she knew who was on the other side of the call.

"Hi, what's up?… Yeah, it sounds like she had a nice day too… WHAT!… Okay, Cree, I'll do that… Yeah all right. Talk to you later."

Ben hung the phone up and turned his eyes on Kate. "Did you forget to mention something about your day, Wildflower?"

Kate snuggled closer and buried her head against his chest. "I didn't want to ruin a perfect day. I'd have told you about the tire eventually, Ben." She looked at the worry lines around his mouth and smoothed them with her finger. His face was so beautiful for a man. It was like sleeping with an overly large warrior.

Kate knew Ben was a protective man by nature. Twenty-two years in the Navy tended to do that to a man, but nothing harmful had happened to her today. The flat tire was a nuisance, nothing more.

Ben sighed and kissed her head. "Cree said the tire was slashed on purpose. He thinks it was Clint and that he must have been following you and Jenny. He and I agree that until we find out what all this is about you shouldn't go anywhere without me, Cree or Jake. Maybe we should even skip the dance Saturday night?"

Kate sat up and shook her head vehemently. "No, absolutely not, Ben. Clint's actions seven years ago put me into a box on this ranch and I'm finally climbing out. No, Ben. I won't get back into that box."

Ben pulled her down into a tight embrace and kissed her softly, licking her lips and the tears from her cheeks she didn't even realize were there. "I want you to be safe, Kate, that's all I'm saying. You're everything important in my life, Wildflower. How can I not try to protect you?"

Kate ran her hand over his muscled chest. "Please don't try to protect me by putting me back in that box. Whether you've lined it with silk or satin, it's still a box. I've given it a lot of thought and I think Clint's been behind the problems here on the ranch for the past year. I'm not sure what he hopes to gain by making my life hell but I've given enough because of that man." Kate kissed the nipple in front of her face. "He cost me my self-respect and my parents, Ben. Help me to stand up to him. Don't ask me to hide from him."

Ben rubbed her back and thought about what Kate had just said. "What do you mean he cost you your parents? I thought they died in a car accident?"

Kate took a deep breath and closed her eyes. She hadn't meant to admit that to him but now she was going to have to explain. "I've never told anyone exactly what happened the day of my eighteenth birthday and what happened afterwards and I will tell you all of it someday. For now I'll tell you about my parents. I was an only child to elderly parents. My mom didn't think she'd ever have children until I came along. She was forty-two when she had me. I was the center of the universe to my parents. The ranch had been in my dad's family for generations but just like before him it was a daily struggle to make ends meet. We've never had a big enough operation on this ranch to make much of a profit but everyone including me had dreams for it. My dad's dream included Black Angus cattle. He knew that if he could just get a good breeding herd this ranch would make a profit. Dad took out a loan to buy the first fifteen heifers and a bull."

Kate looked at Ben and swallowed. "He got the Anguses two weeks before my eighteenth birthday. You should have seen him, Ben. He was like a kid on Christmas morning the day those cows arrived. After what happened on my birthday my dad took me to the sheriff's office to file a report. The sheriff was Clint's Uncle Gus. Gus decided that it would be best for everyone involved if we called Clint and his father down to the station. When they arrived and heard the charges I wanted filed against Clint, his dad went ballistic. He told my father that as the owner of the bank he could find a loophole in his loan papers and demand payment immediately if I didn't drop my complaint against Clint."

Kate started to cry again, thinking of her father. "I'll never forget the look on Daddy's face as he stood there in Gus' office. In that one second he had to choose between a dream and his daughter. I could see the light dimming from his eyes and knew he was prepared to give up his dream for me. I held his hand and told him the success of the ranch would be like a slap in the face to the whole Adams family. I convinced him to just drop the complaint and worry about his new Black Anguses. I assured him that I would be all right."

Ben wiped her tears and kissed her head. "But you weren't all right, were you, Wildflower?"

"No. I wasn't all right. I went home and shut down. For the next two months I cried myself to sleep every night but worked beside my dad all day. My dad saw what the choice he'd made had done to me and became very depressed himself. One day he just wouldn't get out of bed. My mom called the doctor and he said to bring him in. I helped her load Dad in the car and waved them off."

Kate swallowed. Tears ran in rivers down her cheeks but she didn't feel them. "Mom hit a deer on the way to town. She lost control of the car and hit a tree at fifty miles an hour. They both died and I've been trying to keep Daddy's dream alive for this ranch every day since." Kate gave an almost hysterical bark of laughter before she continued. "I had to actually go into the bank and beg Mr. Adams for a loan to cover the funeral and the inheritance taxes. I swallowed my pride for this ranch, Ben. Now do you see why it means so much to me?"

Ben wiped her face and reached for a tissue beside the bed. He handed it to her and tried to regain some control while she blew her nose. "What I see is a sweet, beautiful woman who has been through far too much for her age. You've persevered, Kate. Despite everything this ranch will show a profit by the end of the year. I know now more than ever that you're like the wildflowers growing out on the ranch." He held her tighter and kissed her. "I love you, Wildflower. I'm part of your dream now. I won't let you down. We'll make this ranch profitable beyond anyone's dreams."

* * * * *

Kate finished her chores early on Saturday. She wanted to spend time pampering herself for her date with Ben. Kate drew a hot bath and filled the steaming water with lavender oil. She stretched out in the big claw-foot tub and closed her eyes. Thinking about Ben put a smile on her face and warmth in her heart. She could tell he was still worried about her but they'd finished the week without discussing Clint Adams once. As she soaked in the scented water she felt utterly content. Ben had worn his pirate bandana more and more the last couple of days. Kate smiled. She knew it was because she'd commented on how much she liked it. Boy did she like it. It set off the little hoop in his ear and made him even sexier.

Kate drained the scented water and took a shower to wash her hair. The thick curly hair would take forever to dry but she had plenty of time. She dried off and put her robe on. As she was heading downstairs to get a glass of lemonade the phone rang.

"Hello."

"Hi, Kate, it's Jenny. I just wanted to make sure you were still meeting us at the dance? Although I'm not sure how much I'll be allowed to dance. Jake and Cree are just certain I'm going to hurt myself or the babies if I lift a finger. And boy howdy is my sex life suffering. All they want to do with me is kiss and pet. Not that I don't love that but a girl needs a little boom-boom now and then. The fact that I see their faces when they come back from the barn in the evening doesn't help either. It seems I'm the only one not getting any." Jenny took a deep breath and continued. "I'm sorry to vent to you about my sexual frustrations but what are girlfriends for, right?"

Kate laughed and sighed. "It's nice to have a girlfriend after all these years, Jenny. You can vent to me anytime and yes, Ben and I will meet you at the dance in two hours." Kate saw Ben enter the kitchen looking as sexy as ever. He washed his hands and face and turned to look at her. He walked over to her and opened her robe. Jenny was still talking about all the things Cree and Jake wouldn't let her do. While Ben got on his knees and attached himself to her breast. Kate arched her back, giving him more, and tried to calm her breathing enough to finish her conversation with Jenny. "Men can be really stupid when it comes to pregnant women, Jenny. Maybe you should take them with you the next time you see your doctor." Ben moved to the other breast and began playing with her pierced clit. "Uh...Jenny, Ben's got his fingers all over my pussy so I'm going to have to let you go."

Jenny's voice got dreamy and soft. "God you're lucky. Does it feel as good as I remember?"

"Better. I'll see you soon, Jenny, bye."

Kate hung up the phone and spread her legs even more. Ben was laughing as he attacked her pussy with his mouth. "More, Ben."

Ben twirled his tongue deep into her channel. Kate's legs threatened to give out and Ben helped her down to the floor. Spreading her out on the polished hardwood, he continued with his assault. He stuck his finger deep into her pussy and withdrew it only to replace it once again with his tongue. Ben lifted Kate's legs and put them over his shoulders. He raised her butt up and inched toward her asshole. He stuck his finger in and sucked her clit. Kate stilled at the invasion of her ass. She began squirming and fighting him. "No, Ben, no. I can't….you have to let me up, Ben."

Ben stilled and sat up. "What's wrong, Wildflower? Did I hurt you?"

Kate quickly got off the floor and gathered her robe around her, tying the sash tightly. She got her panicked breathing under control and looked at Ben, totally embarrassed with her actions. "I'm sorry, Ben. I…uh…I can't let you touch me there. I guess I just kind of freaked out on you. I'm really sorry."

Kate started to leave the kitchen but Ben stopped her with a hand on her elbow. "Why, Kate? Why can't I touch you there?" Ben saw the pain in her face. He knew this had something to do with Clint and the night she turned eighteen but he needed her to tell him.

Kate shook her head and buried her face in his chest. "I can't, Ben. It's too ugly. You'll never look at me the same again."

Ben lifted her chin with one finger. He looked into her tear-filled eyes. "Listen to me, Wildflower. Whatever he did to you was his fault, not yours. I could never look at you any way but with love in my eyes. Do you understand?" At Kate's nod Ben continued. "You need to be honest with me, darlin'. I need to know and understand your sexual boundaries if we're going to make this work. Please trust me."

Kate opened her eyes and looked at Ben. "The night of my eighteenth birthday I was in the barn putting away the new saddle my mom and dad bought me. The saddle I've never to this day been able to use. I keep it in the barn to remind me what I'm fighting for."

She shook her head to clear her thoughts. "Anyway, I was in the barn admiring my saddle and showing it off to Ripples when Clint walked in. He was drunk. I remember I could smell it across the barn. He stalked toward me with fists clenched and anger in his eyes. I'd never backed away from anything so I stood my ground. He walked right up to me and kissed me before I knew what was happening. I reared back and slapped him. Told him to get out and never come back. Clint grabbed me by the hair and spat in my face. He screamed that 'no one made a fool of Clint Adams'. He said he was going to teach me a lesson in how to treat my betters. My beautiful new saddle was sitting on a hay bale and he dragged me over to it. When I tried to fight him he punched me in the face twice. One blackened my eye, the other split my lip." Kate put her fingers to her lips, remembering the feeling of the fist slamming into her mouth.

"Clint forced me down over the saddle and pulled my new birthday dress up over my ass. He ripped my panties and dug his cock out of his tight jeans. When I tried to kick out at him and yell for help he twisted my arm up behind my back so hard that I heard the crack as it broke. I nearly passed out from the pain. The whole time Clint was telling me what a whore I was. He said only whores got fucked up the ass. He shoved his cock in me dry and began thrusting in and out. I screamed so loud my dad heard me in the house. I heard the kitchen door slam and my dad yelling my name. Clint must have heard it too because he got off me and pushed me to the ground. He gave me a nice solid kick in the ribs and spat on me again before he ran out of the barn. My dad found me and took me into the house. He didn't know I'd been raped. I was too ashamed to tell him after what Clint had said."

She looked at Ben. Kate buried her face in his chest at the pity she saw in his eyes. "Daddy took me to the emergency room in Santa Fe to get my broken arm set. They stitched up my lip and taped my ribs. The emergency room doctors told me they needed to call the police. I begged them not to, saying I'd go to town the next day and file a complaint with the police in Junctionville." Kate looked up at Ben and shrugged. "You know the rest."

Ben held Kate, but he wasn't with her at that minute. His mind was on murder. Where could he find that little fucker? The blood rushed so loudly through his ears that he didn't hear Kate talking to him. Finally, she shook his shoulders and brought his head down to hers and kissed him. He looked at her and almost fell to his knees. After all she'd been through she was the stronger one of them right now. "I'm going to kill him. I'm going to find him and rip his dick off and shove it up his ass and then I'm going to kill him."

Kate knew he meant every word. She saw the truth in his eyes. "No, Ben. I've lost two people I loved already to him and that night. I can't lose you too. Clint Adams isn't worth giving up the rest of our lives together. He's a self-important man who works at a small-town bank. He's not worth it." She kissed him, sharing her grief and hope with him in that single kiss. Kate rubbed his head, knowing it always calmed him down.

"I'll need to talk to Cree about this, Kate. He needs to know what kind of man Clint Adams really is. I know Cree's suspected a few things about Clint but nothing like this." He kissed her again. "Why don't you go get dressed, Wildflower? I have a date in an hour." Ben turned her around and swatted her ass. "Go. I'll take a shower and try to calm down by the time you're ready."

Kate was ready in forty-five minutes. She slipped the dress on over her head and pulled what there was of it down her body. The pink jersey dress hit about mid-thigh so she decided to forgo hose. She looked at herself in the mirror and decided to be even naughtier by taking off her panties. Kate drew the naughty line at a bra. Her breasts were just too big to go without one in public. She'd chosen her strapless ivory demi-cup because the dress was off the shoulder. Kate applied her makeup and decided to leave most of her curly blonde hair down. She chose a black onyx barrette that had been her grandmother's and put the front part of her hair up. Slipping her new three-inch pale pink heels on, she left the bedroom in search of Ben. She found him in the living room drinking a beer, which he proceeded to choke on when he spotted her.

Wiping his mouth with a handkerchief, he looked Kate up and down. "Damn." Ben shook his head. "Double damn. Woman, I don't know if I want you out of this house looking that good. I might lose you to some fast-talkin' cowboy."

Kate giggled and walked over to give him a hug. "You can't lose me, Ben, so forget it. I've known the people in town all my life and they've never had anything I wanted." Kate kissed him carefully. She didn't think he'd appreciate lipstick all over his face. "Let's go before we're too late to get a table."

They drove the fifteen miles to town in companionable silence. Kate looked over at Ben and smiled. "I think you need to talk to Cree and Jake about their sex life or lack thereof according to Jenny."

Ben swung his head toward Kate. "Men don't talk to each other about their sex lives like that, Kate. We only brag about the conquering part. Not the everyday maintenance involved."

Kate's eyebrows shot up. "So now I'm considered a job? Something you have to work to maintain?"

Ben started to get worried that he'd really stuck his foot in it, but he saw Kate's lips twitch. "You know you're not just a job, Wildflower. You're an adventure," he said and smiled at his funny joke.

Kate rolled her eyes and laughed. "Really, Ben, you need to talk to them. They're so afraid of hurting the babies they refuse to have sex with Jenny and from the sound of her complaints she's about to explode."

"They're probably just trying to be safe, darlin'. I'd be the same way if I were in their shoes."

"Well, Jenny knows they're still fooling around in the barn before they come into the house. Ben, I don't know how to make you understand this but she needs to feel like she's still sexy to them. Her body is changing so rapidly that she's having a lot of self-doubts and I think that's worse for her health than sex."

Ben rolled his eyes and sighed. "All right, Kate. I'll sneak the guys behind the building and tell them all about sex and women." He flashed his straight white teeth in an ornery grin.

They parked the truck and made their way into the dance hall. Kate spotted Jenny and waved. "Over there in the corner." She took Ben's hand and led him through the crowd, totally oblivious to the staring townspeople.

Ben noticed the looks though. Both men and women followed her every step. They reached the table at last. Jenny and Kate hugged, while he shook hands with Cree and Jake. Ben looked at Jake and nodded to the crowd. "What's with all the stares?"

Jake laughed and patted him on the back. "Are you blind, man? Your woman is H. O. T."

Ben smiled and nodded. "Believe me I noticed. Damn near choked to death on a beer when she came down the stairs dressed in that. So that explains the men but what's up with the women?"

Jake shrugged his shoulders. "Jealous I imagine or maybe it's the fact that Kate hasn't been to any kind of social function in years. Who cares, man? She's with you. That's all that matters."

Ben sat down and pulled Jake closer, speaking softly. "Thanks for the advice, cowboy. I've got a little advice I need to impart to you and Cree later regarding sex and the Mrs."

Jake backed up a little and narrowed his eyes. "I don't know that I like the sound of that, Ben. Let's get you and Kate something to drink then we can discuss it." Jake and Ben went to the bar to order drinks.

Weaving through the crowd, Jake noticed Ben garnering a few looks himself. Jake elbowed him in the side. "Don't look now but it seems you're the object of the eyes in the room now." Jake laughed and pounded Ben on the back.

Ben shrugged and smiled at Jake. "They've just never seen a giant in person before."

They got drinks and headed back to the table, handing out bottles of beer to everyone but Jenny who got a glass of ginger ale. Jenny held up her glass and frowned. "This pregnancy thing sucks." She looked at Cree and Jake. "The way things are going you might only get these two babies."

Ben saw it on her face. Kate was right—he needed to talk to his friends. "Kate darlin', why don't you and Jenny go see if they have anything good on the buffet table?" He gave Kate a knowing look.

Kate nodded slightly and turned to Jenny. "Come on, girlfriend, we must gather food for our men." Jenny laughed and took off across the hall with Kate.

Once the women were out of earshot Ben turned toward his friends. He noticed Cree's hand was under the table and Jake had a half-lidded look to his face. He watched as Cree leaned over and stuck his tongue in Jake's ear and whispered something to him. Jake groaned and took Cree's mouth in a deep kiss. Ben decided he needed to break up their little petting session if he was going to help Jenny.

"I don't have much time but listen up and listen good. God I can't believe I'm about to say this. Jenny needs to get fucked. Bad. Kate says she's feeling unwanted." Ben held his hand up to stop them from speaking. "Her hormones are on overdrive right now. Instead of trying to protect her why don't you try fuckin' her? She needs to know she's still sexy to you both. Besides she's well aware of what you two are doing in the barn." Ben gave them a narrowed look. "And under the damn table."

Cree looked at Ben with his mouth open. "Damn, Ben. We've been killing ourselves trying to stay away from her. Her body's been through so much already. We just wanted to make sure nothing happened to her or the babies. That's why we've been waiting until she's not around to fuck and stroke each other."

"She knows that, guys, but it doesn't make her body want you any less. I'm sure she wouldn't do anything to hurt the babies. At least talk to her about it. Maybe go to the doctor with her next time and ask him questions about what you can and can't do." Ben looked at Jake and Cree, who were staring at each other.

Jake got up from the table and pulled his cell phone out. "Next appointment my ass. I'm going to try to get a hold of her doctor now. As far as we're concerned this is an emergency." Jake walked out the front door to use the phone.

Cree looked at Ben and shrugged. "It's been a hard couple of months for us. In more ways than one."

Kate and Jenny returned to the table with trays loaded down with food. Kate handed Ben a plate with four pieces of fried chicken, half a slab of ribs, beans and potato salad. Her own plate only had a chicken breast, coleslaw and a roll.

Cree looked at the differences in their plates and laughed until he doubled over. "Good God, man, where do you put it all? You've got enough food on that plate to feed every one of my ranch hands."

Ben gave him a toothy grin. "I'm still a growing boy, Cree. Maybe if you ate as much as I do you wouldn't be such a tiny little shrimp."

Kate and Jenny rolled their eyes at the good-natured teasing going on between the two friends. Jenny leaned toward Kate and whispered, "Please tell me he burns all those calories up in the sack. I've got a feeling I'm going to have to live vicariously through you for the next three and a half months."

Kate giggled and winked at her. "The night is still young."

The group was joined by Jake who gave Cree a wink and a thumbs-up. They finished their dinner and waited for the band to start. The first song the band played was an old slow country and western song.

Ben pushed his chair back and stood up. "Could I have the pleasure of this dance, Wildflower?" He held his hand out and Kate put her tiny hand in his. Ben led her to the dance floor followed by Jake, Cree and Jenny. Ben looked over at the threesome dancing with Jenny in the middle between the two men. Ben smiled and shook his head. "You gotta love those three. They're so in love they don't care what anyone thinks."

Kate sighed and leaned her head against Ben's chest. "Pay more attention to the woman you're holding in your arms who's not wearing any underwear and less attention to the dancing threesome."

Ben stopped dancing and looked down into her eyes. "Are you kidding me, darlin'? Because if you're not we are so outta here."

Kate looked up at Ben and smiled. "I'm ready to go as soon as this dance is over and I slip into the ladies room." They danced the remainder of the song. Ben's cock was so hard Kate felt sorry for him. After the song ended she kissed him. "I'm going to the restroom. You, my man, are in no condition to wander around in here with all the ladies present. Why don't you go on out to the car and wait for me. Stop by the table on your way out and tell the threesome we're going home."

Kate turned and went down to the basement of the building where the restrooms were located. She finished in the restroom and was coming out the door when a hand reached out and pulled her back by the hair. Kate's hands went to her hair and she tried to turn around to face her attacker.

Clint Adams pulled her around the corner toward the supply closet. Kate kicked him and started screaming. Clint backhanded her across the right side of her face. The impact threw her into the wall. Kate slid to the floor with her hand covering her cheek.

Clint leaned down and came inches away from her face. "Look at you. You filthy whore. Struttin' yourself like you think you're better than everybody else. Well, I've got news for you, slut. Get out of this town. You'll never make a success out of the shithole you call a ranch and if you send that big gorilla after me I'll kill him." Clint looked up and slipped out the back door.

Kate could hear someone's shoes on the tiled floor. She tried to get up when hands gripped her arms. Kate tried to shrug the hands off.

"Easy, Kate. It's me, Jenny." Kate stopped struggling and let Jenny help her to her feet. Jenny looked at Kate and hugged her. "Was it Clint? Where did he go?"

Kate looked at her friend and closed her eyes. "Jenny, please get Cree. He needs to arrest Clint for assault before Ben sees me." Kate looked into Jenny's eyes. "Ben will try to kill him when he finds out what happened."

Jenny found a chair for Kate and set it in the restroom. She got Kate comfortable and went to find Cree. As she approached their table she spotted Ben. He'd obviously come back in to see what was taking Kate so long. Jenny made eye contact with Cree and crooked her finger at him. He must have seen the worry on her face because he tried to slip away unnoticed by Ben and Jake.

He reached for Jenny and pulled her to the side away from the crowd. "What's wrong, sweetheart?"

Jenny looked from Ben back to Cree. "Clint Adams assaulted Kate outside the restrooms. She seems fine other than a backhand to the face but she wants you to arrest him before Ben finds out."

Cree looked toward the stairs leading to the basement. "Where's she now?"

"I sat her in the ladies room on a chair. Please, Cree, find Clint. He went out the back door leading out from the basement."

Cree nodded and pulled Jenny with him to check on Kate. Seeing the byplay between Jenny and Cree, Ben turned away from Jake and followed. He had a bad feeling about what he was about to find. He went down the basement stairs and found Kate being held up by Jenny and Cree. Cree was talking to her in hushed tones. Ben stepped up and took Kate away from Jenny. "What the hell's goin' on?"

Kate didn't look up at him. She just buried her face in his chest. Ben looked at Cree and raised Kate's face. The entire side of her face was turning a bluish purple and her lip was bleeding. "I'll kill him."

Ben tried to hand Kate back to Jenny but Cree stopped him with a hand on his arm. "No, friend, you won't. This is a police matter now. Let me do my job, Ben. I can finally charge that little fucker with something. Don't jeopardize it." Cree looked into Ben's furious face. "Believe me. I know what you're feeling, Ben. I've been through it myself. Take Kate home and keep her safe until I can catch the little fucker."

"There are things you don't know about him, Cree. Things he's done to Kate." Ben ran his hands over his head. He finally nodded to Cree. "I'll take her home for now but you call me the minute he's in custody. We need to talk." Ben bent down and lifted Kate into his arms. "I'm going to take her out the back way. No use in giving the whole town a show." Ben looked back at Cree and Jenny. "Thank you, friends."

Ben carried Kate to his pickup and slid her into the seat. She was unusually quiet and subdued. "Are you all right? Do you want me to take you to the hospital?"

Kate shook her head slightly. "Take me home, Ben."

Ben kissed her forehead and shut the door. He climbed into the driver's seat and put his head down on the steering wheel. "I need to calm down a minute before I drive, Kate."

Kate reached her hand to his smooth head and rubbed. Ben turned his face to look at her. "What an ass I am. Here you are the one who was hurt and you're comforting me." Ben reached for her and pulled her into his arms. "God, baby, I'm so sorry I didn't protect you from him. I'll never forgive myself for it." Ben buried his face in her hair.

Kate kissed his shoulder. "Don't, Ben. It wasn't your fault. I know now it wasn't my fault either. He wants me to leave town. To leave the ranch." She looked into Ben's eyes. "I don't know that he'll stop until he gets what he wants."

Ben squeezed her tighter. "Well, tough. He's not getting rid of us. The ranch is our home." He looked at Kate. "I hope one day it will be our children's home. If anyone's going to get driven out of town it'll be him and you can take that to the bank, darlin'." Ben set Kate back into her seat and buckled her seat belt. He buckled his own and drove home.

He got Kate into the house and guided her to his room. "I'm going to hold you all night, Wildflower."

Kate took off her dress and bra and crawled into bed. She snuggled down into her pillows and sighed. "Thank you, Ben."

Ben undressed and sat on the edge of the bed. "Darlin', I'm going to go find some salve and an ice pack for your cheek. I'll be right back." By the time Ben got back to the bedroom Kate was sound asleep. He carefully applied the salve but opted for a cool, wet washcloth instead of the ice pack he'd fixed. He got into bed and pulled her back up against his front. Cradling her in the safety of his arms, he cried.

Ben cried for the woman in his arms who had been assaulted that night and for the scared eighteen-year-old girl who had been beaten and raped in the barn so long ago. He lay awake and waited for the phone to ring. Finally, at three-thirty in the morning the phone rang. Ben grabbed it on the first ring.

"Hello."

"It's Cree. I found him at his dad's old house. He's locked up for now. You'll need to bring Kate in to the station around nine this morning to fill out a formal complaint against him."

"How long, Cree?"

Cree hissed a breath from between his teeth. "I honestly don't know, Ben. It depends on Clint's attorney, the prosecutor and the judge. He could be allowed to post bond and be out of here Monday. I'll try talking to the judge. See if I can't persuade him to keep the little fucker awhile longer but it's out of my hands after that. I do think Kate needs to take out a protection order against him regardless."

"I'm going to call Gabe and see if he can come out for a while. I'd feel better if I knew she had a shadow at all times. When can I talk to you in private?"

"Why don't the two of you come over for lunch tomorrow afternoon? You can stop by after we finish taking Kate's statement."

"All right, Cree. Get some sleep and we'll see you at nine a.m." Ben hung up the phone and pulled Kate closer. He finally dozed off an hour later.

Chapter Five

ॐ

At six o'clock that morning Kate carefully extricated herself from Ben's arms and went to take a shower. She turned on the shower and looked into the mirror while the water heated. She gingerly touched her bruised cheek. There wasn't much swelling but there was no way makeup would be able to cover the vivid blues and purples. Kate stepped into the shower and gathered her strength like a blanket around her.

Kate knew she'd need to be strong for Ben. He wasn't dealing with this well. His natural instincts were to go after Clint, but he knew he couldn't protect her if he was in jail. Kate shampooed her hair and carefully took off her eye makeup from the night before. The bruise might not be swollen but it was sore. She turned off the faucet and dried herself. Instead of wasting time drying her hair Kate just pinned it on top of her head. She didn't bother with makeup and quietly went in search of her clothes. Kate didn't know what time Ben had finally gone to sleep but she remembered hearing the phone ring only a couple of hours earlier.

Kate dressed quickly and went to the kitchen to make a pot of coffee. While the coffee brewed she decided to start on her morning chores. She headed out to the barn to feed the horses. Whistling for Charlie, Kate entered the barn. Before her eyes could adjust to the dim recesses of the barn she tripped over something. She landed on her hands, just missing hitting her sore face. Turning around, Kate screamed. Charlie came running to her rescue immediately.

* * * * *

By the time Ben made it to the barn he found Kate curled into a ball on the barn floor. He hadn't taken the time to dress properly but he had pulled on jeans and grabbed his gun. He slowly made his way into the barn with his gun at the ready. When he didn't see anyone he called out to Kate. "Kate darlin', what's wrong?" Charlie barked and Ben headed toward him. He walked over to where she was huddled with Charlie by her side and saw the saddle. It had been taken down from the storage hook and placed on a bale of hay in the center aisle. "Damn him." Ben went to Kate and picked her up off the dirt floor. Cradling her in his arms, he whistled for Charlie and carried her to the house.

He entered through the kitchen and carried her to the sofa in the living room. Gently putting her down, he covered her with a throw blanket from the back of the couch. Charlie curled up on his bed under the window. "I'll be right back, Wildflower. I'm going to get you some coffee to warm you up." Ben went to the kitchen and got down two cups. He filled them and headed back to Kate.

"Here, Kate. Drink this. It'll make you feel better."

She took a sip and set the coffee back down on the coffee table. Kate raised her eyes to Ben and the pain he saw brought him to his knees. He picked her up and sat on the couch, bringing Kate down to be cradled in his lap. "Baby? Please talk to me? Tell me what I can do to make you feel better? Damn it, Kate, I feel so fucking helpless." He kissed her forehead and started rocking her in his arms.

Kate was looking down at her hands when a teardrop landed on Ben's bare chest. She cleared her throat. "Ben, I don't know if I can do this again. I thought I was getting over it but every time I turn around the memories are there." She sighed and wiped her eyes. "He told me last night to leave Junctionville. I'm beginning to think maybe he was right. Maybe I should leave before I have a breakdown like Daddy."

Ben embraced her a little tighter. "Please don't give up our dream, Wildflower. We're going to the sheriff's office this morning to file a complaint about Clint. Cree also suggested a restraining order just in case they can't hold him in jail long enough. If you get the restraining order he can't come near you or talk to you at all. If he does Cree can put him back in jail. Please, Kate? Please be strong for me for a little while longer?"

Kate didn't look at him but she nodded her head. "Thank you, Wildflower. I'm going to call Jake to see if he can send one of his ranch hands over to do our chores this morning." Ben started to reach for the phone when Kate's hand stopped him.

"No, Ben. I need to do this. I'd like us to do this together." She stood and pulled herself together. Reaching over to get a tissue off the table, she blew her nose and dried her remaining tears. "I'm ready now."

Ben took her face in his hands, being careful of her bruised cheek. "Let me go out first and put the saddle away. Do you want me to get it out of the barn completely?"

Kate shook her head. "No. I want to see it on the storage hook where it's always been. Someday when all of this is over I'm going to ride in that saddle."

Ben kissed her, softly and sweetly. He put all his love and caring into that one kiss. "You're a brave one that's for sure. I'm glad I've got you on my team." Ben took her hand and walked toward the door. "Let's get the animals taken care of and go to town and see Cree. After we're done in town Cree invited us over for lunch."

* * * * *

Filing the actual complaint was harder on Ben than it seemed to be on Kate. She related the events of the night before with perfect clarity. Kate then described her unsettling discovery in the barn that morning. When Cree was done typing up the official report he looked up at Ben.

"I'm going to fax this report to the judge's house along with another request for a search warrant. Maybe now the judge will be a little more inclined to grant it. My guess is that Clint drove straight from the dance last night to your ranch. He must've known finding that saddle, left like it was, would upset Kate. Clint's already seen his lawyer and the bail hearing will be slated for first thing in the morning." He looked from Ben to a quiet Kate. "He'll probably be released on bail by tomorrow afternoon. I've taken the liberty of drawing up a restraining order on Clint." He looked at Kate, trying to read her emotions. "Would you like to sign it?" Cree cleared his throat and glanced at Ben. "We'll have to go before the judge tomorrow and state the reasons for the order to him but under the circumstances it shouldn't be a problem."

Kate chewed her bottom lip and nodded. "I'll do anything I can to keep that bastard off my ranch and away from me." She picked up a pen and signed the papers Cree had already drawn up. She plastered a fake smile on her face and tried to sound positive. "So sheriff, what's for lunch?"

Cree reached out and pulled her into his arms. He embraced Kate and kissed her on the cheek. At the intimidating growl from Ben, Cree laughed and kissed her again. "You owe me, Ben. How many times did I catch you having a heart-to-heart with Jenny?"

Ben gently pulled Kate away from Cree and into his own arms. "We'll meet you at the Triple Spur. I thought we'd stop and pick up some cool drinks on the way."

"Sounds good, buddy. See you there."

Ben and Kate arrived at the Triple Spur forty-five minutes later. They pulled up to the beautiful log and stone ranch house and Ben turned to face Kate. "Thank you for being so brave, Wildflower." He leaned across the seat and kissed her. Drawing away slowly, he looked deep in her eyes. "I love you, Kate. Thank you for sharing your life with me."

Kate's eyes pooled with tears. She smiled and kissed him back. "I love you, Ben. I've never met anyone I'd rather spend my life with."

Ben got out of the truck and went around to lift Kate down from the passenger seat. They walked hand in hand to the front porch. Blue was in his regular sleeping spot, the front porch settee cushion that Cree had forbidden the dog to get up on. Ben smiled and shook his head and knocked on the door.

Jake answered the door after several long moments. His lips were swollen and his eyes were still hooded from passion. "Hey, guys, come on in. Jenny's in the kitchen finishing up lunch. I'm sorry but things won't be ready for another half hour or so." He looked down at his bare feet. "We...uh...got a little distracted."

Kate smiled and started toward the kitchen calling over her shoulder. "It's about damn time Jenny got...uh...distracted." She waved goodbye to Ben and went into the kitchen to help Jenny.

Ben followed Jake out onto the front porch. Jake took a seat on the porch swing and pointed to the bag Ben held. "Please tell me that's beer? Jenny won't let Cree and me have it in the house anymore." He smiled and shrugged. "She said if she couldn't have any neither could we." He leaned toward Ben and whispered, "Jenny doesn't know it, but I've got a cooler stashed in the barn." He sat back quite proud of himself.

Ben handed him a cold beer out of the bag. "Better drink this six-pack fast then before it gets hot." Ben took a seat in the rocking chair beside the porch swing. "Where's Cree? I wanted to talk to both of you while the women are busy."

Jake took a long pull from the beer bottle and sighed. "Damn that tastes good. Cree should be here any minute. He decided to take the reports over to Judge Hathaway personally instead of faxing them."

By the time they were finished with their first beer Cree was climbing the steps of the porch. "Man that beer looks good." He took a seat next to Jake on the porch swing and wrapped his arm around him. Pulling Jake in, he gave him a deep kiss. He even went as far as quickly running a hand down to the bulge in Jake's jeans.

Jake thrust up into his hand. It seemed they'd both forgotten Ben was sitting right beside them. When Jake reached over to start unbuttoning Cree's jeans, he heard a cough coming from Ben. Startled, he looked over at Ben. "Sorry, Ben. Just can't seem to get enough these days. I think Jenny's hormones are infectious." He smoothed his hand down Cree's torso once more and buttoned his jeans. "Later," he said and licked Cree's lips.

Ben handed Cree and Jake a beer and took another for himself. "How's your prisoner today?"

Cree smiled and took a drink of his beer. "Pissed off. He's been talking to his daddy's lawyer all morning. He's furious he can't get out today. I explained the judge refused to hold a bond hearing on a Sunday but Clint seems to think he should make an exception for an Adams." Cree took another drink of his beer as he played with Jake's hair. "How's Kate holding up?"

Ben sat his bottle between his thighs and ran his hands over his head. "Very well considering the surprise Clint left for her in the barn this morning." At Jake's scowl Ben continued. "Let me back up for a moment. First I need to explain exactly what happened to Kate seven years ago at the hands of that little fucker." Ben told them the story Kate had shared with him. He could tell by the looks on their faces Cree and Jake were remembering what they'd gone through with Jenny.

When he finished relaying the events of seven years ago, he told Jake what happened that morning. Cree of course had already heard the story so he kept himself busy playing with Jake's hair and neck. "This morning Kate went out early to get the horses fed and tripped over a little present. It seems someone put the saddle she'd been raped on in the middle of the aisle on a bale of hay." Ben rubbed his head again and closed his eyes. "I thought she was going to break for good. She was ready to leave Junctionville and the ranch. I talked her into giving me another chance to protect her." He looked at his friends. "I can't let her down again. I'm thinking about calling in one of 'The Team'. What do you think?"

Cree nodded his head and put his empty beer bottle on the porch floor. "I think not only is Clint a bastard but so was his father and ex-Sheriff Adams. I can't officially do anything about the events seven years ago but I might just let a few things slip to Judge Hathaway. And with your permission to a few folks around town." Ben started to protest telling the town's people. Cree could see it in his eyes. Cree held up his hand to stop Ben's objection. "Maybe with a few well-spoken words we can make life a little more difficult in Junctionville for Clint Adams. We'll let him get run out of town by the residents if the law can't take care of him."

Ben began to see the merits of what Cree was saying. "I'll have to ask Kate. It's her story. What about calling in one of the guys?"

Jake reached for the last beer with a pleading face. "Well, I talked to Gabe just yesterday and I can tell you it's not a good time for him. He's got some problems of his own right now. What about calling Nicco? I know his security company is busy but at least he's got a good business partner to take up some of the slack. I'll bet if you call him he'd be on the next flight out of New York City."

Ben nodded and reluctantly handed Jake the last beer. Just as Jake started to take a drink Jenny called through the door that lunch was on the table. Ben doubled over laughing at Jake's panicked face. "Drink fast, Jake, before momma catches you."

Jake opened his throat and poured the beer down. Cree looked at Ben and shrugged. "It's a gift he has." As they got up and walked toward the door Ben caught Cree smacking Jake's ass. "A damn fine gift, cowboy."

* * * * *

After lunch Cree, Jake and Ben retired to Jake's office to give Nicco a call while Jenny and Kate looked at baby furniture catalogs in the kitchen. Jake handed Ben the phone. "You know, Kate could always stay here."

Ben looked at him like he was crazy. "Hell no she can't. I need that woman like I need air. Her place is with me at home." Ben dialed Nicco's cell phone.

"Nicco."

"Hey buddy, it's Ben. How've ya been?" Ben turned his back on the now kissing Cree and Jake. Jake was straddling Cree's lap and from the looks of it he was performing a tonsillectomy with his tongue.

"Hi, Ben, you know how it is. Every day gets a little shorter and the list of things to do gets a little longer. How's ranch life?"

Ben rubbed his earring and put his feet on the desk. "Great. I'm in love with my business partner."

Nicco choked on whatever he was drinking. "That's good, Ben. I'm happy for you. Is that why you're calling? To tell me you're in loooove."

Ben rolled his eyes at Nicco's teasing. "No that's not why I'm calling. I was wondering if you could do me a huge favor." He told Nicco about the problems Kate had in the past and then her present troubles. When he was done he waited for Nicco's reply.

"I'll talk to Mac and be there before midnight tonight. How long do you think it will take? I mean, I'm not going to leave until this thing is settled no matter what, but Mac and I were planning a vacation next week. If it's okay with you I thought I'd ask him if he'd like to take a little trip to New Mexico."

Ben put his feet on the floor and turned toward Jake and Cree, then snapped his head back around. Jake and Cree had obviously forgotten where they were. Cree had his face buried in Jake's naked ass and they were both stroking their cocks. Jake was pushing his ass against Cree's face and begging for Cree's tongue. "That sounds great to me, Nicco. I was just going to tell Cree and Jake but they're otherwise....uh...occupied at the moment."

Nicco laughed and told Ben he'd see him soon. Ben hung up the phone and backed out of the office, giving Cree and Jake a little privacy. He went to the kitchen and bent to give Kate a kiss on the top of the head. "Well, ladies, did you find the furniture you were searching for?"

Jenny's eyes lit up. "Yes as a matter of fact we did. Kate and I agree and we're planning a trip to Santa Fe Tuesday morning to get it. So do whatever protecting you need to do but we're going." Jenny looked behind Ben. "Where are my husbands?"

Ben cleared his throat. "They are...um...occupied in the office." Ben turned back to Kate. "Are you about ready to go home, Wildflower?"

Jenny put her hands on her hips. "Are they fooling around again? Ever since Jake talked to my doctor he can't seem to get enough sex." She looked at Kate and Ben smiling. "Not that I'm complaining. I just can't believe they started without me."

Kate and Ben inched toward the door. Kate waved at Jenny as they started down the steps. "Talk to you later, girlfriend."

Chapter Six

ഇ

Nicco's flight was delayed so he didn't get into the ranch until about three o'clock in the morning. Ben and Kate decided to let him sleep while they went to the barn to do their morning chores. They each picked up a pitchfork and Ben rounded up the wheelbarrow. They started on Too Tall's stall, mucking out the old straw and wood shavings. They worked in a comfortable silence, both deep in thought.

After they finished with Ripples' stall and spread out clean shavings and straw, Kate turned to Ben. "So Nicco is a friend of yours from the Navy?"

Ben nodded and put both of their pitchforks away. "Yeah. He worked under me in the Seal team that included Jake and Cree. You met him at Cree and Jenny's wedding, don't you remember?"

Kate walked over to the grain bin and filled a bucket. "Sure I remember him. It's hard to forget the guy who put a bullet hole between the eyes of a man right in front of me. I just wasn't introduced to him and wasn't clear on the relationship between you all."

Ben got the grooming brushes from the shelf and started brushing down Too Tall while Kate brushed down Ripples. "I'm sorry I forgot to introduce you to everyone. That day was kind of crazy. There were six of us. Nicco lives in New York City now. He's a partner in a personal security company. Then there's Gabe who bought Jake's father's ranch in western Oklahoma. Remy 'The Crazy Cajun' lives in and is part owner of a bar in Key West. And you already know Cree and Jake."

Kate finished brushing Ripples and put her grooming materials away. "Why don't you go and check the water tanks. I'll go start breakfast for our house guest."

Ben pulled Kate into his arms. "First I want some more of those wonderful kisses I got this morning." He parted Kate's mouth and stroked her tongue with his own. "God, Kate, you make me so hard I don't think I'll be able to ride Too Tall out to the pastures today. I'll have to take the truck." He unsnapped her shirt and pulled her breasts out of her bra and latched on.

Kate closed her eyes and arched her back. "Mmm…that's nice, Ben. After this morning I've no doubt that we'll work our way up to 'big blue'. I had no problem with the first new vibrator I bought. The second one was a little tight but you were so gentle with it that it wasn't painful. I think a few more sessions with it and I'll be ready for the big one. Next stop after that is this." Kate ran her hand down Ben's very large, very hard erection.

Ben led Kate up to the hayloft, dragging a horse blanket with him. He spread the blanket out and stripped himself and Kate of clothing. Taking her into his arms once more, Ben began kissing her like a man possessed. He pulled Kate on top of him and positioned her so she was straddling his cock. "You feel so good there, darlin'. Slide back and forth for me. Let me feel your hot wet pussy on my cock."

Kate started a slow steady rhythm, sliding Ben's cock back and forth between the lips of her pussy. The movement rubbed against her clit and she shivered. "So good, Ben. You're so hard and thick."

Ben pulled her down toward his chest. He bent his head so he could get a breast in his mouth. He swirled her areola until goose bumps broke out on her skin. Kate's nipples grew even longer, silently begging for his mouth. He latched onto the nipple, giving it a little nip before sucking eagerly. Kate sped up her pelvic thrusts against his cock and Ben came with a shout to the rafters. He reached down and squeezed Kate's clit between his thumb and forefinger. With his other hand he drove three fingers up into her pussy.

Kate's pussy clamped on to Ben's fingers as she came. She collapsed on his chest, totally replete. Kate kissed and nibbled on Ben's nipples. She looked up at him and smiled. "You know we both smell like horses now, don't you?

Ben smiled and kissed her forehead. "Yeah but it was well worth it. I'll sneak around back and wash down with the hose. You can take a shower before waking Nicco for breakfast. You might make extra. I wouldn't be surprised to see Cree show up anytime this morning." Ben smiled and kissed her again. "If he doesn't show up I'll just have to eat his share. With you around I seem to be burning a lot more calories than usual. I haven't been this active since my Seal days."

Kate got up and put her clothes back on. "How's Big Ben?" She motioned toward his cock. "Are you going to be able to take Too Tall to check the tanks?"

Ben looked down at his still half hard cock and grinned. "I probably could but my condition could pop back up at any time. I'll take the truck. It'll be faster. I'm starting to feel weak from hunger." He smiled and followed her down the ladder.

Kate showered and put on clean clothes. She opted for a pair of shorts since her work was done for the morning. She pulled on her old cutoffs and a red halter top. She put her hair up in a ponytail and went downstairs to cook breakfast.

She had the bacon and sausage done and in the oven to stay warm before Nicco woke up. She'd just started frying potatoes and making pancakes when she heard their house guest enter the kitchen. She went to the cupboard and got an extra large coffee mug down. "Have a seat, Nicco. Breakfast should be ready in about ten minutes." She set the coffee down in front of him and went back to her pancakes. She turned to look at him over her shoulder. "I'm making Ben some fried eggs too, would you care for some?"

Nicco shook his head and looked at the tiny spitfire in front of him. "Um…no thank you. I think the other mountain of food you've prepared will be plenty."

Kate turned and shrugged. "Ben tries to tell me he's still a growing boy and needs a lot of food."

Nicco gave a bark of laughter. "Hell, I hope the giant isn't still growing. Size-wise he's the most physically intimidating man I've ever met." Nicco smiled and took a drink of his coffee. "Excellent coffee, Kate, thank you."

She smiled sweetly and turned around to flip a pancake. "You're welcome. I should be thanking you for flying all the way out here."

Nicco held up his hand taking another drink of his coffee. "No need to thank me. Ben saved my ass more times than I care to count." Nicco's phone started ringing. He took the phone out of his pocket and looked at the caller ID. "Sorry, Kate, I need to answer this. It's my business partner Mac.

"Hey, Mac… Yeah I finally got in around two-thirty this morning. It was later than that by the time I rented a car and drove to Junctionville so I didn't want to call and wake you up."

Nicco continued to listen to Mac. He didn't notice Kate watching him out of the corner of her eye. Kate could see something different in Nicco's face that she'd never seen before, a sort of peace that softened his features. She didn't know Mac but she did know the look of a man in love. Kate just wondered whether Nicco knew it.

"I won't know until later on today, Mac, but it looks like we'll be spending our vacation in New Mexico… Okay I'll call you later today. Bye, Mac."

Nicco flipped the phone shut and shoved it back in his pants pocket. "That was Mac. He just wanted to make sure I got in all right. We've had a vacation on our work schedule for a year now so Mac's going to come in next week."

Kate brought the huge platter of pancakes to the table and sat down. "I'm sorry I'm messing up your vacation, Nicco. Where had you two planned on going?" Kate got up to set the table.

"Don't be sorry, Kate. We didn't have a destination in mind. We just usually get in a car and drive once a year. It's the best way to take a vacation. We were thinking about going up into the mountains and doing a little camping this year but as I look off into the distance I see you have some mountains right here in New Mexico. Maybe if we get this little fucker off your case we'll still have a few days to camp. Either way it doesn't matter. It's just being with each other without all the other stuff getting in the way that's fun for us."

Kate went outside the kitchen door and rang the big old-fashioned school bell. She came back in and grinned at Nicco. "It's like calling the hogs to the trough but don't tell Ben I said that."

Kate finished putting the food on the table and sat down just as Ben walked through the door. He walked over to the table and leaned down to kiss her. He looked at Nicco and smiled. "Good morning. Have you been keeping my little Wildflower company or are you trying to take her away from me?" He looked at Kate's confused expression and shrugged his shoulders. "Nicco has women falling at his feet wherever he goes. Between him and Remy no one else ever has a chance."

Nicco started to sputter a protest. "I've never led a woman on, Ben. I can't help that they see me as some Latin sex machine." He looked at Kate. "Honestly, Kate, I don't encourage them."

Kate smiled knowingly and took his hand across the table. "I totally believe you, Nicco." At Ben's low growl Kate rolled her eyes at Nicco and winked. "Besides you're not a big enough man for me. What are you, Nicco, about six-three or six-four? Why you're just a puny little thing." She patted his hand again and began filling her plate.

247

Nicco looked from her to Ben and broke into a fit of laughter. "I can see you've got your hands full with this one, Ben. She's a regular spitfire."

Ben smiled with pride. "She's my spitfire. Just remember that, Mr. Latin Lover." Ben filled his plate with five eggs, six sausage patties and eight pieces of bacon and then he got up from the table and got down an extra plate for the five pancakes he fixed.

Kate looked at Nicco knowingly. "I told you he was a growing boy." She patted Ben's hand as he gave Nicco a sheepish little-boy grin.

Nicco and Kate finished their breakfast and got up to do the dishes. A knock at the door alerted them to a visitor. Kate looked out the window and smiled at Ben. "Sorry, Ben, but it looks like Cree's here. You'll have to stick with the little measly breakfast you've already had." She left to let Cree in.

Ben eyed the rest of the bacon, sausage and pancakes. "Damn."

Nicco was still laughing when Cree and Kate came back into the kitchen. Kate gave Cree a cup of coffee. "I made extra for breakfast if you'd care for some? We've already eaten."

Cree shook his head and lifted the coffee cup. "Coffee's fine, thanks, Kate."

Ben's face looked like a kid on Christmas morning. "Oh good. I was still kinda hungry." He loaded his plate with the rest of breakfast.

Cree shook his head at his friend. "When aren't you hungry? I thought I was going to have to take another part-time job to feed you when you lived with us. I've never seen you eat like you have lately. Burning a lot of extra calories, Ben?"

Ben looked up from his plate and flashed his teeth in the biggest grin ever. "Shut up, Cree. Tell us what you know so far."

Cree took another drink of coffee and sighed. "Nothing new this morning, Ben. I came to take fingerprints off the saddle in the barn. After that I thought we'd head to town and file that protection order. The bail hearing is at one this afternoon."

Ben finished his breakfast and wiped his mouth. "Well, let's go take a look at that saddle." Ben pushed out from the table and rubbed his muscled stomach. "Damn good breakfast, Wildflower." He looked over at Nicco. "You'll stay in here with Kate, won't you, Nicco?"

Nicco carried Ben's dirty plate to the sink. "Sure thing. I'll just finish these dishes and take a shower if that's all right?"

* * * * *

An hour later Cree pulled out of the driveway in his sheriff's SUV, followed by Ben's pickup truck with Ben, Kate and Nicco inside. They arrived at the courthouse at nine o'clock and filed the necessary petition with the county clerk. She notarized the petition for a temporary protection order as well as the petition for the permanent protection order. The clerk took the paperwork to Judge Hathaway and asked them to wait in his outer office.

Kate's hands were shaking by the time she sat between Ben and Cree. Ben held her hand, trying to give her all the strength he had. "It'll be okay, Kate. You'll be called in to talk to the judge in a few minutes. He'll ask you why you need the protection orders. Just tell him the story you told me. You'll want to include the incident seven years ago as well as the events of the last several months. If he agrees to the temporary protection order he'll sign it and give it to Cree. The permanent protection order will then be scheduled for a hearing. Clint will be served papers on both the temporary order and the hearing date for the permanent protection order."

Kate looked shocked and turned to Cree. "You mean Clint will be in the same room with me during the hearing?"

Cree held her hand and nodded. "Under the law he has a right to defend himself to the judge. Don't worry, Kate, you'll have a room full of people to protect you from that slime."

Kate chewed her lip. "How come Jenny didn't get a protection order against Buck?"

Cree sighed and looked at Ben. "Jenny's situation was different from yours, Kate. Buck was already wanted by the police in three states. Clint Adams may not even be in jail after his bail hearing. If he gets out of jail we need a legal way to keep him away from you."

Kate looked at Ben. Tears welled up in her eyes and slowly ran down her cheeks. "I'm scared, Ben. What if he gets out of jail and comes after me for putting him in jail and filing the protection order?"

Ben enfolded Kate in his arms. "Oh baby, I know you're afraid. That's why I called Nicco. That way one of us can be with you at all times. Clint may be crazy but he's not crazy enough to mess with you with one of us on your arm. I need you to go in there and tell the judge all your fears concerning Clint. We'll be right here when you get out and Nicco and I will take you out to lunch."

Kate giggled and hugged Ben. Patting and rubbing his rock-hard stomach, she cooed, "Is my little Ben getting hungry again?"

Ben looked at Kate and then looked down at his swelling cock. "Your little Ben is always hungry, darlin'."

Kate looked into his eyes and blushed just as the door to Judge Hathaway's chamber opened. Kate took a deep breath and blew it out when the secretary told her the judge would see her now. She turned to Ben for one last quick kiss. "Wish me luck?"

"All the luck I have to offer, Wildflower." He kissed her forehead and turned her toward the judge's chamber.

When Kate disappeared behind closed doors Ben turned to look at Cree. "This better be worth it, buddy. She'll have to relive the whole nightmare over again in that room. I can't even think right now about how she'll get through telling her story during the hearing with Clint sitting there." Ben rubbed his head and began pacing the corridor.

Nicco looked at Cree and nodded his head toward Ben. "Right now I'm more worried about him than Kate. I've never seen him like this before. Usually he's the calmest one of the bunch."

Cree watched his friend pace up and down the hallway rubbing his head. "That's because no one's ever seen Ben in love before. We'll get them both through this one way or the other."

Thirty minutes later Kate emerged from Judge Hathaway's chamber. The secretary motioned for Cree to enter the office. Kate rushed to Ben's arms while Cree went to talk to the judge.

Ben held Kate close to his side as they sat and waited for Cree to reemerge. "How did it go, Kate?"

Kate nodded her head still looking at the floor. "Fine. It was fine, Ben. I just hated airing my dirty laundry to a stranger. Even if he is a judge."

Ben took her face in his hands, mindful of the still sore bruise on her cheek. "I know it was tough, darlin'. I'm very proud of you for sticking up for yourself."

Cree came out and walked up to Ben and Kate. "Well, the good news is he's signed the temporary protection order and set next Tuesday for the permanent protection order hearing." Cree stopped and ran his fingers through his long hair and released a frustrated breath. "The bad news is the judge gave me a heads-up on Clint's bail hearing. He's going to release him with a one hundred thousand dollar bail and instructions to stay away from you." He reached for Kate's hand. "I'm sorry I couldn't do more."

Kate gripped his hand harder. "You've done everything possible, Cree. No one could fault anything you've done. I'll just keep both of these big strong men around and hope for the best." Kate plastered on a smile and looked at Ben. "Did you say something about taking me to lunch?"

* * * * *

After lunch Nicco, Ben and Kate drove home while Cree served the protection order papers on Clint. Kate fought the dirty feelings she always got when she discussed the events of seven years ago. As soon as they got into the house she turned to Ben and Nicco. "If you two will excuse me I'm going to take a shower."

Ben nodded his head and watched her ascend the staircase. He looked at Nicco. "Well, what's your take on the situation? How would you handle this if she were your client?"

Nicco rubbed his already appearing five o'clock shadow. "So far she's done everything I would have advised her to do. I can't figure this Clint guy out. I mean he got away with rape and assault seven years ago so why start stirring up trouble again?"

"I don't know, Nicco. Because he's a crazy mean sonofabitch? Kate told me after he hit her Saturday night he told her to leave town. Why would he care so much that she leaves town? Until I came along she didn't talk to anyone or even go into town more than twice a month for groceries and ranch supplies."

Pouring himself a glass of whiskey, Nicco turned around and looked at Ben. "I think I'll call Mac and have him do a little digging into Clint's life." Ben smiled and raised his glass. "Mac's the best at the digging-up-shit-on-someone part of the job."

Cree called at two o'clock to tell Ben that Clint had indeed been released on bond. "His assault hearing is set for next month, September twenty-seventh. Until then all I can do is keep an eye on him and hope he's learned his lesson." Cree sighed into the phone. "I don't know, Ben. He was pissed when I served him the protection papers. I'm thinking maybe we should call in Remy."

"No, Cree. I don't want to disrupt Kate's life any more than we have already. Emotionally she's on very shaky ground right now. I'll just try my best to keep her here on the ranch by my side."

"All right, buddy. Just call if you need me. I'm going home to enjoy my family. They've had way too much alone time the last couple of days."

Ben hung up and looked at Nicco. "Cree said Clint was plenty pissed when Cree served him the protection order. He thought maybe we should call Remy but I don't want to upset Kate." Ben walked to the bar to get himself a drink.

"I could call and see if Mac could come a little earlier. Kate already knows he's coming and this way he'll be able to do his investigation on Clint right here in town." Nicco stretched out on the couch and picked up the remote. "Do you get any sports channels out here in the boonies?"

Ben drank his whiskey at the bar. He was caught between wanting to go upstairs to make sure Kate was okay and wanting to give her the privacy that he sensed she needed right now. Nicco's questions finally registered. "Yeah go ahead and call Mac and the sports channels are twenty-seven and sixty-three. Don't ask me why they couldn't put them together. I've tried to figure it out since I've lived here." Ben finished his drink and put his glass on the bar. "I'm going out and check the fence. Stay inside with Kate and make sure you answer the phone. I don't think the little fucker is dumb enough to call her but you never know."

Nicco waved his hand as he became engrossed in a NASCAR race on TV. Ben left the room, shaking his head. He headed out to the barn and saddled up Too Tall. Heading out into the pasture, Ben stopped and turned the horse around. He looked at his home. It was the first one he'd ever really had.

Ben grew up the only child of a single mother. His mom was married eight times before Ben graduated from high school. Each new husband was richer that the last. Vera Thomas cared about one thing — money. She died at the age of forty-one, a very rich, very lonely woman. Ben inherited his mother's fortune but it never meant anything to him. Now looking at his home Ben decided to put that money to good use. He would need to talk to Kate this evening.

He rode to the creek and dismounted. Taking off his boots and socks, he rolled up his pants legs and went wading in the stream just like when he was a kid and got to stay with his grandpa in Montana. His Grandpa Joe was the only stable thing in Ben's life when he was growing up.

His mom would send him to his grandpa's ranch when she was on the prowl for a new husband. Vera didn't usually tell the men she had a kid until after the marriage papers had been signed. Needless to say none of his stepfathers had anything to do with him but Grandpa Joe was always happy to see him. When he was fifteen his grandpa died and his mother never even bothered to tell him about it. He didn't find out until two months later when she started complaining she didn't have anywhere to dump him for the summer. Ben asked about going to Grandpa's and she'd sighed and said he'd died. His ranch had been sold by his mother and the money put in a trust fund for him. What his mother hadn't known was that he'd rather have had the ranch. He swore to himself that one day he'd own his own ranch.

Ben dried his feet and slipped his boots back on and whistled for Charlie. That's when he realized that he hadn't seen Charlie all afternoon. Ben had been so wrapped up in his own mind he'd completely forgotten about his buddy Charlie. He got back on Too Tall and rode toward the house.

He rode into the ranch yard and started whistling and calling Charlie's name. He didn't come. Ben jumped off his horse and tied him to the gate. Ben started in the barn and worked his way through all the other buildings on the ranch.

He rounded the back of the house and stopped. He could hear a soft whimper coming from underneath the porch. He went inside the house and grabbed a flashlight. He ran back out and looked under the porch. Ben could see Charlie at the back of the porch breathing erratically.

He called to him but poor Charlie didn't even lift his head. Ben tried to scoot his way under the porch but he was just too big. He knew he had two choices – he could tear up the porch or he could go get Kate. If he'd had the time he would have gladly torn up the porch in order to save Kate from this but he didn't have the time. Ben stood and raced into the house. He found Nicco sound asleep on the couch. "Where's Kate?"

Nicco opened his eyes and sat up immediately. "She must still be upstairs. Why, what's happened?"

Ben headed for the stairs. "It's Charlie, he's under the porch dying and I can't get to him."

He found Kate sound asleep on top of the covers. "Kate darlin', I need you to wake up. Charlie's in trouble and he needs you."

Kate sat up. She registered what Ben said and grabbed a pair of shorts and a t-shirt out of the drawer. She didn't bother with panties or a bra. "Where is he? What's wrong with him?" Kate ran down the stairs while Ben told her what he knew.

They got outside to find that Nicco had pulled the truck up to the porch. He already had a blanket ready. "Kate, take the blanket with you. See if you can lift Charlie onto the blanket. It will be easier to pull him out rather than try to carry him out."

Kate nodded at Nicco and squeezed her way under the porch. Nicco and Ben both held flashlights for her. She made her way to Charlie and managed to get him onto the blanket. She crawled out, dragging Charlie behind her. When she got close enough to the edge Ben reached in and pulled Charlie the rest of the way out. He wrapped the blanket around him and was heading for the truck by the time Kate crawled out. She raced to the truck and got in. Ben placed Charlie on her lap.

They took off in a cloud of dust. They made it to the vet in less than ten minutes. Ben carried Charlie inside and let the vet take over. He turned to find a dirty, disheveled Kate staring after Charlie with her arms wrapped around herself.

Ben went to her and enfolded her in his arms. He rocked her back and forth, murmuring love words in her ear. She began to shake and he held her tighter. Damn, how much more must this one woman survive?

They waited for almost two hours before the vet finally came out to the waiting room. Kate ran up to Dr. Kennedy. "How's Charlie?"

Dr. Kennedy took a hold of her hand. "He's a very sick dog, Kate. It looks like he's ingested poison."

Kate shook her head. "I don't have any poison at my ranch. I don't even use it in the barn. It must be something else he's eaten."

"I'm afraid not, Kate. He had a stomach full of rat poison. I've never seen a dog eat so much and live this long. I've pumped his stomach and I've got him on an IV but I'm not sure if he'll even last through the night."

"Isn't there something else you can do for him?" Kate bit her lip. Her eyes pleading with the doctor.

"I'm afraid not, Kate. Right now we just have to wait and see whether he lasts until morning. If he makes it until then he'll be fine but I just don't know."

Kate thought about what the vet said. "I want to take him home with me. If he's going to die then I want him home with me where he belongs. If he's still alive by morning I'll bring him back so you can check on him."

Dr. Kennedy looked at Kate for a few minutes. "He'll need to finish out his IV before you take him. It should be about another half hour."

"That will be fine, Dr. Kennedy," Ben replied still standing with his arm around Kate.

They took Charlie home forty-five minutes later. He was so weak he couldn't even open his eyes. Kate cradled the big dog like he was a puppy. "It's been me and Charlie against the world for so long I don't know what I'll do without him."

Ben reached over and smoothed her hair back from her face. "Shhh, darlin', don't talk like that. Just pray that he makes it through the night."

Kate looked at Ben and chewed her lip. "I want to sleep with him tonight. If that bothers you we can sleep in my bed."

"It doesn't bother me at all, Wildflower. I'd do the same thing if I were you." Ben pulled the truck up in front of the house. He got out and took Charlie from Kate. Ben carried the big dog inside and on back to his bedroom. He placed Charlie on the bed and turned to Kate. "I'm going to go make us some supper. Why don't you take another shower and change?"

Kate kissed him. "Thank you for understanding, Ben. I love you."

Ben held her tight and kissed her. "I love you too, Wildflower."

Chapter Seven

✫

Ben went down to start supper only to find Nicco in a pretty pink apron stirring what smelled like red sauce on the stove. "Well, don't you look sweet? Like the perfect little homemaker."

Nicco looked at him and grimaced. "Stuff it, Ben. I figured you two would be hungry when you got home. How's Charlie?"

Ben got a beer out of the fridge and sat down at the kitchen table. "Not good I'm afraid. The vet said he had a stomach full of rat poison. He pumped it out but he doesn't know how much had already been absorbed into his system. He said if he makes it through the night he should be okay. Kate insisted on bringing him home with us. If he's going to die she wants him to die here. So it looks as though I'm going to have another bed partner tonight."

Nicco put down the spoon and started the pasta water. "Where'd Charlie get a hold of rat poison?"

Ben took a long drink of his beer. "That's the million-dollar question. Kate said she doesn't keep any poisons on the ranch. What do ya want to bet the little fucker's been out here sometime today and left it out for Charlie?"

"Damn, that would be bold of him. We've been here all afternoon. Sounds like he's starting to get desperate but why?" Ben shook his head. "I called Mac. He'll be out on Wednesday afternoon. I told him I'd pick him up at the airport."

"How'd you get hooked up with a Green Beret for a business partner anyway, Nicco?" Ben asked, getting up for another beer. He offered Nicco one. He knew Nicco hated beer but he thought he'd offer.

Nicco shook his head no to the beer and made a disgusted face. "Mac and I grew up together. Our fathers were both in the Marines stationed at Quantico. They were instructors at the Officer Candidates School." Nicco shook his head. "Harder men you'd never hope to meet. Anyway, Mac and I've been buddies since we were around nine years old. When we graduated from high school Mac did what was expected of him and joined the Marines." Nicco got up and stirred the sauce and added the penne pasta to the already boiling pot of water. "I guess I was the rebellious one because I opted for the Navy." He shook his head. "To this day I'm still trying to make it up to my father."

Ben looked at Nicco. There was a world of information in that one sentence. He wondered how a Marine instructor father would handle his only son's decision to join another branch of the military. Maybe that's where the pain came from that he'd seen in Nicco's eyes since they met on the first day Nicco was assigned to his team.

Ben could see that Nicco was lost in his own thoughts so he got up and stirred the pasta. He tasted a piece and determined it was ready so he got the colander out of the cabinet and drained the pasta. While it was draining he got the plates and silverware out of the drawer and set the table around Nicco.

When a plate was placed in front of him Nicco snapped back to present day. "I'm sorry, Ben. I didn't mean to blank out on you. Why don't you call Kate to supper and I'll fix the drinks."

Ben nodded at his friend and went to find Kate. He entered the bedroom and found her kneeling beside the bed, softly petting Charlie. She was talking in a soft, calm voice to him about getting better so he could help with the chores that needed to be done.

Ben watched her for a minute, not really listening, just watching her. She was so beautiful. He'd never imagined he could get so lucky as to have a woman like Kate love him.

Hell, his own mother didn't love him. Why would this beautiful wounded woman take a chance on such a big man? Ben smiled to himself and decided not to look a gift horse in the mouth. He'd just make sure he was worthy of her trust.

"Kate, supper's ready. Nicco made you some of his famous red sauce." Ben went to the bed and pulled her to her feet.

Kate wiped the tears from her eyes and turned to face Ben. "What's red sauce?"

Ben chuckled at her confused face. "It's just a fancy word for spaghetti sauce without meat. Nicco's sauce is the best. You'll love it." He led Kate out of his bedroom. "How's Charlie doing?"

Kate shrugged and slipped her arm around Ben's waist when they got to the living room. "I can tell he knows I'm there and understands that I'm talking to him but he still won't open his eyes for more than a couple seconds at a time."

Ben squeezed her shoulders a little tighter as they entered the kitchen to find Nicco still lost in thought. Kate looked up at Ben quickly then back to Nicco. Ben shrugged and pulled out the chair for her. "Looks good, buddy."

Kate smiled when Nicco looked over at her. "Yes it does. Thank you for fixing dinner. Ben just told me wonderful things about your red sauce."

Nicco put his hand on Kate's. "How's the dog?"

Kate turned her hand over and squeezed Nicco's fingers. "Charlie's still fighting. That's all I can ask of him. At least he doesn't appear to be in pain anymore. So I'll just keep praying that he'll make it through the night."

They ate their dinner in friendly conversation, no one bringing up Charlie again nor mentioning Clint. After dinner Kate got up to start on the dishes when Nicco stopped her.

"I'll clean up, Kate. You go be with Charlie."

Kate chewed her bottom lip. "I can't let you do that, Nicco. You made such a fabulous meal you deserve to go sit in front of the television."

Nicco chuckled and steered Kate toward the door. "I'm glad you liked my sauce, Kate, but you're not cleaning the kitchen. I'm going to recruit Ben to dry anyway. Maybe I'll even talk him into a game of chess afterward."

Kate looked at Ben. Ben nodded and kissed her cheek. "Go, darlin'. I'll be in later."

Nicco started filling the sink with hot soapy water. Ben started clearing the table, sitting the dirty dishes beside the sink. "So you never finished telling me how you managed to go into business with one of those bossy Green Berets?"

Nicco could tell by the tone of Ben's voice that he was kidding. "Mac was hurt in Afghanistan four years ago. He walked too close to a booby-trapped building and almost got himself killed. As it was he got torn up pretty badly. The right side of his body was pretty much opened up by flying debris. He spent almost a year at the military hospital in Germany. I visited him when I could get leave. When Mac was released to come back to the states I opted to get out of the Seals." Nicco shrugged like it wasn't a big deal. "Mac still wasn't a hundred percent and his father had passed away while he was in the Berets so I came back to help take care of him. He would have done the same for me."

Nicco washed while he continued talking. Ben had the feeling that Nicco had never talked to anyone about this. He always seemed to be so shut down emotionally that Ben figured if Nicco was willing to open up a little he was going to listen. He decided to ask the question that came to mind. "Why didn't your father help Nicco? It sounded like both of your families had been pretty close." At the snap of Nicco's head in his direction Ben shrugged. "I mean most people would gladly have stepped in and helped a fellow soldier."

"My father hates Mac with every fiber of his being." Nicco seemed to think a long time before he continued. "Mac is fairly open about the fact that he's gay. He was willing to suppress his sexual orientation while in the Marines but most people knew." Nicco scrubbed a plate until Ben was afraid the pattern would come off. "Mac was like a second son to my father until he learned of his sexual orientation. He cut Mac out of his life completely. Every picture in our house was altered so that Mac no longer existed to my father. He thought Mac was a disgrace to the Marines."

Nicco handed the last of the clean dishes to Ben to dry. "Anyway, I quit the Navy when my tour was up and came home to take care of Mac. We decided to move to New York City once his physical therapy was over. The security business just came naturally as a vocation to both of us. I usually do the fieldwork if any is involved that our four employees can't handle. Mac takes care of the business side of things."

Ben followed Nicco into the living room and started setting up the chess board. "Do you still see your father?"

Nicco looked up at Ben like he'd grown two heads. "Of course. My father is one of the finest men I know. He still hasn't fully forgiven my error in judgment regarding the Navy but I've worked long and hard to make up for it."

Ben was really confused now. "What about the way he treated Mac? Aren't you angry with him over that?"

Nicco shrugged and made his first move on the chess board. "That has nothing to do with me. That's between my father and Mac."

Ben looked at Nicco for a long time. Nicco was even more screwed up than he had thought. He decided not to rock the boat anymore and just be Nicco's friend. Nicco would figure out sooner or later that his father was not the man he thought he was. Ben moved his chess piece.

After Nicco whipped Ben's butt in chess Ben yawned. "I'm going to bed."

Nicco looked at his watch then looked up at Ben. "I was thinking maybe I'd sneak on over to Clint Adams' house and keep an eye on him for a little while tonight."

Ben nodded. "That's a good idea. Make sure you get back here in time to get a few hours' sleep. We've got a lot of chores to catch up on tomorrow." He winked at Nicco and headed toward his bedroom.

Kate was sound asleep when he stripped and climbed into bed. She had her arm around Charlie and her face in his fur. Ben snuggled his large body in behind hers. He threw his arm over her and rested his hand on top of hers in Charlie's fur.

Ben woke in the same position the next morning. Man he must have been really tired. He felt something wet on his hand and looked over Kate. Charlie was licking his hand like it would make a good snack. Charlie was licking his hand. The meaning finally hit him and he sat up, shaking Kate. "Wake up, Wildflower. It looks like Charlie made it through the night with flying colors."

Kate opened her eyes. She felt Charlie now licking her hand and laughed. "Oh my goodness, Charlie!" Charlie turned over so Kate could rub his belly. "Oh that's my good boy. Are you hungry? Do you want momma to get you something to eat?" Kate jumped out of bed and started for the door.

"Um…Wildflower, you might want to put some clothes on first. Don't forget we have the Latin Lover in the house." Ben smiled and reached over to grab her robe for her.

Kate came back to the bed to get her robe from Ben. She sat on the bed and rubbed Ben's head. "I don't think you need to worry about Nicco looking at me."

Ben's eyes opened wide in disbelief. "Are you crazy? You're a beautiful woman with boobs any guy would drool over. Yes. I do think I have something to worry about."

Kate laughed and kissed him on top of the head. "I don't know how to tell you this but Nicco's in love with Mac. Although I'm not sure he'd admit it to anyone."

Ben's mouth dropped open. "Why do you say that?"

Kate shrugged and stood up to put her pretty pink robe on. "I guess it's a woman thing. I can just tell by the way he talks about him. The way he says his name."

Ben thought for a minute and slowly nodded. "It makes sense. It kind of brings more pieces of the Nicco puzzle together. I don't know why I never saw it before but I think maybe you're right."

Kate patted his cheek. "Well, while you think on it I'm going down to get Charlie some bread and milk. Do you think he needs to go out and potty? Could you carry him outside for me, Ben?" She batted her eyelashes at him.

Ben smiled and put his jeans on. "Anything for you, Wildflower."

She rolled her eyes and left the bedroom. Kate passed Nicco sleeping on the couch fully dressed as she went through the living room. "Good thing I put my robe on," she mumbled to herself as she entered the kitchen.

Ben took Charlie out to take a piss and then took him into the kitchen for a bowl of bread and milk. "Why bread and milk?"

Kate shrugged, "I don't know. It's what my mom always fed small or sick animals."

Ben came up behind her and slipped his hands through the opening of her robe. "Mmm...do you think we have time for a little bit of play before Nicco wakes up?" He moved his hand to her nipple and gently squeezed.

Kate leaned back against him. "I think so. He looked pretty out of it when I passed him a while ago." She turned to face Ben and stroked the length of his erection. "Why do you shove your cock down the leg of your jeans?"

Ben lifted an eyebrow at her question. "Because if I didn't it would stick up out of my waistband every time you're around. Showing you my cock all day is fine for me but not so good when we have company or I'm doing chores."

Kate giggled and put her hand over her mouth. "Well, why don't we go to the bedroom and let that monster out of his cage?"

Ben picked her up and swung her over his shoulder caveman style. He tiptoed through the living room to his bedroom and threw her on the bed. He untied the sash of her robe and pulled it off. Next he went to work on his boots, socks and jeans. He hadn't bothered with a shirt so that was one less thing he had to worry about. Ben jumped on the bed, barely missing Kate. "The beast is free and happy."

Kate laughed. She didn't think she'd ever laughed as much as she did with this man. It amazed her that he could be so big and strong yet act like a goofy teenage boy when they were together. She sat on top of his groin and wiggled. "The beast is so strong and mighty this morning." Kate leaned down to lick the side of Ben's face. She worked her way to his mouth and nipped his lower lip. She soothed the nip with her tongue. She looked into Ben's eyes with her lips still touching his. "Make love to me, Ben?"

Ben closed his eyes and wrapped his arms around her even tighter. "I want nothing more, Wildflower, but I don't think you're ready."

Kate sat up and looked down on him. "I've already proven I can handle your cock's circumference. The only question left unanswered is can I take your length. Would it really be so bad for you if we tried now and I couldn't take all of you? I-I mean if you're unable to come like that I can always figure something else out."

Ben groaned and stopped teasing her breasts to look at her. "I'm about to come just listening to you talk about it. That's not why I don't think it's a good idea, darlin'. I'm afraid if I hurt you..." He stopped talking and closed his eyes taking a few calming breaths. "I'm afraid I'll hurt you and you'll leave me."

A tear slid down Kate's cheek. "Listen to me, you unbelievably thoughtful man. I. Will. Never. Leave. You. I love you more than anything in this world. I just want the chance to feel you inside me. So maybe we have to keep stretching me out with the vibrators. If that's the case okay, I'm willing to do anything to be with you. I just want to try, Ben. Let me try having your cock in me. If it hurts I'll be sure to let you know so you can stop. Okay?"

Ben looked into her blue eyes for a long time. Kate thought he was trying to figure out how to tell her no when she heard one softly spoken word. "Okay."

Ben reached into the bedside table and withdrew a bottle of lube. "If you promise we can use lots of lube and you'll take only as much of my cock as you can without pain."

Kate sat up and looked down into Ben's eyes. "I promise, Ben." She crossed her heart, of course it didn't help Ben's libido that her fingertips skimmed over her nipples when she did it. "Where do you want me, on top or bottom?"

Ben poured a generous amount of lube onto his fingers and started readying Kate for his cock. "Stay where you are, darlin'. It will be easier if you control how much of me you can take in."

He ran his finger up and down her slit, stopping to play with her pierced clit. He moved his fingers back down and entered her channel with first one and then two fingers. Stopping only long enough to pour more lube on them, he continued stretching Kate's channel. When she seemed perfectly comfortable with two fingers he moved to three. When the third finger entered her, Kate tensed on his hand and came. It was so sexy watching her come. "You'd better hop on now, darlin', or there won't be anything left to ride."

Kate repositioned her body. She took his cock into her hand and lined it up with her dripping pussy. Ben put so much lube on his cock she was having trouble keeping hold of it. It was like an oiled-up python. She slowly lowered herself onto the beast, holding her breath as she did. Slowly his cock head entered her passage and she continued to lower herself until about half of his cock was inside her. Kate looked at Ben. It looked like his eyes were crossing. "There's no pain at all so far. I'm going to keep going." Kate laughed to herself and then she laughed out loud. "Listen to me. I sound like an explorer."

Ben's breaths were starting to come faster and faster. "Kate darlin', you feel better than anything has a right to but I'm about to come. So if you want to continue exploring you'd better do it quickly."

Kate nodded her head. She sank down farther until it began to really hurt. Her body just simply wasn't long enough to accommodate such a long cock. "I think that's as far as I can go for now, Ben."

Ben smiled and looked down where the two of them were joined and then back up to look at Kate. "Look down, darlin'. Do you see what I see? You're only about an inch and a half from fully taking me. I think a few more workouts with those vibrators and you'll be able to take all of me."

Kate gave him a pouty face. "Why do I have to practice with the vibrators when there's a perfectly good cock in my bed every night?" She wiggled her ass and rose back up the length of his cock and then slid back down.

Ben reached down and pulled the tiny ring in her clit. She came screaming his name. Ben was a goner when her pussy starting milking his cock. He thrust upward and came. He came so hard his teeth hurt. It was like every ounce of his energy transferred to Kate through his cock.

By the time Kate's breathing returned to normal she looked down at Ben and found him passed out. She didn't know if he'd fallen asleep or fainted but the sight made her giggle. "Yeah you're such a big strong man, honey." She climbed off, deciding to let him sleep. She took a quick shower and dressed in jean shorts and a yellow halter and went to make breakfast.

When she entered the kitchen Nicco was standing at the coffee pot. "Good morning, Nicco. How was your night?"

He raised an eyebrow and lifted one side of his lip, trying his best not to smile. "From the sounds of it not nearly as good as your morning. All I got this morning was a wet Charlie kiss."

Kate turned red from the top of her to the soles of her feet. "Sorry about that. It was our first time. I guess we just got a little excited. As a matter of fact I think Ben may be passed out." She smiled and shrugged her shoulders.

Nicco's jaw dropped. "What do you mean it was your first time? Haven't you two been sleeping together for a while now?"

Kate chewed her lip and got out the bacon and sausage. "Have you ever, um...seen the size of Ben?"

The light finally went on in Nicco's head. "Yeah. Oh. Okay now I understand. Ben thought he was protecting you before, huh?"

Kate nodded and put the breakfast meat on to fry. "He didn't want to hurt me. I finally had to wrestle him down and take what was mine." She giggled and covered her face with her hands. "I can't believe I just told you all that."

"Don't sweat it, Kate. Your secret is safe with me." Nicco sat down at the table with his coffee. "I'll be glad to help you with the chores this morning if sleeping beauty doesn't wake up."

"I'd appreciate that. Ben said something about Mac coming in tomorrow. Are you going to pick him up at the airport?"

A smile spread across Nicco's face like sunshine after a rainy day. "Yeah. I'll leave here around eleven or so tomorrow morning. Why? Did you want to come with me?"

"No it's not that. It's just that I would like to run into Junctionville today sometime and get a new set of sheets for the extra bed. Do you think you could run me in this afternoon?"

Nicco nodded. "I don't see a problem with that if Ben doesn't need us for anything."

Kate turned around and looked at Nicco. "Is that a politically correct way of saying 'if Ben says it's okay'? Because I have to tell you, Nicco, I've made my own decisions for quite some time now."

Nicco spread his hands in a defensive gesture. "We're just trying to keep you safe, Kate. I'm sorry if it makes us seem all 'he-man-ish' but we have to do what we feel is best."

Kate put the bacon and sausage on a platter and put it in the warming oven. "How many eggs would you like, Nicco? I forgot to do my egg gathering this morning so at least you'll know they're fresh." Kate grabbed the egg basket and waited for Nicco's answer.

"You mean you're going to get eggs right now? And then you're going to cook them?" Nicco seemed totally shocked and disgusted by the whole concept of chickens laying the eggs he'd be eating.

"Haven't you ever seen a chicken coop before, Nicco? I thought you stayed on the Triple Spur for a few weeks. That's how most country folk get their eggs. Do you want to come with me?"

"No I haven't seen a chicken coop close up. I did stay at the Triple Spur for a few weeks but I pretty much stayed indoors. And no I don't want to come with you. If it comes to me getting my own eggs or not eating I'll choose door number two."

Kate shook her head and laughed on her way out the door. "What a city boy you are, Nicco. I'll be back in ten minutes."

Kate went to the chicken coop and filled a bucket with cracked corn. She filled the feeding trough and filled the chickens' water. When the chickens left their nests to eat she snuck in and began picking up the eggs. She was halfway through the row when she felt something heavy touch her foot. Kate looked down when she heard the rattle.

Right next to her foot sat a rattlesnake with a full belly. He was eyeing Kate's white sneaker like it was another egg. She knew she couldn't move or the snake would strike. She looked around for something to hit the snake with. She spotted Nicco coming toward the chicken coop and prayed he wouldn't make any sudden noises or movements. Kate slowly put her fingers to her lips and pointed toward her foot. By the time she looked back up at Nicco and down at her foot again the snake was dead. Nicco's knife was sticking through the snake's head into the dirt floor of the coop.

Kate's knees threatened to give way and she started to sag down. Nicco was there in a heartbeat, holding her up with an arm around her waist. "That was amazing. I've never seen anyone so quick with a knife before. Sometimes I forget just how skilled you all are but what a way to remind me. *Wow!*"

Nicco picked up the egg basket and started to head back inside until Kate stopped him. "Not yet. I have to finish gathering the eggs." At his startled looked she smiled. "Why don't you just stand over there by the door. I'll be done in a minute."

When she finished gathering the eggs the two of them went back in to the kitchen. Ben was just coming in from a shower apparently. He smelled like soap and Ben. She walked over to him and gave him a quick kiss. "Morning, sleepyhead. Nicco left a present for you on the floor of the chicken coop. Better get it soon though before the chickens peck it to pieces."

Ben swung his head toward Nicco. "What did you leave for me in the coop?"

Nicco blew on his fingernails and polished them on the front of his red t-shirt. "Oh just a rattlesnake with a knife sticking out of his head."

"A what? Did you say a rattlesnake?" Ben turned toward Kate, looking her over for snake bites.

"Calm down, Ben, I'm fine. I saw the snake at my feet and Nicco threw his knife and killed it. It was all very simple really." She tried to brush off the whole incident.

Nicco chuckled and pointed toward Kate. "Yeah and your little spitfire here insisted on gathering the rest of the eggs."

Kate quickly fried all the eggs in her basket and they sat down to eat breakfast. "I asked Nicco if he would go with me into Junctionville today. I want to get a set of sheets for the other spare bedroom before Mac gets here. He said I had to ask your permission." Kate looked pointedly at Nicco.

"Well, I'm going to work on the fences in the south pasture so I don't see why you can't run to town with Nicco." Ben looked at Nicco with a warning in his eyes. "Don't let her out of your sight for a minute."

Chapter Eight

⁂

Nicco drove Kate to town around eleven o'clock. They'd decided to have lunch at Mabel's before driving back to the ranch. Nicco pulled up in front of the only department store in town and got out. He came around to Kate's door and opened it for her. Bowing as he did so. Kate looked at him and rolled her eyes. "Smart ass."

They went into Jefferson's department store and went directly to the linen section. Kate picked up several sets and turned to Nicco. "What's Mac's favorite color?"

Nicco seemed amused at her question. "Well, that would depend on what you're referring to. In clothes he always wears shades of blue. It makes the blue of his eyes stand out." Nicco looked down like he couldn't believe he just said that. "His apartment is done in shades of gray, black and white with red accents. His sheets at home are plain white." Nicco's face began to color slightly. "I'd go with a simple white, Kate."

Kate grinned and selected a set of white sheets with a crocheted lace edge. "Is there anything you need while we're here? Any special food you or Mac like?"

Rubbing his chin, Nicco thought over what Kate asked. "Well, I might like to stop by a liquor store and pick up a couple bottles of red wine. I'd like to go to the grocery store too. I thought I'd make Mac's favorite dinner for him. Lasagna with homemade garlic bread."

Kate had to bite her cheek to keep from giggling at the thoughtful gesture. This strong, silent warrior was so in love with his best friend it made Kate's heart soar. She wished she could talk to him about it, but she sensed it was a subject he

wouldn't welcome from anyone. Kate took her purchases over to the sales counter and set them down.

The sales clerk, Janie Cosgrove, had gone to school with Kate. "Hi, Janie. It's nice to see you again."

The clerk raised an eyebrow and rang up her purchase without even acknowledging her greeting. "That'll be thirty-eight dollars and forty-seven cents."

Kate looked at Nicco and shrugged. She gave Janie two twenties. "How have you been, Janie?" Kate tried once again to engage the old classmate in a conversation.

Janie gave Kate her change and put the sheets into a bag for her. When she handed Kate the bag she narrowed her eyes. "I don't care to engage in conversation with you, Kate. Now you've made your purchase is there anything else you need?"

Kate shook her head and took the bag. "No. I don't need anything else from you or this store." Kate walked out of the store fuming. When Nicco opened the car door for her she threw the bag inside and stood in front of him. "I'm too pissed off to ride, Nicco. Let's walk to the grocery store. We can stop at the liquor store on the way out of town."

Nicco nodded and closed the car door. He took off down the sidewalk at Kate's heels. "What was all that about anyway?"

Kate spun around and faced him. "I have absolutely no idea. I mean Janie and I were never friends in school but that was a long time ago. I've spoken to her here and there around town and in the store since I graduated and she's always been cordial to me. It's like I've done something to her and I don't even know what it is."

Nicco turned Kate back around and started walking. She followed but he could tell the clerk's behavior was really bothering her. They got to the grocery store and he held the door open for her. He grabbed a cart and went in search of the ingredients he'd need for Mac's dinner. Nicco noticed that everyone they passed in the small store seemed to look away or blatantly stare at Kate. He had a bad feeling he knew what was going on in Junctionville.

When they got to the checkout counter Kate once again tried to engage the older cashier in idle conversation. "Hi, Mrs. Campbell."

Nothing. The woman continued to ring up the groceries with a scowl on her face. Finally Nicco had enough. "Is there some kind of problem here?"

The older woman shot him a look that would kill most people. "I don't like trouble makers, that's all."

Nicco looked around him and behind him. "I'm sorry…Mrs. Campbell isn't it? I don't see any trouble makers in here. I see a hard-working woman trying to buy groceries from a grocery store and a rude cashier. What do you see?"

The cashier clucked her tongue at him and shook her head. "Everyone in this town knows Miss Crawford here is trying to sully the name of a good man just because he's spurned her advances."

Nicco started laughing, almost doubling over. He finally stopped laughing and wiped the tears from his eyes. "Oh you are a stupid one, aren't you?"

Kate pulled on his sleeve. "Let's just go, Nicco."

Nicco batted her hand away and brought his face closer to the old woman. "Listen up and listen good. Clint Adams is finally going to pay for terrorizing this young woman. He hurt her seven years ago and has been stalking her for the past year. If you don't believe me maybe you'll believe Judge Hathaway. He's the one who signed the temporary protection order against, and I repeat against, Clint Adams. Maybe you should get your facts straight before shooting off that mouth of yours."

Mrs. Campbell looked from Nicco to Kate. "That'll be sixty-three dollars and twenty-one cents."

Nicco looked at her and pulled Kate along. "Keep your groceries, lady. We'll get ours in Santa Fe until Kate gets an apology from you and this grocery store." Nicco was so furious he practically dragged Kate to the car.

Once they were seated and buckled in he turned to Kate. "I'm sorry about that. I know I probably overreacted but there's nothing I hate more than a town gossip. There was one on the base where I grew up and she made my life hell." Nicco tried to slow his heart rate. "Maybe I should go back in and apologize?"

Kate took Nicco's hand and grinned. "Absolutely not. I've waited twenty years to see that old woman get put in her place. I wouldn't have missed the last fifteen minutes for the world." She patted his hand. "Good job, Nicco."

They stopped off at the liquor store on their way out of town but Kate opted to stay in the car. "I'm afraid if I go in there with you we'll have to start driving all the way to Santa Fe for Ben's beer." She grinned and waved Nicco out the door.

* * * * *

Kate woke the next morning with the sun shining in her eyes. She stretched her sore muscles and looked at Ben. His face looked so peaceful. The morning light combined with the absolute perfection of his face reminded her of a painting she'd seen once. She ran her fingertips over the planes and angles of his face. Kate softly touched and outlined his lips, marveling at the definition. Kate's finger was suddenly devoured by the mouth beneath the lips.

Ben smiled around the finger in his mouth and sucked as Kate pulled the finger out and then thrust it back in the warm wet depths of Ben's mouth. She finally replaced her finger with her tongue. Tasting and sucking, Kate ate his mouth like a woman possessed.

Ben broke the kiss to catch his breath. "Good morning, Wildflower. I hope you slept well after our stretching exercises last night?"

Kate stretched again. "I slept wonderfully until the sun woke me up. I'm going to have to get you some new curtains."

Ben hugged Kate to his side once again and ran his hands down over her butt, stopping occasionally to squeeze her cheeks. "I don't usually have a problem with the sun. That damn rooster of yours wakes me up before the sun's high enough in the sky to come through the window." Ben finally registered what he'd just said. He quickly turned to Kate. "Why didn't the rooster wake us up?"

It finally dawned on Kate what he was saying. She sat up and pulled her shorts and yellow halter top on from the day before. "Something's wrong, Ben. Special K always wakes me up in the morning." She looked down at Ben who was still stretched out on the bed. "I'm going out to check on him."

Ben sat up and pulled his jeans on. He didn't bother with a shirt but grabbed a clean pair of socks and his boots. "Wait a minute and I'll go with you."

At Ben's slow progress in getting dressed Kate finally couldn't wait anymore. "I'm going out. Just come when you're dressed." She practically ran out the bedroom door.

Kate picked up the egg basket on the way out the kitchen door. She ran to the chicken coop and dropped the basket. The scene before her was too much to stomach and she ran for the side of the coop, dropped to her hands and knees and threw up. When she'd completely emptied her stomach two large arms wrapped around her middle and pulled her up. She turned in Ben's arms and buried her face in his chest.

She hung on to Ben as hard as her tired muscles could. "They're all dead. I've never seen anything like it, Ben. How can they all be dead and we didn't hear anything?"

Ben kissed the top of her head. "I don't know, Wildflower. My guess is more poison. I didn't see any blood so I don't think it was a coyote or other predator. It's like they just died where they stood. Have you found Special K?"

Kate shook her head. "To be honest I haven't really looked for him. I came out and saw the entire coop littered with my dead chickens and got sick." She headed toward the front of the chicken coop again. "My guess is he's dead too."

Ben noticed Kate turn even a paler shade of white than before as they rounded the coop. He was afraid Kate would faint so he steered her toward the kitchen. Taking her hand, he led her into the kitchen and sat her in a chair. "You sit there. I'll make some coffee and wake up Nicco."

When the coffee was ready and Nicco was sitting at the table Ben filled a cup and put it on the table in front of her. "I think you should run to the airport in Santa Fe with Nicco this morning while I call Cree and get the chickens cleaned up."

Kate took a sip of her coffee, rinsed it around in her mouth and placed the cup back on the table. She kept her hands wrapped tightly around the cup to keep them from shaking. "No, Ben. I need to help do this. It's part of ranching."

Ben exploded from his chair in a fit of anger. "What the hell part of ranching is some little fucker murdering your chickens? Kate, stop trying to be so strong. It's okay to let someone help once in a while." He got down on his knees and took her face in his hands. "It's okay to let me help you. Please, Kate. Let me help you." Ben stood up and went to the sink. He held onto the counter and put his head down. "I feel so useless. I've done nothing to protect you from the little fucker. The least I can do is spare you from this."

Kate got to her feet and ducked beneath his arms, putting her body between his and the counter. She ran her hands over his head, trying her best to calm him. "You mean more to me than any protection, Ben Thomas. Clint's sneaky. That's not your fault. How can you protect me against someone that conniving and sneaky? Clint's not man enough to come after *me* with you here. Isn't that the main objective? Keeping me safe? I may not have any animals left by the time he's through with me but I'll still have my life thanks to you."

Kate leaned in and kissed his lips softly just barely touching them. "I need to help you take care of the coop. I need it for me. If I run away even for a day Clint will have won. Does that make sense to you?"

Ben pulled her close and buried his face in her hair. "I love you, Wildflower, and I just want to take care of you."

Kate pulled back to look at his face. She grinned and kissed him a little deeper, aware that Nicco was still in the room. "That's the thing about wildflowers. They don't need a lot of pampering. They just need someone to watch them grow and enjoy the results."

Ben chuckled and slapped her butt. "Okay. I can see I'm not going to win this argument so I'll just shut up. You have to promise me though that you'll let me know if it gets too much for you. I won't have you throwing up again."

"Promise," Kate held her hand up in a Scout's honor gesture.

"Smart ass," Ben said and laughed. Ben turned toward Nicco. "So what do you suggest for breakfast since we're out of eggs?"

* * * * *

Nicco drove into Santa Fe after a breakfast of bacon and waffles. He still couldn't get over the amount of food Ben could consume. Kate must be doing something right because there still wasn't an ounce of fat on the man. He smiled and pulled into the airport parking lot. He sat in his car for a minute and watched the planes take off and land. Nicco realized his palms were sweating and wiped them on his jeans. He couldn't put a reason to it but he'd worn Mac's favorite pair of jeans, the old light blue ones with the rip in the knee and a small worn place on the back pocket. Nicco looked at himself in the mirror. His black hair was in dire need of a haircut.

He got out of the car and tucked his white polo shirt in again. Smoothing the shirt down his chest, he headed for the terminal. When he got inside he looked at the arrival screen and saw that Mac's flight was on time. Nicco looked at his watch. He had another thirty minutes before the flight came in. He looked around and spotted a bar. Nicco decided to get a glass of red wine while he waited. The bartender gave him his drink and he found a little table that looked out onto the tarmac. Sitting down, he let his eyes roam around the room. The room was filled with mostly couples and business men, a few of whom looked back.

Nicco shook his head slightly and took a drink of his wine. He was having a hard time figuring out why he felt such anticipation at Mac's arrival. They'd been apart before when he'd had to go out of town on business, so what was different now? He was afraid of the answer his heart was giving him. Seeing Kate and Ben together was having a direct effect on his willpower where Mac was concerned. Nicco had been fighting his attraction to Mac his entire life. He knew his feelings were wrong — it was not the way Colonel Bellinzoni raised him. Despite what everyone thought, he just wasn't attracted to anyone else, women or men. Nicco tried dating women when he was younger and then again when he got out of the Navy but the satisfaction he gained from sleeping with women wasn't worth witnessing the hurt in Mac's eyes.

Nicco took another drink and looked at his watch. Ten more minutes and Mac would be in New Mexico. He reminded himself to stop by the rental car agency and exchange vehicles. He thought a Jeep would be better if he and Mac had time to go into the mountains camping. Nicco sighed and rubbed his forehead. He wished he had the strength to defy his father and be with Mac, but the Colonel was the only family he had in the world. Nicco's mother left both of them when Nicco was barely two. The Colonel told him she'd died in a car accident when he was eight. Nicco was allowed to grieve for his mother for two hours. That was the time limit set by his father. He always told Nicco that tears were for girls and fags, neither of which had any business in his home. Nicco finished his wine and headed for the gate. He stood toward the back of the crowd gathered there.

Finally the passengers disembarked and one by one Nicco witnessed hugs of welcome and friendly pats on the back from the arriving passengers. He caught a flash of blue and a big white smile and held his hand in the air so Mac could see him. Mac looked damn good today. His shoulder-length deep brown hair was left loose for a change. His golden eyes shone like amber in the airport lighting and that one deep dimple in his right cheek that never failed to make Nicco smile was visible as usual.

Mac came right up to Nicco and gave him a hug. From anyone else's point of view it would have looked like a simple friendly hug between two good friends. Only the two of them knew it was something more. "I've missed you, Nicco." Mac let go and stepped back to look into his friend's dark brown eyes.

Nicco couldn't handle the honesty in Mac's words and he closed his eyes, his long black eyelashes fanning over his high cheekbones. He slowly opened his eyes to look into Mac's golden eyes. "I missed you too, Mac." Nicco turned toward the baggage claim area. "Let's get your bags and we can hit the road."

They started down the corridor and Nicco looked over at Mac and smiled. "I hope you remembered to bring the camping stuff."

Mac chuckled and slapped Nicco on the back. "When do I ever forget anything? Although I had to leave the sleeping bags at home. No way would they fit in my suitcase, but I did remember plenty of bug killer."

Nicco laughed, "Good. I'm so sweet those little buggers love me." Nicco took off so Mac's hand hit only air. Nicco laughed again and circled back around Mac. "Getting slow, old man."

Mac looked at Nicco with raised brows and shook his head. "Let's just get the bags, wise guy."

Forty minutes later after getting Mac's luggage and exchanging vehicles with the rental agency Mac and Nicco were on the road toward Junctionville.

Nicco had the radio on and the top off the Wrangler. He started singing to an old Bon Jovi song and Mac leaned in and turned the radio down. "Who are you and what have to done with my extremely serious and sober friend Nicco?"

Nicco turned the radio back up a little and smiled. "I don't know, Mac. I think that little spitfire Kate has rubbed off on me." As soon as he said it Nicco watched Mac's face fall. The uncertainty in his eyes almost killed him. Nicco reached across the stick shift and put his hand on Mac's thigh.

When Mac turned back to look at him Nicco winked. "No worries, Mac. The lady is very much spoken for. It's just her spirit that's made me different. The woman is only, like, five foot two and maybe a hundred and ten pounds, but she's not afraid of anything or anyone." Nicco continued to fill Mac in on all the events of the past few days. When he was finished he squeezed Mac's thigh. "Now do you understand what I mean by spitfire?"

Mac's hand came to rest on top of Nicco's and squeezed. He felt Nicco tense a little and let go. "I can't wait to meet her and your friend Ben."

Chapter Nine

&

That evening after a wonderful dinner of lasagna and garlic bread Nicco poured everyone an extra glass of wine. "What did Cree say about your chickens?"

Ben helped himself to his third giant piece of lasagna and looked from Kate to Nicco. "He took Special K with him to drop off at the vet. He's hoping the vet can determine exactly what kind of poison they ingested. In the meantime I wanted to talk to you about a little tail detail. Cree and I think it would be easier to follow Clint and catch him the act than to sit back and wait for the attack. I'm sorry, did I just say his name? I meant for you to follow the little fucker and catch him in the act."

Nodding his head, Nicco took another sip of wine. Everyone else at the table had finished eating quite a while ago. Ben, however, probably wouldn't stop until the pan was completely licked clean.

Ben reached for another piece of garlic bread. "I think Cree said he's been staying at his late father's house instead of in town in his apartment."

Nicco got up to take his plate to the sink. "Mac's going to start digging into Cli...the little fucker's past tomorrow." Nicco looked at Mac and smiled. "He's damn good at that. If there's something to find he'll find it." Nicco put a couple of apples and bottles of water in a bag. "I'll catch up with you guys in the morning. Maybe I'll even bring home donuts, Ben."

After Nicco left, Kate and Mac started clearing the table. Ben rolled his eyes. "I guess this means I'm done." Kate leaned down and kissed him. "I'll let you two do the dishes. I need to take some hay to the cattle in the south pasture. I meant to do it earlier."

Kate washed and Mac dried. Handing him a plate, Kate couldn't help asking Mac about Nicco. "Why aren't you and Nicco together? I mean as a couple. It's clear he's in love with you. So why aren't you both together?"

Mac took the plate and began to dry it. "The Colonel wouldn't approve."

Kate's eyebrows drew together. "The Colonel?"

Mac nodded, "The Colonel is Nicco's father. He's the biggest homophobe you'd ever meet. He heard a rumor from a woman on the base once that Nicco was gay and the Colonel beat Nicco so badly he was out of school for a week. That's what prompted Nicco to join the Navy instead of the Marines. Something happened to Nicco though. It was when he was overseas with his Seal team. When Nicco got out of the Navy he was obsessed with making it up to the Colonel. Everything Nicco does now he asks himself first 'would the Colonel approve?' If not Nicco doesn't do it."

Kate wiped the counter and table off and then refilled her glass of wine. "Even though he loves you he won't do anything about it because his father wouldn't approve?"

Mac nodded and sat down beside Kate. "Exactly. I've been in love with Nicco since we were teenagers and I think he's been in love with me just as long, but that's it. He won't do anything about his feelings because he's afraid he'll lose his father. I don't understand it but I know what it's like to lose a father. Just because he'll lose his for a reason other than death doesn't make it any less painful. In the meantime I take what I can get from him. I'll never love anyone but him. Maybe someday things will be different but for now at least I have part of him."

Kate patted the top of Mac's hand. "You're a good man, Charlie Brown." She winked and got up from the table. "What would you say to a friendly game of poker?"

"I'd say it better not be strip poker," Ben said from the doorway. When he saw that narrow-eyed look Kate gave him that meant he'd been rude he laughed and winked. "Unless I'm invited of course."

Kate shook her head and led the men to the living room game table. She dug the cards and chips out of the cupboard and set them on the table. "Ben, you can play for clothes if you'd like, but Mac and I are playing with chips."

* * * * *

Mac was making coffee the next morning when Nicco walked through the door. Mac could see his friend was dead tired. "Morning, Nicco. Did you find out anything?"

Nicco stretched and yawned. He reached for a coffee cup and replaced the half full pot with his cup. He waited while the electric coffee maker slowly filled his cup and then replaced it with the pot once again. Nicco sat down at the kitchen table coffee cup in hand. He took a big drink and closed his eyes. "I saw enough to know the little fucker is up to something else. I followed him to Judge Hathaway's house and took a few pictures of him taking pictures of Judge Hathaway through the window. After he left I snuck up to the window to see what the little fucker was taking pictures of and about lost my eyesight." Nicco stopped to yawn again and take another drink of coffee. "It seems the esteemed judge likes to dress up in women's clothing and get spanked by a guy who looks like he belongs in a motorcycle gang."

Nicco got up and pointed to the camera. "Give that to Cree. I've got a feeling the little fucker is going to try to blackmail the judge." Nicco squeezed Mac's shoulder on the way toward the door. "I'm going to bed. Wake me if you need me."

Mac ate a quick breakfast of toast and jelly and took off in the Jeep. He decided he'd start at the local newspaper office and go from there. He also wanted to check out Bruce Adams, the little fucker's deceased father, to see if he could find anything that would explain Clint's behavior toward Kate.

Kate woke with a smooth shiny head between her legs. Ben's tongue was lapping up her morning juices like they were milk. He ran his tongue from hole to hole, paying special attention to her anus. Kate tensed when she realized where his tongue was.

Ben sensed her fear and lifted his head to smile at her. "Morning, darlin'. I hope you don't mind but I started without you." He licked her anus again. "I know your feelings on this part of your anatomy but I want to help you get beyond your fears. This little rosebud is a very erotic pleasure point. You're denying yourself a great deal of satisfaction because of the events of seven years ago and I aim to change your mind."

Kate shifted uncomfortably. "I don't know, Ben. I know my problem is more mental than physical but it just makes me feel dirty somehow. No, that's not true. I know why it makes me feel dirty. Clint...um...the little fucker told me that whores took it in the ass. Which is why he fucked me there." Kate chewed her bottom lip and looked at him for understanding.

Ben closed his eyes and crawled up beside her. He ran his hand down the side of her face and kissed her. "Oh darlin', I'm so sorry he did and said those things to you but he was wrong. I hate to say this but I've been with a few whores in my time and you're far from being a whore. You're a one-man woman and you're mine." Ben ran his hand down her back until his fingertip rimmed her anus once more. "This is mine too. Let me ask you something. Do you think Jenny is a whore?"

Kate looked shocked at his question. "No of course not. Jenny is one of the sweetest women I've ever met. Why would you ask me a question like that?"

Ben sighed and continued to rim her asshole. "I happen to know that Jenny gets fucked in the ass almost daily. Does that make her a bad person?"

Kate closed her eyes and shook her head. "I understand what you're telling me, Ben, and I know you're right. Please give me a little time to think about it."

Ben kissed her again and slid his finger toward her clit. He flicked the piercing and Kate moaned. "I think I can think of one or two other things to explore during the meantime." He devoured her mouth in a voracious kiss. As he kissed her he slid three fingers into her warm wet channel. Ben pumped his fingers in and out of her while he feasted on her nipples. Pulling and sucking them into his eager mouth.

Kate arched her back and reached for his cock. She wrapped both hands around him and began stroking the solid hard length of his manhood. Her pussy began to quiver and her breathing became unsteady as the first of many orgasms consumed her. She pulled Ben's cock, aiming it for her pussy. "Fuck me, Ben."

Ben levered himself over her and plunged his shaft into her warm pussy. He gave her a moment to become accustomed to his size and then began a steady rhythm in and out of her welcoming channel. Kate moved her legs to his shoulders and thrust upward. "Harder. Fuck me harder, Ben."

Ben smiled and began a more vigorous rhythm. He couldn't believe Kate could take his full length after just a few days of fucking. Her sexual appetite matched his in almost every way but he still hadn't talk to her about his kink for strange places. Ben liked sex whenever and wherever he felt like it. He had decided originally he'd forget that side of his sexuality but he was beginning to think he wouldn't have to.

He continued to pound his cock deep and hard into Kate. She tightened around him and he could feel another orgasm explode from within her, setting off his own. Ben buried his cock as deeply as it would go and pumped his seed into her womb. The thought of her pregnant with his child nearly made him hard again. He collapsed and rolled to the side, taking her with him.

"I love you, Ben," Kate said, scratching his head softly with her fingernails. She kissed the hollow of his throat and followed it with a lick up the side of his face. "I love your cock too."

Ben smoothed the hair away from her sweat-dampened face. He followed the slope of her nose with his finger and outlined her lips. "I need to talk to you, Wildflower. I'm not really sure how to broach this subject so I'm just going to come out with it. You already know how much I like sex but what I've been holding back on you is my dominant side." He held his hand up to stop her from objecting. "I'm not saying anything about ropes or spankings. I'm talking about the fact that I like sex on demand. If I come into the barn and see you and get hard I'd like for you to blow me or let me fuck you then and there." He looked into Kate's face, unable to read her expression. "Am I scaring you, Wildflower? Because I don't mean to. If you're uncomfortable with this side of my sexuality I can try to control it."

Kate shook her head and reached for his hand. She brought it to her lips and kissed his palm. "Unless we're in a room full of people I think I can live with that side of you. It might take me by surprise the first couple of times but who knows? It could become my new obsession."

Ben parted her lips with his tongue and kissed her deeply. "Damn, woman. You are so perfect for me, darlin'. This is not how I wanted to do this but..." Ben got to his knees and pulled Kate up to her knees. "Kate... I love you more than anything in the world. I want you beside me in work and in bed. Would you do me the great honor of becoming my wife?"

Kate took a deep breath. "If you're asking me to marry you the answer is absolutely yes. Besides we've had quite a bit of unprotected sex lately and I imagine eventually there will be a little—God I hope it's little—Ben Jr. born."

Ben stilled, suddenly a spark lit up his eyes. "You think, Kate? You think you might be pregnant?"

Kate giggled and shrugged. "I didn't say that, Ben. I'm just saying that the sooner we get married the better." She threw her arms around his neck and kissed him.

"Well...well, we need to get married right away then. How soon can you put a wedding together? I'll have to call 'The Team' and see if they can all come. Oh and I can ask Nicco to be my best man and you could have Jenny as your matron of honor."

Kate started laughing so hard she fell back onto the bed. "I've never seen a man so excited about getting married. If you weren't such a man's man I'd say you were giddy."

Ben stuck out his lips in a mock pout. "I am not acting giddy. Just happy. I've never really had a family. I feel like all my dreams from my childhood are finally coming true, that's all. So when can we have a wedding?"

"Well, I've already got the dress. I thought I'd wear my mother's and I already know it fits. I'm ashamed to say I tried it on a couple days ago. I'd say we can do it as soon as we can get a minister and your friends out to the ranch. I don't have anyone to invite that you're not already inviting so I'd guess just grilled steaks for the food and a keg of beer. I could even run into Santa Fe and get a ready made wedding cake."

Ben shook his head and held her face. "I want this to be special for you, Kate. Don't rush yourself on my account."

Kate smiled and shook her head, placing her hands on top of his. "I've never been one of those girls to dream about a big fancy wedding. I'll be happy with a few friends and good food and of course the man I love."

Ben bent his head and kissed her ring finger. "What kind of wedding ring do you want, Wildflower? Because it could take some time if we have to special order it."

Kate kissed him back. "My mom always said she could spot a woman who married for love easily. She would be the woman with the simple gold wedding band. I'm marrying you for love, Ben. Not for the diamond. I'd like a simple gold band, which you can pick up in almost any department store in Santa Fe."

Ben was practically vibrating he was so excited. "If we can get the license and the guys here by Sunday is that too soon?"

"That sounds perfect, Mr. Thomas. In the meantime I've got a lot of work to get done. So let me go and come take a shower with me." She pulled herself from Ben's arms and ran for the bathroom.

* * * * *

When Ben and Kate made it into the kitchen they found a note from Mac and a roll of film. Ben picked it up and read the note describing what Nicco had told Mac about the little fucker's activities the previous night. Ben showed the note to Kate and got a cup of coffee. "I think I'll go on over to Cree's and give this to him and invite them to the wedding. Would you like to go?"

Kate took a drink of coffee and started pulling sandwich fixings out of the fridge. "Sounds good to me. Would you like a BLT for breakfast?"

Smiling, Ben reached out and pinched Kate's nose. "I think I'd like about four of them, thank you."

Kate laughed and started frying the bacon. "In that case you can slice the tomatoes. You know we might think about adding a few pigs to the ranch. Otherwise we may go broke buying bacon."

"No. I hate pigs. They'll stink up the whole ranch. I'd rather just find a pig farmer and trade a butchered steer for a big butchered pig." Ben took his coffee and sat at the table watching Kate fry the bacon.

He noticed the short shorts she was wearing looked like she'd had them since she was a teenager. Kate had another halter top on, this one in pink. He loved the way the top bared her sun-bronzed shoulders to his view. Ben's cock started to thicken in the leg of his jeans. He rubbed his cock through the material. Noticing a wet spot had formed in his jeans, he unzipped his pants and pulled the painful erection out into his fist. He began stroking himself and watching Kate's beautiful ass as she cooked the bacon.

Kate noticed Ben wasn't cutting up the tomatoes and turned around to scold him. "Hey, why aren't you..." She saw the look in his eyes first, needy and wanting she could tell. Kate lowered her gaze to the huge erection Ben was pumping under the table. She licked her lips and took the bacon out of the frying pan.

When Kate walked toward him in that sexy way of hers he turned his chair and spread his thighs. "Someone needs a little attention before breakfast. I want you to suck it. I want to come down your throat, darlin'." He pumped his cock a few more times as Kate lowered herself to her knees between his legs.

Without a word Kate reached out and put both hands around the steel pole in front of her. She lowered her head and swiped her tongue across the head of Ben's cock as she continued her two-fisted assault on his erection. Kate enveloped as much of his length as she could into her waiting throat.

Ben began thrusting upward. His hands wrapped themselves in her long blonde curls and he began moaning. "Ah...that's it, Wildflower...suck that cock." He reached behind her neck and released the tie of her halter top. The ties fell and so did her top. Huge boobs came spilling out into his hands. "I love your breasts. They fit my big hands perfectly."

Kate continued licking and sucking Ben's cock but moved one hand down to his sac. She began kneading it. It felt so good to her she wanted to taste it. She pulled her mouth off the head with a pop and ran her tongue down the heavily veined length of his cock. When she reached the base she held Ben's cock against his abdomen and licked his scrotum.

Ben shook and thrust up into her face. "Oh hell yes. Suck 'em deep into your hot little mouth, darlin'."

Ben's balls were too big to get both of them in her mouth so one at a time she licked and sucked the testicles into her mouth. Kate's fingers wandered even farther back and rimmed his asshole. Kate held her hand toward Ben's face without even taking her mouth off the sac in front of her.

Ben licked her fingers thoroughly, knowing exactly what she had in mind. He released her fingers and slid even farther down in the kitchen chair. He spread his thighs wider and presented her with the sensitive pucker of his ass. "Do it, Wildflower. Fuck my ass."

The heated pleas from Ben were taking Kate's level of arousal by storm. She took her fingers and one by one slipped them into his tight hole. When she had three fingers inside him she began to move them in and out.

Ben started moaning and groaning thrusting his hips upward. "Suck my cock, darlin'. I'm gonna come."

Kate moved her mouth back to his cock and swallowed him as far as she could and sucked as hard as she could, all the while slamming her fingers in and out of his ass.

Ben cried out her name and came down her throat. Thick, long bursts of seed saturated her throat and mouth with a musky flavor that she knew she was becoming addicted to. Kate licked him clean and pulled out of his hole.

Ben reached down for her and drew her up onto his lap. "That was hot, darlin'. I could get used to this new arrangement we have." He unbuttoned her shorts and slid his hand to her pussy. "Damn, Wildflower, I thought you were in need of some good strong finger fucking but your pussy is already soaked. Did getting me off get you off too, darlin'?"

Kate licked the side of his face. "I came long before you did. You were right, that was hot." She kissed him passionately and got off his lap, buttoning her pants on her way to the sink. She washed her hands, got out a clean dishrag and ran it under the hot water. She handed the rag to Ben and turned back to the stove. Kate turned the burner back on and heated the grease, adding the bacon back to the skillet when it was hot enough. She looked over her shoulder at Ben. "Time to cut the tomatoes, stud."

Ben chuckled and stuffed his now soft cock back down into the leg of his jeans. He took the dishrag he'd used to clean himself up and tossed it into the laundry room.

Kate smiled at him as he strolled back into the kitchen. "Do you want to go to Santa Fe after we drop this film by Cree's? I thought we could get the rings and order the cake at the same time."

Ben went to the counter and started cutting the tomatoes. He stopped cutting and looked over at Kate. "Why don't you want to get the cake and the rings in Junctionville?"

Kate busied herself getting down a couple of paper plates. No sense washing dishes this morning. She remembered she'd never told Ben about her confrontations in town a couple days ago. She turned to him and cleared her throat. "Um…let's just say the people in the grocery store and department store like to talk too much about things they don't understand."

Ben strode toward her and wrapped his arms around her waist. "What happened, Kate? Was it the day Nicco took you to town?"

She managed a smile, remembering how Nicco had taken care of the busybody in the grocery store. "Yes Nicco was with me." Kate went on to explain everything that had transpired.

When she was finished Ben took her face in his hands and kissed her. "I understand why you'd want to shop elsewhere but Junctionville is your hometown. You can't let the little fucker run you away. I say the two of us go into town after we leave the Triple Spur and put all these rumors to rest. Stand up to those who believe the lies he's spreading about you. Our children will be raised in this town, Kate. We owe it to them to nip this thing in the bud now." He tenderly kissed her closed eyes and then her lips.

Kate nodded her head, never opening her eyes. "You're right, this is my hometown. It's time I stopped feeling ashamed for what Cl… the little fucker did to me seven years ago and hold my head high in town." She looked at the bacon that was now fried to a crisp. "I hope you like your bacon well done."

Ben chuckled and looked at the black strips of bacon. "Well, maybe I'll just have a couple of sliced tomatoes on toast. We can stop in at Mabel's and have an early lunch."

Chapter Ten

ഔ

After doing the morning chores, Kate and Ben pulled up in front of the Triple Spur ranch house. Kate looked dreamily at the beautiful log and stone house. "I love this house. Cree did such a beautiful job designing it, don't you think?"

Ben opened her door for her and grabbed her hand. "Yeah, Cree's talented. This house is big while still feeling homey. There's a trick to that you know. I've lived in enough mansions to know that big usually feels cold."

Kate was surprised by his statement. "You grew up living in mansions? I just realized I don't know anything about your childhood or your family. How can that be, Ben, when I feel as though I've known you my entire life?"

Ben shrugged and started walking toward the porch. "Not much to tell really. My mom moved from husband to husband. Getting all she could from one before moving on to greener pastures. I never knew my real father and none of the men my mom married were interested in having a stepson so I learned to rely on myself. I think I was always the burden my mom begrudgingly put up with." Ben shook his head, releasing the thoughts that threatened his newfound happiness. "None of that matters now because I have you. You and the children we'll have will become my family."

Kate squeezed Ben's hand. She felt sorry for the lonely unloved little boy she could see just under the surface of Ben's strong face. "We'll give you so much love you'll feel like you're smothering." Kate grinned and gave him a quick wink. "Papa Ben."

"Thank you," Ben said and climbed the steps of the porch. He looked at Kate one more time before knocking. "That's all I ever hoped for." Ben knocked on the door and looked over to smile at Blue lounging in Cree's favorite padded wicker sofa.

The door opened and Jenny smiled and threw her arms around Kate. "I'm so glad to see you two. Come in, the boys are in the kitchen eating breakfast."

Jenny walked them into the kitchen but when they got there they found Jake on his knees giving Cree a morning blowjob.

Ben looked from them to Jenny and laughed. "I can see they're having the same thing for breakfast I did. Let's step back out and let them finish."

Jenny put her hands on her hips and stomped her foot. "Hey, guys, you've got two minutes to finish then we're coming back in."

Cree snapped his head in their direction and smiled. "Oh it's not gonna take that long, baby."

The three of them went back around the corner to Cree's moans of pleasure. Jenny rolled her eyes. "Sorry about that. Neither one of them can seem to get enough sex lately."

Kate smiled and winked at Jenny. "It must be something in the air."

Cree called for them to come back into the kitchen. When they arrived Jake was sitting with a smile on his face and a coffee cup in his hand. "Sorry, guys, we got a little carried away."

Ben grinned and patted Kate's ass. "I totally understand, Cree. The reason we stopped by was to give you this roll of film Nicco shot last night of the little fucker. It seems he was taking pictures of Judge Hathaway in a dress being disciplined by a big biker dude. I don't know if Nicco got any pictures of the judge but he did get pictures of the little fucker with his camera pointed in the judge's house. Nicco and Mac think he's planning some kind of blackmail."

Cree whistled and looked at the roll of film. "Do you have any idea how embarrassing it's going to be for me to tell the judge about this?"

Ben spread his hands out in front of him. "Sorry, Cree, I'm just the delivery man." He smiled and pulled Kate tighter in his arms. "We also wanted to stop in and invite the three of you to our wedding this Sunday. That is if we can get a license and a minister by then."

Cree, Jake and Jenny all got up and came over to congratulate the pair. Jenny kissed Ben's cheek and then pulled Kate into her arms in a hug. "I'm so happy for you both." Jenny's belly began kicking Kate's stomach and the two women laughed. "Even the babies are excited and happy for you."

They all sat down at the table and talked about what would need to be done by Sunday. Kate reached out and took Jenny's hand. "I was hoping you would be my matron of honor."

Jenny looked down at her ever growing stomach. "I'd definitely have to make a trip into town to get a dress. The only thing I've been able to fit into are Jake's jogging shorts and t-shirts but I'd be very honored to stand up with you, Kate."

Ben turned to Cree. "We're on our way into town now to pick out a cake and get the rings. How about if we all go and have lunch at Mabel's afterward? I was also hoping to get to the courthouse to apply for a marriage license."

Cree clapped him on the shoulder. "Sounds good to me. What about you, Jake? Can the ranch stand to be without you for a couple of hours?"

Jake nodded. "Only if I get a big piece of pie at Mabel's."

They all loaded into Jenny's minivan and headed toward Junctionville. Ben called Nicco and Mac and they both agreed to meet them for lunch. They pulled up to Jefferson's department store and Kate began to get nervous. She squeezed

Ben's hand and closed her eyes for a minute gathering her strength.

Ben squeezed back and kissed her forehead. "Are you okay with this, darlin', because if it's going to upset you we can always go to Santa Fe?"

"No I'm fine. I was just building up my courage." Kate followed Jenny into the store. Jake went with Jenny to try on dresses while Cree ran down to the drugstore to have the roll of film developed. Ben tugged Kate to the jewelry counter. Kate looked into the display case and saw what she wanted right away. She tapped on the glass counter. "That's the one I want, Ben." It was a thin gold band with filigree etched into the surface. A matching man's ring sat next to it in the white velvet box.

Ben smiled and looked for a sales clerk. When he came back with Janie in tow Kate held her breath. Ben pointed at the set of rings in the case, "We'd like to buy this set of wedding bands please."

Janie, who still hadn't acknowledged Kate's presence, looked at Ben. "Wouldn't you like to see engagement rings also, sir? Most women would prefer a diamond or is that too much money? I heard the Crawford ranch was about to go belly up."

A red flush appeared on Ben's high cheekbones. "Could you get the manager for me please?"

Janie squirmed in her apparently expensive high-heeled shoes. "I'm sorry, sir, there's really no reason to bring the manager into this. I apologize if I've embarrassed you. Now which set was it that you wanted to see?"

Ben put his hands on the glass counter and leaned down until he was nose to nose with Janie. "What I want to see is the manager and I'd suggest you shut your ill-mannered mouth and go fetch him or her. Unless you'd like me to make a scene and call you all the names you truly are?"

Jake and Jenny came up while Ben was nose to nose with Janie. Jenny elbowed Kate in the side and pointed toward the scene. "What the hell is that all about?"

Kate cleared her throat. "Janie suggested that Ben was too poor to purchase me a diamond engagement ring instead of the gold bands I picked out. Seems word around town is that the Crawford ranch is about to go belly up."

Jake started laughing. "I'll go find the manager." He left and came back a few minutes later with a very nervous Mr. Kline, a short middle-aged bald man wearing a very bad toupee.

Mr. Kline stepped behind the counter beside Janie. "What seems to be the problem here?"

Ben looked at the short little man and pointed toward Janie. "Twice this week this young lady has insulted either myself or my fiancée. Today she had the audacity to suggest that I was too poor to buy a proper engagement ring for Kate. Obviously she has absolutely no idea what the hell she's talking about. I've got enough money in my bank account to not only buy this entire store but the entire town." Ben took a calming breath as the manager's brow began to sweat. "I want this employee fired or I will talk to the owner of this department store myself."

Jake rolled his eyes and waited for the manager's reply. *Cree had always said he thought Ben had a secret, now I guess we know what it is. Ben must be rich. Damn, who would have thought it? He sure doesn't act like a rich man.*

The now sweating manager turned toward Janie. "You're fired. Clean out your locker. You can collect your final check at the end of the day." He turned his back on Janie and looked at Ben. "I'm terribly sorry for any inconvenience, sir. What can I help you with?"

Ben looked at Kate and she nodded. "We'd like to buy this set of rings. I'll pay extra to have them sized by Saturday."

Mr. Kline took the small box from under the counter and handed it to Ben. "I'll have to get your finger measurements."

Kate held out her hand and slipped the band onto her ring finger. It was only about a size and a half too big but Ben's ring would barely fit on the tip of his pinky finger.

The manager looked at the size of Ben's finger. "My my, you have large fingers. I'm not sure that we can size this ring up to that extent and still retain the filigree design."

Ben shrugged his shoulders. "Do what you have to do. If you need to special order one that's fine, I'll pay whatever it costs to get it here by Sunday noon."

Mr. Kline wiped his forehead and nodded. "I'll do my very best, sir."

Ben paid for the rings and the four friends left the store, heading toward the bakery located in the back of the grocery store. Kate prayed that Mrs. Campbell wasn't working today. Janie losing her job was one thing but Kate knew that even though Mrs. Campbell was a busybody she needed her job to supplement her Social Security. She put a restraining hand on Ben's arm. "Please go easy on Mrs. Campbell."

Ben winked at her. "I'm always easy, Wildflower."

They managed to order a simple two-tiered round cake with what she hoped would look like wildflowers draped over ivory icing. Kate felt almost giddy by the time they entered Mabel's to meet Nicco, Mac and Cree for lunch.

The waitress showed them to a big round table in the back corner of the café. Kate sat between Jenny and Ben with Mac across from her. Nicco of course took the chair next to Mac and beside him sat Jake. Cree came in a little later and sat beside Jenny.

Cree looked at Nicco and nodded. "Good work with the surveillance, Nicco. I've had the pictures developed and have a meeting with Judge Hathaway this afternoon." He leaned over and kissed Jenny and then leaned over the table to give Jake a deep kiss.

Nicco looked from Jake to Cree. "Don't you two feel a little odd doing that stuff in public?"

Cree looked at him like he was crazy. "What? Showing affection to the two people I love most? Absolutely not. For the most part this is a very liberated town. Junctionville used to be somewhat of an artist commune back in the late sixties and early seventies. Everyone who lives here knows I'm married to Jenny and Jake. To hide my love would be a shame."

Kate looked down at her lap when Nicco suddenly looked very uncomfortable with the conversation. She saw Mac reach under the table and apparently offer comfort to Nicco because he looked up and smiled at him. They ordered their entrees and drinks and Jake began telling the department store story.

Nicco nodded his head. "Good for you, Ben. That little uppity bitch had it coming for the way she treated Kate on Tuesday. I wish I could have been there to impart my own choice words to her manager."

Their food came and the group began discussing plans for the wedding. Ben told them he still needed to call Remy and Gabe to see if they could make it to town by Sunday.

Jake nodded and pushed his plate away, rubbing his nonexistent belly. "I haven't spoken to either one of them in a week or so but I'm sure they'll do everything possible to make it. Although they'll both be shocked as hell that you finally found a woman who could stand you for more than a night, I'm sure they'll love Kate." He winked at Kate and looked at the pie selection on the menu.

They finished their lunch and all fought over the tab. Finally Jake chuckled and handed the bill to Ben. "Word is you can afford to take your buddies out for lunch. Speaking of which, why didn't you ever tell us you were loaded?"

Ben shifted in his chair looking a little sheepish. "I've never really thought of the money as mine. My mother sold her soul time and time again to acquire those millions of dollars. I guess I always thought of it as dirty money but maybe I should find something worthwhile to do with it. It's just been sitting in the bank since her death."

The group nodded. Understanding a little more of what made Ben tick. Kate squeezed his thigh in a show of support. Ben reached down and held her hand on top of his thigh. "Well, if everyone's done I've got some chores to get done at home. Kate, are you going to help me bale that alfalfa this afternoon?"

"Sure, if Mac or Nicco wants to cook dinner?" She looked at the two men with raised eyebrows and a smile.

Mac smiled, showing his deep dimple. "I'm sure we can rustle up something together but first I'm going over to the courthouse to look at the public record of Bruce Adams' will. I think there might be something fishy there. I noticed that the little fucker is his only living relative so it started me wondering why he isn't in possession of the Adams estate and holdings. That's the reason we stopped by the Triple Spur and picked up Ben's truck. I didn't figure you all would feel like waiting on me to dig around in a dark basement."

That reminded Kate of something. "Oh my God, Ben, I can't believe we almost forgot to get the marriage license." Kate got up from the table and started dragging Ben toward the front door.

Ben laughed at his overexcited fiancée. "Okay, Wildflower, I'm coming. You don't have to pull my arm out of its socket."

Cree stood up with the rest of the group. He kissed Jenny and Jake and told them he'd see them after he talked to Judge Hathaway. He looked over at Mac. "Come on, Mac, I'll walk over to the courthouse with ya."

Mac nodded and turned to Nicco. "Why don't you go by the grocery store and pick up something for us to cook tonight. I was thinking something simple like steak and salad."

Nicco slapped him on the back. "Okay, see you later." He turned toward Jenny and Jake. "What are you two going to do while you wait for Ben and Kate? If you want you can run to the grocery store with me then I'll drop you back by the Triple Spur on my way to Ben's."

Jake looked at Jenny and nodded. "That's sounds great, just let me call Cree and let him know."

* * * * *

As Kate and Ben were exiting the courthouse Kate stopped short, causing Ben to run into the back of her. Luckily his reflexes were quick and he grabbed her around the middle before she tumbled down the stairs. He started to ask what was wrong when he saw the direction of her gaze. Clint was standing across the street just staring at them. Ben started down the steps toward him until Kate grabbed his shirt.

"No, Ben. He can't do anything to us and he knows that. Let the protection order do its job."

Ben looked at Kate and then back to the little fucker. "I hate him, Kate. Let him try to say one word to you and his ass is mine. Fuck the law."

Kate steered him toward the bench beside the courthouse where they were to meet up with Cree. Kate sat Ben down and sat on his lap. Ben wasn't sure if she was just being overly friendly or if she was trying to keep him from going after Clint. Ben decided with her ass resting on his cock he didn't much care what the reason was, just that it felt damn good. "You little vixen. You know I won't fuck you in public. Is this your way of torturing me?"

Kate gave her ass a little wiggle. She looked around and didn't see anyone, so she wiggled again and Ben groaned. She giggled and kissed him. "After we drop Cree off maybe I can help you with the little problem you seem to be having with the fit of your jeans."

Ben smacked her ass. "There's nothing little about my problem. That's the problem. I'm going to give Cree quite a show." No sooner had he said it than Cree strolled around the side of the building to where they sat.

He took in the scene before him and smiled. "Ready to go I gather?"

Ben lifted Kate off his lap and stood. Cree took in the front of his jeans and swore. "God damn, Ben. How do you manage to lug that thing around all day?" Cree laughed and headed toward the minivan parked in front of the department store. "Jenny and Jake got a ride with Nicco, and Mac has his own vehicle so we're set to go."

Ben waited until they got in the van before asking the question that was on everyone's mind. "So tell me what Judge Hathaway had to say?"

Cree shook his head and sighed. "Well, he was more than a little embarrassed I can tell you that. At least he knows about Jake and me, so he felt a little more comfortable with me talking to him than if I'd sent someone else. He told me to keep the pictures and he'd wait to see if the little fucker did indeed try to blackmail him. I honestly think he's hoping he will. Then we'll have even more to put him away for."

They drove in silence for a few minutes. "The little fucker was standing outside the courthouse across the street when we came out. He gives me the creeps, Cree. I can't help but think he's planning something."

* * * * *

That night at dinner Mac filled everyone in on what he'd discovered at the courthouse. "Bruce Adams' will had to go through probate so there's a public record of it at the courthouse and you won't believe what I found. Everything he owns goes to Clint, even a presidency position at the bank, with one stipulation."

Mac looked at Kate. "Clint Adams can't get his hands on any of it until he runs Kate Crawford out of Junctionville and off the Crawford ranch. It seems you threw a challenge in Bruce's face seven years ago and he wasn't too happy about it. I'm not sure if that's the only reason behind it but it's the only one listed."

Ben slapped his forehead while Kate sat open-mouthed. "Damn. Kate, didn't all your problems begin after his death? That little fucker has been trying to get rid of you for the past year. He didn't step up his game until I showed up and bought half the ranch." Ben looked over at Mac. "Did you talk to Cree about the stipulation in the will?"

Mac swallowed a drink of wine. "Yeah he said for me to make copies of the will and for Kate to present them to the judge during her protection hearing on Tuesday."

Kate nodded. "Then that's exactly what I'll do. I can't wait to see his face when he finds out we're on to him."

Chapter Eleven

ഇ

Sunday morning Kate woke up alone in her own bed. She hadn't slept well the night before. She had become so used to Ben's strong arms wrapped around her that she had felt cold and alone all night. Kate had no one to blame but herself she knew it but it didn't make her sleep any better. She had been the one to insist on separate beds the night before the wedding.

Kate sat up and stretched her arms over her head. It finally dawned on her what had awakened her. She heard it again. "A rooster," she said aloud, "but I don't have a rooster anymore." Kate jumped out of bed and threw her robe on and rushed out the bedroom door and down the steps. She flew through the kitchen door to find Ben, Nicco and Mac unloading crates of chickens into the coop.

Kate covered her mouth and tears began to trickle down her cheeks. "What have you done, you big wonderful man?"

Ben looked up, surprised to find her. "You're not supposed to see this. It's my surprise wedding gift to you."

Kate put her hands on her hips and shook her head. "It's kinda hard not to find out there are chickens in the yard when your rooster woke me up." She giggled and went over to the coop. There must have been thirty chickens already let loose in the small coop. "How many did you buy, Ben?"

Ben carried another crate over to the coop and let the hens loose. "Fifty. I figured I eat so many eggs fifty was a good number."

Kate rolled her eyes. "Ben, there's no way we can eat the eggs of fifty chickens. I love the gesture, really I do, but maybe you should see if Jake needs a few. The most we should really keep are twenty-five and that's if we hurry and start having big boys like their daddy. Beside there's no way the coop is big enough for fifty."

Ben looked a little sheepish. "I'm sorry, Wildflower. I just wanted to give back twofold what the little fucker took away from you."

Kate walked over to Ben and put her arms around his waist. She hugged his body to hers, burying her face in his chest. "God I love you. This is the sweetest thing anyone's ever done for me but it's just too many chickens. Unless you want to eat half of them. In which case you'll have to do the killing."

Ben turned toward Nicco and Mac still unloading crates. "That's all, guys. We'll have to see if Jake wants the rest of them. If not Jake maybe Gabe would be interested. He's supposed to be here with Cotton and that plant dude anytime."

* * * * *

Kate was just getting her makeup on when Jenny rushed through the bedroom door. "Sorry I'm late, Kate. The guys needed a little TLC this morning." She stopped and covered her mouth giggling. "Actually they needed a lot of TLC but it's better than the alternative, isn't it?"

Going to her friend for a hug, Kate rubbed the growing protrusion of Jenny's belly. "You'd better enjoy it while you can." She turned back to the makeup mirror. "I'm really almost ready. I've just got to finish my makeup and put Mom's dress on."

Jenny looked at the ivory lace gown hanging on the door. "Oh Kate, it's beautiful." She touched the delicate lace sleeves and high neck of the gown. "Is there anything else I can do for you or get for you?"

"Ben was in charge of my bouquet. Could you do me a favor and see if he got it and if his ring has been delivered yet?" Kate started putting her hair up in a loose bun, allowing small curly blonde tendrils to escape around her face and neck.

Jenny waved on her way out the door. "I'm on it."

Kate smiled and walked over to the hanging dress. She took the dress off the hanger and stepped into it. She turned to look at herself in the mirror. "Oh Mom, I wish you could see me today. I wish Daddy could walk me down the aisle the way he was supposed to. I'm marrying a wonderful man. Daddy would have liked him. We're going to make his dreams for the Crawford ranch come true, Mom." There was a quick knock on the door and then Jenny was coming back in with bouquet and ring in hand.

"Oh Kate. You're mesmerizing. It's like you stepped out of a history book." Jenny sat the ring and flowers on the bed and began buttoning the back of Kate's dress.

Kate bent over the bed and picked up the beautiful bouquet of wildflowers, sunflowers and roses. A tear slid down her cheek as she touched her face to the soft flowers. "He remembered."

Finishing the last button, Jenny turned Kate back toward the mirror. "What did he remember?"

Kate wiped her cheek with a tissue, careful to not mess up her makeup. "Ben brought me a bouquet just like this not long ago. It was the first time in my life anyone had given me flowers. He said they each represented a part of my personality. The rose was soft and smelled sweet like me, the sunflower was bright and happy and the wildflowers persevere no matter what nature threw at them. That's why he calls me Wildflower." She wiped her eyes again. "Because no matter what life throws at me I continue to thrive and grow."

Jenny touched Kate shoulder. "You're a very lucky woman to have found him, Kate. According to Cree and Jake, Ben's been a loner most of his life. Always searching for something. It seems he's found what he's been searching for in you. You deserve each other. You both deserve all the love and happiness that life has to offer."

Slipping on her low-heeled shoes, Kate turned and took Jenny's hand. "Did Remy make it in time?"

"Don't worry about anything else. Everyone is here and the cake was delivered by Mrs. Campbell personally with an apology to you for her behavior the other day. It seems Mrs. Donovan from the flower shop set her straight on a few things. Right now though I think your groom is getting a little impatient. Are you ready, Kate?"

At Kate's nod Jenny picked up her small bouquet of wildflowers and went to help Kate down the stairs. Outside the house a tent had been set up with a dozen white chairs. Most of the chairs were full, Kate noticed. The empty ones would be occupied by the wedding party during the wedding meal. Kate peeked through the door and saw Ben standing beside Nicco at the end of the white runner that had been rolled out.

Ben was wearing a tuxedo, which surprised her. She figured he'd just wear a suit or even jeans. She noticed Ben shifting from one foot to the other. Apparently she wasn't the only nervous one. Kate nodded to Jenny who nodded to Cotton. She'd asked if Rex Cotton, Gabe's foreman, could play a wedding song on his guitar while she walked down the aisle toward her beloved.

The music started and Jenny walked down the aisle holding her flowers in front of her stomach. When she got almost there Kate stepped out of the house and walked down the white runner. The closer she got to Ben the more tears gathered in her eyes. She never thought she'd be this happy.

When she reached Ben she noticed moisture in his eyes as well. He bent his mouth to her ear. "You take my breath away, Wildflower." He kissed her forehead and turned them toward the minister.

After they recited their vows the minister gave permission for the kiss. Instead of bending down to kiss Kate, Ben picked her up and cradled her in his arms and kissed her.

The kiss went on so long that the audience started heckling the bride and groom. "Enough already, you two." "Get a room." "Save a kiss for the rest of us, Kate." At that last remark Ben turned around and narrowed his eyes at his friends.

Ben turned with Kate still in his arms and thanked the minister. He turned back around and carried Kate back down the aisle to the kitchen. He set her on the counter and looked into her eyes. "I've never seen anything so beautiful as you coming down that aisle, Kate. I honestly thought my heart would stop beating. Thank you for coming into my life, Kate Thomas."

Kate leaned in and kissed him. "If I remember rightly it was you that came into my life and saved my ranch and my heart."

Nicco stuck his head in the kitchen door. "Sorry to interrupt but the photographer would like to get a few pictures of the happy couple."

Ben kissed her once more and lifted her off the counter. He held out his elbow for her, "Shall we, Mrs. Thomas?"

Kate took his arm, "Yes, Mr. Thomas, we shall."

* * * * *

Later that evening after the gang had taken what was left of the keg of beer and gone to the Triple Spur to continue the party Ben and Kate came down after their first round of exhausting sex.

"It just keeps getting better and better," Ben said as he brushed the hair from Kate's face. He trailed his fingers along the contours of her face. "So beautiful."

Kate sucked one of his fingers into her mouth. She swirled her tongue around it until he moaned. "What did Gabe drag you into the library about earlier?"

Ben took his wet finger and reached down to run it around her clit. "Just some boring business stuff. I'll tell you about it tomorrow when I don't have fucking on my mind."

"Speaking of fucking. I've been giving it some thought and if you're still interested I think I'd like you to fuck me in the ass."

Ben was so startled by her statement he went still. "Are you sure? Because you have to understand it will take quite a while to get you prepared to take the size of my cock. Maybe as long as a month of constantly wearing a butt plug. Are you prepared for all that, Kate?"

Taking Ben's nipple into her mouth, Kate moaned. "Whatever it takes, Ben, I'm willing to do it. I want to be with you in every way possible. I'm not afraid anymore."

Ben bent to her mouth and devoured it, thrusting his tongue into the welcoming depths of her. His cock was already starting to revive itself and he began thrusting toward her still dripping pussy. He broke the kiss and licked his way down her body to her throbbing blood-filled clit. He ran his tongue around the tiny diamond he'd given her for a wedding present. Kate thrust her pelvis toward his hungry mouth.

"Fuck me. Fuck me with that tongue." Kate squirmed and thrust until she came. Ben's tongue eagerly lapped up her cream.

Ben continued his assault on her pussy as he gathered juices from her dripping cunt and ran his finger back toward her puckered entrance. He flicked his tongue against her clit again and sucked it into his mouth, milking it with his tongue and teeth. He pushed one finger into her back entrance. When she didn't tense up on him he pushed in farther. He started pumping his finger in and out of her hole as he sucked her clit.

At her scream of pleasure he lifted his head and looked into her eyes. "Mine. You're mine, Wildflower."

She came again, shouting his name. Before she could come down from her orgasm he crawled up her body and spread her legs back onto her chest. He plunged his hungry cock into her weeping channel. Kate immediately climaxed again.

Ben showed her no mercy and continued to pound into her hard and fast. He seemed to reach depths he never had with another woman. It was like Kate's pussy had formed itself to fit him like a glove. Sweat began pouring down his face as his hips snapped forward one last time before he seated himself to the hilt and pumped his seed deep into her womb.

Ben collapsed on top of Kate and then thought better of it and rolled them over. Kate was still trembling in his arms after the multiple orgasms she'd just experienced. Ben kissed the top of her head. "Damn, Kate, we're so hot together I could almost swear I smell smoke."

Kate shot up and looked at Ben. She raised her nose to the air and sniffed. "Fuck, Ben, you do smell smoke."

Ben jumped out of bed and pulled a pair of jeans on. He stuck his feet into his boots and went to the door. He put his hand on the door and pulled it back quickly. He was cursing himself for making his bedroom soundproof. They'd been so wrapped up in each other they hadn't even noticed the faint smell of smoke, but from the heat emanating from the bedroom door Ben would guess the whole first level of the house was on fire.

He turned back to Kate and grabbed some sweats and a t-shirt from his dresser. He brought them over to the bed. "Quick put these on, darlin'. We'll have to go out the window." He snatched up his cell phone and Kate's wedding dress and headed for the window.

He opened it and climbed through, reaching back in to lift Kate out. He handed her the wedding dress and pulled her out of the burning house. Ben called 9-1-1 and then put a call in to the Triple Spur.

"Who dat be so late calling?"

"Remy, it's Ben. Wake everyone up and get over here. Our house is on fire. Tell Cree I've already called 9-1-1."

Ben hung up the cell phone and shoved it into his pocket. He picked Kate up and carried her to the front of the house. He whistled for Charlie. Relief flooded him as Charlie came running around the side of the burning house. It was just as he suspected, the entire first floor was in flames, rapidly spreading to the second floor. He kissed the top of Kate's head. "We can't save the house, Wildflower, but with your help we can try to save the coop and the barn."

Kate nodded and he put her down. "Be careful with your feet, I forgot your shoes. Go around to the barn and bring me the hose and turn it on. I'll get the coop soaked down first. The chickens I think should be okay in the coop. I just want to make sure a spark doesn't ignite the roof of it." While Kate ran to get the hose Ben managed to clear everything flammable between the house and the chicken coop and barn. He was carrying a load of last year's firewood away from the house when Kate came running back, stretching the hose behind her.

"That's good, darlin', now run into the barn and put the horses into the pasture and bring back some gunny sacks." While Kate was still trying to get the horses out of the barn with Charlie by her side, two SUVs drove up and the gang piled out and ran to Ben's side.

Nicco took the hose from Ben and continued to spray down the chicken coop. "Get the others lined out on what you need. I can handle this."

Ben nodded and slapped him on the back. "Thanks. When you get it nice and wet, wet it again. Kate's chickens are still in there. They are more important to me than saving the barn if it comes to that."

Ben strode to the rest of the gang. "I think the best thing to do would be to pull everything out of the barn of value. It's one thing to lose the structure but the contents hold Kate's heritage. Some of those tools and saddles have been in her family for generations. Once we get everything out of the barn we can wet down gunny sacks and try to keep the errant sparks at bay. The fire department should be on its way."

The group worked as the team they were and cleared the barn in nothing flat. They piled everything on the far side of the ranch yard away from any of the wooden structures. The fire trucks came roaring down the ranch road and pulled up in front of the house.

The fire captain got out and started giving orders to his men. After the firemen went about their various assigned jobs the captain came over to an exhausted Ben. "There's no way we can save the house but at least we should be able to keep the fire from spreading to the other buildings."

Ben thanked him and crossed his fingers that the captain was right. He found Kate with a wet gunny sack slapping at flying sparks before they could land on the chicken coop. He pulled her away from the chicken coop and took her over to Remy's rented SUV. He opened the door and lifted her onto the front passenger seat away from the fire. "Darlin', if you could stop this fire I'd let you but the fire department's here now. Let them do their job. The best thing for you to do right now is to go to the Triple Spur. I'll feel better knowing you're safe. Besides, I bet Jenny could use the company."

Kate put her head to her chest and nodded. Ben lifted her chin with his finger. "I know how you feel, Kate, it was my home too but at least you and I and Charlie are safe."

Kate looked into his eyes. "For how long, Ben? How far is Clint going to go to drive me out of Junctionville? He's already tried to kill Charlie. Are you next? Am I next? When will it end, Ben?" Kate began to sob and held on to Ben.

He wrapped his arms around her and kissed her tear streaked face. He looked into her eyes and nodded. "Tonight, Kate. It ends tonight." He kissed her once more and called Cotton over. "Cotton, I've got something I need you to take care of. Can you drive Kate over to the Triple Spur for me?"

Cotton nodded and ran to the driver's side of the SUV. "Sure thing, Ben. She'll be there when you get done takin' care of your business."

Ben nodded and brushed his fingers down Kate's cheek. "I'll be there as soon as I can, Wildflower." Cotton drove off and Ben went to find Cree. He found him talking to the fire captain. "Can I have a private word with you, Cree?"

Cree nodded and moved to the far side of the driveway. "I think I already know what you're going to say but let me say this. The fire captain thinks the burning pattern of the house looks suspiciously like arson. He thinks some kind of accelerant was used, gas or possibly kerosene. My chief suspect is Clint Adams and as the sheriff it's my duty to hunt him down and arrest him on suspicion of arson."

Ben began rubbing his hands together. "Can I help you hunt the little fucker down?"

Cree shook his head and then looked at Ben for a while and nodded. "Okay but you can't ride in the sheriff's car with me. I'll get the rest of the team to help too. You can ride with some of them." At Ben's nod Cree went to round up the rest of the guys. The fire department had the house fire under control so he thought it was safe for them to leave. Cree already informed the fire captain of his plan to arrest his chief suspect, so they were all free to leave and help in the search for Clint.

As the convoy spread out, one car going to Clint's home and two cars going to Bruce's home, Cree got a call from the dispatcher. "Sheriff Sommers, the hospital in Santa Fe called and they have Clint Adams in the emergency room there. It seems he's got second and third degree burns on his hands."

Cree smiled and picked up his mic. "Ten-four on that dispatch. Tell the hospital I'm on the way. Ask them to take skin samples to try to determine if there are any trace amounts of accelerant on his hands."

"Ten-four, sheriff. Dispatch out."

Cree picked up his cell phone and called Jake who was on his way to Clint's house and then he called Ben. "Ben, I'm turning around and heading for Santa Fe. The emergency room called the sheriff's department. It seems they have the little fucker in the ER with second and third degree burns on his hands. This could be our big break. I asked that the ER doctors to take skin samples looking for an accelerant. If we can match the accelerant on his hands or clothing to the accelerant used at your house we probably have enough for a conviction. Mr. Adams will most likely be charged with arson, stalking and attempted murder to say nothing of the blackmail scheme against Judge Hathaway. Why don't you head on back to the Triple Spur and share the news with your new bride."

Ben hung up and whooped with joy and hit the back of the seat so hard poor Mac was almost pushed into the windshield. "Oh sorry, Mac, I got a little excited." He proceeded to tell Mac and Nicco about Cree's information. "Take me to the Triple Spur. I've got a wife to comfort."

Chapter Twelve

Tuesday morning dawned with an impressive display from Mother Nature. Thunder boomed and lightning lit up the sky. Kate sat at the breakfast table surrounded by the entire "Team". Gabe, Cotton and their friend Boone had stayed on, as did Remy, for her hearing with the judge this morning. Clint had been arrested at the hospital in Santa Fe by Cree on Sunday night but not jailed until Monday afternoon. It seemed his burns were pretty serious. *Good*, thought Kate. *Let him pay for his own crimes a little. Lord knows I've paid enough.*

Cree put down his coffee and looked over at Kate. "Um...Ben suggested I talk to you about designing you a new home. Does that sound like something you'd be interested in?"

Kate's spirits lifted for the first time since the fire. "Really? You'd design a house for us?" She looked over at Ben. "Can I tell you everything I've ever wanted in a house and you can see if it will all fit in one home?" At Cree's nod she jumped up from her chair and went and wrapped her arms around his neck. Kate kissed him on the cheek, noticing as she did so that she was being growled at by both Jake and Ben. She shrugged her shoulders and sat back down. "Sorry, guys, I didn't mean to make anyone jealous. I'm just excited."

They started eating breakfast with jokes and insults being shared across the long country farm table. Kate noticed that Ben was picking at his food instead of eating. She put her hand on his thigh. "What's wrong, Ben?" she whispered in his ear so no one else could hear.

Ben said nothing but he did reposition her hand to rub on his semi-hard cock. After a few strokes it became a full-blown hard-on. She turned his face to hers and asked the question again.

Ben spread his legs a little farther and shrugged. "I'm just not hungry that's all."

Everyone at the table stopped what they were doing and looked toward the end of the table at Ben. Jake's mouth opened and then snapped back shut. He looked at Cree and raised his eyebrow.

Cree cleared his throat. "The hearing will go fine today, Ben. Even though it's only for the permanent protection order the judge will allow Kate to present documentation to support her case. That documentation being the copy of the will and the report from the fire captain I received yesterday indicating arson was the cause of the fire that destroyed your home. We can't link the little fucker yet because that will have to wait until he comes up for trial but Judge Hathaway and anyone else in the room will be able to see the bandages protecting the burns on the little fucker's hands."

Ben squirmed in his seat. His erection had deflated at the thought of Kate being in the same room as Clint. He was relieved at least that the team would be there to surround her. "I'm just not hungry. Get over it." Ben got up from the table and walked toward the kitchen door. "I'm going to wait out on the porch. Come out when you're finished eating." He walked out, letting the screen door slam in his wake.

Kate closed her eyes. "He'll be all right once this is over." She looked at his friends. "At least I pray he'll be all right. I don't know how long he can last without food." She smiled, trying to lighten the mood. She pushed her chair back and followed Ben out the door.

She found him sitting on the porch swing scratching Charlie behind the ears. Blue slept in his customary spot. She approached the swing and sat beside Ben. She reached out and took the hand that wasn't scratching Charlie. Kate didn't say anything she just waited. Finally Ben squeezed her hand and lifted her onto his lap.

Ben buried his face in Kate's hair and inhaled deeply. "I'm so sorry you have to face him today, Wildflower. I wish I could do it and keep you safely locked away until all of this is over."

Kate felt wetness and looked down. A tear had landed on her arm. She hugged Ben closer. "You can't keep me from all the ugliness in this world, Ben Thomas. But you can stand beside me through and though. You can share your strength and your love with me when I need it most. That's all I'll ever ask of you. Just help hold me up when I start to falter and I'll do the same for you."

Ben nodded and nonchalantly wiped his eyes. "I love you, darlin'. I still haven't figured out how I got so lucky but I'm not about to look a gift horse in the mouth." He kissed her, putting all the love he felt into it.

The rest of the gang came out onto the porch and Cree cleared his throat. "Um…we'd better get going if we're going to get there on time."

Ben nodded and set Kate back on her feet. They took the minivan and Remy's SUV. Ben and Kate rode in the backseat with Nicco. Remy and Mac rode up front. The five of them were fairly quiet for the entire ride into town.

When they pulled up in front of the courthouse and got out of the SUV Remy looked at Ben and pulled Kate into his arms. "We gonna be right behind ya, *cherie*. Give dat little fucker what he got comin'."

Remy stepped back and Nicco and Mac both took one of her hands. Nicco patted her hand. "It'll be fine. He's not getting out now."

Kate let go of Mac's hand and wrapped her arms around Nicco's waist. "Thank you for everything. You've become more than just a protector to me. You've become a very dear friend. I just wish you didn't have to go back to New York."

Nicco got a surprised look on his face and hugged her back. He kissed the top of her head. "I've never had a sister but if I did I'd want her to be just like you, spitfire."

At Ben's hand on her shoulder she released Nicco and stepped back. Kate squared her shoulders and thrust her chin in the air. She turned to Ben and nodded. "I'm ready. Let's go take care of the little fucker."

They entered the courtroom as a group. Kate sat at the table in front of the spectator seating. Ben came and sat behind her, close enough for him to put a reassuring hand on her shoulder. Kate spread the documents out on the table in front of her. Her stomach was churning so badly she thought she might throw up.

Judge Hathaway entered the courtroom and gave instructions on how the hearing would proceed. "I'll ask them to bring in Clint Adams in a few moments and then I'll ask you, Mrs. Thomas, if you have anything to present to the court. I'll look at any and all documentation you have to support your case for a permanent protection order. This should include a verbal recounting of any past events that may pertain to the defendant. Then I will ask Mr. Adams if he has anything to say or any documentation to support his innocence. Do you understand, Mrs. Thomas?"

Still standing, Kate nodded to the judge. "Yes, Your Honor. I understand."

Next Judge Hathaway sent for Clint Adams to be ushered into the courtroom. Kate held her breath as a deputy from the Sheriff's Department led a handcuffed Clint Adams into the room. The deputy sat Clint in a chair behind the table across the aisle from her. His handcuffs were removed but the deputy stayed next to him.

The judge banged his gavel and spoke. "I would first like to hear from Mrs. Kate Thomas. After you testify against the defendant Clint Adams, I will ask you to present any documentation you have against him. Is that clear to you, Mrs. Thomas?"

The judge looked toward the bailiff. "You may now be sworn in. Be advised that as long as you are in this courtroom you are to tell the truth."

Kate nodded and was sworn in, then rose and took the seat next to the judge. She recounted in detail the events of seven years ago, stopping several times to compose herself. Kate then proceeded to tell the judge about the occurrences on her ranch in the past year including being struck and threatened the night of the dance. She ended her testimony with the fire that destroyed her house.

When she was finished the judge asked for any documentation she would like to present to the court. Kate walked back toward the table, noticing the steely looks of hatred aimed Clint's way from the team. She picked up the sheets of paper and walked back to the bench.

Kate held up the first document. "This is a report from the emergency room the night of my eighteenth birthday seven years ago." She held up the second document to the judge. "This is an official report from Fire Captain Randolph stating the cause of the fire that burned down my home was arson." Kate swallowed and looked at Ben. Ben nodded, sending her strength. "This, Your Honor, is a copy of Bruce Adams' will. It states that his only living heir Clint Adams is to inherit his entire estate and a presidency position at the bank." At a confused look from the judge she continued. "If you'll please notice, Your Honor, there's a stipulation in the will that must be met before Clint Adams can inherit. That stipulation is that I, Kate Crawford, be run out of Junctionville and off the Crawford Ranch before Clint Adams can inherit a penny. I believe…"

Kate didn't get any further. Clint Adams exploded out of his seat like a wild man. "You fucking bitch. Isn't it enough you humiliated me in front of my father? Now you're going to do it in front of the town? I should have killed you when I had the chance." He pushed the deputy off him, grabbing his gun in the process.

He turned and fired at Kate before Ben could get to him. Ben saw Kate fall as his fist plowed into the little fucker's face. Clint went down and Cree grabbed the gun out of his hand. Ben turned and rushed to Kate. She was sitting up on the floor, holding her arm in a daze.

Ben bent and scooped her up off the floor and into his arms. He looked over and saw Clint Adams still passed out cold surrounded by seven angry-looking men as well as the stunned deputy. "Are you okay, Wildflower?" He turned toward the gathering crowd. "Did someone call for an ambulance?"

Kate put her head down against his chest. "I'm okay, Ben. The bullet just grazed my arm, that's all."

"That's all?" Ben yelled. He looked back toward Clint and then to the judge. "Can I take her out of here please?"

"Yes of course you can. The protection order is granted," the judge decreed so it would be entered into the books.

Ben carried Kate out of the courtroom. "I don't think we'll have to worry about Clint for a long time. I imagine he'll get a nice cell with a nice roommate named Bubba."

Chapter Thirteen
One year later

වා

Ben held his wife's hand in front of their new home. The past year had been a crazy one for the two of them. Kate became pregnant shortly after their marriage and now they had a beautiful little girl named Lilly who had curly blonde hair like her mother. The trials of Clint Adams had kept them both busy as well. He'd been tried separately for the arson and attempted murder stemming from it and the attempted murder at the courthouse. He would not be getting out of jail. Also his father's will had been declared invalid and the entire Adams estate had been awarded to the various charities also listed in the will.

Ben held Kate closer and kissed the top of her head. "Cree did a beautiful job, didn't he?" They had agreed on a Spanish-style hacienda. They even had the old barn torn down and rebuilt in keeping with the Spanish theme of the rest of the ranch. The buttery yellow stucco home with a red tiled roof was a masterpiece. Kate insisted on an open courtyard in the center of the house. The rest of the house opened onto the courtyard with French doors in almost every room. Kate still had plans in the works to add a pool and hot tub area in the back of the house where the large patio already was. She didn't want the pool in the courtyard with children running around. Ben looked down at his wife. She was the best mother in the world. He knew she would be after seeing her help Jenny take care of the black-haired twins Cash and Carson.

Kate leaned her head against Ben's arm. "The house is absolutely beautiful, Ben. I feel like all my dreams have come true in the past year. I'll be glad to move in to our new home tomorrow but I'm going to miss the Triple Spur." She laughed and looked up at Ben. "Although I won't miss having to shield my eyes every time I walk into the kitchen. Who knew that Cree, Jake and Jenny could consider the kitchen an extension of the bedroom? I've seen enough of both of those men's cocks to last a lifetime."

At Ben's raised eyebrows and low throaty growl she ran her hand down the front of his jeans. "There's something I need you to do for me before we move in though. I've got one last demon that I need exorcised."

At Ben's questioning look she pulled him toward the new barn. As she opened the big barn door Ben stopped and looked at her. "Wildflower, what are you doing with that saddle down off the hook?"

Kate ran her fingers over the fine grained leather of the saddle her daddy had given her eight years ago. "I need you to fuck me over this saddle, Ben. I need you to create a new memory on this saddle in our new barn. There are no ghosts in this barn but there's still one riding that saddle."

Ben pulled her to him and starting kissing her, thrusting his tongue as deep into her mouth as it could go. "God I love you, Wildflower." He untied the top of her halter and let the straps fall. Her milk-swollen breasts spilled out to fill his hands. He kneaded them as he lowered his mouth around one extended nipple. He suckled Kate's breast as he slowly unzipped her jean shorts and pushed them down.

Kate threw her head back and held on to his head. Ben had taken to wearing a bandana instead of his old cowboy hat. He knew how much the pirate look turned her on. She tore the bandana off his head so she could touch the bronzed skin underneath. When he stuck two fingers deep into her pussy she cried out his name. "Fuck me, Ben!"

Ben released her nipple and wiped the milk from his chin. "I need to prepare your ass first, darlin'." He ran his fingers, slick with her own juice, back toward her hole. He spread the juices around the rim and inserted first one and then two fingers. He bent his head and took her clit into his mouth and

323

sucked hard. When her climax came he spun her around and bent her over the saddle. He quickly dropped his jeans and lined his heavy swollen cock up with her stretched hole. Thankfully for Kate this wasn't the first time he'd taken her here.

His cock slid in fairly smoothly and he began to thrust in and out of her opening. Ben's cock felt surrounded by Kate's heat. She was still so tight here he felt like he could come any second. Kate slammed her ass back against his cock and soared into another climax. The walls of Kate's ass milked his cock like a vise. He managed to slam into her two more times before his seed was pumping into her channel.

Ben collapsed on top of her and bit her shoulder. "Damn, darlin', that was incredible." Kate kissed his hands where they gripped the saddle on either side of her.

"I hereby declare this saddle exorcised." Ben let her stand and took her into his arms. She reached up and kissed him. "I've got one more present for you." Kate pulled him toward the back of the barn. She went over to the large drop cloth and pulled it off. Under the drop cloth was a new ranch sign to hang over the entrance to the ranch.

Ben smiled and kissed her and read the sign. "Ben's Wildflower Ranch. It's perfect, Kate. I hope Lilly grows up to be just like you. A wildflower in a sea of blowing grass."

Kate laughed, "I have a feeling she will. If you can keep those two Sommers boys away from her. They're already fascinated by her."

Ben's eyebrows drew together and then he smiled. "If they grow up to be anything like their fathers I'll be proud to call them sons."

About the Author

ଚ୍ଚ

I've been a reading fanatic for years and finally at the age of 40 decided to try my hand at writing. I've always loved romance novels that are just a little bit naughty so naturally my books tend to go just a little further. It's my fantasy world after all.

When I'm not being a mother to a five-year-old and a six-year-old, you can usually find me in my deep leather chair with either a book in my hand or my laptop.

Carol welcomes comments from readers. You can find her website and email address on her author bio page at www.ellorascave.com.

Tell Us What You Think

We appreciate hearing reader opinions about our books. You can email us at Comments@EllorasCave.com.

Why an electronic book?

We live in the Information Age—an exciting time in the history of human civilization, in which technology rules supreme and continues to progress in leaps and bounds every minute of every day. For a multitude of reasons, more and more avid literary fans are opting to purchase e-books instead of paper books. The question from those not yet initiated into the world of electronic reading is simply: *Why?*

1. *Price.* An electronic title at Ellora's Cave Publishing and Cerridwen Press runs anywhere from 40% to 75% less than the cover price of the exact same title in paperback format. Why? Basic mathematics and cost. It is less expensive to publish an e-book (no paper and printing, no warehousing and shipping) than it is to publish a paperback, so the savings are passed along to the consumer.

2. *Space.* Running out of room in your house for your books? That is one worry you will never have with electronic books. For a low one-time cost, you can purchase a handheld device specifically designed for e-reading. Many e-readers have large, convenient screens for viewing. Better yet, hundreds of titles can be stored within your new library—on a single microchip. There are a variety of e-readers from different manufacturers. You can also read e-books on your PC or laptop computer. (Please note that Ellora's Cave does not endorse any specific brands.

You can check our websites at www.ellorascave.com or www.cerridwenpress.com for information we make available to new consumers.)

3. *Mobility.* Because your new e-library consists of only a microchip within a small, easily transportable e-reader, your entire cache of books can be taken with you wherever you go.

4. *Personal Viewing Preferences.* Are the words you are currently reading too small? Too large? Too... ANNOYING? Paperback books cannot be modified according to personal preferences, but e-books can.

5. *Instant Gratification.* Is it the middle of the night and all the bookstores near you are closed? Are you tired of waiting days, sometimes weeks, for bookstores to ship the novels you bought? Ellora's Cave Publishing sells instantaneous downloads twenty-four hours a day, seven days a week, every day of the year. Our webstore is never closed. Our e-book delivery system is 100% automated, meaning your order is filled as soon as you pay for it.

Those are a few of the top reasons why electronic books are replacing paperbacks for many avid readers.

As always, Ellora's Cave and Cerridwen Press welcome your questions and comments. We invite you to email us at Comments@ellorascave.com or write to us directly at Ellora's Cave Publishing Inc., 1056 Home Avenue, Akron, OH 44310-3502.

COMING TO A BOOKSTORE NEAR YOU!

ELLORA'S CAVE

Bestselling Authors Tour

UPDATES AVAILABLE AT

WWW.ELLORASCAVE.COM

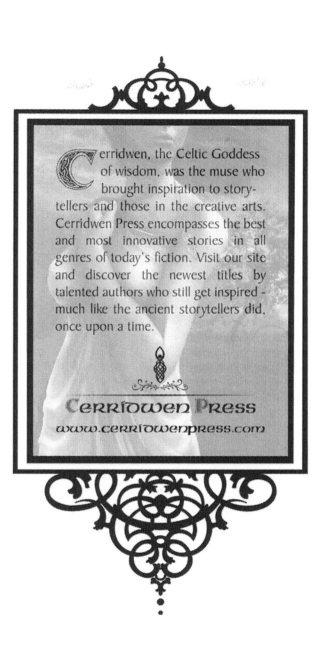

Cerridwen, the Celtic Goddess of wisdom, was the muse who brought inspiration to story-tellers and those in the creative arts. Cerridwen Press encompasses the best and most innovative stories in all genres of today's fiction. Visit our site and discover the newest titles by talented authors who still get inspired – much like the ancient storytellers did, once upon a time.

CERRIDWEN PRESS

www.cerridwenpress.com

*Discover for yourself why readers can't get enough
of the multiple award-winning publisher*

Ellora's Cave.

Whether you prefer e-books or paperbacks,

*be sure to visit EC on the web at
www.ellorascave.com*

*for an erotic reading experience that will leave you
breathless.*

10743929R0

Made in the USA
Lexington, KY
17 August 2011